T0034948

FORGE OF THE HIGH MAGE

Also by Ian C. Esslemont

Night of Knives

Return of the Crimson Guard

Stonewielder

Orb Sceptre Throne

Blood and Bone

Assail

PATH TO ASCENDANCY SEQUENCE

Dancer's Lament

Deadhouse Landing

Kellanved's Reach

FORGE OF THE HIGH MAGE

A Tale of the
Paths to Ascendancy

Ian C. Esslemont

TOR

TOR PUBLISHING GROUP
NEW YORK

This is a work of fiction. All of the characters, organizations, and events portrayed in this novel are either products of the author's imagination or are used fictitiously.

FORGE OF THE HIGH MAGE

Copyright © 2023 by Ian Cameron Esslemont

Maps © Neil Gower

All rights reserved.

A Tor Book
Published by Tom Doherty Associates / Tor Publishing Group
120 Broadway
New York, NY 10271

www.tor-forge.com

Tor® is a registered trademark of Macmillan Publishing Group, LLC.

The Library of Congress Cataloging-in-Publication Data is available upon request.

ISBN 978-1-250-78862-7 (trade paperback)
ISBN 978-1-250-78861-0 (hardback)
ISBN 978-1-250-78860-3 (ebook)

Our books may be purchased in bulk for promotional, educational, or business use. Please contact your local bookseller or the Macmillan Corporate and Premium Sales Department at 1-800-221-7945, extension 5442, or by email at MacmillanSpecialMarkets@macmillan.com.

First published in Great Britain by Bantam, an imprint of Transworld Publishers

First U.S. Edition: 2024

Printed in the United States of America

0 9 8 7 6 5 4 3 2 1

To all those who waited,
my thanks and gratitude

ACKNOWLEDGMENTS

I wish to thank my prereader, Dr. A. P. Canavan. I would also like to thank my agent, Howard Morhaim, and my editor, Simon Taylor. Special thanks to all those fans who came out the summer of '22, and to those of the Malazan online community: Thank you for easing me into your world. Your support and enthusiasm mean more than you can know.

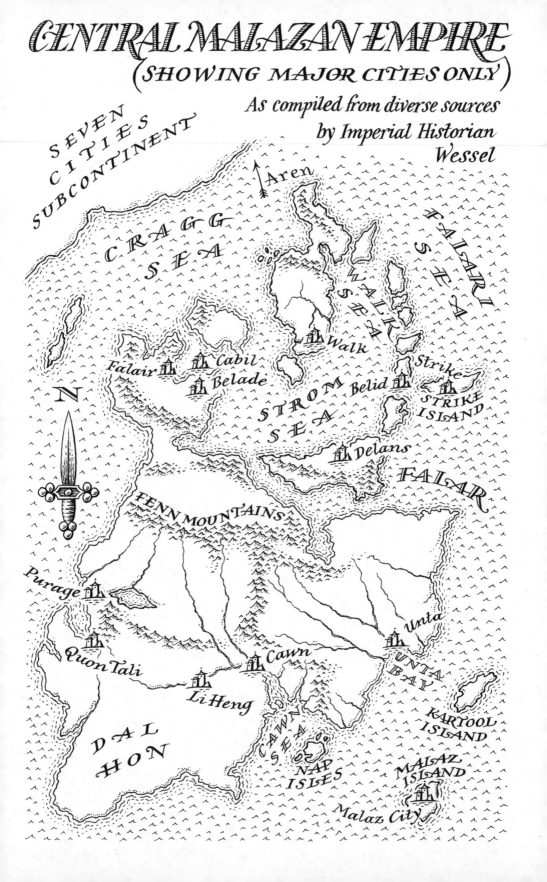

DRAMATIS PERSONAE

In Cabil of the Falaran Isles

Rentil Orodrin	Celebrant of the Faith
Nuraj Senull	Guardian of the Faith
Ortheal Leneth	Proctor of the Faith
Glinith Apanar	Abbess of Cabil
Mallick Rel	Overseer / Purser of Coin
Gianna / Giandra	A runaway from the Faith
Hedran	A priest of Mael
Brother Lethor	A priest of Mael
Jan / Janelle	A washerwoman
Janul	A carpenter

Of Malaz

Kellanved	The Emperor
Dancer	Master Assassin
Surly	Mistress of the Claws
Dassem Ultor	The Sword (Champion)
Tayschrenn	High Mage
Dujek Onearm	A commander
Nightchill	A High Mage
Hairlock	A cadre mage
Sialle	A cadre mage
Ullen	An officer
Orosé	An officer
Ute	A trooper
Missy	A trooper
Karsden	An Imperial Historian
Topper	A Claw

Of the Crimson Guard

Gregar Bluenth 'Blues'	A mage and weapon-master
Smoky	A mage

Gwynn	A mage
Black the Lesser	A swordsman
Jacinth	A swordswoman

Of the Jhek

The Bird Mother / High Priestess	Leader of the assembled Jhek Clans
Looris	Chief of the wolf-warriors
Athan	Chief of the bear-warriors
Ursana	A female bear-warrior

The Shipwreck Survivors

Hessa	The Captain
Turnagin	Ship's mage
Corbin	Mate
Hyde	Crew
Ayal	Crew

Crew of the *Twisted*

Cartheron Crust	A Malazan Admiral
Geddin	Steersman
Creel	First mate
Teal	Quartermaster
The Nose	A talented sailor
Learnan	A sailor/scout
Jill	Ship's cook

Others

Singer	An exile
Koroll	A Thelomen, or 'Fenn'
Bellurdan	A Thelomen, or 'Fenn'
Endest Silann	A Tiste Andii
Feral	A Tiste Andii
Imanaj D'Shren	A Seven Cities fighter
Torva	An elderly smuggler
Brevin	Captain of the *Sea Glimmer*
Realt	Steersman of the *Sea Glimmer*
Brother Rendren	A priest of Mael

Prologue

THE ISLAND OF KYNARL RISES FROM THE OLIVE-GREEN waters of Walk Sea near to the centre of a ring of similar such isles. It possesses its old palace where kings and queens of ancient times once ruled, together with the usual temples and holy shrines dedicated to the region's multiplicity of gods, goddesses, demi-god champions, local noted spirits and honoured ancestors. It is most famous, however, for housing the greatest library in all Falar, and even beyond. A collection rivalled perhaps only by the assemblage of scrolls and elder knowledge rumoured to exist in far Darujhistan.

The fourth, and last, time the priests of Mael arrived at the library to make their demands, its chief curator and archivist was a woman named Leanara of Curaca. Flanked by her staff of sectional librarians, apprentices, copyists and sub-archivists, she met the delegation upon the marble steps to the institution's colonnaded main entrance.

It was a pleasant day, the breeze light but constant. Good sailing weather, as any Falaran would note. The delegation wore the deep blue robes of their order, servants of the ancient sea god Mael, whom they held pre-eminent among the many sundry sea gods and goddesses – the patron and guardian of all Falar itself.

Leanara was clad in plain linen tunic and trousers, the chain and single gold key of her office about her neck. She bowed to the priest leading the delegation, who answered the bow courteously enough. 'M'lady,' this one began, 'we are come for the scrolls of Old Falar.'

'Then I wonder why you came at all,' she answered. 'Our resolve remains as it always has.'

Behind his thick oiled and curled beard the priest smiled thinly. 'The gesture must be made. You must be given every chance.'

'Every chance?'

The priest opened his arms, perhaps to encompass the island. 'Think of the welfare of all these innocents.'

Leanara pressed a hand to her chest, her mouth hardening. 'So. Threats again. You think you can win your way through threats? I thought here among these isles we no longer tolerated tyrants.'

'Yet you tolerate lies – and would have your way by spreading them.'

Now she smiled, amused. 'Let knowledge spread and let the people weigh its merits, and decide for themselves.'

He shook his head, apparently regretful. 'Falsehoods. Deception. A deliberate campaign of defaming.'

'Let the people decide! Let these ancient records be read! If it is false that your cult – this Jhistal – is a distortion and abuse of the true, older worship of Mael, then you have nothing to fear.'

The priest stepped closer to the Chief Librarian and whispered, his voice low and tight, 'It is one thing to flirt with defiance – it is wholly another to endanger everyone who lives upon this isle with your selfish ambition and wilfulness.'

She stared, shocked, searching his face, then hissed, 'You would not dare . . .'

He drew himself straight, smoothing his raiment. 'Do not try us, Chief Librarian. You have five days to hand over the scrolls.' Turning, he waved off his delegation and they marched away in a fluttering of sea-blue robes.

Leanara looked to her staff; all eyed her in varying degrees of dread.

'They really wouldn't do such a thing . . . would they?' stammered the youngest of the sub-archivists.

'No,' she assured the lad. She gestured to the columned front of the library. 'Lose all this knowledge? No. That would earn the condemnation of everyone.'

They, however, did not appear entirely convinced.

Over the next days, she noted how the streets and main markets of the town appeared unusually empty. House fronts stood boarded up, and she overheard talk of people meaning to head off-island for a time – to visit relatives, or to travel.

The priests of the Jhistal, it seemed, had made their intentions public.

But then of course they would, she told herself. How else to put pressure upon her and the library? In the streets, those citizens she knew, instead of greeting her, now looked away, or through her, as if she no longer existed.

Or was already dead.

She kept to the halls of the library after that. Of her staff, only four now remained, two being the young sub-archivists.

She met the dawn of the fifth day on the steps of the library once more. She was expecting another visit from the delegation: they, having made their point, would no doubt arrive demanding delivery. Yet fear also gnawed upon her; the stories of this . . . Jhistal. A monster, an immense beast from the depths that crushes cities and swallows entire fleets.

Folktales surely! None living can claim to have seen this thing! And the cult was cynically exploiting these old tales. No wonder they feared exposure so much.

She waited, but still no one appeared. Indeed, a deathly quiet seemed to hang over the town below – from here a collection of red-tiled roofs – as if it were entirely abandoned.

Her two sub-archivists – last of her staff now remaining – came jogging up the road and climbed the stairs to her side. 'It's empty,' one told her, wonder in his voice. 'There are none there.'

Her brows rose in astonishment. It seemed she hadn't given due consideration to the powers of fear and ignorance, or of superstition.

'What's that?' the older of the two asked, her shock of bright red hair a mass about her face. She was pointing out past the bright harbour below, to the open seas beyond.

Leanara squinted at the shimmering green waters – the sea appeared different. Higher? Closer? An unusually large wave?

Sudden, mouth-drying dread gripped her then and she almost staggered. Swallowing, she looked to her two young apprentices. 'I'm sorry,' she began, 'it seems those with power *will* do anything to hold on to it after all. I underestimated the depths of their selfishness and greed.'

3

The sub-archivists exchanged secretive looks. 'It's all right, m'lady,' said the girl, 'we took precautions. We locked the scrolls in a bronze chest and sealed the lid with lead.'

She rested her hands upon their shoulders. 'Well done, my young archivists.'

They watched, silent now, for there was no time to run or panic, as the sea continued to rise. It towered, far taller than the roofs of the town below – taller even than the peaked stone roof of the library – and she knew then just what this *Jhistal* was.

Not some eldritch beast summoned from the depths. Not some rampaging monster.

A simple wave. An immense mountain of water, leagues high, it seemed to her.

The tales of its enormous destructive power now made sense. Pity she would not live to record her observations. She turned to her two apprentices once more. 'I am so very sorry—'

Their answer was lost as the gargantuan wave swallowed the shore in a mind-numbing concatenation of power. The town disappeared under its skirts while its rearing head was lost above.

The island! was Leanara's last thought. *It will sweep the entire island clean!* Then she knew no more.

Chapter 1

THROUGH DRIVING SNOW A LONE FIGURE WALKED HUNCHED. A long cloth-wrapped bundle just as tall as he was hung cumbrously across his back. He paused occasionally, to adjust this burden, and to shade his eyes against the howling winds to scan the white wastes surrounding him. During one such pause a great fit of coughing wrenched him and he bent even further to spit into the snow, leaving a red blossom of slush. Yet his gaze was drawn ever onwards to a single mountain crag that dominated the western horizon.

After many days the traveller reached the foothills of this lone peak – fields of naked broken rock amid the snow. Selecting one depression reasonably sheltered from the driving winds, he sat against a boulder and drew his long burden from his back. Unwrapped, it was revealed as some sort of musical instrument, a huge horn perhaps, carved from a single gigantic piece of ivory or bone. This he pressed to his lips to blow a few experimental notes, then set aside and tilted his head, as if listening for the winds to respond. With no such response forthcoming, he shrugged, held the instrument to his chest, and closed his eyes to sleep.

So did it go day after day, week after week, and month after month. The seasons did not change; no spring came to lessen the blasts of snow, for the mountain sat at the centre of a vast waste-land of icefields countless leagues across. Thus no beasts accosted the musician, and no fellow travellers appeared. Birds, however, did pass far overhead and these he watched from the corner of his eye, a humourless smile sometimes stretching his cracked lips across his large, upthrusting canines.

But then he would return to his music. And such eerie inhuman music it was – if it may be named such at all. Deep rumbling basso passages too low for any normal ear, or high trilling keening; all mixed together in constantly altering rhythms, beats and progressions. On and on, looping, rolling, changing in pitch and speed, then even repeating for a time.

And always the musician would pause to listen, as if expecting the winds to answer.

As, eventually, they did.

Something far too low for a human ear washed over the piper, making the small stones lying all about him vibrate and jump. The musician perked up, straightened, and repeated his last passage.

The answer repeated itself as well.

Now the musician clambered to his feet. Taking a huge breath, he blew a deep blast upon the instrument that went on and on, for far longer than any human lungs could possibly encompass. Finishing in a flourish, he raised his head to listen. He waited. And he waited, head cocked. After a time he frowned then critically studied the horn.

An immense concussion rocked him backwards on his feet, sent the snow all driving away, and he hunched, wincing and shaking his head. Then he slipped the instrument onto his back and set out to climb the mountain's lower slopes.

He was searching for something, and, eventually, he found it. Through the gusting snow he spotted thin wisps of fog, or a plume of mist, high up one ice-encrusted face of the mountain. This he struggled towards, and, after a time, he reached.

A fresh crack of broken rock it was. A crevasse in the sheath of ice. Steam roiled from far within. At its edge the musician paused, raised a thumb to one up-thrusting canine to scratch it thoughtfully, and smiled, nodding to himself.

Then he slipped within, amid the billowing steam, to disappear.

* * *

Towards the end of the pacification of the northern wilds of Nom Purge, the roving Malazan Imperial Seat settled in next to the confluence of two unnamed rivers to remain stationary for an astonishing fifteen days.

A tent city quickly developed as daily more and more Malazan cohorts arrived to guard the Emperor and his – some said body-guard, some assassin, while others whispered him to be the true cunning and driving force behind the pair's astonishing rise to power – Dancer.

On the fifteenth day the general of the West, Fist Choss, arrived accompanied by his staff and personal guard. Throwing the reins of his mount to a groom, he stomped into the imperial command tent to find the Emperor, Kellanved, sitting at a table heaped with a mess of maps, lists and accounts. Dancer sat aside in a camp chair, arms crossed, his legs straight out before him.

The Fist went to a side-table set with cold meats, breads and fruits. He tucked his gauntlets into his belt and nodded a greeting to Kellanved. Selecting a poultry leg, he took a bite. Round the mouthful, he demanded, 'What's this about you ordering Korelan relief forces north, here, to you?'

The wrinkled, aged Dal Hon mage exchanged a glance with his cohort, who tucked his hands up under his arms. 'I'm redeploying them,' he explained.

Choss coughed on his poultry, wiped the grease from his tangled beard. 'Really?' he answered, incredulous. 'That force is badly needed to relieve those troops. They are hard-pressed, surrounded. All Korel has risen against them.'

Kellanved gave a curt wave. 'Exactly. A lost cause. We miscalculated there. I'll not pour more resources down that hole.'

Choss stared, his outrage obvious. 'But the remaining troops, man! What of them?'

'Word has been sent. They may withdraw.'

'If they can,' the general muttered, darkly. 'And regardless, we can use those forces here. Dujek is still stamping out insurrections in the east, and I'm still trying to pacify the west coast. Surly is camped in Unta to keep it quiet and all the while Dal Hon threatens to explode. Not a good time to start yet another front.'

'Dassem remains in Li Heng,' Dancer put in, speaking softly.

Choss grunted at that, half-placated.

While they had been talking, youths in travel-stained leathers, or hooded in grey robes, silently came and went, whispering with Kellanved, sometimes delivering scrolls. They entered from a rear chamber set off by hangings – a room Choss knew possessed no other exit.

'And where, may I ask,' he said, 'will this new strike force be headed?'

As Kellanved was conferring with a woman whose robes seemed to actually be smoking, Dancer answered: 'Falar.'

The general's thick brows rose in disbelief. He threw the half-eaten leg to the table. 'Falar . . . Really? Why not fabled Jacuruku while you're at it, hey?'

'Falar is no fable,' Dancer observed, calmly and quietly.

But the Fist was shaking his head, hands on belt. 'No. This is madness. We're still not completely consolidated . . .'

'We will never be *completely* consolidated,' Dancer answered. 'We must push on. Expand. Expand or die. It's the nature of the beast.'

'Is Surly for this?' Choss asked, pulling a hand down his beard. The two rulers exchanged another silent glance to which the general nodded. 'Thought not. Then I demand a full council meeting to review this.'

Kellanved flapped his hands in frustration. 'A *full* meeting? Do you have any idea how long it would take to assemble everyone?'

Choss gestured without. 'Your troops are still arriving. We have time.'

The Dal Hon mage raised his chin, half turning away, huffing, 'I'll have you know I don't need anyone's permission.'

The Fist nodded his agreement. 'True. However, as we have all seen over the years, everything goes so very much smoother with everyone's cooperation.'

Kellanved wrinkled up his dark face in distaste. He glanced to Dancer. 'What say you?'

Dancer echoed Choss's nod. 'I agree. We have to have everyone on board.'

The Emperor pressed his hands to his forehead, sighing. 'Oh, very well! If you *must*!' He waved the Fist out – who bowed and exited. Kellanved then snapped his fingers and a leather-clad messenger, a slim woman, emerged from the rear room. 'Send word to everyone,' he told her, 'we assemble here for a full Imperial Council meet.' The woman bowed and ducked from view. Kellanved continued to massage his forehead.

Dancer was studying the tops of his soft leather shoes. 'Told you so,' he murmured.

The Emperor looked to the tent ceiling, sighing anew. 'Oh, *please . . .*'

* * *

A bird winging its way northwards on the updraughts over the Great Fenn Range eventually came to the flat horizon of a continental ice sheet stretching as far as can be seen – even from such a great height.

All was not a wasteland of ice, however. Emerging here and there amid the plain of blowing snow rose islands of heat: fumaroles roiled out great gouts of steam and pits of mud and upwellings of boiling water bubbled. Here lay stone, soil, grasses and low scrub brush. And here could be found game: mice, hares, deer, and the lynx and bears and wolves that preyed upon them.

Impelled onwards, the bird wafted over one such island of life, riding its thermals, to find below huts of hide held down against the constant wind by rings of stones. At the centre of this gathering of huts rose a huge edifice like an upturned ship's hull, with a broad opening at its highest point. And from this maw came and went a veritable storm of birds of all sizes, shadings and kinds. Here the bird flitted within, selected a perch amid the many rafters and hangers, and promptly set to preening its feathers.

The High Priestess of the Great Assembled Clans of the Jhek lowered her face from the opening high above her seat to regard the crowded and this day uneasy court. She wore a scarf of cloth across her eyes yet seemed to peer everywhere and see every shift of stance, every murmur and every furtive glance.

Around her seat perched a multitude of birds of prey: kestrels, falcons, red hawks, and even two of the Great Eagles of the Fenn Range, each as tall as a boy. Their keen gazes darted all about, as sharp as their hooked razor beaks.

Today the Priestess too was nervous, though she strove to hide it. And she may have been able to disguise her emotions from her court, but she could not screen them from her pets, so deep and personal was her connection with them. Her unease spread to the birds and they loosed more shrill calls than usual, half rose from their perches, and shook their wings as if eager to hunt.

Reflexively, she reached out to smooth the plumage of the nearest. All here knew her as 'the Great High Priestess', or 'Bird Mother', but she thought of herself by another name, a name none among her adopted people knew. She also thought of herself as young still, though carrying an ageing frame and iron-grey hair.

And perhaps these differences from her predecessors was why she, inheritor of a near timeless line of priests and priestesses stretching back millennia, had been the first to break with an equally long tradition of warfare and hostility and call a truce with the Jhek's blood-enemy, the giant Thelomen of Fenn.

Now, after a decade of hard-won peace and mutual disregard, they wished to speak. Why? Whatever for? They seemed to need nothing and be content in their isolation.

No, the problem lay among her shapeshifting, Soletaken clans. And she focused upon a group of tall and ropy Jhek warriors among the crowd of her court. The wolf-warriors – most resentful of her peace, and most eager to return to hunting their traditional enemy. Epitomized by their clan leader – white-haired, lean, and ever with a hungry sharp-toothed smile – Looris.

Wiry wolf-soldier scouts came bursting into the longhouse, half loping, wearing loincloths only despite the cold. Her guard of bear-clan soldiers straightened before her, some growling.

'They come, Great Mother!' one scout panted.

She waved them down. 'Very good.' She turned to Looris. 'They come openly, in peace . . . remember that.'

Looris bowed his long and lean head.

The double-door entrance darkened then as huge figures ducked within. Four of the Thelomen, coming through single-file. Shaggy, in ragged hides, but not dull-witted or slow, no, bright and keen, peering all about and grinning as if in jest.

They bowed to her, rumbling, 'Bird Priestess.'

She answered the bow. 'You are well come. To what do we owe this honour?'

One stepped forward, eliciting warning growls from her assembled bear-warriors. This one bowed anew, and even offered a wink; she focused all her sharp eyes upon him to see the dark designs of jagged tattooing thick upon his features, and she thought him strangely familiar.

'We are come, Bird Priestess,' he began, 'because we are troubled.'

'Troubled?' She made a show of glancing about her court. 'Not by anything we have done, I trust.'

'No. Not you or yours. Though we believe you share our disquiet.'

She had indeed been troubled for some time, yet she did not answer. She had kept her unease from her adopted people because, frankly, she was afraid. Afraid of what her suspicions might mean for them. 'Go on,' she invited, her voice a touch fainter.

The giant inclined his head and said, 'No doubt you have heard the strange sounds coming amid the winds from the north. Smelled strange new scents upon the air. Felt the quakes and rumblings beneath your feet.'

She nodded. 'Indeed . . . And what, then, does this portend?'

'That is the question, is it not? We propose an expedition to discover the truth of this. A shared one.'

Looris stepped forward, his teeth bared. 'The northern plain is forbidden to all! None may venture there – upon pain of death!' The assembled wolf-warriors growled their support of this.

'And it is forbidden for a reason, is it?' the giant answered, nonplussed.

She raised a hand for calm. 'So, an expedition to the Broken Plain, and the forbidden mountain within. How is this to be done?'

The Thelomen gestured to his fellows – two other men and one woman. 'One of my kin here shall go accompanying a force of your scouts. They shall cross the plain, examine the mountain, and discover what there is to discover, if anything.'

She tilted her head in a very bird-like manner. 'And you?'

He pressed a wide hand to his chest. 'I shall remain here at your court as guarantor of my people's true intent.'

She nodded. Hostage. 'I see. What, ah, guarantor do you wish of us?'

The giant inclined his head to her. 'Your word, as pledge, is good enough for us.'

She answered his gesture. 'I am honoured by your trust. My word is given. A contingent of our wolf and bear warriors shall scout and guide one of you.'

The spokesman giant waved to the largest of all the four. 'This is Bellurdan, mighty among us. He has volunteered to go.'

11

She nodded to this one. 'Our thanks. May your travels be safe.'

Bellurdan answered her with a slight bow, crossing his thick arms.

She turned to Looris. 'Select our swiftest runners and most cunning scouts. I understand no one has entered the Broken Plain in generations.' She then turned to an older bear-warrior on her right. 'Athan, select our hardiest warriors.'

Athan, chief of the bear-warriors, growled his assent.

Finally, she faced the Thelomen spokesman once more. 'And you? If you are to remain among us, I should know how you are called, yes?'

The great shaggy giant grinned down at her, and again seemed almost to wink. 'Indeed, little one. You should. I am named Koroll.'

The Priestess couldn't hide her startled surprise. 'Koroll? Of Li Heng?'

His grin widened. 'Just so. And I must say, your aura is familiar as well.'

The Priestess raised a hand to her eyes as if to wipe them, but, brushing the cloth of the scarf, she jerked as if stung. She waved her court out. 'Go now, prepare.'

The assembled warriors filed from the hall, as did the three other Thelomen. Koroll moved to go as well, but the Priestess raised a hand. 'Stay. You may stay . . . we must talk.'

Athan straightened to his considerable full height – near to that of the Thelomen Koroll. 'Priestess! I object!'

She urged him down – gently. 'It is all right. They are here among us, outnumbered. None would dare provoke us. They came in trust . . . which I offer as well.'

Koroll bowed to her. 'You are wise, little one. I am happy to speak of anything you wish.'

She paused as Athan lumbered from the hall, the last to go. 'Can you tell me, perhaps, of the south?' she asked, her voice low.

Koroll nodded. 'All I know and have heard. Yes.'

She knotted her hands together. 'You have heard much?'

Koroll nodded profoundly once more. 'Indeed I have, little one. And, as I said, your aura is familiar from the past. You have my name – would you honour me with yours?'

The Priestess let out a shaking breath then lowered her voice to whisper, '. . . Ullara.'

*   *   *

The day Tayschrenn arrived at the newly bustling military encampment and tent city that encompassed the first full imperial war council for some time, he immediately turned his back upon it to walk out onto the rolling grassed hills of Purge to face the north, where, faintly, the jagged teeth of the Fenn Range could just be distinguished.

It was strange, he mused, as the cold winds buffeted him, whipped the tall grasses all about, and sent his long hair lashing, but for some time now something had been bothering him about the north. He could barely put his finger upon it – but where earlier he'd have dismissed it, over the years he'd learned to give greater heed to his instincts.

He crossed his arms and tapped fingers to biceps, frowning. It was all so very irksome – just something in the wind, or thinking he'd heard some distant sound, or felt something, even this increase in minor quakes shivering the ground.

A shadow crossed his vision and he glanced over to see the mage Nightchill standing to one side watching him, her head tilted as she examined him, as if she were amused.

He arched a brow. 'Yes?'

'You are troubled,' she observed.

'Am I?'

She turned her oddly long and narrow features to the north and raised her chin, indicating the distant blue line of mountain peaks.

He frowned anew. 'I am not certain . . .'

'Yet you sense . . . something . . .' She nodded to herself. 'I have watched you grow over these years, Tayschrenn of Kartool. You are coming into your strength, and you are stronger than you know. That you sense anything is a testament to your potential.' She now regarded the north, slit-eyed. 'I, too, am troubled. And now our esteemed leader chooses this time to mount an expedition northwards.' She shook her head. 'Is it prescience? I sometimes wonder.' She gave him another odd sideways glance, almost mocking. 'They say that is one prerequisite for . . . well . . . His and Dancer's time in the Dead House may have, how shall I say it, anointed them?'

He felt oddly offended by the insinuation. 'I received no such special gift or advantage from being within the house, I assure you.'

She nodded her assent. 'Yes. You entered. As did the devotee of Hood, Dassem. And his potential is obvious to all. So, the four of you. Any others?'

'None that I know of.'

She raised a hand. 'Then do not misunderstand me. I do not speak of gifts or aid or any such mundane thing. That would be beneath the Azath. The mere fact that they allowed you entrance means that they acknowledge the *possibilities* of you. Your potential. Do you understand?'

Indeed he did not, but he saw no reason to argue. This was in fact just the sort of vague and airy talk that he despised in magery – and which sadly the field was so very prone to. 'You seem to know a great deal about all this,' he countered, hoping to glean some scrap of further knowledge of the strange woman.

She shrugged, untouched by his challenge. 'A little.'

She turned to the south and the wind-buffeted tent city amid the rolling hills, and crossed her arms. 'Now, dare we descend into the vipers' pit, yes?'

Tayschrenn crooked a small smile and extended an arm, inviting her onwards. 'After you.'

The main briefing tent was lit by candles and braziers and was therefore quite smoky, rather dim, and uncomfortably warm. Dancer and Kellanved waited at the main table, which supported the official Imperial map of the northern regions – which was to say, a cobbled together collection of half guesswork and half legend.

Surly stood to one side, speaking with those survivors of her old Napan associates that could attend: the short and lean Cartheron and his unlikely brother, the gigantic Urko, together with the wind- and sun-darkened Tocaras, liaison with the Seti tribes, and the bearded, wild-haired general Choss.

Also present was the acknowledged 'Champion' of the Empire, Dassem Ultor – who never used the title himself. He was standing by the table, studying the map, his typical stern self. At the

14

sideboard was the newly arrived Eastern Commander, Fist Dujek, squat, half-bald, the stump of his left arm leather-wrapped. He stood alone, perhaps feeling a bit out of place.

Of the mages, there were Tayschrenn and Nightchill – two 'High Mages' of the Empire – plus ancient A'Karonys, and the blunt and bald figure of Hairlock, looking ill-tempered, as usual. The rest of the official Imperial Cadre, including Tattersail, was engaged elsewhere.

Kellanved raised his eyes from the map to regard the low canvas roof above. 'If everyone is *quite* ready, perhaps we can get this over with.'

'Not everyone is here,' Dassem observed. 'What of Admiral Nok?'

'He will remain in the south,' Kellanved answered tersely. 'There is work for him there.'

Dancer eyed Surly. 'And your right hand, Amaron?'

'Too involved in tracking a conspiracy among the Untan nobility.'

Dancer nodded, accepting this. He next eyed Tocaras, or Toc as he was now more commonly known. The man had been living among the tribes for some time and was even wearing Seti hunting leathers. 'Good to see you,' Dancer offered.

The wiry Napan dipped his head in acknowledgement.

'May we begin?' Kellanved cut in. He waved everyone to the table. 'It will be a two-prong assault. A land force and a naval force.' He gestured to the map. 'The expeditionary force will march north through the Fenn Range by way of Eagle Summit Pass.'

'That will bring them past the Guard's Red Fort – this Citadel,' Choss observed. 'Will we finally bring that down?'

Dancer shook a negative. 'No need. We keep a garrison on their doorstep, and word is there's precious few of them left inside anyway. They are dispersed now – a spent force.'

Kellanved raised a hand. 'For the moment, anyway. Now, a second, naval flotilla will then travel along the east coast, timed to arrive just before the land element.'

High Fist Cartheron was shaking his balding head. 'No. Suicide to challenge the Falarans at sea. We'd need a thousand ships – which we don't have to spare. So,' and he raised a finger, 'point two . . . what naval force?'

Tayschrenn recognized Kellanved's cagey look as the hunched fellow's gaze darted about the tent. He tapped his walking stick on the ground – and again Tayschrenn couldn't quite recall just when the thing had appeared. 'Ah, yes. The naval force.' The wrinkled black-skinned mage fiddled with the stick, studying it. 'We will sweep up all the freebooters, smugglers, and remaining independent captains as we go. I believe we'll be able to pull together a fleet of some five hundred.'

'Sea-trash and scoundrels,' Cartheron snorted. 'That's a joke – going up against Falaran galleys!'

'The flagship won't be a wreck,' Kellanved objected.

Cartheron cocked a brow. 'And that would be . . . ?'

'The *Twisted*.'

Everyone objected at once. Urko shouted, 'Ridiculous – unless I'm on it!'

Surly demanded, rather tightly, 'What would be the use of that?'

Kellanved and Dancer exchanged a look. 'It's these legends of this monster. The Jhistal. I would match the *Twisted* against it.'

For the first time Tayschrenn could remember, the Napan woman actually appeared shocked. 'You?' she said. 'You will be going?'

Kellanved shrugged in a too-smug attempt at modesty. 'Well . . . on and off . . . as it were.'

Surly eyed Dancer. 'And you?'

The lean assassin nodded. 'I will go as well, of course.'

Surly was shaking her head. 'I can't permit – that is,' and she cleared her throat, coughing into a fist. 'That is . . . I can't approve of this.'

'Well, we're going,' Kellanved huffed.

'Who is to lead the fleet?' Urko asked. 'You?'

Kellanved flinched. 'Gods, no.' He looked to Cartheron Crust. 'I was hoping . . .'

Cartheron glanced at Surly. 'Well . . . you should have someone with a level head along . . . I can relinquish the title of High Fist.'

'Temporarily,' Surly put in, her expression souring.

The Imperial Champion had been quiet this entire time, but now he extended a hand to speak. 'I too will go. I will accompany the land forces, Emperor.'

Everyone objected further. Once again Surly appeared surprised. 'Whatever for?' she demanded, now rather exasperated.

'This Jhistal. If it is a monster, I should meet it.'

'I shall go as well,' Nightchill announced. 'And Tayschrenn is interested.' She regarded him sidelong. 'Is this not so?'

All eyes turned to him and he cleared his throat. 'Ah – yes. I do wish to take a look at the north.'

'We can't all abandon Quon!' Surly fairly snarled. 'That's more than enough for any expeditionary force.'

'Yet who will command?' Choss put in. 'You still haven't said who will command the land force.'

Kellanved nodded. 'Ah, yes. Well, Dassem, of course.'

'No,' Surly answered, her thin lips compressed.

Dancer and Kellanved exchanged a look, the Emperor's brow rising. 'And why ever not?' Kellanved enquired.

'A commander must have an eye on the entire engagement. Not fight in the front ranks.'

Dassem pushed back the kinky long black hair hanging loose about his shoulders. 'Yes. We've been through this before. I cannot command if I am fighting.'

Kellanved entreated the tent ceiling. 'Well . . . Fist Dujek here then.'

'His wound is still fresh,' Surly objected.

'Well then, he won't be fighting, will he?' Kellanved observed, offering Surly a smile of victory.

The commander of the imperial intelligence – and assassination – service took a breath, her lips yet tighter. 'You are too improvident with our better generals. You have sent Greymane away – now you would take Dujek?'

The one-armed commander pulled his hand down his unshaven chin, glanced between the Emperor and the Mistress of the Imperial Claws. 'Well,' he began, 'if it's all the same—'

'I'm not taking or sending him away,' Kellanved interrupted. 'He's going with me. And anyway, the eastern command can safely go to his Adjutant there, Whiskeyjack.'

Surly started as if stung, and she appended, 'A temporary promotion. Sub-Fist only.'

Kellanved waved a hand to end the meeting. 'Very well. And you can summon us if need be.'

Everyone bowed to him and Dancer, and slowly filed out. Kellanved stood rocking on his heels, walking stick at his back, nodding to himself. Once all were gone, and the heavy tent flap had fallen, Dancer murmured, 'That went far smoother than I'd expected.'

'Indeed.'

Yet Dancer frowned again. 'And the Korel expeditionary force?'

The Emperor shook his head. 'They must withdraw.' He drew a long breath. 'We should've known better than to meddle in that region. Still, lesson learned, hey, my friend?'

'And Falar will somehow be different?'

The mage appeared shocked. 'Why of course! I assure you.'

Dancer crossed his arms to regard his partner steadily. Kellanved hunched beneath the gaze, lowered his eyes to fiddle with his walking stick. After some time, he murmured, 'Of course . . .'

Chapter 2

SUNLIGHT STREAMED DOWN THROUGH THE WATER ABOVE Gianna's head. It rippled like the auroras of magery that sometimes glowed over the great southern ice wastes. She lay upon the sandy bottom, peering up, air bladder in one hand, her other gripping the old timbers of the wreck she'd been searching. As in most of the Falaran archipelago these waters were shallow – relatively – and a pale green, almost olive. Bright fish, like shards of brilliant glass, swam between her and the bottom of the boat owned by the men who'd hired her, that was floating above.

While she lay there she noted a minor quake rolling beneath her. It churned the sands and clouded the waters for a time. After the murkiness cleared, she decided that by now the men who'd hired her must be suitably impressed by how long she could stay under, and so she let go of the timber. The air bladder pulled her upwards – air for her to refresh her lungs, but which she rarely needed, and she began her slow ascent to the surface.

She rose close by the side of the boat, took hold of the low gunwale, and pulled herself up. She found the five men sitting quite calmly, waiting patiently. The boss, a man out of Guando named Obert, merely drawled, 'You were down a long time.'

Rather annoyed by their indifference, she gestured curtly over the side. 'I don't know where you get your information but that wreck's been picked over countless times. There's nothing there but sand. Sorry you had to pay good coin to find that out.'

Obert shrugged his meaty shoulders and glanced to his fellows, all of whom appeared equally unconcerned.

Gianna began to get a very uneasy feeling about this job.

19

Sometimes disappointed clients got angry. Sometimes they accused her of hiding any treasure found – and she had to explain that if she tried that she'd lose her reputation and no one would ever hire her again. A few had even tried to get rough with her. Still, as a free diver she always insisted upon being paid up front, and the side was one leap away should these ones try anything.

'So,' she said, sitting on the gunwale, 'should we head back?'

Obert shrugged again and nodded to his fellows who set to raising the sail and lifting the sea-anchor. Obert had the tiller, which he turned to head them to the nearest settlement, Woad, to the north. She sat close to the stern as well and he pointed to her closely shorn hair. 'White . . . unusual, that.'

Self-conscious about it, she touched her bristling, brush-cut hair. White – she'd paid a lot to have all the colour taken from it. She decided then to imitate their manner and shrugged her own indifference.

Nothing more was said all the journey back to Woad. Obert's crew handled the main and the forestay while she and he remained at the stern of the launch. They entered Woad's busy harbour and approached a pier. Obert expertly swung them in while the crew quickly gathered the sails; pretty much every man and woman in the archipelago was experienced on the water.

She nodded to him. 'Well, better luck next time.'

A small smile crooked his lips and he glanced to his four crewmen also crowding the side. 'Sure, Gianna.'

She nodded again, in farewell, frowning at the strange tone he'd put on the name. She hopped down onto the worn grey-wood slats of the pier then froze as a handful of figures emerged from behind heaped cargo – men and women in the deep-blue, almost black, robes of Mael.

She turned on Obert. '*Bastard!*'

A rope noose tossed by one of the crew slipped over her head, yanking her back from leaping off the pier. She gagged, pulling at it. Obert grinned down at her from the side. 'You see, I *did* find my treasure.'

She drew her knife but one of the priests knocked it from her hand. The priests and priestesses now surrounded her. She recognized one, Hedran of Torn. He gave her a sardonic nod in greeting. 'You ran far, Giandra. But not far enough.'

'It's Gianna now,' she growled hoarsely.

He merely raised his shoulders. 'Whatever. Gianna. Time to come home.'

'Cabil is not my home.'

'It is now. And we've missed you.'

Obert, above, cleared his throat, a hand extended. Hedran glanced to one of the priestesses. She drew a leather bag from her robes and threw it to the man. Coins clinked loudly as he caught it. He gave Gianna a wink. 'Better luck next time.'

'Bounty-hunting bastard!'

The priests tied her hands behind her back. Hedran took hold of the noose. 'Come now. Let us at least have a pleasant sail back to Cabil, yes? What say you?'

She spat upon his robes.

Hedran had requisitioned an old merchantman. He had her locked in the smallest hold, and set sail for Cabil, the centre of the Faith of Mael. The boat's owner wasn't pleased with the arrangement, but he could not argue as every ship that plied the Falaran archipelago, and every isle thereof, owed excises and was held to an honorary allegiance to the Faith. All isles paid tribute in treasure and in the enrolment of youths each generation. All for protection from outsiders, claimed the cult. But every man and woman in Falar knew truly what their coin, food and blood bought them: protection from the cult itself.

The sea journey to Cabil took an unhurried three days and nights. Locked in the hold, Gianna felt the vessel slowly lose all headway as it hove-to before the first of the three immense sea-gates guarding the city. She heard the great iron and oak gates groan and the waters foam as they opened. The vessel edged forward under oar, up what she knew to be a narrow curving channel that boasted an army of guards at catapults, onagers and scorpions. The second gate churned open, and the channel then curved back upon itself to zig-zag its way towards the final gate before the harbour.

These layered defences were considered something of a marvel among the Falaran Isles. No other of the islands possessed walls as high or extensive – save Strike, but that lay open and exposed to the oceans of the east. Any foreign visitor might be forgiven for wondering why a city that served almost exclusively as the main worship centre of the Faith of Mael should require such massive fortifications.

The reason, as everyone in Falar knew well but never dared speak aloud, was that Cabil was much more. It was, in fact, the unofficial capital city of the entire archipelago. An authority monitored, enforced and administered by the priests and priestesses of Mael.

And Gianna loathed all of it.

The vessel scraped to a halt next to a jetty. Bare feet thumped the decking just above her head. Commands filled the air. A gangway banged as it was roughly lowered into place. The hatch opened and sunlight streamed down into the hold. She winced in the unaccustomed brightness. Her hands were still tied behind her back and so she struggled to rise, and couldn't straighten in any case, as the tiny hold was far too short. A priest, Hedran, stooped within. He gestured impatiently.

'Come. Don't make me fetch a pail of refuse.'

'You wouldn't.'

'Yes I would. Now come. You're just delaying things.'

'Fine!' She shuffled forward. She wished her hands were free so that she could toss some of the filth at her feet onto his fine blue robes. Straightening in the hatch she blinked anew, momentarily blinded.

Hedran tied a rope to the bindings at her wrists. Using slow but steady pressure he drew her up the short ladder to the deck. From here she saw the contingent of priestesses awaiting her on the jetty. Her head finally sank; this was it, she was captive again. Once more in their claws and now there would be no escape. Their vigilance would be increased a hundred-fold. Hedran urged her on ahead of him down the gangway.

The tall, grey-haired older priestess leading the contingent motioned to Gianna's hair, then opened her arms exclaiming, 'Oh, Giandra! What have you done to yourself?'

'It's Gianna – as before,' she growled. 'And spare me your false concern, Glinith.'

The priestess, Glinith, swept her into her arms in a hug and Gianna whispered into her ear, '*Horrid bitch.*'

Glinith, in turn, whispered, '*Foolish child.*' She then waved off Hedran. 'That will be all.'

'She may jump,' he warned, indicating the water.

'We are quite enclosed here,' Glinith answered, dismissive.

Hedran ducked his head. 'Of course, Abbess.'

Glinith took Gianna's forearm in a tight bony grip to draw her to the centre of the escort of priestesses and marched her along the jetty. 'Did you really imagine you could escape?' she asked in exaggerated sweetness.

'Every day away from you was a joy,' Gianna answered with equal sweetness.

Glinith simply smiled thinly and tightened her sharp-nailed grip.

The Abbess and escort marched her up wide stairs to a main waterfront walk that led to an entrance of one wing of the extensive complex of buildings that was the Basilica of Mael. This, Gianna knew from painful experience, was the Abbey, which housed the priestesses who guarded the most sacred precincts, including the Sanctum of Mael. Glinith urged her on, through sturdy sets of doors, up narrow stairs, through antechambers – all guarded – to an upper-storey hall lined by doors.

Before one open door, the Abbess yanked Gianna to a halt and pushed her within. Standing in the doorway, Glinith crossed her arms, her lips now drawing down in a disapproving scowl. 'Welcome home, High Priestess,' she announced, and slammed shut the door, locking it.

* * *

The survivors of the shipwreck emerged one by one from the night. They came drawn to a roaring bonfire of driftwood crackling and hissing on the barren shore of rock and snow.

At the fire sat a man and a woman, waiting. The man was quite old, with wild grey and black hair and beard, in sodden brown woollen robes. The woman was of middle age, in leather armour, longsword at her hip, her thick black hair loosened about her shoulders to dry, and so close to the fire did she sit that steam rose like smoke from her leathers.

In all, three survivors came slogging up, making their total number five.

The woman in leather armour tossed a stone into the fire, sighing, 'All right then . . . let's have it.'

The biggest of the lot, a giant fellow with a thick bushy beard, in sodden leathers, peered round at everyone and growled, 'This northern raid of yours isn't going so well, captain.'

The woman looked to the night sky, hissed a long drawn out, 'Yes.'

Flanking the giant were two others, heavy-set and young, male and female, with near identical round chubby faces and brown hair hacked short. They wore darkened dripping leathers, and were in fact twins. 'What now, Hessa?' the lad asked of the captain, peering out at the iron-grey waters.

'Dry off. Rest. Collect what we can.'

'No,' the female twin cut in, 'Hyde means what *now*?'

Captain Hessa dragged a hand through her drying hair, let out a breath. 'We'll find out in the morning.'

They fed the fire with more driftwood. Morning found them dry, though exhausted from hardly managing any sleep among the rocks, and now hungry. Hessa had the twins, Hyde and Ayal, hunt the shore for food then sent Corbin, their best fighter – other than her – inland to scout. She and Turnagin, the ship's mage, searched for anything washed ashore that might be useful.

They salvaged rope and canvas, stripped the corpses of three crew members they found, then piled rocks over the bodies. Hessa was quiet for some time standing over the makeshift graves. Later, two barrels of salted horsemeat were the prize of the day. They set to laying the pieces out to dry in the wind and sun.

During the work Turnagin commented, 'It was a good idea, Hessa.'

'What was?' she answered absently, her mind obviously on something else.

'Heading north. Striking out. The Falarans would've accepted us, I'm sure. She was a good ship.'

She nodded while studying the strips of meat; she hoped they would dry quickly enough not to spoil. 'Yes,' she answered, after a time. 'No room left for us free agents. The damned Malazans are taking over everything.' She shook her head. 'I won't bend the knee to some shadow-pushing mage who knows nothing of the sea.' She glanced over. 'No offence intended.'

Turnagin gave a half-smile. 'Shadow is my talent, yes. But I owe no loyalty. We're a fractious lot, mages. Meanas especially. And it is not my main calling in any regard. I am more scholar and philosopher.' He straightened his back, wincing. 'And since *he* has no time for philosophy – I feel that I must supply it for him.'

Hessa nodded at this. 'I noticed you didn't do much summoning and such. So I always wondered . . . why take service on board a ship?'

He smiled again, though it was wintry. 'Lots of time to think.'

Seabirds were gathering now and she kept a wary eye on them while they eyed the meat. 'And with all that time,' she said, without shifting her attention, 'you didn't see this coming?'

'I am no seer. Should I try I would see no specifics in any case. More like shades. The darker the shade, the worse.'

'So what do you see ahead?'

'Very dark,' the mage answered, softly. 'Very dark indeed.'

Hessa glanced to him; the fellow was resting his chin on his staff, his gaze turned away, eastward, inland. Then he jumped, raising his staff, shouting, 'Get away, damn you!'

Hessa waved her sheet of salvaged canvas at the bold birds, who squawked and screeched back at them.

In the evening they coaxed the bonfire back to life, set meat on sticks over the fire to dry and smoke further, and waited for the other three to return. While they sat waiting the very ground beneath them jumped, almost as if startled; rocks tumbled all about, clattering, and she and Turnagin eyed one another, amazed.

'Burn turning over,' Hessa murmured.

'So they say,' Turnagin agreed. 'She has been markedly uneasy of late.'

The twins Hyde and Ayal appeared first, tracing the shoreline, peering among the rocks. They came to the fire, Hyde looking very pale and ill.

'What happened to you?' Hessa asked.

He held his stomach, grimacing. 'Ate something we found.'

'He vomited like a sick dog,' Ayal put in gleefully. 'It was so funny.'

'What was it?' Turnagin asked, sounding quite concerned.

The lad shrugged. 'I dunno. Something ugly and squishy.'

'Did you cook it?' the mage asked.

The twins eyed him as if he were an idiot. 'How in the name of Hood are we supposed to do that?' Ayal demanded.

'You find a depression. Fill it with fresh water, then drop heated rocks in.'

Hessa nodded to herself, rather impressed by such practical knowledge.

Ayal laughed, scornful. 'An' where do we find this fresh water?'

'Use snow.'

The heavy-set woman lost her sneer. 'Oh. Didn't think a that.'

'Anyway,' Hessa asked, 'did you find anything?'

Hyde shook his head. 'Naw. Just rotting dead fish'n such. Seaweed. People say you c'n eat seaweed – but I don't know what kind.'

'I believe I may,' Turnagin said. He looked to Hessa. 'I'll collect some tomorrow for drying.'

Hessa gave a curt nod. 'Good.' She pointed to the twins. 'You two – go with him.'

They shared a glance and rolled their eyes, then they crouched at the fire to warm themselves and Ayal reached for the nearest strip of meat on a stick.

'Later,' Hessa snapped. Ayal glared, but dropped her hand.

Much later, in the dark of night, Corbin appeared, walking in from the east. He crouched to extend his hands to the fire, rubbing them.

'Well?' Hyde asked. 'Did you see anything?'

'I hiked to the highest piece of land I could find an' looked east.' He eyed Hessa. 'Saw snow. Leagues and leagues of it. On for ever.'

Turnagin nodded. 'Yes. The Ice Wastes. Anything else? Any settlements? People? Animals?'

Corbin snorted, derisive. 'No. Nothing. No soul or beast.'

The mage appeared troubled. 'Really? Nothing? You are certain?'

The big fellow drew a hand down his thick unruly beard. 'Well,' he drawled, letting out a breath, 'far off to the east . . . there was smoke.'

'Smoke,' Hessa echoed. 'One little bit? Or a steady plume?'

Corbin hunched his shoulders. 'A steady plume,' he admitted, grudgingly. He raised his chin to the strips of meat. 'Found some stores, hey?'

Hessa sorted through the pile of canvas strips and handed some out. 'Here. For wrapping the food. And this is all we have for now.

We divide it up. Everyone gets an equal share – so be careful! Eat all yours and I see no reason to give you any of mine.'

Turnagin divided the meat. Hessa wrapped hers in the canvas and pushed it down under her hauberk. Ayal and Hyde each tore into a portion of theirs. Corbin held a bite in one cheek and cleared his throat, asking, 'So . . . what's the plan?'

'One more day on the shore,' Hessa supplied. 'Maybe some more wreckage will wash up – though we went down damned far off shore. Then we strike inland for this smoke. Smoke means fire. Fire means warmth, maybe even life, perhaps even people.'

Corbin grimaced, but said nothing. Hyde shook his head. 'I dunno. Maybe we should just sit tight here an' wait for another ship to come by.'

Ayal laughed her scorn. 'You dummy! No one's stupid enough to sail up this wretched shore!' Then she started, eyeing Hessa sidelong.

Hessa simply cleared her throat, murmuring, 'Point taken. We try inland.' She motioned to the pile of salvaged canvas. 'For now, everyone make yourselves cloaks, or wraps for your feet or hands, or whatever.'

In the end they remained for three more days. Turnagin kept busy drying seaweed over the roaring bonfire, while everyone used the scavenged canvas to fashion cloaks and mittens and foot-wraps. Hessa took the time to hike inland for a look at this smoke herself. She crossed to the crest of a snow-covered hill to peer eastward into a punishing icy wind. It took some time, shading her eyes, but eventually she did spot the plume – slightly to the south. It troubled her that she was able to see it from such a great distance, but it meant heat, and very possibly game, or people.

They built a sledge of driftwood, piled it with as much wood as it could carry, stacked yet more bundles of firewood onto their backs, then headed inland wrapped in their layered canvas cloaks, hoods and swathings.

* * *

Shortly after joining the Crimson Guard, Gregar Bluenth was officially dubbed 'Blues'. Who'd been behind the naming he never did discover. It may have been Haraj, the old friend he'd joined the

Guard with, gone now these many years – the poor fellow's health just hadn't been tough enough for the campaigning life. It was his lungs, the best bone-menders and medicers had all said. The constant damp while growing up in the depths of Castle Gris. Fluid and scarring and a ragged damaging cough that never went away. All growing more and more severe until his lungs filled with fluid entirely; and there was nothing any Denul healer could do as it was the man's own body just naturally breaking down.

Blues pulled his crimson cloak tighter against the freezing northern winds and peered down at the campfires of the Malazan force far below the clifftop tower that was the Guard's Red Fort – that some named the Citadel. And he felt then a faint tremor transmitted up through the very stones of the fortress.

Yet another minor quake; the goddess Burn breathing or shifting in her captivity far underground, some said. A portent to many. To Blues, still exploring his talents as a mage of D'riss – the Warren of earth and rock – perhaps nothing more than the shifting of stone as it heated or cooled.

He heard someone climbing the stairs to the roof and he knew who it was from the slow and hesitant progress. When his fellow mage reached the open doorway atop the circular stairwell, Blues said without turning, 'Good evening, Smoky.'

'Blues,' the lean mage answered, nonplussed. The fellow edged forward to peer over the battlements. He was dressed in dirty old robes but his goatee was crisply trimmed and his long greying hair was pulled back in a neat queue. 'Still here I see.'

'Keeping a wary eye on us,' Blues murmured.

'They *do* know we could leave by Warren any time we wished, yes?'

'But then they'd have the fort, wouldn't they.'

'They are welcome to it.'

Blues sighed. 'Our last toehold on the continent. Hard to let go, hey?'

Smoky shrugged his bony shoulders. 'For some maybe. Myself, I can't wait to head out on contract.'

This was a lingering point of contention among the garrison here at the Red Fort and Blues couldn't help but add, 'Once our relief force arrives.'

28

'It may never come,' the mage answered. 'They may have forgotten about us.'

'They haven't *forgotten* about us,' Blues sighed.

'Then where are they?'

'Busy,' Blues murmured, his tone signalling he'd had enough of the debate.

Smoky cleared his throat. 'In any case,' he said, 'there's something I'd like you to take a look at in the cellars.'

Blues nodded.

Far below – as far as it was possible to descend in the main tower of the Red Fort – Smoky lifted a lit lantern from its sconce and headed up a narrow hallway. Ahead of them the walls glittered in hoar frost.

The mage raised the lantern and Blues understood it was merely for his benefit as Smoky was a master of Telas, the Warren of fire, and could see fine in the dark. At a far door the mage gestured to the wall and Blues edged forward.

The courses of dressed stone blocks were offset in a jagged run that extended like a scar from floor to ceiling. He knelt to examine the dirt and dark moss that had fallen from between the blocks and squeezed the tracings, still moist. 'Recent,' he murmured.

Smoky nodded. 'There's worse within.' He pushed open the door – with some difficulty as the frame was now off-square.

It was a cobwebbed empty storeroom. Not one Blues had ever entered before. One of the lowest in the tower, perhaps even the last room before the foundations. Smoky raised the lantern to the far wall. The dressed stone blocks here were displaced along two verticals. It looked as if a giant had pulled the wall apart.

'When did you find this?' Blues asked, quite alarmed.

'It was brought to my attention today by a servant searching for supplies. These recent quakes, no doubt.'

Blues raised his Warren and pressed his hands to the blocks, casting his awareness outwards, into the solid stone and beyond. He detected no tension, no building potential or stresses – for now. 'The north,' he whispered aloud, mostly to himself.

'The north?' Smoky queried, curious.

'These quakes. They are all coming from the same direction. The north.'

The fire mage nodded. 'The Fenn Range. Perhaps Burn is not yet done with it.'

29

'Perhaps. In any case, we must talk to Gwynn.'

'Very good.' Smoky motioned the lantern towards the door.

As they climbed the narrow stone chute of the spiral stair Smoky peered back over his shoulder saying, 'You know who's supposed to supply the tower's next contingent, yes?'

'No. Who?'

'Skinner.'

Blues felt his lips tighten, but he said, 'Every captain takes a turn. Shimmer has fulfilled her obligation. He'll do his.'

Above, the thin mage shrugged. 'Still . . . they're over a year late.'

Blues raised his brows, surprised. A year? Really? Had it been that long? Time here seemed to speed by so very quickly.

Smoky exited the tight circle of the stairwell at an archway. Down the hall he knocked on a door and together they waited. No answer came. He knocked again. With yet no response the hound-lean mage stroked his goatee in silent commentary, then tried the door. It opened onto a narrow private chamber dominated by a large and heavy table behind which sat a man reading, elbows on the table and head resting on his fingertips.

Smoky cleared his throat and the fellow, another mage, Gwynn, raised his head to blink at them. 'Yes?'

Blues said without preamble, 'You've noticed the quakes of late?'

Gwynn nodded. 'What of them?' He rose and crossed to a small side-table where he poured a glass of wine from a large stoneware jug. He was dressed as was his habit, all in black, with a wide crimson sash at his waist.

'Far below there are cracks in the north wall. New cracks.'

Gwynn leaned up against the table. 'You're certain they're new?' He gestured around him. 'This tower is ancient. It has endured many quakes, no doubt.'

'They're fresh,' Blues insisted. 'I can tell.'

Gwynn raised his shoulders in an easy shrug. 'If you say so. Is it a danger?'

'I believe it could be, yes.'

'Then you'd best keep an eye on it, hmm?' Their commander raised his glass towards the door. 'In the meantime – I have work to do.'

His mouth tight, Blues inclined his head, and exited. On the way down the stairs he couldn't help but snarl to Smoky, 'Who does he think he is? He's no better than any of us. Command rotates.'

'I hear he came from a rich merchant family in Unta,' Smoky supplied. 'He certainly seems used to ordering people about.'

'Too easy with it by half. There's no rank in the Guard!' Blues didn't add that it was this in particular that had attracted him to the mercenary company in the first place. That and all its glory and fame – if he had to be honest.

'There's seniority,' Smoky put in. 'He's been with the Guard for a long time.'

Blues just grumbled under his breath.

In the days and weeks following he did keep an eye on the tower's foundations. Each tremor, some strong enough to knock cups from tables, others so faint no one else even noticed them, brought him down to the lowest cellars, where he inspected the stone walls for new gaps or bulges in their courses. And what he saw developing there did not reassure him.

* * *

Bellurdan did not hurry in the journey north to the forbidden centre of the Wastes. That said, being of Thelomen kind – half as tall again as any man – even his slowest amble was a league-swallowing pace no human could match. He was not hurrying because, firstly, the Thelomen (like their relatives the Toblakai) were a people who prided themselves upon never rushing into anything. Secondly, it was plain that the Jhek warriors accompanying him were in agonized haste to reach their destination.

'Why do you limp along like a cripple!' wolf-warrior Gashar complained for the hundredth time as he'd run back for their lagging companion. 'Are you frightened?'

'Frightened of what?' Bellurdan rumbled mildly, smiling.

The wolf-warrior, naked but for a loincloth, his hair a wild tangle, clambered among the snow and rocks all round the giant, never staying still, sometimes on two legs, sometimes down on all fours. 'The stories,' Gashar leered, baring his teeth. 'The Enemy. The Ancients who mastered the earth.'

Bellurdan nodded his agreement. 'So the stories say. But who

31

has seen any of these Elders? None in living memory. And for the Thelomen, that is a very long time indeed.'

Gashar shook his hair like a mane. 'Faugh! You are frightened. Come! Do not hang back like a coward. There is a hill ahead and a vista of our destination.'

'Is it going anywhere?'

The wolf-warrior paused in his incessant pacing to frown over this. 'Is what going anywhere?'

'The hill ahead.'

'Of course it isn't, you fool!'

Bellurdan nodded sombrely. 'Ah, good. I am reassured. For a moment I thought we must hurry as it was about to disappear.'

Gashar scowled, glaring. He suspected he was being mocked – somehow. Not used to this, he fell back on the tried and true wolf-warrior response to anything more than eating or fighting: 'You're a fool!' he snapped, and bounded off.

Alone once more, Bellurdan continued in his league-eating pace across the flat and windswept wasteland of ice and snow and broken blackened rock. The smile that crooked his mouth from teasing the wolf-warrior quickly faded, as there was little satisfaction to be had from flummoxing the defenceless. He drew a long, low breath; it was going to be a long, dull, and, he suspected, judging from these warriors' limited repertoires, painfully repetitive journey.

How much easier it had been just to fight them!

But the time for that indulgence was passing – so said the ancients of his kind, those whose living memories extended far back indeed. Their vision foresaw a time of turmoil upon them. A time of change. And so old ways must be reconsidered.

Not an easy thing for a people as old as his.

He climbed the slope of the so-called 'hill'. More a rise in the monotonously level plateau. A naked heap of pulverized rock pushed up by the shifting ice that lay as a crushing weight across the Wastes. Here, four bear-warriors awaited him, stolid and silent. Hugely strong and bulking for a human, yes, but nowhere near the might of any Thelomen. One gestured ahead with a thick paw-like hand. Needlessly, as Bellurdan's eyes were no doubt far better than his – bears not being known for their vision.

And there it was, far towards the northern horizon, a thin plume of greyish smoke that rose straight up for some great height. Bellurdan searched his feelings and settled upon . . . unease. For unlike the Jhek's, the racial memory of the Thelomen stretched back unbroken very far indeed. And he had heard stories told of the war that raged across this plain. Stories of one of the seven known K'Chain Che'Malle cities, the Mountains that Move, besieged here by a coalition of races, including his own. Of energies released that blasted this region into the wasteland it had remained to this day. Just like the great plain far to the south of Stratem, where another such mountain city had exploded in an eruption that seared the lands to glass and burned the very skies.

He lowered his gaze to find the eyes of one of the bear-warriors upon him. 'You are slowing us down,' the great man-beast rumbled, resentfully.

'Why? Is it going somewhere?' Bellurdan asked again, smiling.

The creature frowned its confusion. 'Is what going where?'

Bellurdan could only shake his head and sigh.

Chapter 3

To Cartheron's eyes the harbour at Cawn was the ugliest of all the waterfronts of Quon Tali. No effort at all appeared to have been expended in improvements or even maintenance. Instead, raw sewage dribbled in rivulets next to where citizenry – the poorest, admittedly – washed their clothes, their eating crockery and themselves. The main wharf leaned towards the water and the walk was missing a great many boards, making cartage of goods possibly even more hazardous than the sea journey that brought them.

He'd imagined that merchants would be concerned about such things. But not those of Cawn. Each withheld all such expenditures, thinking their rivals would give in first and fund the work. And the result? Nothing got fixed. All of which contributed to an air of general neglect and mean grasping shabbiness that hung over the city like a stink.

Or it could just be his mood.

He shifted his gaze from the piers and dilapidated warehouses to the door of the *Twisted*'s main cabin. *He* was in there now, meeting with a handful of local captains – though captain was far too polite and generous a term for what these were. Lawless seaborne thieves, petty smugglers, coastal raiders and slavers. Men and women too bloodthirsty, drunken or double-crossing to make the cut for the Malazan navy proper.

This brought an ironic smile to Cartheron Crust's lips. Here were trash even ex-pirates like him looked down upon. Imagine that.

Laughter sounded from the cabin, harsh and all too smug for

Cartheron's comfort, then the door opened and out came this most recent handful of such refuse and sea-debris. They emerged winking and murmuring jokes with the short, dark-skinned Dal Hon elder in their midst who smiled benignly and nodded back. He motioned his walking stick to the side where launches and rowboats waited to take them back to their – Cartheron had to pause here to swallow the taste in his mouth – their *commands*. He pointedly turned his back, not deigning to acknowledge them, while they disembarked.

Moments later the Dal Hon elder came to stand at his side: he knew this from the unmistakable power of the man's aura, a puissance that made the hairs on Cartheron's forearms stand on end, though he was no mage. (And a good thing that was too, as he was often in the man's company, for he gathered that the unique strangeness of the man's Warren Meanas, and his mastery of it, often produced skull-cracking migraines, fainting and even nosebleeds in fellow mages.)

'You still disapprove,' Kellanved observed.

Cartheron turned to the Emperor, ruler of all Quon Tali, or at least that portion that could be ruled. 'Does it matter?' he grumbled.

Kellanved shook his greying head. 'No. Just hoping you'd come around.'

'Come around to what?' He motioned dismissively to the scattering launches. 'These so-called *captains* you're recruiting are scum. I know for a fact that at least one of them is an outlawed slaver I'd sink if I came across them at sea.'

The mage raised a placating hand. 'Patience, Admiral. All will be revealed . . . in time.'

Cartheron took a steadying breath. That answer. Always the same damnable answer. Still, they weren't at sea in a leaky boat . . . yet. 'Why, then, am I even here? Obviously you don't need my advice.'

Kellanved appeared genuinely surprised by his words. 'We are going to Falar, Admiral! I will need someone who understands the sea.' He pressed a thin, veined hand to his chest. 'Speaking for myself, I confess that I do not.' He pointed his walking stick east. 'Onwards, then, round the Vorian coast to Unta, yes? We have many more captains to recruit.'

35

'Half the ones you are paying won't even show, you know.'

The Emperor waved negligently. 'No doubt. However, I have their names and will have strong words for them should they disappoint.'

Cartheron had to eye the stooped elder sidelong: he still couldn't tell when the man was being serious. Even Dancer, he knew, was never absolutely sure. 'Well,' he put in, hesitantly, 'I'm certain that will prove cautionary.'

The ancient nodded, quite solemn. 'Indeed. Now,' and he motioned to the cabin, 'I will be within if you would do your sail-orly thing and cast the sails off – or whatever it is one does.'

Dismissed, Cartheron could only bow. 'Emperor,' he murmured.

So the pattern repeated itself, all round the coast: at Vor and Carasin, Aythan and Nure, Gast, Yellows, Larent and Sentry. At some ports no candidates presented themselves. At others, such as Larent, many. However, it was at Unta, the capital, that the most responded. Two separate gatherings had to be organized on board the *Twisted*.

At the second such meeting Cartheron could stand aside no longer and had to find out what all the laughter and glad-handing was about. So, he swallowed his distaste, his disgust and his pride, to slip within the cabin.

The captains sat around a large table with Kellanved, who, amid all the joking and raucous laughter, was distributing pouches of coin. And not just coin, but scrolls as well. Cartheron pushed from the wall, leaning forward over these men and women's heads to take one such parchment, which he read.

It was an official – Imperial – Letter of Marque, endorsing reprisal, raiding, and prize-taking.

With an effort, he managed to suppress his outrage. He dropped the scroll and returned to the wall, where he waited for all these Untan petty shore-raiders, thieves, and damned kidnappers to leave.

And if just one of them were to back-slap him as an equal partner in all this – he'd have that hand. That he swore to himself.

Eventually, the last of them filed out, Kellanved waving them off. Cartheron waited for the door to shut then growled, 'Letters of Marque? We're not even at war with Falar!'

36

The Emperor fluttered a hand, unconcerned. He went to a sideboard where he searched among the various crystal decanters; selecting a tall thin bottle he poured the dark liquid and took a sip. Gagging, he set the glass down. 'Not yet . . . true,' he managed, grimacing at the lingering taste. 'But that *is* the plan.'

'The Falaran navy will destroy these scum. You're sending them to their doom.'

Kellanved raised another decanter. He squinted at the label. 'Whale milk.' He looked to Cartheron, dubious. 'Really? In truth? Or poetic?'

Cartheron suppressed his impatience – this was the Emperor after all – and he was not Dancer, who, unfortunately, had been called away for . . . well, for *work*. 'In truth. A delicacy, fortified and preserved. Quite sweet, I'm told.'

Kellanved shuddered and set the decanter aside. 'Not the Falaran navy, Cartheron. There is no single navy of Falar. Each island fields its own ships.' He raised a quizzical brow. 'Is this not so?'

Lips compressed, Cartheron managed a terse, 'So I understand. Still – people speak of the Falaran navy.'

'A shorthand convenience only, I assure you. In any case, I intend to scatter my fleet, sending them to raid against all the islands, hither or thither as they will.'

Cartheron nodded, seeing the strategy. 'This Jhistal, then, this monster, can only attack a few at a time.'

Kellanved selected another dark liqueur and poured a thick dollop into a tiny glass. 'They will certainly try, I presume. After all, this cult of Mael claims to protect the isles.'

'Then they will select you and the *Twisted*.'

The mage tasted the liqueur and grimaced again. 'Perhaps.'

'And if they do? What will you do?'

The dark Dal Hon elder frowned and opened his arms in a shrug. 'Then we shall see.'

Cartheron could not stop his brows from rising. *Ye gods.* Unimaginable hubris? Or calculated cunning? No one, it seemed – including him – could penetrate the chaos and mystification the man deliberately cultivated.

The Emperor extended the decanter. 'Be a good fellow, Admiral, and dump this over the side.'

Bowing, Cartheron took the bottle. 'Emperor.'

At the half-rotted rail of the *Twisted*, he sniffed the liqueur and was overpowered by some sort of fruity miasma. Passion fruit? Pomegranate? He upended the bottle, and, out of old habit, the ancient rite of propitiation scrolled through his mind: *Accept this offering, Chem. Smooth the waters and guide the winds ...*

* * *

Tayschrenn understood that the armies of Malaz prided themselves on their marching. Convenient, he thought it, given that there was no real cavalry to speak of in the imperial forces – beyond small numbers of Seti or Wickan irregulars. No, the main Malazan horse was wood, and transported them swiftly to every coast. Yet once there, they had no option but to march. Horses were extravagant, costly, prone to sickness, and gods did they eat!

He shared the aversion. He'd never come to terms with the beasts, and as a consequence he rode like a sack of grain. Thankfully, this Fist had no difficulty with marching. And they were headed into mountains after all.

So he paced alongside the fellow, Dujek, just behind the van.

They had served together, of course, over the years. Though never side by side, as Tayschrenn was no battle mage, or cadre mage, as they'd come to be known. Confusing, that nomenclature, since all mages serving under the imperial banner – that is, under him, the High Mage – served in the mage cadre; but such was the precedent and usage, that those serving in the ranks became cadre mages.

He eyed the officer sidelong as they climbed the rugged foothills of the Fenn Range. The twenty-five thousand of his command were strung out in columns to all sides, foraging and hunting as they went. Unshaven this fellow was, most of the time. Laziness? Or cultivating an air of distracted contempt for appearances? Or perhaps he just hated shaving. Burly, with the broad shoulders of a swordsman, though one-armed now, so perhaps those days were over. An old companion to Dassem Ultor, Sword of the Empire, was the common wisdom. Said Sword marched with them now, though he kept to the wilds, hunting with the scouts. Strange how that fellow actually enjoyed running after game all day; for his part, Tayschrenn shuddered at the thought.

This one, Dujek, also shared that natural touch of camaraderie and easy manner of command with the men and women of the ranks. A skill that somehow still eluded him, even when he had bothered to try.

Yes, all in all, some amount to be envious of – if he were prone to envy – which thankfully was a base emotion far beneath him.

So, gloved hands clasped behind the thick cloak at his back, Tayschrenn cleared his throat, saying, 'You have been selected personally by Kellanved a number of times before, yes?'

The fellow tilted his shaven, sun-darkened head, considering. 'A few. Over the years.'

Tayschrenn's own sources hinted at far more than this, but he nodded, accepting the answer. 'You'll have to be careful of that reputation.'

Dujek turned his head, a brow arched. 'Oh?'

'I mean, there will be talk among the officer corps, I'm sure. Some might decide you are the Emperor's favourite, being groomed for overall command.'

He shrugged, unconcerned. 'I've just been on hand when needed.'

'That's not what people will think or remember—' He cursed then, as the heel of one of his tall boots turned on the rough ground. 'People search for patterns,' he continued. 'It's what they do. They will see one here and there will be whispering.'

A half-smile behind the salt-and-pepper bristles. 'You warnin' me?'

'Cautioning, merely. You are close to the imperial inner circle. Succeed here and the coveted rank of High Fist may be yours, yes? The many back at Unta who lust after the rank see you as a threat to their own ambitions, I promise you that.'

Dujek waved his gloved hand. 'I get things done where I am. Why change that?'

Tayschrenn smiled. 'When the Emperor calls upon you for these . . . special missions?'

A chuckle. 'Point taken.'

Runners approached with news from the fore, yet Tayschrenn made no effort to hold back or move off while Dujek dealt with these command matters – strictly speaking, as High Mage, he outranked this regional Fist.

A runner saluted, halting. 'Word comes that Eagle Summit Pass is open, though very narrow.'

'Send lead units through to secure the north end of the pass.'

The young woman raced off. The second announced, 'Spoor has been found of cave bears and what the hunters think might be ice wolves.'

'This far south? Something must've stirred them up. Warn all troops not to wander off alone.' The runner saluted and darted away.

'Eagle Summit . . .' Tayschrenn observed. 'This brings us right past the Red Fort. Their vaunted Citadel.'

The Fist shrugged again. 'What of it?'

'No special orders in dealing with the Guard?'

'No. I have no interest in them. Our mission is Falar.'

'Really? You have the troops.' Tayschrenn gestured east. 'A full-on attack. Overwhelm them. You could be the Malazan commander who finally crushes them. Your reputation would be sealed.'

Dujek gave a snort of a laugh. 'I'd be a general disobeying commands, and a Claw would be sent to collect my famous head.'

From the edge of his vision Tayschrenn studied the man anew. He'd thought he understood the military mindset. Any of the officers back at the capital would jump at such a chance. Fame. Glory. The lust for rank and command. What else drove such men and women?

Still, this one knew Kellanved and Surly well. Perhaps he knew better than most the unavoidable consequences of any misstep. Perhaps the highest ranks had eluded him for so long because of this particular character flaw – timidity.

And yet, such a theory flew in the face of all the other rumours surrounding this man. It was a puzzle; and puzzles interested him.

At least it would help pass the time during the long march.

The Fist gestured north. 'What of beyond? What of these . . . Fenn?'

Tayschrenn nodded and rocked back and forth on his now uneven boots. 'Yes, the Fenn. Giants. Tarthino or Thelomen? Or, gods forbid, Toblakai.'

'Hostile?'

'Little is known. Legends claim so, but no reliable recent information exists. People all say they are – yet no documented encounters can be produced.'

The swordsman grunted, scowling. 'Rumours and say-so. Not

enough. But for the troops' sake I'll have to assume we're facing hostiles and take the necessary measures.'

Tayschrenn inclined his head, accepting this. 'Of course.'

Now the commander eyed him. 'And the cadre's job, then, is to make certain this doesn't become a self-fulfilling prophecy.'

'Oh?'

'Yes. I expect the cadre to make every effort to reach an accord with these locals – if at all possible.' And he walked off.

For a moment Tayschrenn stood wondering: *was that an order? Did a mere Fist just issue an order to him, the High Mage?* But the man was gone and he could only bite down on his affront. He took a moment to look to the cloud cover above and exhale a long breath. Tested. He must welcome this. It had been some time since his restraint had been so tested. He must rise to this.

He wiggled his toes in his too tight boots – and felt sure he was developing a blister.

That evening the servants set up tents for Tayschrenn and the cadre. He usually sat at table with Hairlock, together with the most northerly Quon Talian mage the Empire could recruit: a Seti shamaness provided by Toc's contacts, named Sialle. The last mage of the expedition, Nightchill, being of solitary habits, rarely joined them.

Hairlock had his sandalled feet up on the table and was already into his wine, his reddened face and shaved bald pate glistening in sweat despite the cold. He raised his cup when Tayschrenn entered. 'Come join us, High Mage. We dine well this night.' He waved to the table. 'Some forager took down a wild boar sow.' He held up a cut of meat on a knife. 'Unless you are too fussy for such peasant fare. Perhaps you'd rather a mushroom or a sprig of something.'

Quite used to the mage's jabs, Tayschrenn merely inclined his head at the invitation and nodded to the young and petite white-haired shamaness. 'Sialle.'

She answered the greeting, bowing her head. 'High Mage.'

He sat and a servant brought out a plate of fresh cuts that he examined. 'I have a directive from our commander,' he said, by way of an opening, as he selected a portion.

'Not *our* commander,' Hairlock snorted. 'What d'y'mean, a *directive*?'

He took the time to chew thoroughly and to taste the wine – disappointing – before explaining, 'We are to reach out to these Fenn. Strike an accord if possible.'

Hairlock eyed him, dubious. 'You mean so we can lure them in and exterminate them?'

Tayschrenn looked over the greasy fire-seared meat and sighed. 'No. I mean a true accord. An avoidance of hostilities so that we may pass through quickly to our real objective.'

The squat bald mage snorted his derision again and threw back his wine. 'They are hostiles on the Empire's frontier. They must be dealt with.'

Tayschrenn looked to the shamaness. 'What say you, Sialle? Will these Fenn negotiate? Listen to reason?'

The young shamaness toyed with her bone-handled eating knife. Her gaze became veiled. 'Ah yes,' she mused, 'your *reason*. We Seti know all about your Malazan *reasonableness*. And the Talians before you. All you outsiders. You claim our hunting territory, our pasturage for your farms. And when your sheep or cows wander onto our lands and we eat them because we are starving you take even more lands as reparations. After all, that's only reasonable, yes? And when our villages or people are attacked, we defend ourselves – yet *we* are jailed or hunted for murder. More of your reasonableness, yes?' With the point of her knife she pricked her thumb and showed them blood. 'Jab someone and they will bleed. Take away their hunting way of life and they will starve. A reasonable expectation, wouldn't you say? For my part, I pray to all the gods that the Fenn remain ignorant of your self-serving reason.'

Hairlock sneered, 'Then why in Hood's name are you with us, girl?'

She answered the sneer with a cold, hard smile. 'Some among the Seti must learn your ways. That is, after all, reasonable, yes?'

Tayschrenn returned to his meal and made a mental note that should it come to any negotiations with the Fenn, Sialle would certainly *not* be attending. He cleared his throat into a fist. 'Well . . . perhaps they will remain their characteristically elusive selves.'

* * *

Blues pushed open the door to the fort commander's quarters and announced, 'The Malazans are coming.'

Gwynn peered up from his writing. 'In case you hadn't noticed, they're already here.'

Blues crossed his arms. 'I mean more are coming.'

'Oh?' Gwynn sipped his tea. 'How many?'

'Best estimate is twenty thousand.'

The pale mage choked on his tea. 'Twenty—?' He pushed back from the table. 'Ridiculous. Our little fort is hardly worth the outlay of that sort of resources.'

'Tell them that. Nevertheless, all the scouts agree.'

The commander peered aside, stroked his neatly trimmed goatee. 'We've heard nothing of this. Some massing of troops in Purge, yes. We still have sympathizers in Quon – why have we heard nothing?'

Blues scowled his displeasure. 'We've heard nothing from no one for too long. What's going on? Where's our relief from Skinner? Cal-Brinn's out of touch, and Smoky says he's heard nothing from Shimmer for over a year. I don't like it at all.'

Gwynn nodded, distracted. 'Yes, yes. So you've been saying.' He tapped a finger to the scarred wood of the tabletop. 'Very well. Send Smoky to me. Tonight we will make a collective effort to contact Skinner. And you will attend as well.'

Blues shook his head. 'Not my sort of thing.'

Gwynn smiled, perhaps at Blues's discomfort. 'Nevertheless, I suspect we will have need of your strength.'

That evening Blues joined Smoky and Gwynn in the commander's quarters on the top floor of the tower. Once he arrived Gwynn had them pull the large heavy table to the wall, to clear the centre of the room. He then had them stand together facing west. At Blues's quizzical look the dour mage explained, 'I believe he's in that direction.

'Now,' he went on, 'Smoky and I shall reach out as we have had more experience at this. You, however, must be ready to lend your strength.'

Blues nodded, and together they raised their Warrens to their furthest height. The table juddered on the stones of the floor as the room began to vibrate with the power it contained. Dust swept up all about and a wind now rushed past Blues from behind, as if being sucked into some sort of gap in the air before them. Darkness gathered at the room's centre and Blues recalled that Gwynn's Warren was that of Rashan – Night itself.

Smoky grunted then as if gut-punched, hissing, 'There's a powerful aura near. Shielding this place.'

Gwynn cut a hand through air and the darkness parted, revealing a scene as if through a window: large green leaves dripping water, a thick jungle, as of southern Dal Hon. Then came the clash of battle nearby.

Blues now sensed something behind him, approaching. Something immense and very powerful. He resisted the urge to glance over his shoulder.

'Skinner!' Gwynn yelled. 'Your brothers and sisters seek you!'

'Come!' a voice commanded from the dense leaves and hanging ropy vines. The view shifted as they seemed to jump, then there stood Skinner, wearing now a coat of fine dark mail armour, and at his feet the tangled coils of a snake, its girth as great as Blues's thigh. Nearby, half-hidden amid the jungle, there fought other brothers and sisters of the Guard. Skinner drew off his full helm and pushed back his long sweat-soaked hair and seemed to glare right through them. 'You should not be here,' he growled. 'You must go.'

'The Malazans are coming for the fort!' Blues shouted.

'Then slay them all,' Skinner answered.

Somehow, Blues wasn't surprised.

'We need reinforcements,' Gwynn ground out, his teeth gritted with effort.

Skinner shook his head. 'I am sorry. We are hard-pressed here. I have accepted a challenging contract.'

'And just where is this?' Smoky gasped, sounding as if he were drowning.

The man's slash of a mouth crooked at some hidden joke. 'Jacuruku.'

The darkness wavered then, Gwynn perhaps losing his focus in shock. 'And your patron?' he grated, renewing his effort.

Skinner waved them off. 'Go now! She comes and allows none to trespass on her demesnes.'

'But—' Gwynn began, only to grunt in psychic pain, as some

44

thing tore the connection from him and Smoky and was now in the process of brushing aside all their frantic efforts to sever the link.

Blues had one last glimpse of a renewed attack on his brothers and sisters as what looked like gigantic butterflies came hovering down upon them, before Smoky, tottering, clutched his arm and he had to throw all he had against the titanic tsunami of power about to smother them.

An instant's hesitation of surprise, or uncertainty, was all he bought with his entire might but it was enough for Gwynn to cut the connection. The three of them collapsed, while the room rocked as if slapped by a giant.

Black the Lesser, Lean and Jacinth burst in, swords bared. 'What is it?' Black demanded.

Blues could only lie blinking to refocus his vision. The big swordswoman Lean yanked him to his feet and he nodded his gratitude then went to see to the others. Black raised Smoky who stood dazed, blood running from his nose and eyes. Gwynn was on his feet, and strangely his clothes now smoked as if he'd just emerged from a potter's kiln. The mage of Rashan dabbed at his own bleeding nose.

'Well,' he croaked, 'I believe we now know who Skinner's patron is.'

'Who?' Blues demanded; his ears still rang from that blow of stupendous power.

Gwynn appeared amused by Blues's lack of knowledge. 'Why, Ardata, of course. Whom some name the Witch Queen of Jacuruku.'

Blues managed to stifle his laugh of derision; after all, they'd just had a demonstration that this Ardata was no myth.

'Will there be any relieving force?' Jacinth demanded. Her thick mane of red hair was all a tangle, and she wore only a thin linen shirt and cotton trousers. Blues found himself admiring the curved musculature of her shoulders.

Gwynn drew out a handkerchief that he pressed to his nose. He shook his head. 'No. There will be no relieving force for us. We are on our own.'

'And our orders?' she asked, her gaze narrowing.

'We are to resist.'

45

Jacinth snorted, 'Against twenty thousand?' and she stormed from the chamber.

Black scabbarded his sword, saying, 'Well, they'll sing a song of the engagement . . . but it will be a very short song.'

Blues wiped his wet nose and tearing eyes and silently agreed with that sentiment.

*   *   *

The Golat family villa stood upon a cliff on Cabil Isle, with a view of the Old Guando Sea. This day, Trehan Golat, patriarch of the family, had been surprised by a noontime announcement from a servant that Mallick Rel, priest of Mael and Overseer of Coin, had arrived for a visit.

This was quite surprising to him as no such arrangements had been made between his secretary and this fellow's servants. Nevertheless, while the Golat family was very old and possessed a permanent seat upon the island's guiding council, this Mallick Rel was an important priest of the cult of Mael and had risen very fast within that organization to now be in charge of all its finances.

Also, troubling rumours circulated concerning the man and the numerous deaths and disappearances of individuals who happened to stand in the way of his advancement.

So, that noon, Trehan stood waiting in the villa's gardens over-looking the sea, waiting and wondering what possible reason could lie behind the visit.

The priest's rather large party came filing along the cobbled walk that led from the front main entrance to twist its way between pools, plantings of rare flowers, and twinned fountains. All wore the long flowing blue robes of the cult of Mael. The man himself was by far the shortest of the group, nearly all the others being his personal guard of burly priests.

Trehan bowed, calling out, 'Welcome to the Golat family villa. To what do we owe the privilege of your visit, honoured priest?'

At a small wave from the short and chubby priest his escort of guards and servants dispersed, leaving the two of them alone. The priest crossed his arms across his wide stomach, slipping his hands into the robe's broad sleeves. He peered about the gardens, blinking in the sunlight like some underwater creature drawn up from his accustomed darkness. 'I have heard much of the beauty of these grounds and would see for myself,' he said, his voice so faint Trehan could barely hear his words.

Trehan beamed, inwardly relieved, and raised his arms wide. 'Of course, sir. A tour perhaps, before a meal?'

The suggestion of further physical activity made the priest wince. His greased flat hair and pale skin made Trehan think there was something slimy and lizard-like about the man. 'Later, perhaps,' Mallick said. 'I have decided that I do indeed like the grounds and the villa, and that they will do just fine.'

Trehan stood blinking his uncertainty. 'Ah, fine, sir? Fine for what?'

'For myself, of course.'

After staring for a time Trehan offered up a nervous laugh. 'You must be misinformed, sir. The villa is not for sale.'

Mallick sighed heavily, as if already exhausted by the day's efforts. 'Patriarch Trehan. I have recently come into a position of some responsibility with our good faith and now require a residence reflecting said position.'

Trehan was now losing his patience; this was all just too outrageous – even for the high-handed priests of Mael. 'Well, I wish you luck with your search, father priest, but this villa has been in our family for generations and is not for sale.' He pointed to the front. 'You know the way out.'

The priest did not move; his gaze did not even shift from Trehan – who became a touch uneasy beneath the man's odd slit-eyed stare. 'It is my humble duty to know the finances of the Faith, and it sorrows me to say that your family has fallen into debt in this regard.'

'Ridiculous! We have kept up in all tithes and taxes.'

'Said duties have been your son's, yes?'

Trehan now frowned, troubled by the man's direction. 'Yes . . . what of it?'

The priest raised a pale stubby hand and studied his blunt nails. 'Sadly, none of such monies have reached the temple's coffers. While your son has hosted many extravagant parties of late, has he not? And gambled a great deal. And lost a great deal.'

'These are lies, sir. I will thank you to leave.'

The squat priest merely stared back with his half-lidded eyes.

'Said debt must be covered and the Faith shall accept this property – in lieu of other payments. In kind or chattel.'

Trehan found his hand going to his throat. 'Chattel?' he managed, his voice hoarse. 'What other payments could you mean?'

Mallick slid his hand back into a wide sleeve. 'Your younger children – all daughters, I understand? They could be accepted into the Faith. Such a service would be an honour to the family, yes? Scullery maid, or floor scrubber, or prostitute. No doubt some use could be found for them.'

Trehan could not find any words; he gaped, stunned. Finally, he hissed, 'You little shit. The council will hear of this outrage! You cannot simply—'

The priest had waved and strong hands took Trehan by the shoulders and marched him up the walk. He shouted as he went, all abuse and insults. Mallick sighed, peering round the gardens. One of the priest's servants approached and bowed. Ignoring the servant, Mallick mused aloud, 'It suits, but I doubt I shall spend much time here.'

'And the council, father?' the servant enquired.

The priest blinked at the servant. 'The council only listens to men or women of property. And Trehan Golat is no longer a man of property.' He waved the servant off. 'Now go prepare a bath. I am much in need of one.' He extended a limp beringed hand.

The servant bent to one knee, kissed the ringed fingers, and backed away, murmuring, 'Of course, good father.'

Chapter 4

ABOUT TWICE EVERY MOON A RITUAL OF SORTS WAS OBSERVED on a pier of Cabil's enclosed harbour. An elderly washerwoman of the temple, her hair all a tangle, would arrive at the waterfront to sit with her equally unlikely paramour, a greying, heavy-set carpenter. Together they spent the evening, he smoking a pipe, she mending bits of cloth, as they shared one another's company.

For observers and other passers-by it was a test of one's character and outlook on life. Those without compassion or any generosity in their souls found the sight revolting. Those labouring under an excess of optimism or a romantic inclination were warmed by the example of enduring loyalty and friendship. Realists saw few other options available for either. As was usual, none saw the entire truth. The two were not lovers – though they did love one another – nor were they even of Falar.

'They are coming,' Janelle announced to her brother, Janul.

'It's about time,' he grumbled. 'We've been saying this place was ripe.'

'The same was said about Korel,' Janelle put in.

Janul blew out a snorted gout of smoke. 'Different. How could anyone predict they'd be so stubborn?'

'People are always stubborn in the face of change. Especially change from the outside.'

Janul began, 'I'm sure this—'

Footsteps on the boards sounded behind and a voice snapped, 'Don't you two have duties?'

Janul peered up over his shoulder where a priest of Mael in his deep sea-blue robes stood glaring down. 'After this dinner hour, good father,' he answered round his pipe.

The priest's glare turned even more sour and he wheeled away in disgust. 'Well, see to them! Don't fritter all your time away here,' and he marched off.

'Fritter?' Janul murmured. 'Did he say *fritter*?'

'Indeed he did.'

'Hunh. People say the oddest things . . .'

'A black heart in that one,' Janelle observed. 'No generosity of spirit.'

'A characteristic of the order, I'd say. No one will miss them.'

'That's what they said about—'

Janul threw his hands up in surrender. 'I know! I know.'

'Anyway,' Janelle continued, 'anything to report?'

'Another quake. Quite strong. Shacks nearly collapsed. A big wave took out a dock.'

'I felt it too. Pots and pans fell everywhere.'

'Burn fighting her captivity,' Janul sighed.

'Mael,' Janelle corrected. 'They say it's Mael here.'

'Hunh. They would, wouldn't they.'

'Nothing else?'

'Well . . .' Janul answered thoughtfully, drawing on the pipe. 'Heard some strange talk on the waterfront. Parties sent into the southern mainland wilderness are overdue. Some say they've disappeared. Natives, or something.'

'But the southern wilds are unpopulated.'

Janul shrugged. 'So they say.'

'Anything else?'

'Not that I can think of right now.'

'All right then.' Janelle pressed her hands to her thighs. 'Next week. I tell you, I'll be glad to finish this assignment and move on.'

Janul shook his head; his greying brush-cut hair gleamed in the sunset. 'Not me. I kinda like it here. I sense . . . possibilities.'

Now Janelle shook her head and, rising, flexed her back with a groan. 'Gods! Getting old is not for the faint of heart.'

'We've lived twice over, you and I.'

She grunted a laugh. 'Hunh. Maybe so. Magister protect you, brother.'

'And you, sister.'

A woman's voice called loudly from along the pier: 'Oh, look at you two lovebirds!' A very wide woman in a cook's apron came over to smother Janelle's hands in her own. She beamed down at Janul. 'It warms the heart, it does! Gives us all such hope.'

Janelle ducked her head shyly while Janul looked away.

'Here you are, you two!' and the woman produced two buns from pockets in her apron. 'Fresh from the oven, stuffed with sweetmeats.'

Janelle curtsied, taking them. 'Thank you, ma'am.' Janul, she saw, was hiding a wide grin behind his hand.

*　*　*

It was Hyde and Ayal's turn to pull the sledge. Hessa scouted ahead with Corbin, while Turnagin lagged behind as always: the cold, the poor fare, the constant labour of struggling on, all was taking a toll on a man not used to hardship.

Hessa herself was feeling the strain, and she a toughened veteran. She paused amid the snow to hug herself and rest for a moment. The roiling plume of what was obviously a giant volcano now churned overhead. Large flakes of ash and soot fell as if new snow, and here and there amid the ice and bare black rock steam curled and vented. At least they no longer froze at night; they merely had to select one of these hot flues to huddle about. Sleep could come then, without the fear of never awakening again – if one could sleep with the now near-constant rumblings and shakings that juddered the land beneath their feet.

And as usual, when she paused she began to think and with thought the doubts came rushing in. It was bad enough the way they all looked at her – as if she'd condemned them to die – though none said a thing of it. At least not to her face. But what had been their choices? Being marooned on the shore or marooned inland? Did it matter at all? At least they had the promise of warmth here, which was sent by the gods, as their wood was running out.

Corbin appeared from scouting far ahead. He was wrapped from head to foot in a long canvas cloak. His thick beard and wild shaggy hair glittered white in frost.

'Any sign or spoor?' Hessa called, as they all did every day.

The big man came close, rearing taller than Hessa who was

considered unusually large – especially for a woman. His face held a strange expression as he studied her for a time silently, then he spoke, his voice hoarse and faint. 'Aye.'

Hessa was actually surprised, and she sighed, feeling the enormous pressure upon her relenting a fraction. *At long last.* 'What game?'

'The big shaggy ones, like oxen.'

'Really? Close?'

Corbin nodded. 'Just beyond the rise ahead.'

Now she frowned, a touch puzzled. They'd heard nothing. 'Did they catch wind of you?'

Again the man's strange haunted expression, but tinged by a dark humour. 'No. They did not.' He gestured ahead. 'You'll see.'

Turning, Hessa waved to the distant figures of Hyde and Ayal, each leaning forward, lashed to the sledge, and she gestured for a halt. They eased up and Hessa nodded to Corbin. Together, they advanced to the slight rise ahead.

Once they made the high ground Hessa had to pause to let what was confronting her sink in. A valley of white snow and black rock misted by steaming flues stretched out before them; dotting it lay a swath of dark shaggy bodies, an entire herd perhaps. All dead.

After a time Hessa managed, her voice a croak, 'Who would do such a thing?'

'All left to rot,' Corbin added. 'No meat taken.'

That, she had to admit, shocked her the most. Thinking of her duties, she turned and waved the rest forward. They stood silently studying the slaughter while the others gathered with them, Turnagin the last. After a few gasps and muttered curses Ayal started forward only to halt as Turnagin thrust an arm in front of her.

'Wait!' he commanded, then he turned to Corbin. 'This mist – was it always here?'

'Aye.'

'And you entered into it?'

'Aye.'

'Any dizziness? Shortness of breath? What did it smell of?'

The hulking fighter pulled a sour face. 'The usual stink. Shit and rot and farts.'

'You examined one of the bodies?'

'Un-huh.'

'And? Any sign of how it died? Any wounds?'

Corbin laughed at that and ambled forward. 'Oh, yes. There's wounds all right . . .'

When they reached the first of the field of shaggy oxen corpses Hessa saw that Corbin had not been exaggerating. The massive animal had been hacked nearly in two by one great slash of some large cutting weapon. After that, it had been left to rot – or in these temperatures freeze solid – amid its own spilled viscera. No feeding at all, as far as she could see, though from blood splashes it did look as if some carcasses were missing. She motioned to Hyde. 'Butcher this one. Pile it all on the sledge.'

'Must be as hard as a rock,' Hyde complained.

'Then chop hard.'

Grumbling, Hyde set to work. Hessa crossed to Corbin and muttered under her breath, 'I wouldn't want to meet what did this.'

'Don't know what did it but there was somethin' else here.'

'Something else?'

Corbin nodded to where Turnagin crouched, examining the snow. Hessa went to look herself. There were tracks in the snow, but this spoor was like nothing Hessa had ever seen before. Enormous claws, or talons, was all she could make of the traces.

Turnagin pointed to one particular track. 'See the depth? Very heavy, whatever it was.'

'What was it?'

The elderly mage sighed his discomfort and rested his hands on his thighs. 'Well. This will sound outrageous, but from what I can see these tracks resemble those of birds – monstrously huge birds.'

Hessa gave him a very hard look. He raised a hand. 'I know, I know. But look . . .' He indicated a wide imprint. 'Three forward raking clawed toes; one rear claw. Looks like a very large bird foot.'

'Could these claws have made these wounds?'

Turnagin pulled his fingers through his wild unkempt beard, thinking. 'Possibly . . .'

Hessa straightened. 'So . . . huge carnivorous birds.'

The mage rose as well, blowing on his hands. 'No. Not just carnivorous. Murderous and bloodthirsty beasts that walk on two clawed feet . . .' The mage paused, his voice trailing off. His gaze swung to the volcano peak and the man visibly paled. 'No . . .' he murmured.

'What?'

'We must avoid the mountain. Go around.'

'Turnagin . . . It's been our goal for weeks.'

'I know! But now we have food, yes? We can carry on to the far coast. Or the north.'

Hessa was shaking her head. 'I can't just order everyone to turn around. Not after we've come so far.'

The mage swept out an arm to encompass the killing field. 'What more do you need?'

She blew out a hard breath, considering. Her gaze lingered on the trail of bodies. So many! All left to rot. Why? She nodded then, curtly. 'Very well. This I can sell.'

The mage relaxed, nodding his gratitude. 'Very good. I'll start working on disguising our presence.'

Hessa raised a brow. Really? He was that worried? 'Should we move at night?'

But Turnagin just shook his head, moving off. 'No. It would make no difference.'

She watched him go, rather bemused. She'd never seen the fellow so unnerved. Still, she had commands to give so she slapped a hand to the grip of her longsword and ambled over to where the twins were butchering. 'As much as you can,' she told them. 'We're heading north to Falar.'

The two gaped up at her. '*What?*' Ayal burst out. 'Why don't we just walk in fucking circles?'

Hessa pointed to the carcass. 'Turnagin says whatever did for these will get us if we don't swing away.'

Ayal sneered, 'How the fuck does he know?'

Hessa gave a curt wave, ending the conversation. ''Cause that's his job. Now you do yours,' and she walked away.

She didn't mean to join Corbin where the big fellow stood staring off at the mountain, his arms crossed, but it was the direction she'd swung into and so she ended up stopping at his side. After a silence, she asked, 'What do you know of the Wastes?'

'I've heard rumours,' he allowed.

'Such as?'

His gaze lowered to one of the carcasses. 'Of death – and of monsters. But more than that as well.'

'Yes?'

He lifted his chin to indicate the mountain. 'Of treasure and lost knowledge beyond anything anyone can imagine. Enough to buy a kingdom.'

Hessa couldn't tear her gaze from the hacked corpse. 'No good to you if you're dead.'

Corbin didn't answer, and after a time she gave him a glance to see his jaws working and bunching, perhaps in frustration – or hunger.

*　*　*

Gianna wandered the halls of the sprawling temple complex at Cabil. As the entire series of buildings, walks, yards and temples was walled and closed off, she was allowed to go pretty much wherever she wished – though shadowed by four priestesses chosen from the guard regiment of the order. She knew that to the Abbess and the guiding priests of the Inner Synod of the Faith she probably resembled an animal prowling its cage, seeking escape, which of course was very much the case.

Her pace was fast, stiff-legged, as she stalked hallway after hallway, endless staircases, and countless rooms after empty waiting-rooms. Her escort was sometimes hard-pressed to keep up. She stopped only at windows that offered a view of the waters far off beyond the walls that stood between her and the sea. There, she would stand for a time staring, hands pressed to the rough and gritty stone ledges.

On one of her rounds far down in the lower kitchens her escort was particularly delayed by the curved narrow servants' stairs and she made it clear to the far side of the broad kitchen before they appeared, hurrying now after her. She turned to run but a crash and yells of pain brought her up short: the priestesses had run into or tripped a servant carrying a large pot of steaming soup, drenching their blue robes even darker and eliciting yells of pain. She glimpsed the kitchen labourer – an older, dumpy, wild-haired woman – before turning again to run. Oddly, the woman gave her a broad wink as she yanked and pulled on robes to wipe them with a dirty rag and the priestesses fought to slap her away.

She eluded her escort for the rest of that afternoon, and as she walked, hands at her back, feeling more carefree than she'd been since her arrival, it occurred to her that there were clearly more prisoners here in this complex than just her.

The next morning when the lock to her cell rattled and the door was yanked open it wasn't the usual escort of brawny, dull-witted priestess guards awaiting her; there stood Glinith, the Abbess herself, the habitual scowl upon her tight lips, arms crossed over her thin chest.

'It has been decided,' the Abbess began, 'that your time would be better spent in meditation and prayer, rather than racing about the complex like a spoiled child.'

'Or like a prisoner?' Gianna suggested.

Glinith did not deign to acknowledge the comment, gesturing her into the hall instead. 'This way.'

'I know the way,' Gianna snarled.

'Really?' The Abbess arched a brow. 'I am quite astonished.'

Gianna bit down on any further comment, growling under her breath, as she had to admit that the damned woman had won that round.

She was escorted through the broad colonnaded Basilica itself, which hosted all main public ceremonies, to the private worship centre beyond, one open only to those sanctified in the worship of Mael. This circular space held a pool sacred to the sea god, and offered many stone benches all for meditation and prayer. Beyond this, Gianna knew, lay the most sacred Inner Sanctum of the Faith – a great drop to the secret Holy Waters of Mael – where, it was said, the Jhistal itself was summoned of old.

Her escort pushed her down onto one of the cold stone benches where she pulled her robes tighter about herself. After a warning glance to the four guards, the Abbess offered Gianna the sketch of a bow and withdrew. Gianna resisted sending her on her way with a few choice words – thinking that would come across as merely petulant.

Instead, she considered the Abbess's injunction: prayer and meditation.

Very well, Mael – I'll offer you up a prayer.

She clasped her hands before her lips, fingers entwined, and clenched her eyes shut. *Oh, Great Ancient One, Mael . . . May you dry up and blow away.*

May you be forgotten. May your worship be destroyed. May you diminish and be forgotten to all.

It is I, your High Priestess, who offers up this prayer – grant it, be you a god! If not, I curse you as a fraud, a fake, and a sham!

I, Gianna, so pray!

For the first time in her life she prayed with fierce conviction, and she pressed her fingers and nails to her forehead with all her force until she felt hot wet blood warm them.

*   *   *

After the fifth bird the Priestess, Ullara, sent after the northern scouting force was somehow turned away – or her vision was somehow torn from it, leaving her momentarily blind – she sent for the Thelomen Koroll.

The giant appeared, ducking his head through the wide entrance, and offered her a bow. 'You sent for me, Priestess?' he rumbled.

She realized she had her fingers entwined before her and she pulled her hands apart, pressing them to her lap. 'Yesterday and today I find that I can no longer follow the party. My pets are brushed aside. *I* am even balked somehow. Do you know anything of this?'

Koroll nodded his shaggy head. The tattooed lines all across his face twisted and writhed as he rubbed a cheek. 'Aye, little bird. That does agree with what my kin find. For some time now we've been unable to probe northwards to the mountain.'

'Yet you said nothing of this?'

'I hoped that perhaps you would be able to pass through whatever this is that has been raised against us.'

'A warning would have been—' Wolf-warriors came loping through the entrance, followed by their chief, Looris, who came panting. He glared at the giant. 'We do not like you being here alone with our Priestess, Thelomen.'

'I summoned him,' Ullara explained.

The old wolf-warrior inclined his long head to her. 'Priestess. We have advised against such meetings, have we not?'

'You have. And I have taken that under advisement.'

'We consider it dangerous.'

Ullara indicated the entrance. 'Would you leave us for a moment, Koroll?'

The giant bowed. 'Of course, Priestess.' He shambled from the hall.

Ullara turned on Looris. 'I *know* you think it dangerous. You have been more than plain in your warnings.'

'And yet?' the lean chief asked, tilting his head.

'You did not say please.'

The chief's teeth, almost always bared, now disappeared behind his lips as he pressed his mouth shut, ducking his head. Ullara waited, silent. A long and slow growl escaped those lips and the man straightened, pushing his shoulders back. 'Very well,' he ground out. 'Will you *please* not meet with this Thelomen alone?'

Ullara answered with a considered nod. 'Thank you. I shall try to have guards present in the future. Now, please have Athan attend me.'

Looris bowed, his teeth bared once more. 'Of course, Bird Mother.'

The wolf-warrior chief motioned for two of his men to remain then marched out, attended by the rest of his guard.

Athan, the bear-warrior chief, entered shortly after. Hugely tall, with great rounded shoulders and thick arms heavy, all covered in greying pale hair, he bowed to Ullara. 'Yes, Bird Mother?'

Ullara clenched her lips. She knew what she would say would now make its way to Looris, but the wolf chief would have learned of this eventually, in any regard, so she let her breath out and said, 'I have seen a great deal of smoke far to the south, round the pass at Eagle Summit. Send two of your most cautious warriors to investigate. What is it? A Seti war party? Malazan scouts?'

Athan bowed once more. 'At once, Priestess.'

She watched the huge man – giant she used to call him, until the Thelomen arrived – lumber from the hall. Please let it be nothing more than a lost party of some sort, or miners, or anything, she wished for the hundredth time. Anything other than the Malazans exploring the northern routes. This was frankly the last thing she needed right now – possible threats from both sides?

Through the eyes of the many pets she kept about the open-roofed hall she saw that she'd twined her fingers together once more and she yanked them apart.

*   *   *

The flotilla of vessels newly commissioned in service to Malazan imperial forces made poor progress northwards round the east Quon Talian coast. Cartheron wanted to blame the poor sailorly skills of these sea-scum; but he had to admit that the weather and the sea were against them.

First there were the currents; the further north up the Wickan coast they pressed, the more turned-around and unpredictable the waters became. None of the known currents were in their seasonal place. Instead, the waters churned as if unable to find their way. And this was as nothing compared to the winds. These lashed and turned all about, far stronger than any records indicated of the region. They were also unseasonably warm, and sometimes dense with smoke – Cartheron wondered if perhaps there were forest fires in the Fenn Range.

Because of this he had the *Twisted* showing very little canvas. Its bow-wave was hardly discernible. The fleet of some four hundred followers milled to the rear, and he wouldn't be surprised if some of the soft-spined weaklings had already turned back.

And all this was before the ice.

He'd been belowdecks. It was night, just before he was to turn in, but their slow progress had sent his mind to supplies; had they brought enough for this extended journey? How was the sweet-water holding out? They could hardly count on known stops for resupply between here and the Falaran Isles.

Then the call had gone up from the watch – the shout that freezes the blood of any experienced mariner: '*Ice ahead!*' Cartheron ran for the ladder, sailors scrambling from his way.

At the rail he scanned the dark waters and it took him some time to understand what was confronting them. Broken crags of ice floated like a serried mountain range for as far as he could see. Not one berg, or sheet of flat sea-cover: a flotilla that far dwarfed his own, comprising chunks of all sizes, all gently bobbing and bashing one another as they rocked amid the steely grey waters.

'Drop all canvas!' Cartheron called. 'Ready belaying poles!'

The Malazan sailors, who had all been staring too, ran at his command. He sensed a new presence at his side then, as the small hairs of his arms and neck now stirred: he glanced over to see the Emperor, Kellanved, walking stick planted on the decking before him, hands crossed over its silver hound's head.

'We have slowed even more,' the Emperor observed, with no small amount of disapproval.

Cartheron gestured ahead. 'A field of icebergs.'

The dark-skinned mage squinted then flinched as if offended. 'This is not mentioned on any chart nor in any traveller's journal.'

'I know . . . yet here it is.'

'These shakings of the earth of late, perhaps,' Kellanved mused.

Cartheron nodded. 'Perhaps.' He pointed again. 'Can't you do anything . . . ?'

The ancient-looking mage raised an eyebrow. 'I can't just wave them out of existence, if that's what you're hoping. No, Shadow can have no effect here. I am quite out of my field.'

Cartheron sighed – he could never get the hang of this spookery-jiggery stuff. All too abstract for his liking. 'Very well.' Bowing, he moved away, forward, to direct those sailors and marines crowding the bows, poles extended.

Over the next few hours he had everyone pushing away the smaller shards of glittering ice, while shouting directions to the steersman, Geddin, to avoid the larger. In this fashion they threaded the maze of bumping, aimless wanderings of the bergs until it was time for the next hands to take over. Cartheron then stumbled, exhausted, to his bunk.

Morning's light revealed the sea still awash in bergs of all sizes – from tiny slivers to fortress towers. Silvery glare shone from their smooth facets and fractured sides. One nearby, as large as a castle, showed rounded shoulders and glass-like curves; water dripped from its lower edges just above the reach of the waves.

'They're melting,' Cartheron announced to no one in particular.

'Not fast enough,' a passing sailor answered.

Cartheron agreed. Jill, the ship's second cook, handed him a glass of hot tea and he turned to examine the south: his – and here he hung his head for a moment – *his* command looked to be strung out over several nautical leagues. The craven worms seemed to be trying to follow the *Twisted* through this maze single-file, like ducklings after their mother. Mouthing a silent curse over their yellow hides, he drank the tea then looked to the mainmast, calling, 'Can you see an end to the damned things?'

No answer came and he squinted more closely: no one appeared to be up on the top spar. He peered about for Creel, the mate. Spotting him, he shouted: 'Creel! Why is there no one on damned lookout?'

The mate came to him, looking abashed. His wild unkempt hair blew about in the contrary winds. 'Beggin' your pardon, Fist, but, ah, *it's* up there. The, ah, *thing*.'

Now Cartheron rolled his eyes. *Oh, by the Seven Daemons of Kan!* He stomped to the captain's cabin, currently occupied by Kellanved. Knocking on the door, he received no response, and so very slowly, and carefully, he swung it open to peer inside. The cabin was very dark, seemingly shrouded in gloom. Cartheron squinted, his eyes adjusting. 'Ah, Kellanved . . . you are here?'

A slight hint of movement there in the murk; a faint shift of cloth and a clearing of throat. 'Yes, Cartheron?'

'Sorry to interrupt . . . whatever. But your ah, pet, is in the shrouds and the crew won't go near it.'

'Ah.' The walking stick appeared from the darkness, pointed to a corner. 'You see that keg there?' Cartheron nodded. 'Walnuts. Take a sack and lure him down.'

Like some damned bird? But he nodded, doing so. He emerged, canvas sack in hand, and crossed to the mainmast. Here he shook the sack, the walnuts chattering within. Other than this he didn't know what to do. Should he call? *Here, boy! Good boy!*

As it was, there was no need: the creature came swinging down with astonishing agility and speed. Before Cartheron could react, it snatched the sack from his hand, gave him a sort of wild fanged grin, and took off for the stern, crew men and women ducking and jumping from its path. The thing resembled a small ape. Nachts, they were called. Native to Malaz and other remote locations, favouring, he understood, dense forests or steep cliffsides.

Shaking his head, Cartheron waved the nearest sailor up the mast. Soon the shout came down that the field of ice crags extended for as far as anyone could see. He resisted pounding a fist to the rail at this. Already they were far behind schedule, and they hadn't even met the enemy yet! They would have to get word to the expeditionary force – and he supposed that was another reason why Kellanved was with them. At least they should be able to coordinate through him.

*   *   *

While waiting for Eagle Summit Pass to clear completely, Command of the Falaran Expeditionary Force encamped with the small Malazan garrison nearby that was tasked with keeping an eye on the Crimson Guard's Red Fort, or Citadel. It was a contingent of some seven hundred, a backwater command of no potential note, the sort of post usually assigned to veterans close to retiring or, conversely, used to bury incompetent officers where they could do the least harm.

Tayschrenn, however, was extraordinarily pleased to find that command here was currently held by one of Kellanved's Imperial Historians – a veteran of the wars of consolidation named Karsden – as something of a quiet sinecure to enable him to work on his writings. Officially, the man's rank was captain, but unofficially his title of Imperial Historian, as bestowed by the Emperor, gave him the status of Imperial Fist, or higher.

For the first time in many months Tayschrenn spent hours in pleasant conversation in the captain's command tent discussing matters ranging from imperial domestic policies to the possible establishment of schools of magery, to general governance and political philosophy.

Sadly, however, the captain suffered from the flaw of being an inveterate prestige-chaser and fawner. Whenever Dassem was present Karsden inevitably turned to reminiscing over old campaigns, and who outgeneralled whom, or outfought whom, or the merits of this duel or confrontation over that. It frankly all bored Tayschrenn to tears. Rarely having spent much time with the Sword, either in the field or otherwise, it occurred to him now how little he'd seen of the sycophantic worship that the man's reputation – and title – could sometimes elicit.

This evening, while the braziers of the command tent grew dim, Karsden was questioning Dassem regarding this very title – all very respectfully, of course. Present also were Hairlock, Sialle and, for once, even Nightchill. The slim dour woman sat upright, arms crossed, saying nothing and thus casting something of a, well, a chill in her corner of the large tent.

'And what of the legendary encounter with Bors Lengst, the Boar of Bloor, as the noble was styled,' Karsden asked of the Sword. 'Was he not favoured by Fener? Did Hood not stir within you at this fell meeting, Lord Dassem?'

Tayschrenn resisted looking to the ceiling – this Imperial Historian was laying it on rather thick. Hairlock, he noted, was openly smirking at the man.

Dassem raised a hand and said, 'Not *Lord*. Just Dassem. Or Sword – and even that title is not official.'

Karsden appeared openly shocked. Sitting back, he rested his hands on his paunch. 'Really? Not official? Do forgive me, but what exactly does that mean?'

Dujek, still working on the dinner of venison, looked up. 'It means it stands apart from the established chain of command.'

Dassem nodded at this. 'Exactly. The High Fist commands. "The Sword" is merely an honorific.'

Peering about, the Imperial Historian huffed, 'Well . . . I should think it *superior* to any mundane title or rank, dealing as it does with matters of the gods.'

Now even Nightchill rolled her eyes to the ceiling.

With something of an evil leer Hairlock threw back his wine and asked of Karsden, 'Didn't you pen *The Fall of Li Heng and the Rise of Malaz*?'

Now Tayschrenn put it together – a blatant piece of flattery that had been. An open entreaty for favour and patronage. And it had worked. The Emperor had bestowed the title of Imperial Historian as a reward. But then, he reflected, Kellanved seemed to collect historians the way other rulers collected mistresses.

The fellow pressed a hand to his chest, beaming. 'You have read it?'

Hairlock shook his bald blunt head. 'No.'

Karsden's face fell. 'Well . . . you are no doubt quite busy, being such a high-ranking imperial mage.'

Hairlock continued shaking his head. 'Naw. I just heard it was shit.'

Dassem shot Tayschrenn a pained look and he took the hint, clearing his throat. 'That's quite enough, Hairlock.'

The squat mage surged to his feet and scooped up a carafe of wine, grumbling, 'Too stuffy in here for me.' He pushed aside the heavy flap and exited to the night.

Following the mage's departure Karsden sighed, 'Everyone is entitled to an opinion – I suppose.' His tone made it clear he did not think much of Hairlock's literary credentials.

'I enjoyed *Commentaries on the Eastern Campaigns*,' Sialle offered to the lengthening silence.

Karsden gave a small dismissive gesture. 'Duiker is wise to remain active in imperial service. He is, I think, a better soldier than scholar or writer.' The historian turned to Dassem. 'I would, however, be very keen to hear *your* opinion on the campaigns, Lord Dassem.'

With another pained face, the Sword rose. He offered Karsden a polite bow of the head. 'Thank you for hosting us, Historian, but I believe I shall retire for the night. Tomorrow I may scout the—'

He grabbed for the main tent post to steady himself as the ground beneath them jumped and fell like waves at sea. The table was thrown upwards. Plates and glasses smashed everywhere. The tent swayed as if caught in a raging storm. Tayschrenn fell while the ground kicked him. Dassem and Dujek made for the entrance, both tottering and staggering like drunks. Karsden rolled on the ground, head in hands, crying his fear.

The noise was tremendous – like a thousand continuous rolls of thunder.

Then it was over, so very suddenly, and the land was stable once more, as it should be. Tayschrenn rose cautiously to his feet. Dassem and Dujek were gone. Sialle and Nightchill stood, the shamaness peering about, warily.

Tayschrenn dusted himself off. 'The strongest one yet,' he commented.

'I heard rocks falling,' Nightchill observed.

He wondered how she could've heard anything at all.

Karsden offered everyone a hurried bow, saying, 'I must see to my command,' and rushed out.

Dassem re-entered the tent. 'Few casualties,' he reported. 'Dujek is restoring order and receiving damage reports.' He studied the wreckage in the tent then looked to Tayschrenn. 'Your evaluation, High Mage?'

Tayschrenn raised his brows, surprised by the request. 'My evaluation? Whatever do you mean?'

The Sword cut a hand through the air, impatient. 'Was it natural or not?'

'Ah. Natural, I assure you. Entirely natural.'

'Not entirely,' Nightchill said.

Tayschrenn looked to the tall thin sorceress. 'Not entirely? How so?'

She extended an arm to the entrance in an invitation. 'Let us look to the north.'

'Very well.'

Sialle stepped up. 'May I join you?'

Tayschrenn shrugged. 'If you wish.'

The pale sorceress led them out of camp, climbing a nearby overlook that offered a better view north. Immediately east of them rose a series of steep cliff-like mountain slopes, and high amid these slopes was perched the Red Fort. The Malazans garrisoned here said one could see the glimmer of its torches and lanterns on the darker nights.

Below them the expeditionary force was a dark milling anthill of torch-bearing men and women rushing about. The winds were strong, icy, and gusting contrarily. Tayschrenn pulled his thick cloak tighter about himself. Neither Sialle nor Nightchill appeared to feel the cold.

'Why are we up here?' he asked of the sorceress – trying not to sound as if he were complaining.

Nightchill raised a thin arm, clothed only in a ragged linen shirt, to the north. 'Cast your senses northwards, High Mage. What do you perceive?'

Sighing, he complied, raising his Warren to throw his senses to the north. He felt the shamaness Sialle at his side doing the same. After a time of reaching out further and further to the north and detecting nothing of a sorcerous or theurgic tinge, he dropped his questing to look to Nightchill. 'I sense nothing untoward.'

'Nor did I,' said Sialle.

The sorceress's strangely shaped eyes appeared to hold disappointment. Her thin pale lips turned down. 'You are thinking of this as an exercise. I have been watching you for some time,

Kartoolian. You approach magery too intellectually. There is another entire side to it. One you seem afraid of.'

Tayschrenn could not help but answer, irritated, 'I like to think I know a good deal about the subject. What aspect is this I'm afraid of?'

The sorceress was untouched by his tone. 'You should ask Hairlock. He knows all about it.'

He frowned, puzzled. That loathsome creature knew more of magery than he? Whatever could this woman be speaking of?

'Try harder,' she urged. 'Push yourself. Go as far as you dare and then onwards.'

'And why should I do that?' Tayschrenn asked.

'Because there *is* something there. I have sensed it. As, I believe, you have, if not consciously.'

Ah . . . those itches and hints that he had spoken of as troubling him. 'Very well.' He sat cross-legged and wrapped his cloak about himself. 'I shall have another try.'

'Sialle and I will keep a watch.'

He did not answer; his eyes were shut already and he was closed to the outside world. He cast his senses very far – very far indeed. Vastly further than he considered prudent, and, to his surprise, he found that he *could* cast his awareness much further than he ever had before – he had simply not forced himself to do it.

Eventually, after an amount of time unknown to him, he opened his eyes. It was the dawn of a new day. Wan sunlight bathed his numb face. Sialle and Nightchill still stood with him. The sorceress sent him a questioning, searching look.

'There *is* something there,' he murmured, his voice thick and hoarse, yet full of wonder.

'What do you make of it?' she asked.

He tilted his head, thinking. 'It is . . . strange. Like nothing I've ever sensed before.'

The sorceress gave a curt nod. 'Indeed. It is strange.'

He struggled to rise on numb, tingling legs. Sialle took his arm and he nodded his thanks. 'Let us return to camp,' he croaked through cracked and frozen lips.

A grim-looking Dujek was awaiting them back at the Malazan encampment. Runners came and went, giving whispered terse messages that he answered then waved the men and women off. 'Word has come,' he announced as they approached, 'that a land-slide has blocked the pass – and swept away a good three hundred troops.' He gave Tayschrenn a hard look. 'Is there someone who doesn't want us getting north?'

Tayschrenn rubbed a hand over his shaven cheeks. 'Hard to say. There *is* something there in the north, but it is so very far off. I don't see it having any direct attention here. These quakes may just be a symptom or byproduct of what is going on there.'

Dujek grunted, dissatisfied with such vagueness, but sensing this was all Tayschrenn had to offer. He shook his head. 'Well, keep an eye on it. Now I have to get us working on digging out.'

Tayschrenn nodded in acknowledgement of this very delicate dismissal, murmured, 'Fist.'

Chapter 5

BLUES STAGGERED UPRIGHT AMID THE FALLEN ROCK CHOKING the Red Fort's small court. He was extremely relieved to feel the ground beneath him stable once again. Guardsmen and women came running to move brick and rock to aid those struck or buried. After standing for a moment, stunned by the power of the quake, he then realized what he had to do and ran for the stairs to the lowest levels. He grabbed a lantern along the way and fought to light it as he descended.

Fortunately, the narrow spiral staircase was extremely sturdy. Some of the dressed stone blocks of the walls had shifted, and a few steps were misaligned, but he was able to reach the lowest level of storage rooms.

Light flickered high above and behind him in the circular stairwell. 'Coming!' came an echoing shout from Smoky.

The mage emerged, a ball of flame in one hand. 'Saw you go down – thought you might need some help.'

'Yes. Thanks.'

'How does it look?'

'Let's see.' He raised the lamp and advanced up the hall. It was worse than he'd imagined. The walls bulged inwards, stone blocks thrown like toys. Nearly impassable. He pressed a hand to the walls only to pull it away as if stung – the strain was immense, poised, ready to shatter – perhaps at the next merest shake or push. It felt as if it could all come roaring down upon the two of them at any moment.

'We have to evacuate,' he breathed, awed and terrified.

'Have to convince Gwynn.'

'I will.'

He found the commander overseeing repairs to the battlements of the outer curtain walls.

'There you are,' the dour mage called to Blues. 'Worried you'd taken a block to the head.'

'We all will if we don't get out of here right away.'

Gwynn arched a brow. 'Oh? There's damage, yes. But, as you see – we are still here.'

'One more quake like that one and we're done for. The foundations are shattered. Cracks have riven them completely.'

'Every time I hear that same thing from you. Yet here we are.'

'Not like this. The tower can take no more. We'll be tumbling down the mountainside next time. We must evacuate.'

But the mage frowned and half turned away as if to end the conversation. 'Orders. You heard Skinner.'

'We can't *attack*, man!' Smoky put in.

Blues had to shake his head at the stubborn futility of it. 'Well . . . if you won't evacuate, I will. I'm ordering the regulars away to return to Shimmer's command.'

Gwynn turned on him. 'You would defy orders?'

Blues pointed down. 'Because I know for certain this structure will *not* stand.'

'I will have you confined to quarters.'

'There may be no quarters tomorrow.'

'What does it matter, man?' Smoky entreated. 'Today, tomorrow, a month from now. We must abandon the fort eventually. It is indefensible with these numbers.'

But Gwynn was now peering north, hands clasped at his back, his expression thoughtful. He gave a small, almost wistful smile. 'The north, you say?'

Blues nodded. 'Yes. Whatever's causing this is coming from the north.'

The man smiled again, as much as he could – a thin humourless twitch. 'Strange. Many years ago I, too, defied orders here in this very fort. I knew I was right, then.' He eyed Blues speculatively. 'As you must be convinced you are now.' He rubbed his thin pale

69

hands together. 'Very well. Begin the evacuation. I will remain till the end, of course.'

'As will I,' said Blues.

'And I,' added Smoky.

'Who of the Avowed will command those going?' Gwynn asked.

'Lean and Shell. They'll rendezvous with Shimmer . . . wherever she is now.' He gave a bow – in gratitude for the man's change of heart – and turned to go. He halted, though, and returned. Gwynn had already brought his attention to the repair work. 'A question, if I may,' Blues asked.

Gwynn looked back. 'Oh?'

'May I ask – why the change of heart?'

'Ah.' The man arched a brow once again. 'Well, let's just say I have something of a personal interest in the north.'

* * *

Bellurdan walked with the core of the Jhek scouting force, the stolid bear-warriors. The wolf-warriors now ranged far and wide, loping back with reports of the landscape, and of the looming, smoking mountain ahead. They passed patches of naked rock where cracks cast clouds of steam into the cold air, where mud boiled and evil-smelling gases fumed.

He indicated one such collection of small cones tinged by yellow and white deposits and addressed the commander of the bear-warriors, one Hirsen. 'I do not recall reports of the lands here being so warm.'

Hirsen nodded grimly. 'It was not so before.'

Bellurdan cast him an inquisitive look. 'Before . . . ?'

The great hairy fellow almost seemed to blush behind his thick beard. 'When I was young – we dared one another to see who would travel the farthest into these lands.' He sighed ponderously. 'A foolish game. We have since stopped such things.'

'You grew up.'

He shook his head. 'No. Four of us did not come back.'

'Really? So, there *are* inhabitants.'

'No.' Hirsen pointed to low-lying mud flats to one side. 'In deeper hollows and low valleys such as these the fumes can be poisonous. You notice we skirt them. Walk there and you may not walk out.'

Bellurdan nodded. He'd heard of such things. 'I'd wondered about our rather circuitous route—'

He steadied himself as the land bucked once more beneath them. The bear-warriors all went down on all fours; Bellurdan barely managed to keep his footing. Rocks bounced and crashed about them. The ground roared as if being tortured.

Slowly, in waves, the tumult subsided until Bellurdan could again stand easy. 'A strong one,' he observed to Hirsen, in a lightly joking tone.

'They trouble me . . .' the bear-warrior growled.

Me also, my literal friend, Bellurdan added silently.

The noise of drumming and thunder, however, did not recede completely. Bellurdan and the bear-warrior exchanged an uneasy glance. Wolf-warriors appeared in the distance, loping on all fours, racing at a rate Bellurdan had never seen from them before. The lead one was yelling something as she came, waving an arm when she could, as if to warn them off. Bellurdan backed up a half-step, peered about warily.

Then the reason for the utter panic of these ferocious warriors became plain: rearing up behind came long and narrow towering saurian shapes in great ground-eating steps, grey blades at their forearms slashing. Even as Bellurdan gaped, disbelieving, a wolf-warrior was sliced in half at mid-leap.

The very eldritch horror itself, Bellurdan thought to himself, stunned. Alive. He'd never actually seen them himself, never imagined he would ever do so, either. But he recognized them easily from all the stories and descriptions he had heard: *The K'Chain Che'Malle. But how? How could this be?* He'd expected to perhaps discover a few bones, dust, and the broken remains of enigmatic machines. Not *this*.

Hirsen was shouting at him and he blinked, focusing. 'Run!' the bear-warrior bellowed. 'You Thelomen are faster than us when you want to be. Now go! Warn the Bird Mother! We will try to slow them.' So stunned was he that Hirsen actually managed to push him back a step. 'Flee, damn you!'

Bellurdan nodded. *Yes, of course. Warnings. Everyone must be warned of this.* He turned and ran, legs loping.

A great roar of battle went up behind him as the four bear-warriors loosed their challenge and joined the fray. Yet Bellurdan did not turn to look. He knew they would not last long. Slow *them* down? K'ell Hunters? Not by much.

One such horror now rose up before him – an encirclement! He snatched up the largest rock he could manage and closed upon the monster. He summoned his personal powers to strengthen himself, and, with all his heightened might, he heaved the great rock at the thing's head.

With a shattering report the beast was knocked back, head lolling, to crash to the steaming ground. Bellurdan leapt it to carry on his charge south.

As he ran, arms pumping, he noted several things he'd witnessed of the Hunter. Sickly, it had looked to him. Thin, with rents in its hide. Bones poking like tent poles. Its forelimb blades tarnished and corroded. And it had fallen too easily – weakened perhaps, or ill. Whatever was going on with these returned fiends, their nest was not a healthy one.

And so he ran, his great giant Thelomen legs loping, eating league after league, and he knew he would not stop until he reached the home of this Bird Priestess – and that there Koroll would get word immediately to his own people high in the Fenn Range. If they did not know already. For who could not be aware of such an epoch-making event? The K'Chain Che'Malle resurgent? Perhaps this age of peace between the many peoples, that had reigned all his life, was now fraying apart.

* * *

When Dancer returned to the *Twisted*, by way of Kellanved's use of the Imperial Warren, he trained belowdecks. He exhausted himself to keep from being driven to distraction by the long enforced captivity of the crossing. And whenever he found himself resenting the inactivity, he would remember his hard-won training in patience and waiting – the core of any true assassin's efficacy. And that waiting and watching paid off as, so had been his experience, it generally did.

It had become usual for whichever of these pirate – or freebooter – captains were nearby to come and go visiting Kellanved on board the *Twisted*. This day, three of the largest vessels of their rag-tag flotilla were alongside the *Twisted*. Their crews crowded the decks, idle and curious, while the captains and their first mates came aboard.

Dancer watched all this from close to the stern cabin – Kellanved's quarters. The three freebooter captains, laughing and talking amongst themselves, handed over their weapons, longswords and daggers and such, to Cartheron's guard of marines, then headed onwards to the cabin for a meet with the Emperor.

However, from years of observation, and personal experience, Dancer could tell by the way they walked and moved that each carried hidden weapons. While, it seemed to him, their first mates watched rather tensely from the deck.

Moving casually, Dancer stepped in front of the cabin door. The three pulled up abruptly, surprised to find him in their way. 'You are supposed to hand over *all* your weapons,' he observed.

The three exchanged sharp glances, and the lead one, a huge bearded fellow, puffed up angrily. 'We have indeed! Now, if you will stand aside, your ruler awaits us.'

'Not my ruler,' Dancer answered, and he made a feint to the side that they shifted to answer, then he bent the other way, taking the lead man's elbow, to turn him around and end up behind, a blade under his chin. 'Last chance,' he said. 'Hand over your weapons.'

The other two shared a narrowed glance, then went for their blades themselves.

Dancer slit this first one's throat, threw the knife into the second's, pulled another knife free and, lunging, sank it up under the last's chin.

'*Ware!*' Cartheron bellowed even as the three thumped to the deck, dead.

Dancer stood relaxed, arms loose at his sides, and regarded the three first mates at the *Twisted*'s rail. He cocked his head as if to ask, *Well?* These three bowed their heads as Cartheron's marines grabbed their arms.

Cartheron stomped over. 'You okay?'

Dancer nodded. He motioned to the mates. 'Let them go.'

'*Let 'em go?*' Cartheron answered, outraged. 'They're obviously in on it.'

'No matter. I think they are now suitably . . . chastened.'

Cartheron was shaking his head. 'Well . . . it's your call.' He waved his marines off. 'Let 'em return to their ships.' And he shouted after them: 'Congratulations! You're captains now!'

'What's all this bellowing?' Kellanved yelled from within the cabin and the door flew open. Out peered the diminutive, hunched figure of the Emperor, squinting in the unaccustomed brightness. He glanced down to the fallen bodies, then up to Dancer. He arched a brow. 'Really? Dancer? Must you?' He slammed the door shut.

Dancer blew out a breath in silent comment and took hold of the latch. 'I'll be inside.'

Cartheron nodded then pointed to the spreading pools of blood. 'Bring mops, dammit to all the sea gods!'

Within, Dancer squinted in the darkness, for the cabin was unlit but for the weak light from two small windows of murky glass.

'Must you kill all my captains?' Kellanved complained from darkness.

'They were planning to kill you.'

'Really?' The Emperor sounded genuinely baffled. 'But why? I'm leading them to the richest pickings of their wretched careers.'

'Perhaps it's the kingdoms offered for your head.'

'Ah.' Movement. Dancer could now make out a table and Kellanved behind, fiddling his fingers at his stomach. 'But how would they get away with it? Cartheron is outside the door.'

'Their three crews were poised to attack and take the *Twisted* at a given signal.'

'How do you know this?'

Dancer shrugged. 'Because that's how I'd have done it.'

'Ah.' A sigh. 'This crossing is clearly taking too long – these fellows have entirely too much time on their hands.'

'Agreed. But Cartheron is confident we're almost through.'

'Good. Good.'

'And then?'

A long pause, Kellanved's tiny eyes glistening as he peered right and left. 'Then what?'

Dancer suppressed a hard breath of frustration. 'Falar.'

'Ah, yes. Well, then I loose the hounds, ha! Metaphorically speaking, of course.'

Dancer nodded. In the gloom he could make out the side-table and carafes of watered wine. He poured himself a glass. 'Speaking of hounds and such ... can we count on our hidden allies for help?'

Kellanved looked to the ceiling; Dancer could almost hear his teeth grinding. 'No. Remember what happened the last time I summoned – they almost took my head for bothering them!'

Dancer swirled the weak wine. 'Well. Falar has no real army to speak of anyway. It's all down to controlling the seas.'

'Exactly. Sea power.'

Dancer crossed his arms and leaned back against the side-table. 'So this had better work.' The Emperor stared back, looking shifty once more. Dancer waited – he could always wait the man out.

'Of course!' Kellanved finally expostulated. 'Why ever would you doubt me?'

'Korel.'

'Greymane—'

'Greymane is not to blame for our failure,' Dancer cut in.

At some time Kellanved had summoned, or fashioned from shadows, or pulled out from under the table his walking stick, which he set his hands upon and rested his chin there. 'But he must be, dear Dancer. I can't possibly be. That's what historians are for.'

'Your hired pamphlet-hacks, you mean.'

Kellanved pursed his lips in disapproval. 'Let us just say they know who pays their bills.'

* * *

As she had these weeks past, Gianna sat hunched on a marble bench beside a reflecting pool in the Sanctuary of Mael. She no longer bothered to pray for the destruction of the cult of Mael, or the death of the hoary old sea god himself. She prayed instead for escape, and her prayers were wild schemes, each more extravagant than the last. And each, she knew, less likely to succeed.

So she did not even look up when food was offered her by a servitor – some sort of baked bun. She bit and chewed indifferently, mechanically. Until her teeth came down on something thin and wide and she nearly choked right then and there.

Gasping, she peered about; her minders were eyeing her curiously, and she waved them off. She swallowed the chewed pulp of the bun but pushed the flat, thin object – a piece of

75

parchment? – to a cheek. The servitor stood at the door, peering back at her narrowly: the shaggy-haired old kitchen maid who'd helped her before. She offered the woman a nod that was ignored as she was hurried out.

Gianna faced the reflecting pool – which also put her back to the guards. She pressed her clasped hands to her lips and pushed the slip between them. She then brought her hands to her lap and lowered her head – as if in devout prayer.

Gently unfolding the piece of heavy parchment, she read, in a childish ill-educated hand, the message: *Come to kitchen. Talk.*

Slowly, carefully, she tore the slip into tiny pieces that she did then eat, one by one.

Come to the kitchens? Talk? But why? What help could some slave servitor possibly be to her? Still, what options did she have? She might as well hear what the servant had to say. And she mustn't get her hopes up – the poor old woman might just want a blessing.

She waited until midnight then slipped from her room; she'd behaved these last weeks and her captor, the Abbess, had allowed her some limited movement – to the lavatory and the upper hall walks – though all stairs were watched by her hefty female guards.

There were other ways out, however, for those resourceful or desperate enough to try. Short jumps down to an open-air arcade, for example, below two southern windows. Gianna had been holding back on this route – reserving it for a future escape – which, she had to admit now, was looking less and less likely.

So, she decided to use it, risking its exposure. First, she made certain the room, a workspace for weaving, was empty, then entered and latched the door behind her. At the window, she peered down to the moonlit arcade, listening. Hearing no footsteps or talk, she swung her feet out and over and let herself down as far as she could. Arms extended, straining, she tried to look down past her feet but couldn't see what lay below. Finally, fingers aching, she had to let go.

She struck the stone paving of the walk far harder than she'd imagined and fell flat, hammering the breath from herself. After a moment to regain her senses, she pushed herself up but winced, one ankle flaming in pain. Staggering, an arm against a wall to brace herself, she limped onwards to the kitchens.

At each corner and turn she halted, listening for footsteps, but heard nothing. *Mael must be looking away*, she thought to herself. She made it all the way to the lowest of the kitchen spaces – the meanest preparation counters and pantries closest to the wharf entrance where all the fresh produce, fish and fowl, was transferred within. Here she found the woman sitting at a banked fire, poker in hand. Gianna took breath to speak but silenced herself as an enormous wet snoring sounded from next to them. There lay a fellow flat out on a cot, mouth open.

'The night steward,' the woman supplied to a staring Gianna. 'Don't worry, I put a little somethin' into his drink.'

Gianna nodded her understanding and ran her sweaty hands down the front of her skirts, wincing as her weight rested on her bad foot.

'You're hurt,' the woman said, rising.

'Just my ankle.'

'Let me see it.'

Rather peremptorily the woman took hold of her leg and raised it up to rest her foot on one of the tables. Gianna had to steady herself against an opposite table. 'What do you think you're—'

The woman cut in, 'Was a churgeon's assistant a time once.' She examined the ankle. 'Not broken. Twisted bad. Swelling already.' She let go of it. 'I'll prepare a poultice to wrap round it. Reduce the swelling.'

Gianna bit back on her affront at the woman's high-handed manner. 'You *do* know whom you are speaking with . . . ?'

A strange knowing smile from the woman. 'Oh, aye. Here we are. You the highest of the high, an' me the lowest of the low.'

Gianna tilted her head, examining this washerwoman anew. She appeared old, but none of her movements betrayed infirmity at all. Her face was dirty, yes, but not nearly so lined as she'd imagined. And her accent was strange. 'You're not from Falar, are you? What's your name?'

The woman smiled, as if in reminiscence, as she worked, gathering ingredients and tearing a cloth into strips. 'No. I'm from Genabackis. You know it?'

'It's far to the east.'

The woman nodded. ''Tis that. Name's Jan. Me an' my brother, we was children when our ship was driven here in a storm. We was taken, sold as slaves to the Faith. We want to return home.' She was kneading the poultice ingredients in a ceramic bowl now, adding water. 'We help you – you help us, yes?'

'I understand. But how? How am I to help?'

A soft bitter laugh was her answer. 'Child, you may be the High Priestess, but you are so naive. My brother is a carpenter repairing ships. He can get us on board an eastbound trader. But it will take coin.' Jan rubbed her raised fingertips together. 'You understand?'

Gianna nodded her understanding. 'I see.'

'Yes. Eyes must be paid not to see certain things. Guards must be paid to look the other way. But most of all,' she continued as she now pressed the poultice paste to Gianna's ankle, 'we mustn't arrive poor, yes? Otherwise we are no better off than as now, yes?'

'I see . . . I think,' Gianna hissed, wincing. 'But I have no coin. Nor do I ever handle any – how can I be of help?'

Jan wrapped the ankle in the rags – rather savagely, as she shook her head anew. 'Gods, child! An' you a High Priestess? That silk and cotton shift you wear right now is worth more than I would ever earn if I was a free servant. You have gold necklaces, yes? Gold wristlets? Gems in your rings an' pendants an' such?'

Gianna nodded, rather embarrassed – she hadn't thought of that – in point of fact she never thought of any of that. Such finery was always pushed on her by the priests for the public audiences; she herself wanted none of it. When she'd escaped, she earned her way by diving and there had always been work. Money, or an income, had never been a problem. 'I'll collect what I can,' she promised.

'Without makin' no one suspicious, yes?'

Gianna let down her leg, tested her weight. 'Yes. Of course.'

'Good.' Jan handed her a rather large pie on a cloth. 'Now go.'

Gianna peered at the greasy thing. 'What's this?'

'A leftover meat pie. Take a bite.'

Gianna's stomach rebelled. 'It's the middle of the night. I'm not hungry.'

The older woman looked to the ceiling and Gianna could tell she was working hard on controlling her temper. 'Gods below, girl,' she growled. 'You were hungry, so you came down to the kitchens for a bite to eat. Do your best not to limp. If one of them guards asks, you say you stubbed your toe in the dark – yes?'

'So . . . I should walk right up the main stairs?'

'Yes.'

'But the guards will ask how I came down . . .'

Jan crossed her arms over her thick bust. 'Well . . . you say you came down the stairs, a course.'

'But I didn't . . .'

She gave her a glare and Gianna nodded. 'Ah – I see. Okay. Right. Good.' She took a bite of the cold greasy pie.

It went just as Jan said it would: the guards gaped at her, starting from their benches as she came up the stairs.

'Where did you come from?' one demanded.

'The kitchens,' Gianna answered, doing her best not to favour her wounded ankle, and she continued right on without halting.

'How did you get down there!' asked another.

'The stairs, of course,' Gianna answered, putting a laugh into her voice.

These tall priestess guards eyed one another, frowning their uncertainty. Gianna kept on going up the hall.

'Well . . .' one shouted after her, 'return to your room – m'lady.'

Gianna nodded as she went.

Downstairs, in the lowest of the kitchens, Jan – as Janelle was known in Cabil – went to a rear door and opened it to reveal her brother Janul standing in the rain. He stepped inside and gently shut the door behind him. 'You told her a great deal of us,' he observed, his tone disapproving.

Janelle nodded. 'She's sheltered, but still a High Priestess. She had to hear some truth behind my words.'

He accepted this without argument. 'Will she bite?'

Janelle laughed throatily. 'Oh, she has bitten, brother. Now we must play the line.'

He nodded. 'I will watch for a proper vessel.'

Her gaze rose to the stone ceiling, as if imagining the floors far above and the High Priestess's room. 'Good. She will make for a great prize. The Magister will be pleased to have her in hand when he arrives.'

*   *   *

79

Hessa did not know what threat Turnagin feared, she knew only the deadly earnest of his dread of it, and that was good enough for her. The others, however, were not convinced. So she spent what energy she could spare chivvying them along. The twins could be urged to put forth more effort, but Corbin was sceptical. He clearly wished to make a run for this mountain and the storied riches it contained. Hessa, then, when they'd been aside, had struck a deal with him to organize a return expedition, but properly provisioned next time. That promise – only half in expediency from her, truth be told – had been enough. And now they trudged along, still taking turns dragging the sledge though it held hardly any provisions at all.

Sometimes, when the winds shifted, curtains of choking ash and dust rained down upon them and they had to halt, coughing, cloths pressed to their faces. It was during one of these showers that the ground shook nearby and Turnagin's head snapped up, dust shaking from his hair. 'We must move!' he shouted.

'Oh, put a cork in it would you!' Ayal complained.

'No! We must.' He squinted into the drifting haze.

Hessa peered up as well – the ground was shaking, but not from the usual tremors and quakes that were quite common now. Rather, it was as if huge heavy beasts were passing.

Corbin now stood, hand going to the heavy broadsword at his waist. He turned a slow circle, gazing out. 'Perhaps,' he mused, 'we'd best remain where we are.'

'No,' Turnagin hissed, 'I—' He stopped himself as the pounding, now all around, abruptly halted.

Hessa slowly drew her longsword, taking hold with a two-handed grip. Enormously tall shapes loomed through the drifting dust and ash. She turned a full circle as well; it appeared they were surrounded.

'Do something!' Hyde snapped to Turnagin.

But the mage was shaking his head. 'It's too late. They know we are here. There is nothing we can do.'

Corbin hefted his broadsword. 'We'll see about that.'

'What are they?' Hessa called to Turnagin.

The mage's shoulders had slumped and his head hung. 'Something that should no longer walk the earth,' he murmured.

Hessa struck a ready stance, sword high and to the left. She would not give in so easily. If these things walked then they could be struck – at least such was her reasoning.

The shapes advanced and as they parted the intervening curtains of drifting ash and dust, her confidence died within her. For she recognized them – not from ever having seen them, but from their descriptions in countless stories, songs, and myths: the ancient K'Chain Che'Malle. Rearing near twice the height of any man, saurian, up on two thick legs with enormous clawed feet, and steel blades affixed to their upper limbs.

Even Corbin flinched back, snarling, 'What in the name of Hood . . . ?'

Hessa remembered her place then, and raised her sword higher, leaned forward. They were looking to her. 'Steady,' she called out. 'Form circle.'

Ayal had her twinned needle-sharp blades out, and Hyde his long-hafted war axe. Recovering from his shock, Corbin gave up a great shouted challenge.

'*Hold!*' came an answering bellow from the distance, followed by an eerie sing-song hooting, and as one the creatures paused in their cumbersome advance.

Hessa snapped up a hand. 'Who's there?'

'Wait!' sounded another shout, and presently another form came limping forward: a man, yet taller and broader than any man Hessa had ever met, even Corbin.

As this figure neared, Hessa heard a loud hiss of shocked recognition escape Turnagin. This fellow, whoever or whatever he was, was a mess. One leg was twisted and he walked with the aid of a staff; burn-scars marred one side of his face and half his scalp; these scars appeared to cover most of him as they extended to his hands; oddly prominent upward canines pushed forward from his mouth. He eyed them in turn, nodding at what he saw.

'So,' he rumbled, 'raiders, hey? A pack of thieves. Came to try for the mountain?'

'And you are?' Hessa answered.

'Call me Singer.' He jerked his head to the surrounding Che'Malle. 'They do.'

'What do you want?' Turnagin called.

Singer eyed him. 'You are in no position to demand anything of

81

me. I, however, know what you want – beyond your continued existence, of course.'

'And that is?' Corbin growled, still glaring a challenge.

Singer swept an arm behind, to the bulk hidden behind the hanging curtains of ash. 'The Mountain. I assure you, all the stories and legends of it are true. They barely touch the surface of the truth, quite frankly.' He gestured to Corbin, Hyde and Ayal. 'Riches beyond your dreams! Boatloads of gold. Precious gems beyond count.' He turned an eye to Turnagin. 'The secrets of the K'Chain Che'Malle. The forces of nature they mastered. The mysteries of their power.' Lastly, he turned to Hessa. 'Fame and glory. Discoverer of the Mountain! Songs will be sung about you.'

Sword still raised, Hessa eyed him in return, sceptically. 'Why?'

He held out his scarred and rather twisted hands. 'I have only two hands. And there is much work to be done. Serve me and you will be richly rewarded. All the riches you could possibly heap on that sled, actually. A very beneficial arrangement . . . considering the alternative.'

Hessa glanced to her crew to see them eyeing her. Deciding, she slammed home her longsword, sighing, 'What choice do we have?'

Singer quirked a lopsided smile. 'Indeed. Very wise.' He threw his head back and let loose a great loud series of hoots and bellows. Hessa cocked a brow at this, thinking him touched, but then as one the surrounding Che'Malle turned and lumbered away. Singer gestured for them to follow him and he set off at a good pace, despite his limping.

Hessa fell in with Turnagin and held him back from their guide. 'You recognized him?' she murmured to the mage.

'Not *him*,' Turnagin answered, 'but his kind. He is not human. He is of the Jaghut.'

Hessa just stared at the bearded mage. Normally, she would've considered the man addled for such a statement. However, given that they had just faced an even more mythical race, she decided to accept this – for the moment. 'And his claims? What do you think?'

'I think we must play along and discover whether he's telling the truth.'

'And if so?'

'Then we must escape to bring warning.'

'Warning? Really? To whom?'

Turnagin cast her a desperate glance. 'Everyone. The entire world.'

Now Hessa raised both brows. Was everyone and everything going mad? Ancient myths were walking the land and a broken-down failed scholar now had delusions of self-importance? As far as she was concerned, they'd do whatever donkey-work this fellow had in mind for them, then pile up their gold and go. If, however, he betrayed them, or reneged on the deal, *then* she'd give him the edge of her Darujhistani-forged blade.

* * *

So gentle and seamless was his sliding into wakefulness that it seemed to Endest Silann that he still slept. Or that perhaps his waking was no different from his long sleep. The distinction being unnecessary, or a self-delusion, raising all sorts of philosophical conundrums. Questions that the Tiste in general, and the Andii in particular, did enjoy musing upon – during their long sleep.

Something had woken him. Some preset condition he himself had established within Kurald Galain to prod himself, should it transpire. He wondered then, with quickening and awakening interest, what in the name of Eternal Night it could be.

He opened his eyes to complete darkness; which was reassuring as this was as it should be. Not the black depths of Night itself, simply fathomless comfortable darkness – the normal mantle of the Tiste Andii.

He swung his legs down from the plinth of stone he rested upon and sat up. He remained in this position for a time, allowing his body to catch up with his mind. He would investigate this, for it was one of his duties as his Lord's right hand in these matters, keeping an eye on events below the Andii adopted home of a float-ing shard of rock some named the Moon's Spawn.

Once his legs had regained their strength, he set out pacing the quiet echoing halls. All seemed to be as it should. His brothers and sisters slept on. Even his Lord, high above in the throne room, still slept. For all would know it should Anomandaris, the Son of Dark-ness, Mane of Chaos, have awakened to the world.

Something else then; something less . . . pressing. Which was strange as he would not awaken to a trivial matter. He continued

83

pacing, arms crossed now, fingers to his chin. The only sound that disturbed the dark was of long robes brushing the smoothly polished basalt floor as he passed along.

Then he remembered. His dream thoughts had been troubled of late by stirrings within Tellann and the rousing of the T'lan Imass.

A matter of historical note, certainly, but of no direct interest to the Tiste Andii. Some meddler, it seemed, had incited them, or perhaps provoked them. As wise as sticking one's finger into a hornet's nest, in his opinion, but irrelevant to his Lord. The Imass would merely return to hunting down their old blood-enemies, the Jaghut.

He paused in his pacing to wonder whether there were even any of the Jaghut left in the world at all. Then he shrugged and continued on.

No, this surely could not be it. He would continue to consider the matter and send his senses outwards. The answer would come. For he was of a patient people, and he, High Mage to Lord Anomandaris, was even more patient than most.

Chapter 6

WHEN WORD CAME TO TAYSCHRENN THAT A SLIM PATH north had been cleared and that troops were being sent through as quickly as possible, he was in the cadre tent taking tea. Hairlock sat at the open flap, leaning back, glaring at the mountains as if they were a personal insult to him.

Dujek came thumping in. 'You've heard?' he asked of them. Tayschrenn nodded, sipping. 'I'd like eyes in the north.' He glanced about the otherwise empty quarters. 'Where's Sialle?'

'With the troops,' Tayschrenn supplied.

'And Nightchill?'

'Oponn knows,' Hairlock growled.

'She seems to do as she wishes,' the Fist mused.

'She can do no wrong in Kellanved's eyes,' Hairlock leered. 'At least he's still *that* human.'

Dujek ran his hand over the greying bristles of his pate. 'Well, I guess that means you two.'

'You are asking us to travel to the north staging grounds?' Tayschrenn asked.

The Fist did not answer right away. His gaze steady on the High Mage, he offered, 'If you would be so kind . . .'

Tayschrenn returned the stare while, ever so slightly, inclining his head in acquiescence.

Dujek gave a terse nod, saying, 'Good,' and ducked from the tent.

While Tayschrenn packed, Hairlock sat picking at his teeth until finally saying, 'Ain't no use butting heads with that one. Strictly by the book, I'd say. An officer's officer.'

'I *am* the High Mage,' Tayschrenn sniffed.

'Don't think he much cares.'

'I find his manner . . . verging upon insolent.'

'Why? 'Cause he don't bow to you like them noble-born com-manders? You're used to them kissing-up, bowin' and such. Trying to ingratiate themselves. Curryin' favour. Now this one don't and it gets up your butt.'

Tayschrenn paused in his work to regard the squat grinning mage. 'Try not to enjoy it all too much, will you?'

The march clambering over the fallen, broken rock and heaped rubble of the pass took three full days. They travelled with a guard of medium infantry, some fifty men and women. The third day's end found them arriving at the northern staging grounds. Tayschrenn walked onwards through camp; Hairlock went to see to having decent quarters raised, and a meal.

These northern slopes of the Fenn Range, Tayschrenn now saw, descended rather smoothly to a broad plain of ice and snow below. The sunset was a lurid red, the tell-tale sign of dense smoke in the air, and a haze darkened the purple of dusk across the northern horizon.

All this gave him pause, as what he saw before him did not conform to the official Imperial map of the region. A narrowing, or a secondary mountain range, should lie before him . . . somewhere or other . . . he was no expert in the field. It would have to be brought up with the Fist; word would have to be sent to the Archives. A cartographic expedition would have to be assembled. And gods knew how long that would take.

The Malazan regulars walked by without acknowledging him, and he was both relieved by this – not having to make the effort to communicate – indeed, what *does* one say to such riff-raff? Yet at the same time a touch irked, or more, if he must be honest with himself, perhaps even wounded. It wasn't that he wanted their friendship – by all the gods, no – yet . . . something. He identified a deep down longing that would not go away.

What he wished for, he realized, was their respect.

How pedestrian and insipid. Yet there it was.

Facing the north, he squared his shoulders, clasped his hands behind his cloaked back. How, then, did one go about achieving such a thing? This was a puzzle to be examined. Bribes and gifts?

No, that only gained fawning followers. Joking repartee? He hoped with a horror that that would not be the case.

No, he would have to think on it. Perhaps in time the answer would come – some appropriate course of action to put into place.

He came upon a detail of troopers digging a trench for the defensive earthworks and raising cut logs for a palisade wall. One, head down, shovelling, called to his companion in the trench, a slim female trooper, 'Thinks he's the lord of all he surveys, or some shit – hey?'

The young woman shot Tayschrenn a glance, paling, and waved for the fellow to keep his voice down.

'Don't kid yourself, Missy,' the trooper went on, grunting as he dug. 'His showing up just means things're gonna get worse for us.' He stabbed his shovel into the stony ground. 'More work and more holes in the ranks, I'm tellin' you.'

The young trooper, *Missy?* Tayschrenn wondered, just lowered her head to take a strong interest in the mud.

He simply walked on. As he'd thought: what could one possibly say to such riff-raff?

*   *   *

Ullara did not need to wait for word from the scouts sent to the south. Through her numerous bird eyes, she saw events unfolding day to day: she saw Malazan lights – scouts themselves – eyeing the slopes just beyond the mountains; she saw Malazan troops, marines, establishing some sort of forward camp guarding the northern mouth of the route to Eagle Summit. Clearly, the Malazans were coming. And if all the tales she'd heard from numerous travellers – including Koroll – were any indication they would be coming with or without her permission.

However, unlike the chief or hetman or priestess ruler of any other small clan or tribe in the Malazans' path, she had a potential connection within the highest level of that Empire. A connection she frankly dared not reveal to any of her adopted tribe.

Therefore, one day, despite the silence from the north, she announced to Looris, 'I will travel south to deal with the Malazans.'

The wolf-warrior clan chief gaped at her, astonished. 'That is lunacy. They will be sure to try to take you captive, or slay you!'

87

She gave him her hardest eye. 'They may try.'

This was a language the clan chief understood, and he chuffed, growling. 'You must go well guarded,' he finally snarled.

'I will take twenty bear-warriors with me,' she answered. 'Will this suffice?'

Looris growled anew, but did not object. 'And the Thelomen? What of him?'

She shifted, uncomfortable. 'I would like to take him with me, but that would be too much for you, would it not?'

'It would indeed.'

'So he must remain. But no harm is to come to him without my approval – is this clear?'

Looris bowed. 'Athan and I will make the arrangements.'

'Very good. I will leave on the morrow.'

Ullara, however, did not leave on the morrow. It took two days to make the arrangements, including the construction of a litter for her, as she could never have maintained the pace the bear-warriors intended to keep. The column left at dawn. The giant Thelomen Koroll was among the last to say farewell. He knelt next to the covered box on twinned poles that was the litter, saying, 'Safe travel to you, little one.'

Ullara, among her layered blankets, reached out to touch the hard, leathery skin of his enormous hand. 'I told them not to harm you in my absence.'

'Do not worry about me, little bird. And remember, you are not without allies among all beasts – you merely have to summon them.'

She did not know what to make of that, thinking perhaps he meant her pets, but he'd said *all* beasts. The litter rose, however, rocking on the shoulders of her bear-warrior carriers, and she waved farewell. They made quick travel south in the tireless rolling gait of the bear clan.

* * *

In the administrative wing of the Basilica of Mael, the Guiding Council of the Faith sat for its weekly consultation. Present were Proctor of the Faith Ortheal Leneth, responsible for guiding the souls and the structure of the Faith itself; Guardian of the Faith Nuraj Senull, responsible for the arm militant; Abbess Glinith, warden of the mysteries of the Inner Sanctum of Mael; and Overseer, or 'Purser', of Coin Mallick Rel, responsible for all finances of the Faith.

These four sat awaiting the arrival of the head of their order, Celebrant Rentil Orodrin, who had led the Faith these last two decades. Presently, the door to the sunlit chamber opened and the Celebrant entered. All four rose to their feet and stood bowed until he sat himself at the head of the table.

The Celebrant dipped his leonine head in answer to their obeisance, his great long grey-shot beard nearly touching the tabletop. 'May we convene with the wisdom of Mael,' he intoned.

The four echoed the invocation and the Celebrant turned to Ortheal. 'These rumblings and shakings of the earth,' he began, 'they have not decreased at all. If anything, they have gathered in strength.'

Ortheal nodded fiercely. His halo of thinning and unkempt hair floated about his head and he raised his thin pale arms, now animated. 'Exactly! Mael is letting his displeasure be known! We must act – and quickly.'

'What do you propose?' the Celebrant asked.

Aside, Mallick and the Abbess Glinith shared a glance and Mallick raised his eyes to the ceiling in silent commentary.

'Sacrifice, of course,' Ortheal enthused. 'Blood must be given! Every isle should contribute. It is for their own protection after all.'

Mallick raised a pallid hand. 'Ah, question, good Proctor of the Faith . . .'

Ortheal's gaze narrowed on Mallick. 'Yes?'

'Should said blood be spilled – soothing the waters,' he began in his soft, sibilant voice, 'what if such shakings and quakes continue? What does one do then?'

Ortheal blinked, his wrinkled brow creasing even more. 'Well . . . even greater sacrifice of course! The offering obviously was not sufficient to answer Mael's ire.'

Mallick nodded thoughtfully. 'Ahhh. Of course. Thank you, good Proctor.'

The Celebrant's gaze lingered on Ortheal as he stroked his long and thick beard. 'We mustn't rush into anything,' he murmured.

'However, you have permission to begin a search for further candidates.' Ortheal sat back, a smile stretching his thin lips. Rentil looked to Glinith. 'You have the High Priestess in hand?'

She bowed her head. 'Yes, Celebrant. She is under constant observation.'

'Good. Do not let her fall through your fingers again.' He eyed Ortheal. 'We may have need of her.'

Glinith ducked her head once more. 'Of course, Celebrant.'

From beneath his thick bushy brows Rentil peered about the table. 'Now, if there is no other pressing business . . .'

Guardian of the Faith Nuraj Senull raised a hand. He was as lean as a starved dog, his sun-darkened pate shaved, his mouth perpetually downturned and sour. 'Timber,' he announced.

Celebrant Rentil frowned, uncertain. 'Timber, Nuraj?'

The Guardian of the Faith stared back, the sharp angles of his face giving nothing away. 'Timber. We need more.'

Rentil gestured weakly. 'Well, then . . . I suggest you collect it.'

'From where?'

The Celebrant laughed uncertainly. 'Well, from where it grows, I should imagine . . .'

The Guardian's harsh gaze slit even further and he drew breath to answer; Mallick, however, shot a hand up, announcing, 'A matter for the coinbox no doubt?'

Nuraj's thin gaze slid to Mallick and he eased back in his chair. The Celebrant nodded sagely, 'Ah – of course. Purchasing and budgeting.' He pushed himself up from the table and all the others rose with him. 'I leave you to it.'

The four bowed their heads, murmuring, 'Celebrant . . .'

The moment the door closed behind the head of their order Ortheal threw his shoulders back. He waved a curt dismissal to the remaining three. 'Timber and gold will not save us. Only blood.' He shook a damning finger. 'You will see!'

Mallick smiled in answer, revealing his greying, greenish teeth. 'Perhaps you should be first in line, good Proctor . . . To prove your peerless devotion.'

Huffing, Ortheal stormed stiff-legged from the chamber.

Once the three were alone, Glinith warned, 'Do not push too hard, Mallick.'

Mallick opened his arms. 'He invites it so earnestly.'

'He has Rentil's ear.'

Nuraj growled, 'And must we endure that oaf?'

Mallick raised a pale pudgy hand for calm. 'He suits the part of the strong patriarch so well. His . . . presence . . . is an asset.'

Glinith nodded her agreement. 'As we have discussed.' She turned to Nuraj. 'So, timber . . .'

With a curt nod Nuraj leaned forward. 'There's none left, frankly. The islands are all too small and there have been too many generations of shipbuilding. We must regain our foothold on the mainland to the north.'

'What of the southern coast?' Glinith asked. 'It is forested.'

Nuraj shook his head. 'Picked over for generations. Only unsuitable types remain. Softwoods, curved trunks. Not enough good wood.'

Mallick's thick lips drew down in displeasure. 'Too many times have we tried to establish a colony among those barbarian tribes, and each time the howling savages have beaten us back.'

Nuraj cut a hand across the tabletop. 'We go only for the timber. We cut, haul, load and go.'

'While under constant attack night and day from screaming human waves of foaming madmen and women?' Mallick shook a negative. 'No.'

Snarling, Nuraj fell back in his chair. 'Then what? We need ships, man! Desperately. Sooner or later others will take notice. Even your savages, the Seven Cities natives – they raid us as well, you know!'

Glinith raised a thin hand for peace. 'What of it, Mallick? You have a proposal?'

The fat priest offered her a nod of gratitude. He straightened the many layers of his fine robes. 'Indeed. It just so happens that this one does have a proposal.' He steepled his fingers. 'Trade. We purchase it from our savage friends in the north.'

Nuraj sneered. 'We need a huge amount. Years of backlog in building.'

'Indeed. Several hundredweight in gold by my calculation.'

Glinith felt her mouth tighten as she eyed Mallick. 'That would be an enormous expenditure. You would ruin us?'

A raised hand. 'Temporarily only. I propose we then use said built ships to raid our savage friends in the north to recover our expenditure.'

Glinith and Nuraj shared a glance. One side of the Guardian's thin lips drew up; a smile grew upon the Abbess's mouth. She nodded. 'You shall have my support in this.'

Nuraj waved a hand. 'Done,' he announced, and he pushed back his chair.

Mallick waved a limp hand. 'Until next time, my friends.'

But the other two had already turned their backs on him, exiting through separate archways.

*　*　*

Singer guided – or guarded – them southwards back towards the mountain. A snow of pulverized rock fell nearly constantly now and smoke and sickly mists churned all about the bare rocky landscape. These monstrous K'Chain tromped about, appearing suddenly from the choking smoke only to disappear once more. Hessa noted how her crew crowded close now, worried, no doubt, about what might happen should they wander too far from Singer's protection.

As to their guide, where at first he was voluble, he now strode in silence, grimly it seemed, teeth clenched, and Hessa thought him struggling with his twisted leg.

The closer they approached the mountain the more the falling ash and smoke hid it, until they walked in what seemed a perpetual gloom of low boiling clouds. Stretches of the landscape glowed now, the stone cracking and heaving to reveal molten rock beneath.

'What is this?' she whispered to Turnagin, indicating the shining landscape.

The mage pointed ahead to the vast bulk of the mountain, now filling the south. 'The source of the heat,' he answered, sounding resigned, yet touched by wonder.

'A volcano? Erupting?'

Turnagin shook his head. 'No. Not a volcano. Artificial. A mountain that is a K'Chain city – well, a nest.'

'Then why all the smoke and molten rock?'

'I am not sure, but from legends I have heard and read, I suspect it has to do with its movement.'

A harsh cackle sounded from Singer's direction and their guide emerged from the coiling mists. 'Indeed! The mountain floats on a sea of molten rock. Energies released from its machines melt the ground beneath and so it moves! Nothing can stand in its way. Ha!'

Hessa and Turnagin eyed one another in silent commentary. Singer limped onwards, cackling as he went, and Turnagin shook his head. 'That we are led by a Jaghut is bad enough. But this one I suspect is mad.'

Hessa eyed the bent and twisted figure as he went, limping along, nearly hopping, and she had to agree.

The next day they came to shimmering, open pools of molten rock. Corridors between the pools formed wide paths leading to and from the mountain. Their escort of K'ell Hunters left them here, thumping back to the south, perhaps returning to some sort of patrol or scouting. Singer was alone with them then, but Hessa reflected that there was probably little they could do against him – should all the legends of his kind be true.

He led them onwards, up a slope of beaten rock and gravel, to a narrow ingress into the very rock of the mountain. They passed through broad and tall halls, all carved to suit the size of the K'Chain. Down side halls lights glittered and the sounds of heavy machinery echoed, but Singer led them upwards, climbing sloping curved ramps, or very shallow and broad stairs, ever upwards. Exhausted, and sweaty in the constant heat, Hessa finally called for a halt and Singer grudgingly allowed it. He led them to a smaller chamber and motioned for them to lie here, then walked on. They dropped their packs and sank to the bare stone floor.

Hessa noted raised plinths round the border of the room, moulded strangely and radiating a dull heat. She wondered if this was a K'Chain Che'Malle sleeping chamber – if they did indeed sleep.

'Well,' Hyde opined, yawning, 'no one's tried to eat us yet ...'

'It's early still,' Ayal snapped.

'This place is immense,' Corbin murmured. 'I can see why he'd need help.'

'What about them K'Chain themselves?' Hyde answered.

Corbin shrugged. 'Don't know.'

'Sleep,' Hessa ordered.

Despite her order she barely slept at all. Sitting up, nerves on edge, she couldn't relax enough. Hand on the grip of her sword, she sat tensed, half expecting one of those monsters to come barging in, jaws agape. Yet she must have dozed, for there was Singer at the open portal, gesturing. 'Come! Time to move on.'

Amid groans and coughs, they pushed themselves to their feet.

On and on they walked, passing corridors, serried chambers, and twisting interconnected ramps, always moving upwards. They all shrank to the walls to allow lumbering K'Chain Che'Malle to pass; yet they saw far fewer than Hessa expected. She almost asked Singer about this, but caught herself at the last moment, thinking it better to keep her suspicions, and observations, to herself.

'Where are we headed?' she finally asked as they marched.

He waved vaguely ahead. 'The Node – the centre. What you'd think of as the throne room, I suppose. There we can control the main instruments for heat and such.'

Eventually, the halls they walked levelled off and they came to a large vaulted chamber hewn from the granite rock of the mountain. She saw that Singer had not exaggerated when he'd said instruments: banks of box-like daises or plinths lined the room. Gems glittered embedded in the rock and the breath hissed from Hyde who ran to the nearest.

'Gemstones!' he exclaimed. 'A king's ransom!'

'Touch these not!' Singer commanded. 'There are others below – broken – for you to salvage if you choose.'

Hessa approached one of the tall plinths. Reaching up, she could hardly even touch the top. It was obviously not built to human scale.

Singer led them across the immense chamber to a wall studded with levers and circular controls for making some sort of adjustment, like ones she'd seen on water-driven mills for grinding flour or hewing wood. Next to these panels of levers and such ran a series of wide wells that led down into empty darkness where the sounds of metal clashing and roaring echoed far below. Steamy heated air rushed up here to the ceiling where openings took it away. Chains hung over the wells, rattling and clunking as they appeared to descend all the way to the unseen depths.

'Your captain and I shall remain across the complex at the main controls,' Singer explained. 'The rest must manage these controls for the engines.'

'I stay with my crew,' Hessa answered.

Singer scowled his displeasure. 'I need someone who can remember complex series of movements and actions.'

'Hey!' Hyde objected. 'What d'ya mean by that?'

Hessa indicated Turnagin. 'He can serve.'

Turning to use his better eye, Singer looked the mage up and down. Finally, he grunted, 'Very well. He'll do. You three,' he indicated Corbin and the twins, 'will work the engine controls. You, captain, will be our go-between conveying commands addressing more complex problems or corrections.'

Hessa inclined her head in agreement.

'And our payment?' Corbin growled.

Singer opened his arms. 'You've seen the gems. There are thousands. More than you could possibly carry. You can have your pick – but only when we're finished.'

'Finished?' Hessa asked.

Singer must have smiled, but on his twisted scarred face the expression resembled more a manic grimace. 'Why, bringing this enormous machine, a Mountain that Moves, back fully to life.'

Hessa caught Turnagin's eye and she saw that despite the heat, the mage was deathly pale.

'Now we must return,' Singer announced. 'And I will show you what must be done.'

* * *

The Falaran fishermen and women of tiny War Isle were not used to visitors. No one ever visited as there was nothing there. Merely a few small coastal fishing villages, each so paltry as to barely be worthy of a name. The collection of huts on the south shore was, for example, known as South village. The collection on the west shore was known as West village, while the huts along the eastern deep cove were known as Deep Cove. This hamlet was the largest of the three, boasting a long pier, the isle's temple to Mael, and even a ramshackle tavern where the men and women of the island could sit over tiny glasses of the clear fiery drink called *ikkor*.

It was here that the stranger sat, day after day, drinking glass after glass of ikkor, yes, but also tea, and fermented goats' milk, while also smoking pipe after pipe of d'bayang poppy and durhang.

He was a Seven Cities native, that much was obvious to everyone: swarthy, sun-darkened, and impressively lean and muscular. He was also quite young, perhaps just out of boyhood, still carrying the downy pale hairs of a first moustache.

He was here on the island not because he chose to be – which would make no sense, as no one *chose* to come to War Isle; he was here because he hit rocks in Walk Sea and barely managed to limp to this, the nearest land, before almost sinking. His crew abandoned him immediately, stealing a vessel and disappearing. He waited now for the island's best boatwright to repair the small launch, which could take some time as this fellow was also the island's most irredeemable drunk.

At first no one troubled him, for Seven Cities natives were notoriously short-tempered, quick to take offence and easy with violence, and he did carry two of the traditional curved daggers of his kind, ivory-handled, sheathed high on his leather vest.

So the regulars satisfied themselves with watching him sidelong where he sat next to an open window overlooking the bay. Brooding, it seemed to all. Bored, no doubt. Considering violence, likely. Though some of the women did think his expression wistful.

Every day, late in the afternoon, as the shadows lengthened, he would walk the rocky path down to the cove, to where the launch lay on its side high on the strand, and he would talk with the boatwright. Every time a few of the island's children followed him, just out of kicking range, whispering and giggling among themselves, fascinated by the foreign stranger.

This day, like most, he had to kick the man awake where he lay in the shade of the boat. The fellow jerked up, hitting his head and swearing. He emerged from the shade smacking his lips and rubbing his balding pate.

'How goes the work?' the young stranger asked in his barbarously accented Falari.

The boatwright bobbed his head, nodding. 'Oh, it is going fine. Yes. Working on it now.'

The stranger nodded, rather dubiously. He looked over the stove-in planks. 'Forgive me,' he said, 'for I am not privy to the mysteries of boat repair, but everything looks the same.'

The boatwright bobbed his head again, weaving slightly. 'Wood, good sor. Wood.'

'Wood?'

'Yes. Wood for the repairs. I need some.'

'Ah. Then get it.'

The man grimaced, peered round as if searching for something. 'I have sent for some, but good lengths for boats are scarce these days. And pricey. Who knows how long it will take for the pieces to arrive? Ah!' Brightening, he bent down, weaving again, and pulled a large earthenware jug from the sands. He extended it to the Seven Cities youth. 'Ikkor?'

The stranger shook his head. After one last look at the boat, he turned on his heels and retraced his steps, back to the tavern where he sat again, staring out over the bay. Brooding, it seemed to everyone.

*   *   *

Long before Bellurdan reached the main village of the Jhek he gathered guards and out-runners who jogged along all about him: lean wolf-warriors who ran panting, tongues lolling, sometimes on all four limbs, sometimes on two.

He shuffled along, nearly spent, a red mist of exhaustion before his eyes, his stomach clenched and writhing in protest. As he approached, he saw through his blurred vision a contingent of the wolf-warriors blocking his way. With them stood their war-chief – someone or other – Koroll had told him his name. Oh yes, Looris, or some such thing.

'You come alone!' this one bellowed, a hand raised for a halt. 'Where are the brothers and sisters we sent with you?'

Bellurdan nodded, bent over, fighting for breath. 'I would speak with the Bird Priestess,' he gasped, his voice weak.

'No doubt you would,' Looris growled. 'Answer me!'

Bellurdan swept a hand. 'Dead. Killed by an enemy – I must speak with your priestess!'

The war-chief was nodding to himself, his gaze slit. 'Yes, killed by an enemy in truth . . . you! And now you would trick your way to our Bird Mother.'

Bellurdan could only gape. 'What . . . ?' He searched the hut fronts, called, 'Koroll! What insanity is this?'

'The other comes,' a wolf-warrior murmured.

'Good,' Looris answered. He threw up a hand and on all sides warriors, both of the wolf clan and the bear clan, emerged from around and within the huts.

Bellurdan backed away, as a tall figure now straightened from exiting the main longhouse to raise his tattooed head and plant his tall staff. 'What is this?' Koroll called.

'K'Chain Che'Malle awakened!' Bellurdan answered. 'We must bring word!'

Even from this distance Bellurdan saw the powerful mage of his people stagger as if struck. 'But how . . . ?' he gasped.

'I know not . . .'

The wolf war-chief Looris cut his clawed hand down. 'Enough of this trickery! Your plan to take the Priestess has failed.' His lips drew back in a savage smile. 'Kill them both.'

The gathered wolf-warriors howled their bloodlust and launched themselves upon Bellurdan. They transformed in mid-leap, chests thickening and jaws strengthening into their full wolf forms. He swung as they came, his giant Thelomen fists shattering skulls and breaking ribs, but they were too many and he went down amid a horde of snapping rending jaws tearing and pulling at his legs and arms.

He protected his throat from their driving snapping teeth, strove to rise to his feet, but the ground gave way beneath him as if it were water, and he immediately relaxed into the morass as he recognized the Elder earth magics of Koroll. Long had it been since he had witnessed the full ancient lore of his kind unleashed, the root rock of all Earth magery; his assailants were torn from him, swept aside like dust, and he found himself panting, wincing in pain, upon a hillside beneath a darkening sky.

'Where are we?' he gasped.

'Not far,' Koroll answered from the near distance.

He rose, almost snarling from the many deep bleeding bites and gashes. 'Damn those fools!'

'They can only follow their nature.'

He spat blood from a torn lip. 'You are too forgiving.'

'I know. You are much more the warrior than I.'

'What now?'

Koroll raised his staff to the south. 'I shall return to the heights.

Warn the elders – though I assume they know well enough by now. You must remain. Your strength will be needed.'

He spat again. 'I'll not help these fools!'

'Ullara – that is, the Bird Priestess – is no fool. Help her. And . . . there are others coming.' Koroll turned his tattooed face to the south. 'The Malazans. They may be induced to fight.'

Bellurdan drew a hand across his mouth to wipe away the blood. 'Those southerners? They care only for gold. They know nothing of honour or loyalty. I will not help them.'

His companion turned a hard eye upon him and Bellurdan ducked his head. 'Apologies. What do you advise?'

Koroll looked to the north. 'You have *seen* the K'Chain? Awake?'

He spat again. 'I had to bring down a K'ell Hunter to escape.'

Koroll eyed him narrowly. 'Indeed . . . a mighty feat. Remain, then. Look to Ullara and these Malazans. Perhaps an alliance could be arranged.'

Bellurdan snorted his disgust. 'Greedy, grasping empire . . .'

'They *all* are,' Koroll answered, loftily, and he started walking south. Bellurdan watched him go, shaking his head – Elders! How can anyone make them understand? And *he* goes to talk to those who would consider *him* a child! He shook his head anew. *Well – better him than me!*

Chapter 7

OVER THE NEXT FEW DAYS GIANNA TOOK TO HANGING about the Abbey's kitchens. The Abbess, Glinith, challenged this of course, with an eye on how near the waterfront lay, but Gianna explained that she wished to learn baking. An arched brow from the woman answered the claim – she obviously wondered why any High Priestess would desire to learn servant's work – but seeing how the newfound interest seemed to divert Gianna, and keep her busy, the Abbess relented.

Four strong priestesses of the militant arm of the Faith, however, remained on constant guard.

At first the washerwoman Jan had looked at Gianna strangely. Finally, she realized the problem: she'd been forced to have a haircut – her natural straight, thick, black hair was growing in strongly and she looked rather strange with her white tips. Still, they'd had to hold her down to do it.

Eventually, after a week of struggling with the mysteries of proportions and dough kneading, the word that she'd been hoping to hear whispered to her came. Jan brushed up against her and murmured, '*Tonight*.'

So startled was Gianna that she almost dropped the clay pot of milk she held, but she recovered, shooting nervous glances to the guards – had they seen? Had they noted? The four, however, appeared quite content to sit at a corner table near the door, eating and drinking all day.

The rest of the afternoon she was a wreck, unable to concentrate on any of her tasks, and so she cast up her hands instead, pleading tiredness. She retreated to her room where she threw herself into preparing for the evening. She assumed Jan meant midnight, as they usually met in the middle of the night when she had some few stolen rings or bracelets to hand over – nothing so large that it would be noticed as missing, she hoped.

She pulled on sturdy street clothes – trousers and a shirt – beneath her finer priestess robes, rolled her few remaining stolen items in rags and secreted these about her person, then she ordered a large meal – as who knew when the next time would come that she could eat?

After the meal she could no longer contain her nervousness and she spent the gathering dusk pacing her rooms, back and forth, pausing at each narrow window to watch the sky deepening into night.

* * *

North of Eagle Summit Pass, Tayschrenn pulled up a camp chair and sat overlooking the slope where it descended to the northern icy wastes. The Malazan encampment was growing around him now as the majority of the expedition force had marched through the pass. Hairlock and Sialle sat within the canvas tent nearby that glowed a warm amber, lit by lanterns against the gathering dark.

He could sense the alien presence far to the north quite readily now. Nightchill's challenge to him to stretch his abilities had indeed been a kind of revelation; he recognized that he'd always been a touch frightened of what his powers might do – to others, yes, as violence was distasteful, but perhaps most personally to himself.

It was strange, but he'd always feared that if he extended himself too far, wandered or dared reach out too intensely, he might not ever return. Or return changed – *different*. It was an odd fear. More of a troubling suspicion, really. Yet at the same time it was almost seductive. He wondered, perhaps, if he was sensing what so many named the lure of power.

How prosaic then, after all.

He drew the long edges of his cloak about his knees against the chill winds and studied the common soldiers cooking and settling in about him, and the wide berth, the *distance*, they kept from him. He let out a long breath. How ironic. This path of exploring, and

101

realizing, more and more of his greater potency was taking him farther and farther away from the goal he truly wished – becoming one of them.

So be it. He was committed. He tilted his head upon hearing a light tread and sensing an approaching presence. And how odd that this path should be taking him farther from being human, to being . . . and he turned to see the slim figure that seemed to radiate cold, Nightchill . . . to being more like *her*.

He inclined his head in greeting. 'Nightchill.'

'Kartoolian.' She raised her sharp chin to the north and the distant dark clouds. 'You sense it?'

'Of course. But, just what is it?'

She nodded, accepting the question. 'You would not know, would you. There are few these days who would. That, dear High Mage, is the aura of the K'Chain Che'Malle.'

Tayschrenn felt his brows rising. *Indeed* . . . He let out a breath as if punched. 'I find that difficult to believe.'

'Yet you sense that it must be true, yes?'

He considered the alien presence; it was so like a distant lurid glow, or pulse. So unlike anything else, yet so oddly similar to others of the Elder races he had encountered. 'I see,' he finally decided. 'What, then, are we to do?'

'Proceed with caution – I should imagine,' Nightchill answered.

Tayschrenn turned to eye her more closely. Had that been sarcasm? Even irony? He returned his attention to the north. 'Things,' he murmured, 'have gotten far more complicated than our plans supposed.'

'Isn't that always the way?'

Now he frowned; he wasn't certain he liked this new, voluble Nightchill.

*

From the outer crenellations of the Red Fort overlooking the Malazan camp, Blues watched their torches and lanterns sway and bob as the last elements joined the march northwards. He pulled his thick crimson cloak tighter against the cold. Next to him, Smoky stood peering down, looking satisfied.

'We've faced each other for so long we now know each other too well,' Blues said.

Smoky nodded. 'A mutual, unspoken agreement to withdraw. Not worth it.'

Blues smiled, remembering briefings with professional officers. 'A redeployment of resources,' he offered, quoting some long-ago officer.

'Almost finished.'

'Who's left?'

'Other than us? Maybe twenty regulars. Gwynn's in quarters. Probably composing a greeting for whoever the Malazans eventually send up here for a peek.'

'Nothing useful left?'

'Nothing. Place is emptier than a merchant's heart. Shellarr and Lean took all the stores with the garrison.'

Blues leaned on the gritty cold blocks. 'They'll need them. A long journey ahead.'

'You really think something's in the north?'

'*Something* is.' He nodded to the valley below. 'And the Malazans are going north.'

Smoky gave him a look. 'You think it's connected?'

'I don't know . . . but I think I'd like to see.'

'Hunh. Thin.'

'You don't have to come.'

Smoky laughed and pushed away from the wall. 'Better your company than Gwynn's!' He went inside. A while later Blues decided to go scrounge up something to eat. The fort was on skeletal staff – most followers having been sent off. He descended the stairs to the kitchens wondering whether to wait a while longer and follow along behind the Malazans to see what they were up to. Or to get out front to try to thwart whatever it was they had in mind.

Follow, he decided; seeing as he had no idea at all what they might be up to.

*

A tumult of yelling and raised voices brought Hessa running. This section of the chamber was a maze of towers encasing rods and chains and other blocks of steaming, clanking machinery. She rounded a final series of enmeshed gigantic gears taller than herself to find Singer arguing with Hyde and Ayal.

'No, no, dammit, no!' The Jaghut was his usual apoplectic self. He slammed a hand to the metal wall of levers before them. 'Look at our drawings! This top one first down twice!' He pointed along the row. 'Then that one – *up* – till the centre chain starts descending. Then reverse the series!'

Hessa stepped up, hands raised. 'Slowly, yes? Slowly?'

Singer pulled a scarred hand down his face, almost weeping with frustration. 'You said you were literate, yes?'

The twins exchanged quick glances. Hyde shuffled a bit. 'Actually,' he began, '*mostly* literate.' He peered upwards, squinting at the charcoal drawing next to the lever. 'So, down is that one, hey?'

'Yes,' Singer sighed. 'And the two lines means twice.'

Hyde nodded animatedly. 'Oh, yeah. I know that one.'

Ayal was smirking throughout. Singer shot her a glare. 'Help him out.' She rolled her eyes.

Hessa crossed her arms. She asked of the twins, 'So, we're good then? We can start again?'

Ayal waved them off. 'Yeah, sure. From the beginning.'

Singer straightened slightly, coughing into a fist. 'Very good.' He thrust a finger to the banks of levers. 'Reset positions then.'

Hyde dragged over a box of folded metal that they used as a stool to reach the highest levers and toggles and began resetting them one by one. Grudgingly, Singer turned away and limped off. Hessa followed – after one last warning glare.

'We are so close,' the Jaghut growled to her as they walked. 'One good run-through without any major mistakes and we may awaken the engines fully.'

'And then?'

The Jaghut laughed – rather manically, Hessa thought. 'Yes! Then!' And he laughed anew.

At the main banks of controls Hessa nodded in answer to a worried look from Turnagin. Singer took up his long horn. 'Opening positions,' he announced. Hessa and Turnagin began reviewing all the various metal switches, knobs and levers before them.

Singer raised the horn and blew a series of blasts and rippling notes upon it. Three lumbering K'ell Hunters came thumping up a wide ramp then stood waiting; these carried no blades upon their small forearms – for managing the controls, Hessa assumed. Their wide chests barely registered any shallow breaths and their large black lizard eyes seemed dull and lifeless.

Singer blew further warbling and hooting notes upon the instrument. The three turned and thumped off without any visible response. Here Turnagin shot another significant glance to Hessa. *He's commanding them*, the mage had whispered to her days ago. *He shouldn't be doing that. Only the matron commands.*

For her part, Hessa had no understanding of it. Turnagin had explained, when Singer was absent, what he knew of K'Chain Che'Malle society. Apparently, this matron was like the queen. She would be in command of any installation as important as this. This Jaghut had somehow replaced or usurped her.

The answer, Hessa assumed, might lie up one distant narrow ramp that Singer had forbidden any to enter. She *was* curious, no doubt of that. But curiosity alone was not enough to risk the lives of her crew. Not yet, at any rate.

After this long series of notes Singer turned to them, but grimaced and bent nearly double, coughing into a fist, convulsing. He leaned against a wall to steady himself, panting. The fellow, Hessa had already surmised, was not well.

Eventually, he straightened and raised his own hands to the controls. He sent them a slow nod. 'Now . . . begin.'

A third or so into the series of switchings and turnings, Hessa decided that it was like a dance – a damned ugly and awkward one, but a piece of choreography just the same. She traded off with Turnagin, then the two waited for Singer to perform his series of hoots or pushing at crystalline levers; then it would be her turn; then Singer blew a trumpet-like blast that was the signal for Hyde and Ayal to begin their moves. For his part, Corbin waited at a huge gear that he turned by grasping a cog and raising his entire weight upon it to get it to move – a turning that she knew any Che'Malle could manage easily one-handed.

All about them chains began heaving, descending or rising among their wells and tubes. Steam shot from tall openings; gears turned squealing and grinding. Hessa shot Singer a worried glance. 'Should they sound like that?' she tried to yell over the cacophony.

The bent-backed Jaghut was laughing now, quite manically. 'It is – how do you say – in very poor repair!' And he cackled on, coughing. 'We are close! The last sequence!'

Hessa returned to concentrating on her complicated dance of motions. The vibration rising up from the very rock of the mountain beneath them was enough to nearly throw her into the air. A strange glow now shone up from the larger wells. The chains then all rose at once, pulling to their maximum height.

Singer staggered backwards, raising his horn, and, taking an enormous breath, he blew an ear-shattering blast that made Hessa swear and cover her ears.

The detonation of power that answered that blast swept Hessa's legs out from beneath her and rammed her to the floor. The screeching and grinding of tearing metal drove her to scream in agony and she watched her vision tunnelling into grey, then thickening into darkness.

*

It was long into the night and Tayschrenn was still in his camp chair, and Nightchill standing. They had moved on from the revelations of what lay to the north – which he assumed would prove to be nothing more than yet another enigmatic slumbering ruin – to talking of the imperial mage cadre, recruitment and training, when he detected a sudden new tension in the woman and she turned away to face the north once again.

'What is it?' he asked.

'Do you not sense it?'

He returned to studying the north. And he had to admit that, yes, there was . . . something. 'Stronger . . .' he murmured.

She nodded. 'Yes. Stronger.' She narrowed her gaze. 'In fact . . .' She threw an arm across her face, turning her head: 'Look away!'

Startled, he did as she commanded, but an instant too late. Shining white light dazzled and blinded him just as he hid his eyes. Even from this great distance the power was enormous – like the aspect of an unleashed Warren, yet different – pure streaming energy. 'What is this!' he yelled, pained.

'The mountain awakened!' Nightchill yelled in answer, and he was even more alarmed to hear the awe in her voice. 'Astonishing!'

Then the ground kicked Tayschrenn from his chair.

*

Blues was in the kitchens, dipping a crust of hard old bread into a bowl of lukewarm soup he'd poured from a pot over one of the banked hearths. He was alone, the kitchen lit only by a sole candle and the low glow of the darkening hearths.

An eruption of power caused him to surge to his feet, throwing the chair careering backwards; he faced the north. *What in the name of Burn . . .*

Then he felt the entire tower leap like a startled animal.

He was thrown into a wall. The very dressed-stone blocks beneath his feet fought each other as if they wished to escape the floor. Dust choked and blinded him. An avalanche of stones crashed around him. Then, the entire edifice itself, all of it – he *felt* it – began to tilt outwards from the heart-rock of the mountainside it had been built into.

Overcoming his stunned amazement, and coming to his senses, Blues snapped up his D'riss Warren and strained, screaming with the effort, reaching out to every life spark he could find in the tower, and brought them with him through the Warren to fling himself clear. Never having dared do anything so reckless, so excessive, he felt his consciousness being stretched near to breaking – and then it did.

*

In the valley below Eagle Summit Pass, Karsden, Imperial sanctioned Historian, came stumbling from his tent, struggling to retain his footing while the ground juddered beneath him. Distant roaring sounded and in the half-light he saw the slopes over the valley shudder and writhe. Clouds rose, seemingly from every direction, as avalanches of rock came hurtling down upon the valley.

We are all dead, he thought to himself, oddly calm, as if detached from the event. *Shame I shall not be able to record—*

He froze, staring upwards as the mountain slope supporting the Red Fort, the famed Citadel of the Crimson Guard, appeared to slide down as if cut, severed somehow, as if by a god's sword slice:

107

down the immense length of the mountain's face, onwards, tumbling, and the thought came, exultant – *Yes!*

Then the avalanches struck.

*

Tayschrenn rose unsteadily to his feet. Continuous rumblings and echoing, cascading roars pulled his attention to the mountains and he gaped, blearily. *Gods! The pass!*

The troops around him were running now, southwards. He found Dujek amid a crowd of staff and officers, yelling orders. Catching sight of Tayschrenn, the commander snapped, 'What in the Abyss was that!'

Tayschrenn held his aching head. 'I have to say I am not certain.'

'An attack?'

'I do not believe so. Not . . . deliberate, no.'

The blunt fellow pulled his hand down his face to wipe away the sweat and dust. 'Gods! Hate to see a deliberate one.' He eyed him. 'The thing in the north?'

'Yes.'

Dujek grunted at that. 'Keep an eye on it.' And that was a dismissal as the commander turned to creating some order from the chaos.

A thick mane of white hair marked the Seti shamaness, Sialle, and Tayschrenn pushed his way through the milling soldiery to her. When they met, the young woman said, dryly, 'I certainly sensed *that.*'

He nodded his commiseration. 'Have you seen the Sword? Is he safe?'

'The Sword is in the pass helping to dig out troops and find survivors.'

A curt bob of approval. *Good. That is where he should be.* Though in Tayschrenn's mind another less charitable voice whispered, *And he would be – wouldn't he?*

'And what of us?' Sialle asked. 'What should we be doing?'

'Keeping watch. Guarding the perimeter. Make certain no one takes advantage of this.'

She inclined her head in agreement and jogged off.

He returned his attention to the north. He felt his shoulders almost slump with a presentiment of what awaited them. Was it hostile? *Overtly* hostile? Or perhaps this was all just the gods playing with them for sport, as some philosophers contended. He took a long breath. Whichever. It had to be dealt with regardless. It was too close to Malazan lands.

Or, perhaps more accurately, Malazan territory was advancing too close to *it*.

*

Gianna was on the Basilica's main harbour waterfront, crouched behind cargo with Jan and her brother, eyeing the marina of quiet vessels. 'Which one?' she asked of the brother.

He shushed her, which rather irked her. These foreigners had no manners or proper respect. The harbour night watch passed with their lanterns on poles and she ducked while Jan and her brother did not. 'Can't they see us?' she whispered to Jan, but it was her brother who answered by making the common sign of rubbed fingers for graft. Gianna was quite shocked; she thought the watch beyond reproach.

Still, the brother and sister waited until the watch was long past before urging Gianna onwards to scurry out towards one particular pier. She supposed there was no sense in being *too* bold.

Halfway up the pier she halted as a jolt cleaved through her; it came from the water of the harbour, the bay, and the seas beyond that. She did not know how to understand it save that the water seemed to flinch as a shock pounded through it. Then the stones of the pier leapt sideways to send her stumbling. Jan and her brother fought to retain their footing. Wood crashed and iron screeched as the boats rocked, bashing the stone pier. Masts waved like saplings in a wind-storm. From the shore came the worst: the avalanche-like crash of brick and stones tumbling as arches collapsed and walls fell. Screams sounded even from this distance.

The sharp jolts subsided; only smaller shudders rumbled beneath Gianna's feet now. The entire calamity must have taken only a few instants, but it had seemed to go on almost for ever. She made a wobbling turn, though the ground continued to buck at random moments, and began making her way back to the harbour-front.

'What are you doing?' Jan called after her in wonderment.

She pointed. 'There are wounded! I can heal!'

'No, damn you – now's our best chance!' The High Priestess did

109

not answer or slow her uncertain progress. 'Little fool,' Jan snarled and the auras of Warren magics bloomed round her hands. She raised a fist to gesture but her brother Janul rested a hand upon her shoulder.

'No. She's strong in Ruse, remember. We could lose her. And so much for any quiet getaway.'

Janelle snorted her frustration at that. The blooms of power dancing at her hands dispersed. 'But in the chaos . . .'

Janul shook his head. 'The gates aren't opening now, are they.'

Janelle looked to the night sky, her jaws writhing.

Behind them a concatenation of power and water sprayed high above the sea-walls as a monstrous wave crashed into the outer defences. A heavy mist from the spray hissed down around them; Janelle wiped the cold salt water from her face while glaring back at the wharf.

Janul gestured her onwards. 'Come, let's make a show of helping – get into her favour, yes?'

She looked again to the night sky. *Gods! The things she did for the magister!*

*

Blues awoke at a blow to his chest. He raised his dizzy, throbbing head to peer around; he was on a rocky forested mountainside, probably not too far from the Red Fort – or rather, where the Red Fort *once* stood. Groans sounded, announcing the presence of others, and he pushed himself to his feet to find them.

After searching among the rocks and brambles he gathered together Gwynn and Smoky, and Black the Lesser and Jacinth joined them. Blues eyed the four; every one of them, including him, carried deep cuts, were covered in rock dust, clothes torn from savage blows. 'Is this all?' he panted, wincing. 'Any others?'

Gwynn shook his head. 'Fell in the landslide. Only we survived.'

Blues felt his shoulders slump. He turned away. *I tried. Gods I tried. But it wasn't enough.*

'So . . . you were correct,' Gwynn murmured.

Blues winced anew.

'Now what?' Smoky asked. 'We're not exactly well equipped.'

Blues turned back; the mage of Telas was right. None carried any armour or a weapon more than a dagger. He was dressed in leathers; Gwynn must have still been up as he wore his usual black. Smoky was barefoot, in nothing but trousers and a long shirt – he must have been in bed – while Black the Lesser and Jacinth both wore only their padded belted gambesons and boots.

No food, no water. No armour or weapons.

Blues shook his head.

Black the Lesser seemed to read his mood as he pulled a hand down his thick black beard, observing, 'We're alive, Blues.'

'Question still stands,' Smoky reminded.

'I'm going north,' Blues answered, rather surprising himself.

'As am I,' Gwynn added. Blues looked to him, surprised again.

Smoky set his hands to his hips. 'Really? Like this? What in the Abyss for?'

'The Malazans are going north.'

Smoky snorted, 'They're going *everywhere*.'

'We should investigate – off contract,' Gwynn put in.

All four eyed Gwynn, startled. 'Really?' Jacinth asked for them all. He gave a sombre nod in answer – much more his usual self.

Blues rubbed his shoulder where a stone had hit a glancing blow. 'Well, the Malazans have stores . . .'

The tall and hulking Black the Lesser stroked his beard and crooked a smile. 'And armour.'

Grinning, Jacinth chimed in, 'And weapons.'

*

Imperial Historian Karsden awoke in a cot in a tent alongside a crowd of other cots and bedding occupied by wounded. He raised a hand to find sticky cloth wrapped round his head. 'Medicer!' he yelled, and winced with a groan.

A private came to him. 'Yes, Commander?'

'A quill, lad! And vellum!'

The young soldier demurred. 'You are wounded, sir. A severe blow to the head.'

'Never mind that! Do it! Now!' The young fellow peered round, perhaps for help, but finding himself alone, he bobbed his head. 'Very well, ah, sir.'

Karsden rearranged his bedding so that he could sit up. The private brought a flat board, vellum, an inkwell and a quill. Karsden nodded his thanks then shooed the lad off. He dipped the quill then raised his eyes for a time, arranging his gyring flying thoughts, then set tip to vellum and wrote:

The Fall of the Crimson Guard.

So did Glorious Emperor Kellanved finally set his troops 'gainst the last foothold of the defeated Crimson Guard upon the Quon Talian mainland. And seeing their petty and sullen defiance of his honourable claim to all lands, was reluctantly forced to bring his righteous might down upon their rebellious heads. Raising his puissance, he smote the mountainside with his dread power and crushed the last great fortress of the Citadel. Its broken stones came raining down upon the valley below. And though some Malazan forces were lost in this great siege, and some wounded, it remains a great victory, and a final death-blow to that wicked order.

Setting down his quill, Imperial Historian Karsden sat back with a sigh. There, a strong beginning to a true recording of events. He gently pressed a hand to his bandaged head. Yes, he could probably anticipate a new posting for this work. Perhaps even at the capital.

He smiled then, easing even further into the pillows, and shut his eyes imagining the luxuries and fame that most certainly would be his.

*

Dancer braced himself at stanchions on board the *Twisted* as yet another monstrous wave bore down upon them. Holding tight while the bows rose up the great sweep of water, with Cartheron yelling commands to the steersman and the crew in the sheets, he was beginning to wonder whether there really was some antagonistic force opposing their advance. For no sooner had they left the fields of ice-crags behind, and reorganized their rag-tag flotilla, than a series of gigantic waves had now come storming down upon them.

Their fleet – if you could call it that – was scattered across the seas again. Gods knew how long it would take to herd them together once more; and some, no doubt, had already decided those very gods were against them and had turned tail to return to home ports.

The *Twisted* seemed to fly, as, for an instant, only clouds and sky showed before the bowsprit. Then the ship tilted and fell bow-wards, gaining momentum, charging down a broad mountain-slope of mottled green and blue. Dancer swallowed hard to ease his queasy stomach: most comfortable in the city, he'd never found his true sailorly legs.

The *Twisted* levelled, yawed slightly with its speed, and Cartheron stomped by, shouting commands but grinning; he shot Dancer a wink. Dancer carefully unlatched his hands from the wood and eased his shoulders. He shook his head. Grinning? These Napan sailors were mad.

The cabin door banged open and out staggered Kellanved, looking very green around the gills – as these sailors would say. He made for the side, gasping, 'Sea power! Outrageous foolishness!' He leaned over the railing, groaning. 'Whose idiotic idea was this?'

Dancer felt no need to answer that.

Kellanved vomited over the side, wiped his mouth with a handkerchief, and moaned anew. Then he straightened, waving the stained cloth. 'Where is our glorious fleet? Have they all bolted? Disloyal scum!' He pointed to Cartheron. 'Round them up!'

The Napan admiral was still grinning behind his scraggly beard. 'Oh, we will all right.'

Kellanved nodded at this, swallowing. 'Good, good.' Then he bent over the side once more, gagging. Above the bent and heaving form, Dancer and Cartheron's gazes met, both men grinning now, and both looked to the sky.

From the shrouds above came an eerie, nearly human, mocking laugh from that odd creature, the sometime pet nacht.

Chapter 8

FOR ULLARA, THE GREAT KICKING AND SHAKING OF THE EARTH had been terrifying – the worst she'd ever experienced in her life. But at least she and her guards had been on open ground. She lost none of them to this fit of Burn's wrath. When it struck she'd been asleep, surrounded by her guard of bear-warriors. After those first shocks passed and the embers of the fire stopped bouncing, she immediately cast her vision to the night-hunters ranging round the home village. The night-eyes of owls revealed little damage; the huts were small and light after all, of wattle and daub. A few had fallen, but the main temple of thick wood pillars still stood. The wolf-warriors were all astir, hurrying about. Strangely, though, she saw no sign of the Thelomen mage, Koroll.

'Home is safe,' she told Ursana, the leader of her guard. The huge bear-matron grunted her relief at the news.

'We should return,' the giant growled, eyeing the south.

'But we are so close!'

'Exactly. After this, they may not be in the mood to talk.'

'So, we just turn around?'

The huge matron of bears nodded ponderously. 'Yes. They will be worried for you. They do not know what has happened.'

'We could send a messenger. One of your warriors.'

Ursana shook her head. 'No. You must return to the people. They have had a shock.'

'But the Malazans . . .'

The bear-warrior snorted her disdain. 'They will keep. Now, we must go.'

'What? Right now?'

114

'Yes.' She gestured for the litter to be readied.

Ullara almost – but not quite – stamped her foot at this, this, *defiance*. 'I am the Bird Priestess. You must do as I say.'

A small upturn of one edge of the veteran's lips was all this stirred. 'And I am charged with your safety for the people. So . . . we leave now.'

The guard of bear-warriors had broken camp and four brought the litter. Ursana gestured her in with one broad paw-like hand.

Ullara twisted her hands together. 'Well – if I must. But I think this is a mistake: the Malazans must be dealt with.'

'These Malazans,' Ursana judged, 'will no doubt come to us.'

Settling into the blankets and cushions within the narrow litter, Ullara reflected that, yes, that was most likely to be the case. As the bear-warriors set off at double-pace she banged her head against the wall of the covered box.

The journey back took half the time; even the preternatural stamina of these Jhek bear-warriors was tested for Ullara could hear them panting and chuffing through the last portion of the way. They reached the village the dawn of the fourth day. Wolf-warriors bounded about them – some no doubt running ahead to bring the news.

Looris met them before the entrance to the temple. 'We are glad to see you unharmed,' he said as Ursana helped her from the litter; she leaned on the bear-woman, her legs numb and tingling.

'My thanks,' she answered. 'And you as well. Everyone?'

Looris nodded. 'Everyone is well. There were no deaths.'

Ullara felt her shoulders ease. 'Good, good.'

'And these invaders? You simply returned, I take it?'

Ursana walked her into the temple. 'Yes,' she told Looris. 'But they *are* coming. Have no doubt of that.'

'Good,' he answered, sounding pleased. 'We will meet them and destroy them.'

Ullara almost fell – Ursana holding her up by an arm. '*No!* You most certainly will not!'

Looris waved a dismissal. 'They are mere men and women – no match for us.'

Ullara halted abruptly just inside the temple. Her pets cawed and screeched a welcome, many flying tight circles within the

115

broad vaulted chamber. 'They are normal men and women,' she said, 'this is true. However, they fight differently from you: not as warriors but as soldiers, together, organized.'

The wolf war-leader raised his bony shoulders in a shrug. 'This may be true but it will make no difference.'

Ullara resisted raising her eyes to the ceiling: *how to penetrate such self-satisfaction?* She pointed a finger. 'I forbid you to challenge or attack them, Looris. We must talk first. Spread the word.'

He gave his typical toothy grin, bowing his head slightly. 'As you wish.'

'Now . . . where is Koroll? I would speak with him.'

'Ah.' The war-leader gestured her inside. 'Now *we* must talk.'

She allowed Ursana to guide her to her seat. The largest of the hunting birds flapped down to perch about her: mountain eagles, red falcons and giant owls. She reached up to stroke an eagle. 'Yes? Where is Koroll then?'

Looris cleared his throat. 'Troubling news, Priestess. The Thelomen Bellurdan returned alone from the north and tried to force his way inside these precincts. No doubt he killed all those we sent with him and was intent upon attacking you.'

Ullara stared, unable to form a reply. 'I find that hard to believe,' she managed after a time.

'All witnessed it.'

'But *why*? Why did he? Did he give a reason?'

'Faugh – just stupid lies. The old tales of monsters at the mountain.'

Ullara stared anew. *Oh no.* Finally, blinking, she asked, 'And Koroll?'

'He aided his brother, raising his magery against us here within the village.'

Looking down upon the wolf-clan leader from her seat, Ullara nodded to herself. 'I think I see, Looris.'

'Yes. They betrayed us.'

'Did they? I wonder.'

'Yes, Priestess. Like all outsiders.'

She pressed a hand to the cloth covering her eyes, whispered, 'Leave me.'

Looris bowed and backed away. Ursana bowed also and briefly

rested a great paw on her shoulder, rumbling, 'I am sorry, my priestess.'

Alone in the great vaulted space, her pets eyeing her, Ullara covered her mouth to stop from crying out loud. The same thought circled in her mind over and over: *Gods! What am I to do?*

* * *

In the throne-room of the mountain, or navigation-deck – call it what you will – Hessa sat with the twins and Turnagin, awaiting dinner. They sat leaning up against the panels of tall machinery, which hummed and clicked and shuddered with their mysterious tasks. The fronts of some were too hot to touch and the general heat of the chamber was rising steadily; Hessa was down to a loose shirt and trousers, as were the others.

'What do you think Corbin's cooking up?' Hyde asked with a chuckle.

Ayal rolled her eyes.

'That is a point,' Turnagin answered thoughtfully, and he stretched his back, wincing. 'We can't just keep eating meat.'

'Meat's a gods-given treat,' Hyde objected. 'I c'n remember not getting any for months.'

'You'll sicken on a meat-only diet,' Turnagin answered.

Hyde raised a brow. 'Damn – what a way to go.'

Hessa just shook her head. Corbin came round a corner. He carried a metal shield on which a large cut of meat steamed. 'Dinner,' he announced.

'You used that flat metal plate to cook it?' Turnagin asked.

Corbin waved the question off. 'Yeah, yeah.'

The mage caught Hessa's eye, saying, 'I wish I knew what was heating that plate.'

Hessa just lifted her shoulders as if to say: *What can we do?*

Everyone tore off pieces of the seared haunch of shaggy beast. Hessa ate sparingly. The diet was palling on her. 'Anyone have any personal stores left from what we found from the ship? Twice-baked biscuit? Dried fruit?'

The twins shrugged. 'Some,' Ayal answered.

'Take a bite of it with each meal, okay?'

Hyde made a face. 'That dry crud is disgusting.' He licked his greasy fingers. 'This is much better.'

'Have some anyway.'

Turnagin leaned back, wiping his fingers on a rag. 'What of our monster-friends? Anyone ever see them eating?'

Corbin nodded. 'Down by the rooms below where they keep the frozen carcasses. I sometimes see them eating there.'

'They eat them? The frozen carcasses?'

'Yeah.' Corbin looked aside, thinking. 'But hardly, y'know. Like they're not interested.'

Turnagin again gave Hessa a significant glance.

The uneven thump and slide of Singer's limping gait sounded as he appeared from a file of the tall control-plinths. He was actually humming to himself as he came, looking quite pleased.

'Singer,' Hessa called, 'how much longer? The machines are up and running. We've done our part.'

The Jaghut paused, then approached, hands clasped at his back. 'True,' he nodded, 'they are warming. But we have yet to move. Once we get moving, then you will have done your part.'

'*Moving?*' Turnagin echoed.

Singer nodded again, cracking what could be called a sideways smile. 'Oh, yes, my friend. Moving. And once we begin there will be no force in the world that will be able to stop us.' And he laughed, limping away, humming again.

'Moving?' Hyde said. 'How long is that supposed to take?' He leaned forward, lowering his voice. 'I say we cut out now.'

'Them Che'Malle would slice us to pieces,' Corbin answered. He dug into a pouch to pull out a small stone that he tossed to Hyde. 'Been poking around.'

Hyde examined the reddish pebble. 'What's this?'

'A ruby.'

'No it ain't! Don't look like no gem.'

'It's uncut, unpolished. These Che'Malle use them in their natural state.' He gestured to Turnagin. 'Take a look.'

Hyde passed the stone over. Turnagin examined it. 'Looks like it could very well be.'

'Where'd you find it?' Ayal demanded.

'Just lyin' there on the stone floor in one of the hallways.'

The twins jumped to their feet.

'Don't—' Hessa began, but they were already running. She yelled after them, 'Stay away from the Che'Malle!' She turned her attention to Corbin, staring long and hard at the big fellow – he appeared uncomfortable under her steady regard. 'How long you been holding on to that?' she asked.

He shrugged his beefy shoulders. 'Long time. If I'm gettin' out of here I mean to leave filthy rich.'

Hessa sighed and waved him off. 'Fine. Then go look.'

He got up, stretched. 'Yeah. Might as well. See ya later.'

Hessa leaned her head back against the warm stone slab behind her. She didn't mind. Singer had practically invited them to pick up all they wanted. And if they gathered a stash it would make it easier to convince them to cut and run when the time came.

When was right; she was beginning to suspect that Singer had no intention of actually letting them simply walk out. It would be up to them to be ready to dash at the best opportunity. They'd have to be ready, and recognize the moment when it came. Personally, she suspected it would have something to do with any opposition; she imagined this monstrosity must've gathered *some* attention by now.

* * *

Two days after what was coming to be known as 'the night of Mael's Wrath' Gianna sat in her room at a window, staring, lost in thought. The clinking of metal on stone and the yells of labourers marked the repairs going on below, but she hardly noticed the noise.

It was the words of the city-folk, the common men and women of the town, that she could not get out of her head. She would never have imagined it had it not happened, and she wondered, was this why they kept her locked up and separated from everyone?

She had healed all through that night. Fires that had broken out in homes and shops lit her work as she pushed her meagre Denul skills farther than she ever had before. And she'd been startled – so many of the folk she worked on or who were helping had grasped her bloodied and dirtied shirt and trousers, whispering: *Save us from this damned Jhistal!*

119

One old woman had reached up almost reverently to touch her black hair as she numbed the pain from a shattered leg and staunched the bleeding. *The mark of the old ones*, the old woman told her, even as she lay dying from loss of blood. *The first people . . . favoured of Mael.* Yes, Gianna had silently agreed. For all the good it did us. And the woman gasped, *Rid us of this Jhistal!*

Her dying words and her dying breath.

She wondered now whether all these years she'd been wrong in running away. Perhaps she should've stayed; perhaps she should've fought.

So distracted was she that she did not note the door to her chambers opening and now the Abbess, Glinith, was with her – together with the usual four guards.

'The capital is abuzz with word of your healing, Priestess,' the Abbess said. 'Congratulations.'

Gianna frowned her puzzlement. 'What do you mean, "Congratulations"?'

'I mean it was well played. You have enhanced your reputation greatly.'

'*Reputation?* I didn't do that for any *reputation*!'

The Abbess smirked her disbelief. 'Come, come, girl. We are alone. You needn't play the innocent with me.'

Gianna stared at the woman, thinking, *What an appalling monster!* 'People were hurt – I went to help them.'

The Abbess's thin lips quirked. 'Whichever. Regardless. You appear to be growing up and accepting the reality of your situation. No more childish escape attempts. Therefore,' and she gestured to one of the priestess guards who gave her a cloth-wrapped object, 'I am here with a gift for you. Congratulations again . . . you have earned it.' And the Abbess offered the object, folding back the cloth to reveal a cream-hued, curved, serrated knife that appeared to have been carved from some sort of large seashell.

Gianna sprang from the woman and bit back a shriek. '*Get that thing away from me!*'

'But it is yours, High Priestess. The Blade of Offering.'

Gianna continued backing away. 'I know what it is! I won't touch that thing.'

Glinith sighed, rewrapped the opalescent knife. 'In time you will carry it, Giandra. It is your duty as High Priestess.'

'Never.'

The Abbess crossed her wiry, thin arms, sighing. 'Still this obstinate foolishness. You will carry it – I promise you.'

'Never.'

Shaking her head, Glinith signed to her guard and they left the rooms. Gianna stood frozen, her blood pounding, her hands cold, sweaty and shaking. *That thing has done monstrous crimes.* She peered round the chamber as if seeking escape that moment.

She realized then what she had to do.

That night Jan actually jumped when Gianna stepped into the kitchens. The old washerwoman stared about, almost guiltily. 'What are you doing here?' she asked, and steered her to a side-larder.

'I have to escape,' Gianna whispered, fierce.

Jan nodded, glancing behind. 'Yes, yes. We tried. That was, how would you say – poor timing.'

'Well . . . can't we try again?'

'Yes. You are fortunate. All ships are stuck in harbour until repairs on the sea-wall can be completed. So, at that time I believe we can try again.'

Gianna nearly hugged the old woman. 'Thank you! You have no idea what this means to me.'

Jan waved her off. 'Yes, yes. Until the harbour is opened once more, hmm?'

Gianna turned and headed to the door, almost running into a plump older priest who started as if stung. 'High Priestess!' he stammered, and bowed. For a moment she thought he'd been listening in – but he'd seemed so surprised to see her.

'Ah!' Jan announced. 'Brother Lethor. I am honoured.' She addressed Gianna: 'You are so kind to have come but there is no need to thank me for helping with the wounded and the healing. I was glad to.'

Gianna stared for a moment, then jerked a curt nod. 'Ah! Yes, well . . . thank you in any case.'

Jan bowed deeply, and Brother Lethor bowed again. Gianna backed away. 'Very well – good evening then.' She headed for the back stairs, hurrying, but trying not to appear to be hurrying.

On the way up she placed Brother Lethor: high up in the Coin of the Faith, an assistant to Mallick Rel. What would he be doing down in the kitchens? After pondering on it for a time, she shrugged. Abyss, the man was quite heavy – perhaps he actually *was* hungry.

*　*　*

It was an exhausted and subdued group gathered at the command tent north of Eagle Summit Pass. Everyone rested themselves on whatever could be found: stools, kegs, crates, all together under the tent. Present were Fist Dujek, who sat slumped in a camp chair, Dassem Ultor, and two young regular captains, Ullen, out of the officer academy, and Orosé, a tall, broad-boned female war-leader from Dal Hon. Of the mage cadre, present were Tayschrenn, Hairlock and Sialle.

Dujek roused himself to rub the stump of his lost arm and looked to Tayschrenn. 'So, here's the brief. Lost most of the rear echelon and baggage train. Some two thousand men and women. Most of our supplies. The pass is—' and here he paused, snorting, 'a field of rubble, near impassable. But got crews working on clearing a path through. Gods know how long that will take. Maybe a full season.' He rubbed his hand over the greying bristles of his pate, sighing. 'Abyss, if this were any other sort of expedition I'd turn round right now. But we can't. We're just one pincer in this invasion. Got an entire naval force counting on us holding ground for them. Ports for resupply, refit, shelter. Can't just turn round.'

Still eyeing Tayschrenn, Dujek leaned back, absently scratched the stump where his arm ended. 'So, we face a forced march across a wasteland where some sort of hostile force awaits us. Is that an accurate evaluation?'

Tayschrenn cleared his throat. 'Well . . . not necessarily hostile. It is possible that they may not even know we're here. May even consider us beneath their notice—'

'Beneath their notice!' Orosé cut in. She thrust a finger towards the pass. 'That was beneath their notice? Just what are we dealing with? I demand to know!'

Dujek nodded his support and raised a questioning brow to Tayschrenn. 'And just what does the great and powerful mage cadre have to say about all this?'

Tayschrenn compressed his lips. Revealing information – Hood, revealing *anything* – was against his nature, but he relented. 'It is not certain yet, but north of us I believe there lies a nest, or hive, or colony – call it what you will – of the K'Chain Che'Malle.'

Hairlock grunted a coarse laugh. 'Wouldn't you know it!'

Dujek turned an eye on the mage. 'You have something to add?'

Hairlock was nodding now, snorting. 'Yeah. I knew something was there. Could sense it. But couldn't place it. Not like anything I've ever seen afore.' He tilted his head, narrowed gaze on Tayschrenn. 'Who identified it? You?'

Tayschrenn shook a negative. 'Nightchill.'

Hairlock grunted again, spitting aside. 'Figures.'

Dujek looked to Dassem. 'What of you, Sword? What say you?'

The Champion uncrossed his arms, sat forward. 'If this is true then we certainly cannot turn around. K'Chain Che'Malle so close to Quon lands? We must scout this out, evaluate the potential threat – if any.'

Dujek inclined his head in agreement. 'Yeah. My thoughts as well. What of Falar?'

'Secondary.'

'For now – very well.' The Fist turned to Ullen and Orosé. 'All right. Marching orders. We head north as quickly as possible. Send scouting parties out. Rations will be cut a third, but we'll double the hunting and foraging parties. Very good?'

Both officers saluted, fist to chest. Orosé marched out, but the lean, newly promoted Ullen lingered. Dujek raised his chin. 'Yes?'

'A minor issue – but I ought to report it. Theft and rummaging has already been reported at the materiel depot.'

Dujek scowled, disappointed. 'Already? Thought that would wait a few weeks. Post guards.'

Ullen bowed, and departed.

'I would like to join the scouts,' Dassem put in.

The Fist sighed. 'Don't know if I have the authority to stop you. Just don't take any unnecessary risks, okay?'

'Agreed.'

Dujek now turned his attention to the mages. 'Looks like you lot are gonna have your work cut out. Not what you were expecting, hey?'

Tayschrenn grimaced at the casual tone, but inclined his head. 'We will do our best, of course.'

'I think you may have to,' the Fist answered. He gave a wave. 'Dismissed.'

Outside the tent Tayschrenn nodded good night to Sialle then walked for a time with Hairlock. 'What was that back there,' he asked, 'about Nightchill?'

A strong cold wind blew between them, coming down from the mountain heights. The Seven Cities mage walked with a splay-footed swagger, his arms loose at his sides, like a wrestler. 'How much you know about that gal?' he asked.

Tayschrenn almost laughed at the question. 'Virtually nothing.'

'Exactly. She comes and goes as she wills. Disappears for years at a time. Most have forgotten that she goes way back – maybe even before you'n me.'

'What of it?'

'*What of it?*' the mage repeated, almost affronted. 'So, what's her game? What's she up to? Has to be something, a sorceress as powerful as that. Why's she content just to kick around as an imperial mage so long when she could accomplish just about anything?'

'Perhaps she has no ambition.'

Hairlock made a farting noise. 'Plans. She's running some long game. You can be sure of that.'

'Such as?'

The mage rubbed his wide jowls. 'Dunno yet. Thinking on it. I'll let you know.' He eyed Tayschrenn sidelong. 'An' you too, *High Mage*. Content takin' orders from some jumped-up sell-sword?'

'We're in a battle theatre now. It makes sense that the military commander take charge.'

Hairlock snorted his scorn anew. 'Have to say, I don't under-stand you.'

Tayschrenn took a moment to eye the fellow. 'Nor I you.' He paused here, wondering whether to continue, then ploughed on. 'Nightchill did make a claim regarding you.'

'Oh?'

'She said you knew more about magery and power than I.'

The squat mage grunted his agreement. 'That gal's been watching.'

'What does she mean?'

The sun-darkened Seven Cities native gave him a smirk. 'I know

124

where real power comes from, friend.' He slapped a hand to his wide belly. 'It comes from here. From the gut.' He tapped a blunt finger to his temple. 'Not here.'

Tayschrenn stared his obvious and complete disbelief.

Hairlock gave a disgusted, 'Good night!' and swayed off in his straddle-legged walk.

Tayschrenn remained for a time, raised his gaze to the night, clasped his hands at his back. He shook his head. *Ridiculous nonsense that. Yet, what of me as the fellow asked? What are my plans? My schemes or games?*

Mentally, he raised a tally of such and frankly came up empty and he wondered: *Is it complimentary that one has none such? Or a condemnation? Is it even desirable that one could be so distanced from one's self that such a question could even be asked? Or is it yet another trap of self-delusion?*

He let out a long breath to the chill night. *How is one to know? One simply cannot.*

*   *   *

Beneath the sheltering slab of rock they'd chosen as their base camp, Blues and Gwynn sat awaiting Black the Lesser and Jacinth. It was the third day since the two had left to scavenge or steal from the Malazan force and Blues now was at the end of his patience. He'd start from his rock seat at every minor sound to peer to the west. Finally, towards noon, he muttered aloud his misgivings. 'I should've gone with them.'

Gwynn hadn't shifted from his perch where he was poking at the dirt with a slim poplar branch. He asked, 'How is your woodcraft?'

Blues slumped back to his seat: whatever his many other talents, mage, weapon-master to the Crimson Guard, his woodcraft was a joke to everyone. He eyed Gwynn. 'You are calm enough.'

'What will happen will happen. Our presence would only be a hindrance.'

This was true. Either of them might be tempted to raise their Warren, and the moment one of them did so every mage the Malazans had with them would spot their presence, plain as a bonfire on a prairie night. He and Gwynn were strong; but they weren't *that* strong.

A bird trilled from a tree nearby and Gwynn rose to stand and stare intently, searching for it. Blues watched him, mystified. He finally asked, 'Why do you do that all the time?'

'Do what?'

Blues waved a hand. 'Stare at the birds. Is it a hobby or something?'

After peering closely a while longer, Gwynn sat once more. He asked, 'Have you read any of the accounts from sailors or travellers who passed through this region?'

Blues almost snorted his dismissal. 'Gods no.'

'I have.' The pale mage, whose grim and dour demeanour was something of a joke among the Guard, gave him a glance. 'Sort of a hobby.' He returned to poking with the branch. 'Most are uninteresting and not worth the effort. However, one did mention something intriguing. A marooned sailor who walked south through the Fenn Range mentioned encountering beast-men. That is to say, men who are also beasts.'

Blues rolled his eyes. Fanciful nonsense. Sold some pamphlets though, no doubt.

'This sailor also mentioned hearing of their Queen, or Priestess. A sorceress of great power who – these beast-men claimed – could speak with birds.'

Blues shrugged, bemused. 'So?'

'So, that particular detail interests me. It interests me a great deal. Suffice to say, it has always intrigued me. And now I finally have the opportunity to investigate.'

Blues shook his head. For the life of him, he could not understand this fellow. Here they were stranded next to an army of Malazans, without any food or gear, and he was going on about birds? He blew out an impatient breath. 'Well . . . I think we have more pressing concerns.'

Gwynn nodded his easy agreement. 'Oh yes. Indeed we do.'

Blues sat and returned to waiting. He now began to wonder just how long they *should* wait. What if the two had been caught? Another day, perhaps, he judged, nodding to himself. Then a thump made him start to his feet, swinging round: there stood Black and Jacinth, each burdened with bundles and large travelling pouches and sacks. 'How do you *do* that?' Blues demanded.

'Do what?' Black answered, dropping his bundle.

'Sneak.'

'Sneak?' Black echoed, outraged. He and Jacinth exchanged a bemused glance. 'We do not sneak. We move quietly.' He and Jacinth began untying and opening all the pouches. Black handed wrapped sacks of supplies to Blues. 'Food. Armour – such as we could find. Weapons.' He and Jacinth set to trying on the various hauberks, mail shirts and greaves they'd pilfered.

'You see,' Black went on – and Blues crooked a smile, for Black did enjoy going on – 'you see . . . Jacinth and I hunted as youths. Have you ever hunted?'

'No.'

Black strapped on a hauberk faced in metal banding. 'There you go. You mages have no idea of the hours, the years of effort that go into things. You just snap your fingers and whatever you wish happens – like magic.'

The hauberk was obviously woefully small and he yanked it off. 'You are spoiled by that.'

Now Blues and Gwynn exchanged an amused glance. 'Is that so? Well, there's a bit more to it than that . . .'

Black waved the objection aside. 'For now, you two are going to have to learn to do things the hard way. No more magicking for either of you.'

'Oh? None at all?' Gwynn asked.

'That's right,' Jacinth put in. She'd used a long wood stave to carry her burden of gear and supplies and this she extended to Blues. 'You're the mere weapon-master for now.'

He took the stave, nodding his thanks. 'Just how many damned mages are with the Malazans?'

'Not how many,' Black answered. 'Who.'

'Who?' Gwynn asked.

'The mighty High Mage himself,' said Jacinth. 'Tayschrenn.'

Gwynn sat back on his rock, his brows rising. 'You saw him?'

'Yes. Walking across the camp.'

Blues let out a snarled breath. Damn. They sent *him*? Just what *was* north of them? 'So, we keep our distance.'

Jacinth was strapping on a long coat of layered leather armour laced with lozenges of bronze. 'Damned right.'

Black gave a curt nod of agreement. 'We'll trail them. Every other direction is crawling with Malazan scouts. They'd trip over us eventually.'

Blues extended the stave to touch the silver sceptre sigil at Black's breast. 'But will they know it when they do?'

Looking down, Black grunted a laugh. 'Hunh! Well, maybe it'll buy some time.'

Jacinth examined her own Malazan armour. She shot Black a questioning glance. 'Just what do they do to spies?'

'Kill them.'

'And what do they do to the Crimson Guard?'

'Try to kill them,' Black answered, and the two bashed forearms in a loud thump.

Blues and Gwynn both looked to the night sky and shook their heads.

* * *

Resolution of his uncertainty came to Endest Silann as the faintest of distant pulses, or waves, that propagate themselves in some enigmatic manner through the unknown Aether, or perhaps chaos, that is said to fill the voids between the Realms. He was not certain as he was not a scholar of such mysteries.

All he knew was that the answer to his vague unease, his wariness, was finally delivered by a particular taint: a certain unique flavour, if you will, of one unmistakable race, the K'Chain Che'Malle.

He rose then, from his chair in the darkened, otherwise empty room, and made for the chamber that his Lord had adapted as his main reception hall. Walking the wide and empty echoing tunnels, he savoured the irony, or poetry, of this particular verification of his suspicions: given that the Andii now occupied a floating fragment of a blasted K'Chain Che'Malle stronghold. Otherwise known as the Moon's Spawn.

Reaching the adapted reception hall he strode up to the main raised stone plinth that his Lord used for a seat – no actual chair per se being available as the Che'Malle had no use for such things.

He paused upon finding it empty.

This was not what he'd anticipated nor been told; he understood that the current watch was his responsibility alone. His Lord could rest at ease under his vigilance – and he was proud of the confidence so implied.

128

Then all tension and unease fled as realization came: he was not the only one with particularly heightened senses. Turning on his heel, he headed for where he suspected his Lord was no doubt to be found.

Another long walk through darkened halls and tunnels brought Endest Silann to a narrow way that led to a pale wan glow of starlight. Ahead lay a small opening, a ledge, something of a watchpost, that afforded a view of the outside: rare in a K'Chain Che'Malle construction as they had little interest in what lay without their demesnes. A racial flaw? he wondered, in passing. Something to set aside for later speculation, perhaps.

As he'd suspected, here stood his Lord. Upon the ledge the winds were fierce and howling. His Lord's cloak whipped about, as did his long mane of white hair. Endest Silann knelt to one knee, calling, 'M'lord . . .'

Anomandaris turned. A smile crooked his lips. 'You felt it too, of course.'

'Yes, m'lord.'

The Son of Darkness, Lord of the Tiste Andii, beckoned that he should rise. 'No need for that, my friend.'

'No need perhaps,' he answered, 'but it is your due.'

The Son of Darkness gestured that he should join him upon the ledge. 'Far to the west, I judge.'

Endest nodded his agreement. 'Yes. First the Imass – now this. Someone is meddling where they should not.'

'Who are we to complain of the actions of others?' Anomandaris murmured in answer, almost to himself.

'This may lead to much worse . . .' Endest offered.

Anomandaris nodded agreement. 'True. There are worse Elders to rouse.'

'We should investigate.'

His Lord gestured his consent. 'Very well.'

Endest clasped his hands at his back. 'I will waken Orfantal and Horult, then.'

Now his Lord shook a negative. 'No. Do not disturb them. You are awake. You may go.'

He found himself at rather a loss. 'Myself, m'lord?' he stammered. 'Leave . . . you?'

Anomandaris set a hand upon his shoulder. 'Who better? You

have leave to go. Investigate these disturbances. Report back on what you discover.'

He bowed his head; his Lord was showing him great confidence. 'I shall evaluate the situation. Thank you, m'lord.'

But Anomandaris had returned his gaze to the surface so very distant below them. Given that they had withdrawn for a time from the irritations of all the clamouring below, the Moon's Spawn now floated extraordinarily high; the lands and seas below lay like a carven tabletop far off beneath ribbons of cloud.

His Lord regarded this gods-like vista with narrowed gaze, one hand upon the hilt of the blade at his side that even now after all these centuries still unnerved Endest: Dragnipur itself, which some named the Prison of Souls.

He bowed. 'I will prepare.'

Chapter 9

DANCER STOOD WITH CARTHERON AT THE SIDE OF THE *Twisted*. The ship's frayed lines thrummed their strain about him while ominous creaking and groans sounded from the deck and hull at his feet, and he wondered – not too idly – whether the old girl would hold together. It was an overcast morning and they were headed south at all speed, returning towards the ice fields, and he was not pleased.

'How many are left to round up?' he asked of the Admiral.

'Ten. There are supposed to be ten more of them. That's what the lookout said.'

Dancer squinted to the southern horizon where tiny discolorations marked the sails of distant vessels against the iron-grey waves. 'I see six.'

'The slower ones.'

Dancer now looked to the heavy cloud layer above and mouthed a curse. 'Hood damn this! All the others must be making a break for it.'

'To where?' Cartheron asked. 'They're too frightened to go north into Falaran waters. A barren hostile coast bars the west. There's uncounted leagues of open ocean to the east. That just leaves the south – and we're between them and it.'

Dancer could only shake his head. 'We were leading them . . . now we're cajoling.'

''Bout what I expected from scum like them. No backbone. Opportunist thieves who'd abandon anyone to save their own skins.'

Dancer crooked a one-sided smile. 'You've made your opinions plain, Admiral.'

'Admiral, hunh,' he snorted. 'Never did agree to that.'

'You did some time ago.'

'Musta bin drunk.'

'Can we overtake the leaders in the *Twisted*?'

Cartheron rubbed the bristles of his cheek. 'Don't think so. She's known for all kinds a things, but speed's not one of them.'

'Damn.' Dancer looked to the main cabin's door. 'He'd better have a plan, then.'

'Good luck,' Cartheron murmured.

Dancer grunted his acceptance as he headed to the cabin.

Closing the door behind him, Dancer found himself in darkness. He called, 'Would you stop it?'

'Stop what?' came Kellanved's surprised answer from somewhere within.

'The darkness.'

'I'm not doing a thing – it's just dark in here.'

Dancer's eyes were adjusting from the dusk to see his partner, the Emperor, sitting behind a table, head cupped in hands. 'Cartheron doesn't think we can catch the fastest of them.'

Sighing, Kellanved came around the table. His walking stick appeared. 'Well then, let's see what can be done . . .'

Out on deck, it seemed to Dancer that even though Kellanved had the dark skin of his Dal Hon descent his face appeared greyish, and he walked very slowly and unsteadily, leaning heavily on his stick. The Emperor made his uncertain way on the canted vessel to the bow where Cartheron awaited. Dancer followed, wondering what the fellow had in mind – if anything.

The mage peered ahead for a time, squinting and covering his gaze. 'Can you get them all in sight?' he asked of Cartheron, his voice still a touch weak; despite being ruler of a sea-power, sea-travel, it appeared, most certainly did not agree with him.

'I don't think we could get all of them,' Cartheron supplied.

Kellanved sighed again. 'Well, the most that we can . . . yes?'

Cartheron nodded his assent and moved off to give orders. Bare feet slapped the decking as sailors ran to lines to tease more speed from the winds. The *Twisted* soon leaned even further to the bows. When Cartheron returned, Dancer asked, 'Will she hold?'

The old-hand sailor gave an eloquent shrug.

By noon Dancer counted eight sails of this small fleet, the last of the deserters they could reach. Cartheron rejoined them at the side and he called above the winds, 'They'll soon respond and put on any more sail they might have.'

Kellanved grimaced. 'Very well.' The walking stick had disappeared at some point; Dancer knew that sometimes it was real, and sometimes it wasn't, but he was never quite sure which. The Dal Hon mage gestured, letting out a hissed breath. Cartheron and Dancer exchanged uneasy glances. Ahead, quite suddenly, like passing clouds, darkness enveloped the leading vessels. Cartheron let out a grunt of amazement.

It was almost as if, Dancer reflected, each ship was under, well, thick shadow. Even from this great distance he could see that these three had now lost headway. The five fleeing privateers caught in the middle waters between now eased up as well, perhaps reluctant to invite a similar fate.

The *Twisted* cut a path through these and Cartheron made a show of gesturing northwards. Dancer caught glimpses of pale and wide-eyed faces at the sides of vessels as they passed.

'One should come with us to see this,' Kellanved told the commander and Cartheron hurried off to the steersman. The *Twisted* came about, circling one of the privateers, which was named, rather jauntily, the *Best Regards*.

Dancer meanwhile kept an eye on the three lead vessels; the darkness was gone but all three now wandered, sluggish and every which way, as if no one had a hand on them. The *Twisted* headed southwards once more and slowly came abreast of one of the three. It was dangerous work as the deserter ship was lurching this way and that in the winds; Dancer saw no one at the sails or moving on deck.

Cartheron gave the order to come alongside. Eventually, they were close enough for Dancer to see that indeed there was no one in evidence. It was as if the ship had somehow been abandoned.

'Ahoy!' Cartheron called. '*Ahoy!*'

No voices responded.

Sailors jumped aboard, went belowdecks to investigate. Across the water the *Best Regards* was warily approaching another of the idle ships.

'Where are they?' Dancer asked of Kellanved.

'Elsewhere,' the elder answered, rather tightly; Dancer could tell he was irritated.

133

The sailors returned, looks of stunned wonder upon their faces. They shook their heads. Cartheron turned to Kellanved with a questioning look.

'Take it under tow and order our compatriot to do the same,' Kellanved told him. 'Now, if we can *quite* return to our prior heading . . . ?' and he headed to the cabin, pulling the door shut behind him.

'Tow it,' Cartheron passed along to the crew.

'It will slow us down,' Dancer objected.

Cartheron, a fair bit shorter than Dancer, rubbed his balding pate, his gaze on the closed cabin door. 'Aye, but it's proof. Proof of the tale that the *Best Regards* will bring to the rest of 'em.' He let out a breath, shaking his head. 'They might be fearful of what's awaiting them in Falar – but they'll be a fair more fearful of what's behind them now.'

Dancer reflected that that was probably an accurate assessment.

* * *

Tayschrenn marched, or rather walked, with the main body of the expeditionary force, which constituted the majority of the heavy infantry and held their commander, Fist Dujek. This was surrounded by further spread-out columns, skirmishers beyond these, and far-flung scouts and hunters and foragers.

A continuous string of messengers, scouts and staff came and went, relaying observations, reports, and in turn conveying orders and such. Tayschrenn himself paid little attention to it all; 'High Mage' of an expansionist empire he might be, but he'd never developed an interest in military matters and nor did he wish to.

Therefore, later in the third day of march, when he happened to find himself near Dujek's walking command, he was rather surprised to find it quite busy, with messengers and scouts rushing in, and the burly one-armed fellow giving constant orders.

'What is it?' Tayschrenn asked.

A harried Dujek cast him a quick glance. 'Multiple contacts all about.'

Tayschrenn raised a brow. 'Really? I've not seen nor heard a thing.'

134

Dujek ignored him for a time, murmuring orders to waiting messengers who darted off. 'The foragers and hunting parties were targeted first – they're getting slaughtered. I'm ordering them back in and the scouts to pull back.'

'But we'll be blind then.'

'That's probably their intention.'

'Who are "they"?'

'Some sort of beasts. Large wolves, apparently. Perhaps who-ever's out there breeds them.'

Tayschrenn opened his mouth to ask another question but the Fist had turned away, dismissing him; which, he reflected, was understandable. The man was quite busy after all.

Later that afternoon he came across Nightchill walking alone. He hadn't seen her for some time. She was dressed as always in a plain dirty shirt and trousers; her bare feet were blackened in dirt. She could almost be mistaken for some poor ragged camp follower and Tayschrenn wondered if perhaps some unlucky trooper had done so – and where he, or she, was now. Joining her he did not bother to ask where she'd been, or what she'd been doing, as she never gave a straightforward answer. Instead he began, 'Have you heard the news?'

'What news?' she responded, uninterested.

'Some sort of large beasts are attacking our scouts and foraging parties.'

She nodded absently to this. 'I sense the Beast Hold.'

'The Hold? So, not normal wolves.'

'A mere distraction.' She raised her chin to where the plume of black and grey smoke marred the sky. 'We mustn't be diverted.'

He murmured, 'I don't think our esteemed commander will agree.'

'We shall see.'

Tayschrenn had nothing to add to that and so they walked in silence for some time. Towards dusk the main column halted and preparations began to establish camp. A messenger ran up to him and saluted. 'The Fist bids you come – we have a corpse to examine.'

Tayschrenn cast a glance to Nightchill who shook her head, uninterested. Bowing slightly, he turned for the command tent which had been raised and glowed now with multiple lanterns.

Within, he found Fist Dujek, captains Ullen and Orosé, Dassem Ultor, Hairlock and Sialle, plus Dujek's staff and usual personal guards. They stood, or lounged in the case of Hairlock, round a central table upon which lay an unusual corpse. Dujek gestured to it. 'Cadre mages, if you would . . .'

Tayschrenn bent to the hacked body. It was a man, who, despite the cold and snow, wore only a tattered and dirty loincloth. He was extremely hairy; Tayschrenn lifted one shoulder and peered beneath: he bore a thick ridge of hair down his back. Sialle lifted a hand, examined it, and nodded to herself; she showed a finger to Tayschrenn. The nail was thick and extended, more like an animal's claw or talon. Hairlock pulled back the lips and grunted his surprise. Tayschrenn peered closer: far oversized teeth, canines upper and lower very robust, without molars to speak of: all rear teeth ridged and sharp for tearing.

Tayschrenn turned to Dujek. 'A shapeshifter. A type of Soletaken.'

'The ritual?' Dujek asked. 'Then why didn't you sense it?'

Sialle shook her head. 'No. A true beast-human. In the blood. Born. The Jhekal, Jhek, or Jhall. They have many names.'

Now Tayschrenn was nodding. 'Ah. There are reports of enclaves on other continents and such. Just not here. That they've managed to remain hidden is a testament to how desolate and untravelled this region is.'

'Can they be negotiated with?' Dujek asked. 'Bought off?'

'Not from everything I've heard,' Tayschrenn answered. 'They are territorial, aggressive. Do not back down.'

'I agree,' Sialle added.

'They are very fierce fighters,' Dassem said from where he stood aside, his arms crossed. 'Stronger and faster than any man or woman. Our regulars do not stand a chance against them individually.'

Dujek nodded at that while eyeing the Champion; some sort of understanding passed between them and he turned to his staff. 'Pull everyone back. We move in column ready for any attack.'

Captain Ullen saluted, but hesitated, saying, 'We are still very low on stores . . .'

'We'll just have to tough it out for a time.'

The captain saluted once more, but looked grim as he exited.

The Fist stared after him and ran his hand over his balding scalp, sighing. 'The lad's right. We are damnably low on provisions.'

Dassem nodded his assent. 'Let's hope we do not have to wait long.'

Dujek looked to Tayschrenn and the other mages. 'Thank you for your help, cadre. And be ready to defend if we are attacked.'

Tayschrenn simply inclined his head, and exited. Outside, he fell in with Hairlock who walked in his usual swinging swagger. 'What do you think about all this?' Tayschrenn asked.

''Bout what?'

'These Jhek.'

The burly mage cut a hand through the air. 'Faugh. We'll annihilate them.'

Tayschrenn happened to glance aside to Sialle and was surprised to see her watching the Seven Cities mage with a slit-eyed glare that could only be described as disgust.

* * *

When the great doors to the temple were thrown open and in strode the wolf-clan leader Looris accompanied by his picked warriors, Ullara knew exactly what the man was going to say; after all, she'd been watching everything. As she thought, the chieftain was clearly elated. His broad toothy grin was almost creamy in its self-satisfaction.

'So much for your dreaded Malazan soldiers,' he announced. 'They die like any other man or woman beneath our nails and teeth.'

'I know,' she answered tightly, 'I saw.'

He nodded, not the least bit troubled. 'Good! Then you saw how they fled from us.'

'They've withdrawn, Looris. That is altogether different from fleeing.'

He waved her misgivings aside. 'They've clumped together like fearful sheep. We will fall upon them soon.'

Ullara surged to her feet. 'Do not attack that main body, Looris. I forbid it.'

The clan-chief's look turned condescending. 'This is a matter for warriors, Priestess. Keep to your birds.'

She raised a finger to the roof and the circling birds. 'Through eyes like these I have watched countless engagements and battles all across the lands to the south. And believe me, war-chief, that main column will be your ruin. Those soldiers you attacked – did they carry shields?'

He shook his head, bemused. 'No. No such things.'

'Well, you will meet those who do and they will repel you.' She softened her voice, 'Please. I beg of you, do not do this.'

Now his gaze hardened. He snorted, 'Begging. Clearly you carry no warrior's heart. Begging only wins you contempt.' And he turned away.

'You are making a terrible mistake, Looris,' she called after him. 'Remember my words!'

The doors boomed shut behind him and the birds sent up a squall of complaint.

After sitting for a time Ullara headed to the doors. She pushed one open a crack only to see two wolf-warriors on guard. 'What is this?' she demanded.

The young warrior would not meet her gaze. 'Apologies, Priestess. Orders from the clan-leader. You are to be kept safe within.'

'Imprisoned, you mean!'

The young fellow blushed his embarrassment. 'I am sorry.'

'Well, at least send Athan to me. You can do that, can't you?'

'I am sorry, Priestess, but he is in the field.'

'Ursana then?'

The two exchanged uncertain glances then this one nodded. 'I will send for her.'

Ullara straightened, raised her chin, and said coldly, 'My thanks.'

Back in her seat she let her head fall to her hands and wept again, shuddering, in an agony of dread. Later that afternoon the doors opened and in lumbered the bear-warrior Ursana. The huge warrior knelt to one knee before her, saying, 'You sent for me, Priestess?'

'Yes. Can you stop this insanity? Stop any further attacks against this foreign army?'

The bear-woman slowly shook her head. 'No. I am sorry. Looris is war-chief. I am bound by honour to follow his commands.'

It was all Ullara could do to stop herself from screaming at the woman. She reached out, clasped a hairy forearm. 'Then at least do this for me. Be ready. Ready to withdraw. Salvage all that you can when the battle turns. Will you do that for me? Promise?'

The warrior was clearly troubled. She nodded, rumbling, 'I will keep your warning in mind, Priestess.'

Ullara would've kissed the woman, could she reach so high. She gave the broad muscular forearm a squeeze. 'My thanks. The priestess of your people thanks you.'

Ursana bowed her head and withdrew.

Alone, in the fading light, Ullara couldn't stop the tears from returning. She let her head fall back, staring sightlessly, roving from eyes to eyes: watching the implacable advance of the Malazan infantry, watching the smoke plume of the K'Chain Che'Malle mountain thicken and darken, watching her poor foolish people in their preparations to encircle the Malazan force, watching a stream cut a new channel through the wreckage of Eagle Summit Pass, watching—

She nearly fell as she surged to her feet, gasping her disbelief.

'*Gwynn?*' she yelled to the empty hall.

* * *

In the mountain's main control chamber Hessa stood waiting with Turnagin. 'You sense nothing?' she asked of the mage again.

He gave a grimace of assent. 'Nothing. These alien energies play havoc with my abilities. Also, I dare not strengthen my attempts as Singer would probably detect them.'

Hessa just shook her head; it would all be so much easier if Turnagin could simply use his talents. But they would have to make do. She straightened then, at the sound of running footsteps.

Hyde appeared round the towering plinths and instruments. 'Yeah,' he called, panting, 'he's long gone down below.'

She jerked a nod. 'Good. Keep a lookout. Call if you see him.'

Turnagin cleared his throat. 'You do not have to do this . . .'

'I know. But perhaps I should – I don't know.'

The mage just clenched his lips, lowering his gaze.

Hessa turned and jogged for the one ramp that rose from this chamber – the one Singer forbade them entering. Its dimensions were gigantic, tall and broad. Its walls the bare heart-rock of the mountain, but smoothed as if by great heat. She started up it at a lope, to find it gently spiralled like a circular stairway.

Some turns later, panting, she cursed: she'd not expected such a long way. She kept telling herself: just the next turn. See what's round the next curve. But so far it had been just more of the same. The heat was intensifying, however. It was like breathing inside a kiln.

Finally, the sloping rise levelled off. She spurred herself to more speed. A broad hall of rock ran straight ahead. To either side opened alcoves, or caves, each sealed by some sort of soft waxen barrier. Within lay immense K'Chain Che'Malle shapes, but different somehow. It was hard to tell through the obscuring barriers, but these ones appeared to have more limbs and be longer and leaner than the other ones, more serpentine.

The hall ended in another alcove, the full width wall to wall, where the largest shape yet lay curled up, dark and blurred behind its soft barrier. This wall, waxen, or some such material, was not solid and unmarred like the others. A hole had been cut in it, one large enough for a hand – a rather large hand.

She knelt at the hole, peering within. She saw nothing but darkness, though the Che'Malle dry stink was pungent here. After a time, it wasn't what she saw that made her flinch away; it was what she heard.

A single long and low rasping breath – as of a long slow exhalation.

She turned and ran.

Exhausted, dragging her feet, she finally arrived back down at the ramp's base. Here she found Turnagin and the twins, Hyde and Ayal, waiting. None spoke as she approached, but Ayal glanced aside in a significant stare. Hessa felt her shoulders drop. *Damn.*

Singer stepped out from round the wall. He crossed his arms. 'So . . . as you suspected, no?'

'Yes.'

He gave a shrug. 'Then this changes nothing.' He waved them to follow. 'Come. Let us see about raising the energy levels.'

Turnagin fell in step with her. '*The Matron?*' he hissed.

'Alive. Sleeping, maybe?'

The mage nodded. 'Hibernating. As all these should be. This Jaghut has—'

'Enough whispering, little mice,' Singer called to them.

Hessa mouthed, *Later.*

They crossed the broad, maze-like chamber with its rows of

plinths and standing gears and chains, and Hessa was surprised to smell that strong Che'Malle stink that had filled the uppermost hall. She raised her hand to her nose and realized, *It's me.*

She also remembered another time she'd smelled something similar – when she'd happened to be quite close to Singer.

*   *   *

Blues lay flat out on the slushy snow and mud, chilled to the bone, hands numb, and tried to catch sight of the Malazan scouting party they'd been shadowing all morning.

'This is stupid,' he hissed to Black, 'we're too far away!'

'Have to be – you and Gwynn move like great hairy bhederin.'

Blues glanced back to where Gwynn and Jacinth waited, crouched in a slight hollow. 'Ha! Very funny.'

They were wary because twice already they'd come across scenes of slaughter where Malazan light foragers, scouts and hunters lay scattered, literally torn limb from limb, throats savaged and abdomens ripped open. Black believed it some sort of pack of hunting beasts, perhaps set upon the invaders by whoever, or whatever, lay to the north.

Blues returned his attention to the rolling wasteland to the north where the Malazan scouting party appeared to have gone to ground, or moved at speed too far off. He opened his mouth to complain to Black once more but silenced himself, for the fighter lay frozen, tensed. Then he felt it too. Company.

He held a hand out to the side in a sign: *contact*. The two rose slowly and casually rejoined their compatriots. Blues, Jacinth and Black then straightened in a tight circle around Gwynn, hands on weapons.

Their company closed from all sides. Even the north; which soured Blues's mood as he'd just been scanning it. Scrawny they seemed, all wiry naked hairy limbs. They moved low, sometimes on all fours.

'Shapeshifters. Soletaken!' Gwynn warned. 'The very beast-humans of old accounts.'

'Just passing through!' Blues called out. None answered, as he'd expected.

They closed just like a pack: one darting in quickly then

141

retreating, drawing attention, then another darting in from the opposite side. But he and Jacinth and Black held their tight circle, weapons bared, waiting for the full rush.

After more baiting and a number of false charges, at some signal the full numbers fell upon them. Blues knocked aside raking slashes of nailed hands, stop-thrust snarling mouths, gut-thrust leaps. One beast-woman clamped a hand on his forearm and even through the leather armour he felt the inhuman strength of the grip as the fingers and nails gouged deeply. He twisted his stave between their arms and wrenched, snapping the creature's wrist.

Then it was over. Black and Jacinth stood over the dead, their scavenged Malazan shortswords bloodied to the hilts.

'I'd give anything for my old longsword,' Jacinth complained, and she cleaned her blades on the thick pelts of their attackers.

'They were strong,' Black observed, impressed.

'And fast,' Jacinth added. 'The lights never stood a chance.'

'We should move,' Gwynn observed. Jacinth grunted her agreement and sheathed her blades. They jogged north-east, following the slight depression between spare hills.

After a few moments a white blur shot across the trampled mud of the skirmish. A long pale body that twisted nimbly. It rose up on its hind legs, sniffed the air with its pink nose, then blurred. An instant later a young woman in a plain jerkin and trousers bearing a wild and thick mane of pure white hair stood among the dead. She examined the wounds of the fallen, then the footprints that told the story of the engagement, then she looked to the north-east for some time, a thoughtful expression upon her pale oval face.

* * *

The residents of Deep Cove on War Isle were now deeply worried. Just as they had gotten used to the presence of a foreigner – a Seven Cities native no less – five more such foreigners arrived in a hired boat to climb the stone stairs to the single tavern of the town and sit at the first's table.

There they sat, speaking in their guttural uncouth tongue, which every resident understood as it was a dialect close to their own.

'Imanaj,' a newcomer said as he sat down.

142

'Kor'th,' the first foreigner responded. 'Legor ... Cresh ... Sethen ... and L'Orth,' he lastly greeted a large and alarmingly burly woman.

The one greeted as Kor'th – a bearded and very hairy and large fellow bearing twinned axes at his belt – peered about the tavern, his distaste and disapproval obvious. 'Imanaj,' he grunted, 'just what are you doing here?'

'Waiting.'

'Do not play coy,' snapped the one named Legor. Skeletal he was, with a sharp hatchet-like face, in leathers, with twinned hook-knives at his belt. 'You ran – but you did not run far enough.'

'I hit a rock. Stove in my boat.'

'Imanaj,' sighed the third, named Cresh, in a loose dark cotton shirt over trousers, long thin blades at his belt, 'you may be a great champion, but you are obviously no sailor.'

Imanaj tilted his head in agreement. 'Few of us desert-dwellers are.'

'You abandoned your place, your Holy duty and obligations,' said the fourth, named Sethen, in leather armour, a long two-handed blade at his side.

'Another will arise to take my place.'

'In the meantime Aren is defenceless!' cut in the last, the woman L'Orth, in heavy leathers with shortswords at her belt.

'Do the great sea-walls still stand?' Imanaj asked. She nodded, grudgingly. 'Do the great gates remain guarded?'

She looked away, grimacing. 'A city may challenge – what then will we do without a champion?'

Imanaj slowly shook his head. 'L'Orth, the days of city challenges are long behind us. It has been, what? A generation since the wars for pre-eminence? No, the Holy cities no longer war or challenge one another as in the old days. And thank the Seven for that.'

'He is afraid,' judged Legor, sneering. 'Afraid to face Yrgell of Ubaryd, or Sianna of Ehrlitan. Afraid to fight.'

Imanaj merely turned the small glass of ikkor before him. 'Think what you wish,' he murmured.

Sethen had been studying him closely and, having reached some sort of conclusion, now nodded to himself. 'You have doubts,' he said. 'Doubts are normal – but not for a Holy City Champion. You must have no such weakness.'

143

'Doubts are what keep us human,' Imanaj murmured, looking out to sea.

'You do not understand,' L'Orth said, her voice tight. 'We judge you unworthy of the honour.'

Imanaj gave an amused half-smile. 'Then by all means – bestow the honour upon someone else.'

'You are being obtuse,' Kor'th grunted. 'You know full well what this means.'

Sighing, Imanaj squinted at white seabirds hovering over the bay. 'Yes. No chance, then, that you may return and say you did not find me?'

Legor snorted at that. 'Let's get this over with. You now sicken me.'

Imanaj gestured to the open portal of the door and they all slowly rose from the table, hands near weapons. 'After you,' invited Cresh.

Imanaj walked out, headed down the beaten path to the shore, crossed the cluttered strand near the village, and continued on to an untrammelled stretch of sandy beach. The five followed at a discreet distance. Curious villagers stopped to watch from the cliff heights above.

Turning to face the five, Imanaj tapped the hilts of his daggers. 'As you see, I am not properly armed. Where is your so-called honour in this?'

Cresh unhooked one of his sheathed swords and tossed it to Imanaj who inclined his head in thanks. He drew it and examined the blade. 'An excellent weapon. My—'

'Enough of this!' Legor hissed, and he charged, his hook-blades flashing. Imanaj gave ground, parrying slice after slice – but only just enough so that the keen weapons passed a bare finger's breadth from their mark. The blades moved in a blur between the two fighters. Imanaj kept moving, circling, giving ground. Legor followed relentlessly, his face set in a rigid snarl.

None of the villagers watching could say what happened next, or how it happened, but in one instant Legor staggered back, blood flew in an arc, and he fell to the trampled sands, weapons still in his fists.

Kor'th stepped forward. He peered down at the body. 'Legor's weakness,' he opined, 'was too much faith in his savagery.' He raised his gaze to Imanaj. 'You will find no such weakness in me.'

'We all have our weaknesses,' Imanaj returned.

Kor'th drew his two axes and advanced.

So the villagers of War Isle watched with growing amazement and stupefaction as this fearsome-looking axe-wielder and the armoured newcomer with a two-handed blade both fell to the blade of the placid slim fellow who'd sat among them for weeks, quietly watching the sea from his seat in the tavern.

The woman strode forward now, large and heavy-set, in leather armour of the loose Seven Cities style. She drew two shortswords and struck a ready stance.

'L'Orth,' Imanaj greeted her. 'We need not do this.'

'I am afraid we must,' she answered, sounding regretful.

Imanaj tilted back his head to the sky, sighing. His shirt was torn and bloodied and a sheen of sweat glistened upon his face and arms. 'Please—' he began, but L'Orth charged in.

The duel between these two was the longest so far. The woman tested again and again, easing in, then out, constantly probing. Imanaj appeared reluctant to initiate and held back, waiting.

The better part of an hour passed in this manner; the sun lowered towards the horizon. Twice Imanaj wiped sweat from his eyes. The second time his face changed as a realization came. 'You would wear me down,' he told L'Orth, who did not answer, remaining crouched, thrusting, forcing him to parry, and circling.

Imanaj shook his head. 'Sound strategy . . . but I cannot let that happen.'

Again the villagers could not see it. This visitor, Imanaj, darted forward, closing the space between him and the woman. The blades flew as a blur then she, too, staggered backwards, dropping one shortsword, a hand going to her chest.

That bloodied hand then reached out to Imanaj, entreating. 'Do not leave Aren defenceless,' she gasped, and fell.

Imanaj then turned to face the last of them: the lean and rangy one, Cresh, in a black shirt and trousers. He pursed his lips and peered down at the one weapon at his hip. 'I suppose I should ask for my sword back now,' he said, and crooked a grin. 'But that would be dishonourable.'

Imanaj stood waiting, breathing deeply.

'Also,' Cresh added, 'I suppose I should give you time to recover . . . but that would be foolish. Therefore,' and he raised a

145

finger, pointing to the alarmed villagers above. 'You there!' he called. 'Go to this man's room. Search it. You should find a long bundle somewhere – under the cot perhaps. Bring it.'

Three of the villagers ran towards town.

'Also,' Cresh called to the rest, 'bring torches.' He eyed Imanaj. 'This may take some time.'

Indeed, it did take some time. The two fought on through the night, lit by torchlight and the silvery glow of the half-moon. Each fought with twinned blades, light and slim. The song of these brushing and touching as they parried and blocked was like high-pitched music. It occurred to some villagers that – had they been fighting men or women themselves, or connoisseurs of blade-craft – they were now being treated to the greatest spectacle of their lives. But it was all lost upon them: none had ever fought, nor did they wish to.

It ended before dawn, and before the remaining few villagers noticed. The one in black, Cresh, simply suddenly remained still for a time; his arms slowly lowered. He fell to his knees, may have whispered something to Imanaj, then toppled over into the wet sands near the surf.

Imanaj then slowly, and very stiffly, came walking up the path to the village. The first inhabitant he came to ducked his head and murmured, 'We'll take care of them – don't you worry.'

'Take care of them how?' the man answered, his voice faint and hoarse.

'We'll dump the bodies at sea.'

Their visitor weaved then, blearily. He swallowed to wet his throat, said, 'You'll do nothing of the sort. You'll bury them. It's the Seven Cities way.'

The villager bobbed his head respectfully. 'Very well. Yes. We'll bury them.'

Their visitor staggered on towards the tavern. Left behind, the few remaining villagers exchanged glances that said: *We'll dump them at sea. After we strip their gear, of course.*

Chapter 10

Tayschrenn stood with Nightchill on the crest of a modest moss-covered hill at the centre of Dujek's command. The Fist himself stood nearby, surrounded by his staff and guards and messengers. Around the hill stood the encircling ranks of the expeditionary army, heavies deployed to the outer ring.

They had marched three days further north; three days and nights of constant harassment, raids, and contact by these Jhek warriors. Many troopers had been taken, picked off one by one. All this time Dujek had refrained from any punitive counter-raid or trap to push the enemy away or bloody them, and Tayschrenn had to admit that the Fist's strategy seemed to be working: these warriors were becoming more and more bold, more sure of themselves, more certain of victory. More likely to commit to a standing battle. Or such, it seemed, was Dujek's hope.

Yesterday's march had been something of a running battle: Jhek warriors darting in, dragging troopers off – even from the arms of their squad-mates; pulling down withdrawing marines from behind; contact had been thick on all sides. Then late yesterday Dujek cast about and selected this small hill as his apparent 'last stand'. Or so he no doubt hoped it would look – that they were exhausted, at bay, with nowhere to run.

The Malazan force endured a chaotic night of raiding and quick darting attacks. With dawn they straightened, readied their shields, and formed ranks. Tayschrenn had to admit being quite impressed with these troops' discipline and morale. No fear showed in any eye that he saw, only a slow simmering rage and the flat, hard resolve to deliver fearsome payback.

147

Dujek ordered Tayschrenn and Nightchill to hold back in reserve, in case something unforeseen should arise, or the battle go horribly wrong. Hairlock and Sialle stood closer to the front, ready to intervene if necessary to prevent any major incursion or breach.

Tayschrenn did not resent any such 'orders'. This was battle, the Fist's purview, not his.

So he watched, waiting, gauging the actions and preparations on both sides. Out beyond javelin range the Jhek circled, running and bounding, sounding their chilling war-calls. As they never stood still it was difficult to estimate numbers, but Tayschrenn thought them woefully under-strength to assault such a large force. But they'd tasted blood and wanted more, and, admittedly, man for man or woman for woman, they were more than a match for any one trooper.

Now that they were standing their ground, he noted many more of the larger of these Jhek. A different breed of Soletaken perhaps, far taller and heavier, and obviously slower. Bear-warriors, Sialle had named them, and their appearance worried him.

For their part, the marines waited in silence, the outer ranks with shields readied. Dujek stood waiting silently as well, eyeing the enemy, absently rubbing the stump of his arm, or the greying bristles at his chin.

These enemies were obviously in the process of whipping themselves up into a frenzy, readying to throw themselves upon the marines, and it seemed to Tayschrenn that the more ferocious and savage they became, the more animal-like: far hairier, more on all fours, their sharp teeth more pronounced. A wolf-type of Soletaken indeed. The larger bear shapeshifters waited further out, rearing up on their legs then slamming the ground and chuffing and roaring.

He turned to the slim figure of Nightchill next to him, who stood quiet as well, her thin arms crossed at her narrow chest. He asked, 'How do you think this will go?'

Without removing her gaze from the bounding, howling warriors, she replied, 'I think we will be hounded every step of the way to Falar unless this ends here.'

He believed she was probably right.

When the attack came he had no idea what had triggered it. In one instant the warriors were circling, the next, seemingly as one mass, they charged snarling and raging in from all sides.

148

He felt the impact as a physical blow to his chest. The ranks seemed to waver slightly backwards then straighten once more, leaning in to respond to the challenge. The Soletaken clawed at the outer rank of heavies, snagging shields, even troopers. He saw men and women flying through the air. The clamour, screaming, howling and clash of armour and shield was a tumult that made talk impossible.

Every marine heavy, however, was thrusting back with shortsword, stabbing over and over, punishing anything before them that moved.

Then drums sounded a battle order and the second and even third ranks behind thrust their javelins over and between shields, and the ring of Jhek warriors physically recoiled.

As if waiting for that counter, or the wavering of their brethren, the huge and lumbering bear-warriors came charging in. Watching, Tayschrenn tensed for the impact. The smashing shock was like an avalanche. He saw some of the immense creatures break through three ranks deep, sending great swathing blows side to side before falling under countless swordthrusts. The impact pushed the very rear soldiers back a step and made him glance worriedly to Nightchill: the woman was betraying no emotion, only a narrowed critical gaze, as if studying events somehow wholly unrelated to her.

The outer borders of the defence were now a milling chaos. These Jhek were savaging the foremost ranks. Tayschrenn was beginning to wonder if perhaps Dujek might actually have to call upon him and Nightchill. Instead, the burly commander gave a hand-sign and the drums sounded once more.

At this signal a portion of the ranks surged forwards, shields locked, pushing outwards, the rear ranks following, splitting left and right. Tayschrenn watched, fascinated, as the marines all fell into place one rank after the other, shields locked, to begin to unwind themselves like a fruit in the gradual process of turning itself inside out.

Slowly, foot by foot, the attacking Jhek warriors found themselves fighting on both fronts as the advancing arms enveloped them from behind.

Tayschrenn continued to stare, now well beyond fascination and into reluctant appreciation of the close-order formation. *So all*

149

that ridiculous marching about actually has a purpose. Well done, Dujek.

But the tactic was not a success yet; even as the rear arms were closing the front ranks thinned, and Jhek warriors were pushing through. At one of these breakouts Tayschrenn glimpsed some of the huge bear-warriors attacking their brothers in stiff and awkward motions and he thought Hairlock behind that.

Just before the englobing arms met, a large party of Jhek warriors, mostly the bear Soletaken, were able to pull away from the engagement and break out of the closing circle. The majority, however, found themselves surrounded, without retreat. Yet they fought on – even to the end when the last few were cut down, wounded, alone – none surrendered, none asked for quarter.

Ferocious, and foolish, to the last. Implacable and resolute. A pity they have made themselves an enemy.

He turned to Nightchill meaning to offer a comment but stopped himself upon seeing the sour disgust in her face. 'What is it?' he asked.

'What is it?' she echoed, a touch angrily. 'Can you not see it? Such a waste. Such a stupid needless waste.'

He returned his attention to the piled fallen Jhek warriors. 'Ah . . . of course. Yes, a waste.'

Dujek was still surrounded by guards and his staff while messengers still came and went. He was talking with the captains Ullen and Orosé and looked more relaxed now, his one hand tucked up under the stump of his arm. Tayschrenn crossed to him.

'Track them down,' he was saying to Captain Orosé. 'Find their lair, or home, or whatever.'

The impressively large Dal Hon warrior woman saluted and jogged off.

'Perhaps we have done enough . . .' Sialle called as she approached. 'You have delivered your lesson, Fist.'

'Can't leave them behind us,' he answered gruffly.

The Seti tribal shamaness let out a hissed breath. 'And what will you do with the children and the elders? What of Malazan justice and forbearance?' She pointed to the corpses. 'Is this not blood enough for you?'

Amazingly, the Fist did not lose his composure – even in the face of such direct insubordination. He nodded, his jaws working. 'Very good, cadre mage. You've had your say as is your right. Now it's my turn. We're trespassing on their land, that's true. Blundering through. But they chose how to respond, what to offer. We merely reacted to their choice. Now I have to follow through. Can't leave a wounded enemy at your rear – ain't sound tactics. Invites trouble.

'You have a point about the bloodshed though. I don't like it either. So, I'll give the order for no more hostilities. But we will have to drive them off.'

She drew breath to argue further but the Fist silenced her with a cut of his one good arm. 'That's the best I can offer.' He marched off, surrounded by his guards and aides, giving orders as to repositioning the ranks. Sialle watched him go, her lips tight, her hands pressed to her thighs.

Tayschrenn studied her curiously. 'You really didn't think it would end here, did you?' he asked.

'Oh, shut up,' she snarled, and marched off.

He raised his brows; he thought it a perfectly sensible question.

He watched while, towards noon, burial details were at work. They would resume the march on the morrow. His thoughts went back to the battle and he turned it over in his mind, thinking it through. He decided that perhaps he'd underestimated this jumped-up hiresword commander. And wrongly too; as, after all, he was one of the Emperor's favourite officers.

Also, he'd heard nothing of the Sword. The man had participated in the engagement – and in the front ranks, too. Yet he'd heard nothing of it so far. He decided to seek the fellow out.

In truth, the Champion was not difficult to find; Tayschrenn merely had to look about for a certain sort of tension among the men and women, where all eyes were turned in one direction. He sought out that epicentre to discover Dassem walking among the troopers, squeezing a shoulder here, kneeling with one wounded lass to exchange a few words, then moving on to share a small chuckle with another group.

Maintaining morale, was Tayschrenn's constructive take on it. The man's job, after all. But another far less generous voice whispered: *Cultivating adoration.*

Frankly, he wished he could be certain which to believe. But there was something impenetrable about the man. Rigid. Oddly unreasonable – and this was coming from him.

151

The Champion moved on and after him came trailing two swordsmen and one swordswoman – his self-elected unofficial bodyguard who tagged along after him whenever he entered the ranks. Tayschrenn had a less than complimentary term for them as well, but refrained. Called themselves the 'Sword'. Rather confusing that, since Dassem was the Sword. He shook his head as he turned away: the unimaginative soldier's mind.

After some searching, he finally discovered where the servants had pitched his tent. Entering, he sat on a collapsible camp stool to think. Much later, and with few conclusions regarding his colleagues – and their impenetrable preoccupations – his eyes began to droop and he realized he should rest.

He blinked heavily once more then saw that he was not alone.

A tall, thin, quite dark individual stood facing him, wearing dark green velvets and silks, multiple rings on his fingers and a self-satisfied smirk on his lips.

'Topper,' Tayschrenn greeted him.

'High Mage. My mistress grows impatient for news.'

'Never sneak unannounced into my quarters again.'

The smirk turned down. 'Perhaps you did not hear me.'

'I heard. And I reiterate: never ever sneak up upon me again – or I will treat you as a hostile. Is that clear?'

An impatient wave of one beringed hand. 'If you insist. Again, any news?'

'Nothing your operatives have not doubtless already conveyed.'

'What is your conclusion? Is this thing, this Elder construct, is it Kellanved's true target in travelling north all along?'

Tayschrenn blinked, surprised. In truth, the idea was so outrageous he hadn't even considered it. 'I do not think so.'

'*You do not think so,*' the assassin repeated, mockingly. 'Well, my mistress is not interested in opinions. She wants facts, information. You should try to collect some.'

Tayschrenn prided himself on his dispassionate detachment, but this man was trying his patience. Despite his best efforts, a note of displeasure tinged his response: 'I am not one of your mistress's operatives to be told what to do. You have my professional evaluation. That should suffice.'

The smirk climbed Topper's lips once more. 'And we shall see what she thinks of it – won't we?'

The High Mage pointed to the tent flap, but the fellow snorted at the idea, and faded away into Rashan. Tayschrenn remained still for some time afterwards – having been given more to think about.

Kellanved's true target all along? Really? He shook his head. The growing mutual suspicion and paranoia among the top echelon was beginning to be a concern.

* * *

Eventually, Ullara stopped weeping. For a full day and night she'd lain on the floor of the Great Temple, a handful of cloth pressed to her face, sodden in tears. It was now night again and she sat in her chair. The day-hunters slept on their perches and the owls were out. She knew she had to push herself to her feet: she had a people to lead – a people who had just taken a terrible blow. And Ursana, she could see, would be here soon.

Levering herself upright she staggered to the doors and pushed one open a crack. The village was quiet; no one had any idea yet of the catastrophe that had occurred, though they suspected the worst. The two young guards were no longer at the doors; they were in fact now dead. Ullara walked out into the night to await Ursana.

At the village's edge she paused. The night air was cold against her wet face. Through her night-hunters she watched the laboured advance of the small band of mostly bear-warriors Ursana had pulled free of the slaughter. Many limped, some held others up as they loped along. She also watched the progress of the numerous small scouting parties the Malazans had sent tracking them. It occurred to her then, that if the Malazans had the advantage in battle, she had the advantage in being elusive.

The small band closed and Ursana pulled ahead. She came to a halt before Ullara and knelt. Blood caked her fur and deep cuts still oozed on her arms and body. 'I am sorry, Priestess,' Ursana rumbled. 'You were right. I should have listened to you.'

'There is nothing to be sorry for, Ursana. Rise. I am heartened that you have saved lives.'

The exhausted woman rose unsteadily to her feet. 'We must flee at once. These Malazans are no doubt coming. They cannot leave us here.'

Ullara nodded. 'I know. I have seen them.' She invited the band onwards. 'Rouse the village. Pack all that can be fitted onto sledges and shoulders. We leave at once.'

'And where can we possibly go?' Ursana asked, despair creeping into her voice.

'We will head to the west, hide ourselves there until these Malazans leave. There is nothing for them here. I do not think they intend to stay.'

Ursana nodded almost sleepily – she had clearly pushed herself beyond all endurance. 'It will be done,' she said. 'And may I add that *I* am heartened to find you here watching over us.'

Ullara reached out to squeeze a very hairy forearm. 'And you must lie down and rest until we leave. *That* is an order.'

It was not until dawn that the column of all remaining Jhek of both clans, bear and wolf – the young, the elderly, and the mates, male and female, who had remained behind – set out. Many pulled sledges and travois. Ullara travelled in her litter, on the shoulders of four bear-warriors. All those who could fight now ranged about her, wolf-warriors scouting ahead and behind.

Within the litter, jerked about and wrapped in blankets, Ullara cast her vision all around, watching the advancing Malazan scouts, the Malazan main column as it continued its northwards march, and a small party of four that followed it at some distance.

* * *

There were no bodies to be seen, but the meagre hillock and surrounding grassy slopes was clearly the site of a battle, especially to the eyes of those who had known many. Black the Lesser brushed the ground, pointing here and there. 'Looks like the Malazans bloodied these shapeshifters.'

Jacinth nodded. 'A decisive victory. Few got away.'

Gwynn, who had found a broken stave that he now used as a short staff, leaned upon it, a gloomy look upon his pale features. 'This is regrettable,' he murmured.

'True,' Black agreed. 'I would've liked to see the Malazans get their arses kicked.'

Gwynn winced. 'That's not what I meant.'

154

Jacinth traced a path with her finger. 'Then they marched north.' A bruise of smoke darkened where she pointed. 'Looks like they're headed to that peak.'

Gwynn nodded. 'The Mountain of Gold.'

Blues, who had been scanning the horizons, turned. 'That old story?'

'What story?' Jacinth asked.

'A mountain of untold riches – in the centre of a wasteland, guarded by monsters,' Blues supplied.

'Sounds like a story all right,' Black sniffed.

Gwynn raised a hand for patience. 'This particular region has always been considered one of its possible locations.'

'Well, it's a wasteland all right,' Black said, and he sent Jacinth a sceptical look.

'How in Hood's name did he get here?' Blues suddenly called, pointing south.

Everyone turned. There stood a huge man – a giant of a fellow – and now that they were watching him, he advanced.

'How did he *do* that?' Blues complained.

Gwynn, his gaze narrowed, nodded to himself. 'He is Thelomen.'

'Damn!' Black snarled, and he drew his blade.

The giant, for he was a giant, at least half again as tall as a man, extended his arms out from his sides. 'I am unarmed,' he rumbled.

'He could twist our heads off,' Jacinth hissed in warning, and she drew her weapon.

The Thelomen pointed at them. 'You are no Malazans.'

'This is true,' Gwynn answered.

'Then who are you? Why are you here?'

'That's close enough,' Blues shouted and the giant halted. 'Why should we answer you?'

Black and Jacinth slowly spread out to either side of the Thelomen. He watched them, a grin upon his wide lips. 'Because I think these Malazans are no friends of yours.'

'What of it?' Blues answered.

'I think we can come to some sort of an alliance.'

'Not interested,' Black called. 'Get going your own way.'

The giant tilted his shaggy head. 'Why are you following them? Why spy upon them?'

'Not interested,' Black repeated. He waved his blade. 'Back up.'

The Thelomen lost his grin. 'I do not like your tone.'

Black and Jacinth both struck ready stances; Blues stepped in front of Gwynn, staff readied.

'Wait!' Gwynn called, and he was peering up at the sky. Blues followed his gaze, squinting; something was there, flying – a tiny bird. Blues traced its path as it circled them, all of them, repeatedly, drawing closer with each pass.

The little ball of brown and grey fluff finally alighted on one of the giant's outstretched hands where it hopped about, tweeting loudly, looking this way and that. Gwynn stepped closer, peering hard. 'A chickadee,' he announced. 'By all that is holy . . .' He looked to the giant. 'What do you know of a girl – well, a woman – who can speak with birds?'

The giant's grin returned, and he snorted a deep laugh. 'I know a fair deal . . .'

*　*　*

Far later than Gianna wanted and hoped for, Jan finally passed her closely in the kitchens and gave the word that they were ready. She felt herself almost leap, tensing, her heart hammering. She shot a glance to the guards who always shadowed her, but again they were all too happy just to sit and eat.

That night she prepared herself once more, wearing regular street clothes, hiding small cloth-wrapped pouches about her person containing bits of jewellery, gold rings and bangles. She ate a large meal after dusk, then waited, pacing. She knew why Jan had given the word, it was all the news in the capital: the repairs of the sea-wall were complete and ships could now navigate the defences.

At the midnight call she slipped out into the hall to her fallback escape route, the drop to the south arcade below. She hadn't used it since that first time, as of late she openly descended to the kitchens to pursue her 'hobby' of baking.

She lowered herself down as far as she could then hung for a time, straining; finally she let go, trying to roll with the impact. Perhaps she succeeded; all she knew was that while the wind was knocked from her by the blow, at least this time she didn't twist an ankle. She headed for the kitchens.

She found the broad main kitchens dark but for the dim glow of banked cooking fires and a few trimmed lamps. She drew breath to give a gentle call for Jan, only to almost leap as a hand closed upon her mouth from behind. She spun, her eyes wide, to see the very servant-woman herself. 'How did you do that?' she hissed once the woman removed her hand.

'A lifetime of hiding,' she answered, sounding a touch bitter. She waved Gianna onwards. 'Now come. We go.' She went to a cabinet near the door and pulled out a large travelling bag bound by a leather belt. This she hung over one shoulder then she opened the door a crack, peeking out. After watching for a time, she opened the door just far enough to squeeze out and waved Gianna to follow.

Stopping at each corner, keeping to the deepest shadows, the servant-woman led her down to the wharves and out onto a pier crowded with waiting cargo. They inched their way between piled barrels, crates roped together and covered in sail-cloth, even wicker baskets and wooden cages of murmuring ducks, until Jan motioned for a halt, peering ahead.

Gianna dared a glimpse over Jan's shoulder; a ship lay ahead, just past a short set of stairs to the lower dock. A gangway was even down. One sailor, a woman in the short-sleeved cotton shirt and short sashed trousers that was the Falaran unofficial uniform, stood at the ship's side, a lantern next to her. The night watch, perhaps.

Jan made a small gesture, a slight wave of her hand, and the female sailor straightened from the side, picked up the lantern, and wandered off out of sight.

The deck of the vessel now appeared empty. Jan glanced about then waved Gianna onwards. 'Come.'

They made it to the gangway and Jan started up. Gianna couldn't stop herself from hissing, 'Where is everyone?'

'Paid to be elsewhere,' Jan snapped, and she urged Gianna to hurry. On deck, she gestured her to a companionway leading belowdecks. She pushed her along all the way to the lowest stern deck where the dim yellow glow of a lamp flickered. Here they found Jan's brother waiting. He pointed to a small square dark opening. 'In there.'

Gianna balked. 'There? What's there?'

'A hidden room, small, yes,' Jan's brother explained. 'No one will know you are here. Inside is food and a honey-bucket. You can come out when we are far enough away.'

'Ah, I see . . . How long?'

The brother shrugged. 'Days, I think.'

Gianna suddenly felt very troubled by these arrangements. She felt her heart fluttering. 'Isn't there any other way?'

The brother looked to Jan, impatient.

'We haven't much time, lass,' Jan said. 'This is the best we could do.'

Gianna nodded. 'I understand. It just seems . . . like a prison.'

'Just a few days, lass,' Jan urged. 'Until we are far enough from Cabil.'

She jerked another nod. 'Yes . . . all right.' She bent down and crawled within. In the faint light of the lamp she found bedding, a pack – presumably of food – and the proverbial bucket.

'I will close the opening now,' the brother said.

'Wait!' Gianna called.

'Yes?'

'What about a light?'

'Ah,' he answered. 'During the day some light should stream down through cracks in the timbers above. Yes?'

Gianna sat back, hunched in the tiny space, and clasped her hands. 'Well – if you say so.'

'Yes.' He raised a square of wood and set it into the opening. Gianna immediately found herself in complete darkness. Light hammering sounded as the fellow sealed the opening, then silence. She raised her head, hoping to see some lamplight, but saw nothing.

She knew they were trying to help her – and themselves – but she couldn't shake her unease. Perhaps it was because her current situation reminded her so strongly of how she was brought *to* Cabil not so long ago. After some time she did manage to relax enough to lie back and try to sleep. As the brother and sister had said, it might be days, so she ought to get used to it. She stretched out as much as the cramped space allowed, and shut her eyes.

At least she was now just above water, and this water was an extension of the sea just beyond, and somehow this brought her great comfort.

* * *

158

Upon a northern slope of the Fenn Range the darkness of a starry night swirled and thickened. An owl nearby flew off and a red fox scampered away. The thickening darkness coalesced into a deep utter black far denser than any night. A gust of air sounded and a thin figure stepped from the upright pool like a man emerging from a doorway. He wore long robes of silk and cotton, tailored to his slim form. His skin was as black as the night he'd stepped from though his brush-cut black hair was shot with grey.

The pool of night dispersed and the man turned to face the north. He clasped his hands at his back and cocked his head, his almond-shaped eyes narrowing, and he nodded to himself.

Endest Silann was firstly gratified to see that his journey to these wild regions was not for naught. A nest, possibly a city, of the K'Chain Che'Malle did indeed exist to the north. And, judging from the glow of energies revealed to his questing, it was roused.

And who, he asked himself, in all the Seven Realms would be so foolish?

He studied the plain of snow and ice below and saw there far off the heat-glow of a presence. A large body of entities, humanoid? Perhaps these were his aforementioned fools. He gestured and the pool of night re-formed in front of him. He stepped through—

To emerge upon the plain of snow. Though not just snow: patches of grass and moss now showed, even tiny delicate flowers of blue and red. Off to one side steam rose from a bubbling patch of heated mud. Endest nodded to himself; such were common near the larger Che'Malle enclaves.

He also noted the very faint, and failing, glow of bodies a way off down the shallow valley he occupied. He started in that direction, hands clasped at his back. He came to a single body first; it lay sprawled out on the surface, slowly rotting. He recognized the type immediately: a descendant of Soletaken, a true-breeding man-beast, what some name a 'shapeshifter'. Their kind could be found here and there about the lands, usually in isolated regions. They went by many names. Woefully degenerate and fallen, to his eyes.

He moved on and eventually he came to the site of a struggle. The corrupting bodies of dead humans lay here. They had been torn apart, apparently, by the Soletaken kind he'd found. He studied the wounds, untroubled by the horrific stink, lifting limbs and pulling at rotting flesh. Large tearing teeth, rending claws . . . yes, enemies.

He also noted that the dead wore a type of uniform. Black sur-coats, or black armbands, each emblazoned with a silver sceptre – or a kind of a sceptre: an orb held by three gripping bird's claws that descended to a limb, or handle.

Interesting. The army of a political entity, here upon this waste-land, within reach of a K'Chain Che'Malle enclave. And fighting a presumably native population of Soletaken. What were the dynam-ics? Was one of these parties an enemy or ally of the K'Chain Che'Malle? Or neither? Too soon to say. He would have to wait and watch and continue to study the situation.

He noted a patch of the tiny blue flowers and knelt to pluck one. He held it close, studying it. Admirable. Delicate, yet hardy. Per-fectly adapted to its place. Yes, admirable. He drew a breath of bracing air and walked onwards, blossom in hand.

Chapter 11

CARTHERON LEANED ON THE RAIL OF THE *TWISTED* AND enjoyed the cool night winds. They were finally making good time north. The smoke and rains of soot and ash had fallen behind. And these raider captains – as he'd come to call them, because 'freebooters' was just too damned dignified – were for the time being behaving themselves.

Understandably. Word of the mysterious fate of the three deserter crews had spread through the fleet. As Kellanved no doubt intended. Now they were behaving like good little ducklings, sailing all in line; but he knew this would pass. He knew the type; lessons faded quickly, and their true nature would always reassert itself. It was only a matter of time.

He just hoped they'd make the Falaran Isles before having to deal with yet another rebellion or mass desertion, or some other damned failure of nerve.

A contrary wind blew then across the deck and sailors cursed. Cartheron turned, hands on the horn grips of his knives as that wind had been bone dry. Someone new occupied the deck, a tall slim woman in old, torn and dirty clothes, barefoot, and he relaxed, grunting a greeting, 'Nightchill.'

'Admiral.'

'Hardly.' He jerked a nod to the cabin. 'He's in there.'

She padded past him and he chose to follow. She knocked and a muted voice murmured some objection within; she pushed open the door regardless. Cartheron followed.

Kellanved swept his feet from the desk within and quickly stood. 'Nightchill! Greetings.' He gestured to a chair. 'Do have a seat.'

She did not answer this; nor did she sit. Cartheron pushed the door shut behind him. Kellanved went to a sideboard of decanters. 'Wine? Liqueur?'

'I bring news of the expeditionary force.'

The Emperor was studying a tall decanter. 'Yes, of course,' he answered distractedly.

'It is delayed.'

'Oh?'

'We met local inhabitants. Hostile. But we have dealt with them.'

The Dal Hon elder nodded, half-listening. 'Good, good.'

She crossed her arms. 'However, we have also encountered an enclave of K'Chain Che'Malle.'

Kellanved fumbled among the decanters, knocking several over. '*What?*'

At the door, Cartheron stiffened, his breath catching.

'You did not know?' she observed, surprised. 'You have been complacent.'

Straightening his shirt and vest, Kellanved moved to the desk. 'Not my speciality, that.' He leaned against the desk. 'Do tell me all about it.'

'The cadre are in agreement that a large Che'Malle enclave, a city or nest, lies at the centre of the wastelands. The expeditionary force is advancing towards it.'

The Emperor was nodding to himself. 'The Mountain of Gold,' he murmured.

'Of legend,' she agreed.

'And so?'

The woman crossed her slim arms. 'And so we expect a delay.'

Cartheron couldn't help himself; he muttered: 'Rather an understatement.'

Kellanved pressed a hand to his brow. 'Funny – I was about to say the same thing. We too have had our delays.' He sighed. 'Nothing ever goes as planned – as is well known.' He dragged the hand down his face. 'So, we are to hold back, then? Is that what you are getting to in your rather roundabout way?'

The sorceress raised her thin shoulders. 'That is for you to decide.'

Kellanved pinched his chin, obviously displeased by the vague response. 'Thank you, High Mage, for your advice.'

Bowing very sketchily, the woman turned on her heels and headed to the door. Cartheron hurriedly moved out of her way.

'Do keep in touch,' Kellanved called, just as she reached for the latch.

Pausing, she tilted her head in acknowledgement, and exited.

Into the silence following, Cartheron let out a long breath, murmuring, 'K'Chain Che'Malle . . .'

Kellanved waved a dismissal. 'Nothing to us. I do hope Dujek is wise enough to just go around.'

'That may not be possible.'

The Emperor now pressed both hands to his temples. 'This is not what I wanted at all. Are the gods just playing with us?'

Cartheron decided the Emperor was being rhetorical.

Stabbing out a finger, Kellanved ordered, 'Have the fleet shelter on the coast. Send out search parties for water and food and such. You know what to do.'

Cartheron nodded his understanding. 'I see. Hold back. Well, for a time, anyway . . .'

Kellanved slumped into his chair. 'Yes. For a time.'

'Very good.' Bowing, Cartheron exited. Outside, on deck, he shook his head in disbelief. *K'Chain Che'Malle!* Well, better Dujek than he! Not that he'd wish anything like that upon the commander; he rather liked the gruff fellow. For his own command, he decided that tomorrow morning, with the dawn, he'd relay the new sailing orders. With that in mind, he went to find the sailing-master – the *Twisted* would have to approach from the east . . .

* * *

Gianna's unease did not fade away. In fact it grew. Over the next few days she became convinced that they were not travelling east, as the brother and sister had told her, they were actually travelling *south*.

She knew this, for a priestess of Mael and mage of Ruse knows the seas – knows their character, their moods, their sounds and their nature. Her instincts told her they were travelling Lure Sea when they should be crossing Old Guando Sea.

At first she tapped lightly upon the barrier of her hiding place, hoping Jan or her brother would answer. With no answer for two days she began banging. Soon after this a voice – Jan – called to her from beyond: 'Quiet, lass! You must remain hidden, yes?'

'Jan! Thank Mael. Tell me . . . why are we going south?'

The old washerwoman laughed. 'South? Ridiculous, child. We are headed east.'

'No we're not. I can tell.'

'Really? And how can you tell hidden away in there? Can you see? You are being foolish. Now be quiet.'

'Jan . . . *Jan!*' No answer. She had gone. Gianna pressed her forehead to the wood. Gods and daemons, what was she to do? She wasn't strong enough to force this barrier. What was going *on*? Were they headed south or not? She was beginning to doubt herself.

But no. She knew the sea. It was in her blood. She was right.

She glanced up to the cracks between the thick wood timbers of the ceiling. It seemed to her now certain that the brother had lied. No daylight had, or would, seep down to her. Her instincts told her it was night in any case. She'd wait for the day. She might not be physically strong enough to force this issue, but she was perhaps strong enough in another way.

She lay back to try to sleep for a time; she'd need all that strength tomorrow.

When next she opened her eyes she felt she might have slept, but she wasn't sure. Her dreams had been troubled of late. Perhaps she'd dozed. In any case it was time – no more delaying.

She sat up, crossed her legs, and readied herself to summon her Ruse Warren.

At first nothing happened and she wondered if perhaps it had been too long. But soon enough she started to sense the depths beneath her and felt as if she were inhabiting those limitless leagues rather than the pathetically tiny wooden construct that floated upon its thin surface.

Bringing her Warren to bear, she began to squeeze that poor little box of wood.

Groans and creaking sounded all about her; she kept up the pressure, intensified it. Poppings and crackings burst out now, as if planks were snapping.

Water came swirling round her legs, rose past her lap. Still she pressed. Only then did it come to her that she was imprisoned – her hope was that with her Warren she'd be able to somehow break her way out.

Frantic banging penetrated her concentration. Someone yelling. She raised her head, grunted through clenched teeth: 'Yes?'

'Stop this!' It was Jan. 'What idiocy is this?'

'Get me out!'

'Don't worry, child.'

'I mean it! We'll all go to the bottom!'

Silence for a time. The water churning around Gianna reached her stomach.

Then came a snarled, '*Very well!*'

Creaking sounded, wood snapping, then the small barrier was pulled away.

Gianna slowly relaxed her concentration; the groaning of the stressed planks eased. Water, however, continued seeping in through sprung seams.

Gianna pushed herself out through the small opening. Rising, she found Jan and her brother facing her – from a respectful distance. She also noted the auras of raised Warrens shimmering about them both.

'You are mages,' she observed, startled.

'As are you,' Jan answered, rather resentfully.

'What is this then?'

A shrug from the woman. 'As we promised. We are helping you escape.'

'Escape to where and to what?'

Neither answered that. Jan sighed, 'What do you want?'

'I want to be on deck.'

The siblings exchanged glances. The brother said, 'There's no getting away, you know. There's no land in sight. Nowhere to go.'

Gianna struggled to keep her expression flat. 'Please. I'm suffocating in there.'

'Fine,' Jan growled. 'But we're both watching you. Don't do anything foolish.'

'Thank you.'

The siblings parted, backing away to leave room for her to reach the steep stairway-cum-ladder. She climbed to the deck to find that the brother and sister hadn't been lying: they had crossed through Lure Sea – perhaps into the southern passage.

She was also surprised to find the sailors of the vessel simply continuing about their duties: giving her wary glances, but otherwise ignoring her. Bought – the entire crew – bought. This must have taken far more than the pitiful sum her trinkets could have come to.

She turned to face the siblings. 'So. Where are we headed?'

'Never you mind that,' the brother grumbled. 'You're on deck, right? So sit and don't cause any more trouble.'

'I think not.'

Both of the siblings' Warrens blazed to light at their hands. Jan warned, 'Do not challenge us, child.'

'Who said anything about a challenge?' And she turned and dived over the side.

Flames roared about her even as she slipped into the welcoming embrace of the cool waters. She sent a great wash behind, rising over the vessel in a wave, and swam as hard as she could for the bottom.

On board the ship, Janul and Janelle and the sailors picked themselves up from the water still swilling about the deck – all had been hammered flat by the gigantic wave. Janelle lunged to the side to search the waves. '*Dammit to Hood!*'

Janul joined her. He pushed back his sodden hair, let out a long grating snarl. 'Teach us to try to kidnap a mage of Ruse at sea. I told you we should've taken her into the Warren.'

'The moment we did that we'd have had a battle on our hands,' Janelle answered. She waved at the waters all about. 'And she has the advantage.'

Janul grunted his sour agreement. 'Now what?'

'We return. Our mission remains.'

He nodded. 'Yes. Lower profile, though, hey?'

'Yes. Lower profile.' She continued studying the waves, and after a time she shook her head. 'Could she really swim all the way to land?'

'I suppose we'll find out, won't we?'

She snorted a short laugh. 'Yeah. I suppose so.'

Still shaking her head, Janelle went to order the captain to turn around.

*

A touch woke her. She opened her eyes to look into the face of a gaping, staring child who promptly screamed. She fell back into the cold water just gratified to be alive.

Hands gripped her shortly afterwards, carried her from the rocks to a shore of grass. She roused herself enough to gasp, 'Where? Where am I?'

'Quiet now,' a gruff older man said. 'Rest.'

'No! Where?'

A reluctant answer of, 'Big Island. South coast.'

She relaxed then, and allowed herself to fall back into darkness.

Some time later she awoke again on a pallet of straw stuffed into old blankets, inside a small cottage. Probably a fisherman's. She raised the thin and tattered coverlet to see that her outer clothes had been removed. Peering round she found them laid over a chair before the hearth.

Very slowly, and carefully, she forced herself from the cot, swung her legs down, and straightened. The pain from much abused muscles lanced her, but it was welcome. It meant she was alive. She hobbled to the hearth and dressed.

Outside it was raining in a light mist. The day was overcast, grey; combers sounded nearby striking a shore. Following the sound, she descended a path down a cliff to the strand. Here she found a man hunched over repairing nets next to a small beached dory.

Hearing her approach over the broken rock of the shore he looked up. 'Ah! With us again I see.'

'You . . . ?' she asked.

He nodded. 'Aye. And my granddaughter. Gave her quite the fright, you did. Thinks you're one o' them Mael's daughters. Them sea-people.' Gianna's lips tightened as she remembered her mother's tales. The fellow's gaze narrowed upon her. 'You have the hair,' he observed.

She reflexively touched her thick black hair. 'Just a castaway – as you see.'

'Castaway?' the fellow repeated, doubtful. 'No ships pass this coast. Only the Ice Sea beyond.'

'And the Southern continent,' she added.

He allowed himself a judicious bob of the head. 'Aye . . . so they say.'

She cleared her throat. 'My thanks. I owe you much.' He just gave a shrug. 'So – we're on the south coast?'

He nodded, 'Aye. South of Ictor.'

'I have to go there.'

He shrugged again.

'I'll go in the morning . . . I suppose.'

The fisherman returned to his work. 'If you must,' he answered.

She paused here, waiting for more, but the fellow did not look up. She turned her attention to the sea beyond. Somewhere out there she'd jumped ship and remained far below the surface long enough for the vessel to travel some distance. When she'd surfaced it was gone, and, following her Ruse instincts, she'd struck out for the west, sensing that this was the closest landfall.

She believed that was five days ago. By the third day she'd hardly been swimming; drifting, really. Barely staying afloat. She'd been so exhausted and starved she'd passed out when her limbs had finally struck rocks. At the end there she really hadn't known what had kept her afloat. Her own will? Or was it that she was just so at home in the waters?

Again, her mother's tales of the true first people of Falar returned to her, and she shivered. Gone. All gone. She returned to the cottage and rested some more.

In the morning she kissed the granddaughter – who could not stop staring at her – on the brow and headed inland up a path that the fisherman said led to a climbing rutted road that itself led to Ictor. Near noon she found what looked like a road – three lines through rising hills that denoted horses or mules leading carts; this she followed north-east. Near dusk she came to a lean-to shelter next to the path she'd been following – she really couldn't call it a road. A rickety enclosure for any mounts stood next to the hut and she imagined this must be a wayside stop for any travellers. Just how far she was from the civilized centres of Falar couldn't have been more strongly borne upon her, and the hard-scrabble poverty of the lives she was seeing saddened her.

In the morning she woke on the raised wood cot to see that another traveller had arrived in the night. That she hadn't woken was a testament to her exhaustion: a two-wheeled cart now rested a short way off while a mule chewed grass in the enclosure.

Rising, she came to the cart to find a young boy asleep across its burden of a tall heap of hay.

'Morning,' she offered.

The youth rubbed his eyes and nodded. Without a word he went and grabbed hold of the mule and set it to its harness. He invited her into the cart and she bowed, accepting.

The rest of that day she sat with her feet dangling over the rear wood slats of the cart while hay tickled her arms and neck.

Ictor was small for a Falaran city; more of a frontier outpost, or colony. Its collection of stone and wood buildings descended a slope down the waterfront where vessels rested at anchor. The town seemed to Gianna uncommonly quiet and subdued as she walked the dirt ways. Many of the citizens stopped to stare at her as she passed and, her hand going to her hair, she realized why. Her thick black hair was long now, impossible to hide: a mark of the Old People, the folktale first inhabitants of the isles.

She stepped up onto a pier that led out to boats waiting to load or unload, each tied off at the thick butts of the support timbers. She walked to the very end, the last vessel, where four men and a woman stood watching over a file of sitting children. As she closed, her breath caught and she almost staggered; the youths all bore that same mark: thick black hair, some matted, some luxuriant and long, even curled.

'What is *this*?' she gasped, her voice actually catching.

The four men turned, and she saw their brows rise in surprise as their gazes settled upon her own dirty and unkempt mane. The woman pointed a thick stick, a cudgel, to the file of youths. 'Don't make no trouble. One of these yours?'

'What do you mean is one mine? What's going on here?'

'There's been a new Call, fool,' one of the burly fellows growled. 'If none o' these is yours, then get lost. Ain't no business of yours.'

Gianna now understood. A Call. The Faith's 'recruitment' of those of the old blood – so-called *favoured of Mael*. Or, as her mother used to name it: a Cull. 'There's been a Call already this year.'

'Orders of Ortheal Leneth, Proctor of the Faith. Mael has need.'

She crossed her arms. 'Mael has no such need. Release them.'

The four eyed one another, amused. 'Early in the day to be so drunk,' one drawled.

Gianna felt as if her black hair was now standing on end; she sensed the power of her Warren rising, unbidden. The hairs of her neck and arms seemed to be crackling with energy.

'By my order you will release them,' she fairly snarled.

More amusement. 'And you are?' the woman asked.

Gianna opened her mouth to answer only to snap it shut – perhaps it would be best if she did not reveal that just yet. 'A citizen of Falar who has no tolerance for slavery . . . of any kind.'

The burliest of them slipped his cudgel into his hand and waved her off. 'Just walk away, and maybe we won't report this to the priests.'

She'd had enough. She swept an arm and a wall of water rose from beside the dock to sweep the four into the sea.

Rising amid the waves, gasping for breath, one growled, 'You stupid bitch!' and grabbed hold of the dock edge to climb back up.

Gianna gave a slow pushing gesture and the woman cried out, alarmed, 'I'm sinking!'

'Swim away now,' Gianna called, 'or drown.'

Reluctantly, cursing her up and down, they swam off. Gianna watched for a time to be certain.

'Finally!' yelled out a loud woman's voice, 'someone's found the spine to kick back!'

Gianna turned; there on board the vessel stood a very large woman, both tall and broad. 'May I speak with your captain?'

'You are.'

Gianna pointed to the file of children staring up at her, blinking in the sunlight, looking fearful. 'You were to take these youths to Cabil?'

'Had no choice.'

'Well, you'll be taking us, but not to Cabil.'

The captain set her fists on her very wide hips. 'Really? And where will I be taking you? And why should I?'

'Anywhere else. You can say I threatened you.'

The captain snorted a laugh. 'No need for threats. No sea captain argues with a mage of Ruse. None still afloat, anyways. And I'll be honest, I hated to take 'em. But they invoked the requisition for the Faith.' She shrugged. 'One cannot refuse.' She tilted her head, examining Gianna. 'Unless one is a complete fool.'

'Fool or not, we're going – now.'

The captain peered round at the staring ship's hands, many of whom, Gianna saw, looked on in disapproval; the woman waved them back to work. 'What's your name, lass?' she called.

'Gianna.'

The captain nodded. 'Well, I'm Brevin and this here's the *Sea Glimmer*. Welcome aboard.'

Gianna answered the nod. 'My thanks, captain.' She turned to the sitting children. They stared up at her, confused and wary. 'We're not going to Cabil,' she explained. 'You're going home.' She waved them off. 'Go on. Go back home. You're free to go.'

Not one of them moved; all stared back, squinting their confusion.

'Don't know where home is,' one whispered, fearful.

'I understand this lot's been pulled together from all over,' Brevin explained. 'Gathered here.'

Gianna pressed a hand to her brow. *Gods curse it!* 'Is no one from here?' Two timorously raised hands: a boy and a girl. The rest, twelve of them, peered back with wrinkled brows. 'Okay. You two. Go home.'

'But my ma would beat me!' the boy exclaimed. 'She told me to go. She's bin paid and everything!'

Gianna pulled her hand down her face and bit back a curse.

'This whole setting-the-world-to-rights thing is a lot harder than you'd think, hey?' Brevin drawled, setting a foot up on the railing.

Gianna shot her a dark look. 'Thank you.' She clapped her hands together. 'Okay. We're just getting out of here. As fast as we can.' She waved them aboard. 'So . . . let's go.'

None moved. Gianna urged them onwards. 'C'mon.'

'We don't wanna go!' one wailed and covered her face in terror.

Gianna raised her face to the sky. *Burn forgive me! How do parents not strangle them?*

'Hey, kids,' Brevin called. 'Who's hungry?'

Every youth surged for the side of the *Sea Glimmer*. All clamoured for food and besieged Brevin, who laughed and sent Gianna a wink – who could only shake her head.

'Got a whole tribe of them myself,' the big woman explained.

* * *

On the second day they walked the mushy, melting ice and snow of the wastelands, Blues leaned closer to Gwynn and murmured, 'You realize we're following a bird.'

Hands clasped at his back as they tramped the boggy ground, the dour mage nodded very solemnly. 'Oh, yes.'

'And this doesn't trouble you?'

The thin fellow blinked back at him, quite sincerely. 'No. Should it?'

Blues resisted raising his gaze to the thickening black clouds of soot and ash roiling above. 'I can't imagine why,' he answered, rather dryly.

The pale mage quirked a smile. 'As I said, I believe I know who has sent it.'

'This sorceress. So you *believe*.'

Gwynn nodded sagely. 'With some degree of certainty – yes.'

Blues now directed his gaze to the back of the giant Thelomen leading them in their march. 'And our friend?'

'He may be a friend or ally as well.'

Clenching his jaws against any further questioning, Blues peered about warily, stave over one shoulder.

Later that afternoon, as the dimmed sun fell towards the horizon, Jacinth came jogging in from the east. 'We're being shadowed,' she announced, joining Blues and Gwynn. 'A few of the wolf-boys, but mostly bigger bear-fellows.'

Blues shot a glare to Gwynn who shrugged, saying, 'She *is* their priestess.' Blues cupped a hand to his mouth, calling to the giant, 'Hello! Thelomen! How far?'

Their towering guide turned, strode back towards them. 'I know not,' he answered, unconcerned.

Blues planted his stave. 'Then this is far enough for today. I'm not going to walk into any ambush.' He eyed the giant. 'What's your name, anyway?'

'Bellurdan.'

'You have anything to eat?'

'Sadly, no.'

'Well . . . we have a few scraps. You eat dried meat?'

'If there is nothing else.'

'You're welcome,' Blues answered. He pointed his stave to a

minor rise. 'Might be drier ground up there.' Jacinth nodded and jogged off in that direction.

They sat on the driest spots they could find. Blues pulled together handfuls of grass to sit on cross-legged, then draped a scavenged cloak over himself, held up by the stave, as a tent. Gwynn sat brushing the grey ash from his black Malazan cloak. They ate a small meal of Malazan dried rations, taken from bodies they'd come across. The giant, Bellurdan, stood keeping lookout; apparently his kind needed little sleep. One of them would join him through the night on watches.

In the morning Blues was woken by a touch from Black, who glanced significantly to the west; a large creamy-white figure was approaching their camp, its rolling walk and bulk announcing it as one of the Jhek bear-warriors, and a very big one at that.

Black and Jacinth drew their weapons and spread out to either side. Blues, Gwynn and Bellurdan went to meet their visitor. Coming close, the bear-warrior reared up on its hind legs and Blues couldn't help noting it was female, with just two heavy teats – so, perhaps still more human than bear. Also, it now stood nearly as tall as the Thelomen, but carried far more bulk.

'I bring greetings from my mistress, the Bird Priestess,' this Jhek announced.

'Greetings,' Blues answered. 'And you are?'

'Ursana.'

'Greetings,' Bellurdan rumbled.

Ursana nodded to the giant. 'Yes. I bring apologies from my mistress for the unwarranted attack upon you and Koroll.'

Blues noticed Gwynn start slightly at the mention of that name.

Ursana continued, 'I also bring two names.' She pointed a heavy, hairy, clawed hand to Gwynn. 'You are to give them to me. One is yours. The other hers.'

Gwynn was peering around and Blues followed his gaze to find the tiny puffball of a bird circling them, only to come to rest upon the shoulder of Ursana. Gwynn lowered his head in welcome. He placed a hand to his chest. 'I am Gwynn. Gwynn of the Crimson Guard. And another name was, once, long ago, Ullara.'

The bird flew off, heading west. Ursana followed its path for a moment then returned her attention to them. She gestured them onwards. 'You are welcome to join my mistress's camp.'

* * *

From the verges of night Endest Silann kept a distant watch on the advancing army. He'd had little interaction with the political entities of this era and so could only speculate. However, the more he observed, the more he settled upon the working hypothesis that this invading force was a punitive action intended to cow or eliminate these local inhabitants, the Soletaken shapeshifters, from the region. Perhaps they'd proved hostile, or had been raiding southwards. In any case, the larger, more organized force was now aware of the much greater potential threat posed by the K'Chain Che'Malle and were warily advancing towards the enclave.

Or so he surmised.

It seemed to him after some thought that if the Che'Malle were indeed rousing and did prove to be a nascent threat, then this force could be used to weaken or blunt it. All without any cost to his Lord or his people.

A plan came to him, then, of approaching them and offering his services, all with the intent of throwing them against the Che'Malle in order to test the strength of both.

Therefore, one dusk, he left behind all aspects of his Elder magics to enter entirely into the mundane realm and headed towards the army encampment. It was a cool night; the wind was against his back flowing towards the distant smoking mountain. This, he noted, was not uncommon, as K'Chain Che'Malle structures often dominated their local environment.

Approaching the first of the outlying pickets of the camp, Endest paused to send the most cursory and light glance across the field ahead, for he'd sensed mages among these invaders. All simply as a preparation.

What he glimpsed surprised him in the extreme and he immediately cloaked himself entirely in Elder Night. The aura of one of the human mages within hinted at astonishing potential and power, which itself was reason for caution, but this was as nothing compared to another aura he sensed within – one he'd not encountered in a very long time indeed – and one which advised caution in the extreme. The hint of an Elder.

Which entity he could not be certain. But undoubtedly one did not simply come blundering up to such a being. Due observation would be necessary. He would have to withdraw to a discreet distance and be as wary as possible – such a confrontation was not the errand his master had sent him upon.

Having made his resolution, Endest withdrew fully into Elder Night, Kurald Galain, to consider his next move.

*

Within the cadre mage tent, Tayschrenn was surprised when Nightchill rather suddenly lurched from her seat and marched out through the open flap. Such behaviour usually signalled something significant – if obscure – and so, curious, he followed.

He found her standing near the edge of camp, facing south, arms crossed, her thin mouth pinched and eyes slit. He followed her gaze to see nothing but night-darkened gentle hills tufted in grass and mounds of moss.

'Something?' he murmured, now willing to respect the woman's instincts, however abstruse.

She nodded. 'We are not alone here,' she answered.

'Who?' he asked, but she'd turned and marched off once more. He sighed and sent a glance skyward; was a normal, helpful, communicative ally too much to ask of the world?

And what would he do should one be forthcoming? Fall off his horse?

Chapter 12

Tayschrenn was definitely missing the Emperor's taste for the finer creature comforts. And Dujek's coarse soldier-habits were definitely beginning to wear. Command tent, for example, was nothing but a staked-down large canvas drape over bare earth. Not a rug or throw or animal fur in sight. A few charcoal braziers for heat, a few camp stools and benches; a cot to sleep in.

The High Mage stood rather awkwardly among this sparse arrangement, not sure whether to occupy one of the few chairs, or ease himself down on a bench. Their commander ate his meal one-handed, standing at the one slim table, receiving messengers and giving orders.

Hairlock slumped down on a stool; captains Ullen and Orosé stood near the open flap; Sialle stood with crossed arms, legs straight; Nightchill hadn't appeared.

'These Jhek have retreated to the west, you say?' Dujek asked of Orosé.

'Yes. They appear to be withdrawing.'

Hairlock gave a sceptical snort.

'And what of the north?' Tayschrenn asked. 'The mountain?'

'We're waiting,' Dujek answered round a mouthful of sliced meat.

'Waiting?'

'The Sword has been scouting,' Ullen supplied from the tent entrance. 'He's due.'

Tayschrenn raised a brow. 'Ah.' He'd wondered where the fellow had got to. He went to a side-table and poured himself a glass of watered wine. 'Will he be long?' he asked of the captain.

The young officer had an eye on the open flap. 'No. Scouts report he is close.'

Tayschrenn gave a noncommittal grunt. So, the troops were keeping an eye on the man. Well, appropriate enough, he supposed, given what his reputation meant to them.

Just a few minutes later he heard distant shouts that clarified into greetings and calls of 'Sword!' raised among the camp beyond.

The two captains straightened as the Sword entered. He wore plain leathers, mud-caked, his longsword at his side. The man went straight to the side-table, took up a stoneware jug of water, and drank. Tayschrenn noted how his thick black hair hung lank, sweat-soaked. 'Where is your bodyguard?' he asked. 'Your, ah, Sword, Sword?'

Dassem smiled, amused, and glanced back to the opening. 'They are not so used to running.'

Orosé laughed. 'They are certainly not Dal Hon.'

The Champion gave her a nod. 'True. I am certain you could give them a lesson in endurance.'

Tayschrenn saw the effect the small, off-hand compliment had upon the experienced officer; he swore she nearly blushed. But Dassem's back was turned as he now looked to Dujek. 'They're out there,' he said.

'You've seen them?' Tayschrenn asked.

Dassem glanced to him. 'No. The mists ahead are thick. But I have seen their fresh tracks in the muck and melt. I suggest you withdraw the scouts – they'll just get mauled.'

'Advance blind?' Dujek objected.

'Advance in line – as if anticipating contact.'

The Fist's broad and blunt face turned sour. 'That bad, hey? How wide?'

The Sword appeared a touch uncomfortable. 'You are the Fist. However, I would suggest as broad as possible. But no less than ten ranks deep.'

Dujek nodded his reluctant agreement. 'Three phalanxes then, with a small reserve behind. Captain Ullen, you will take the left. Orosé, the right. I'll be at centre.'

'And I will be centre front,' the Champion added.

'You will not,' Dujek growled.

Dassem gave another small smile. 'It is my place.'

Dujek let out a long hard breath. 'Gods, Dancer will have my head if I lose you here.'

'And the cadre?' Tayschrenn asked.

'You and Nightchill at centre – should you be needed,' Dujek answered. Then he cleared his throat, adding, 'If you would so please. Hairlock and Sialle on flanks.'

'Fine,' Hairlock answered, leaning forward from his seat. 'You got two High Mages here with you, so in the meantime I'd like to take a small force out west to make certain these Jhek don't plan on taking advantage of the situation.'

'They've withdrawn,' Sialle pointed out.

'Not far enough,' Hairlock answered. He looked to Dujek. 'Can't leave hostiles to come at our rear.'

Now the Fist looked uncomfortable. Tayschrenn imagined he'd prefer to leave the locals alone – but Hairlock did have a point. Dujek finally nodded. 'Fine. A small force – just to make certain they don't come at us.'

Hairlock quirked a lopsided smile.

'I would like to go as well,' Sialle put in. Dujek sent her a questioning look and she gave a small shrug. 'Tracking is something of my speciality.'

Dujek waved for an end. 'Fine. Just be aware that Tayschrenn here may have to call you back at an instant's notice.'

Hairlock rose with a grunted, 'Right.'

The briefing was at an end and everyone went their way to prepare for the morrow. Tayschrenn was surprised to find Hairlock fall into step with him. He gave the squat, deeply tanned mage a sidelong look.

'Been thinking about our mutual friend,' Hairlock murmured.

Tayschrenn assumed he meant Nightchill. 'What of her?'

Hairlock rubbed his unshaven jowls. 'I think she's after your boots.'

Tayschrenn lifted a brow. 'My boots? Really?'

'Yeah. I think she wants to fill them.'

'She's a High Mage,' Tayschrenn pointed out.

'Yeah. But she's not *the* High Mage. The Imperial Mage. If you know what I mean. Never will be, neither. So long as you're wearing the boots.'

'So you're warning me, are you? As a friend?'

A snorted laugh answered that. 'Just something to keep in mind. A word to the wise – as they say.'

With that the Seven Cities native trod off without a farewell. Tayschrenn watched him go and it occurred to him that should he move against Nightchill, or she him, then that would place Hairlock one step closer to those selfsame boots. Not something the mage would regret, no doubt.

And he had to shake his head: so this was how the game was played. Pitching people against one another. Sowing suspicion and division. Yet the warning might be true. People had their ambitions; she must have hers. It occurred to him then that thinking of such eventualities, and motives, meant that he too was now playing the game.

This saddened him, obscurely, and he drew his cloak tighter against the chill night.

* * *

For four days the huge Jhek bear-warrior Ursana led them northwest. Jacinth and Black reported their party was being shadowed by wolf- and bear-warriors. Blues accepted this as an appropriate precaution on the Jhek's part; while Gwynn remained unperturbed in his confidence of a friendly reception.

Bellurdan kept up his steady pace, always just behind the Jhek, and by the next day Blues smelled smoke from cookfires – as distinct from the smoke that billowed overhead in waves from the far mountain. The Jhek warriors walked nearby openly now, closing in upon them.

When they reached the camp, Blues was surprised to see that it was just that, a temporary camp, like a hunting site. He hadn't known what to expect, but had assumed they were being guided to a permanent settlement of some sort. Obviously, this was not the case; living in hide tents, out of packs and sledges, the Jhek looked like a population in migration.

The Thelomen, Bellurdan, went up to an old woman and sketched a small bow. Blues noted that she was not Jhek at all, but plainly human, a blanket about her shoulders and a cloth wrapped across her eyes. He followed Gwynn's lead and slowly approached. Bear-warriors crowded close in front of them, rumbling warnings, but the woman called out something and they were allowed to pass.

Gwynn stopped before the old woman, a good few arm's lengths off, and gave her a long hard look. She seemed to return the favour.

Finally, the woman smiled, which took years from her, and shook her head. 'You have changed little, Gwynn of the Crimson Guard,' she said.

Gwynn clasped his hands behind his back, lowering his head slightly. 'You, I am sorry to say, have changed much, Priestess. Gone is the young woman I let travel north – you have given too much of yourself.'

'I give all of myself to my people.' She turned her face to Blues. 'And who are your companions?'

'This is Blues. The woman is Jacinth, the other fellow Black the Lesser.'

She nodded at the names. 'Ah. All famous and storied members of the Guard. You are here because the Malazans are, yes?'

'We are here because of the mountain,' Gwynn said.

The smile fell and the woman looked old once more. 'The mountain is too much for you, Gwynn. Leave it for the Malazans.'

'It may be too much for them as well.'

These words appeared to trouble the Priestess and she looked away, to the west. 'We,' she said, 'are journeying away for now. There is game in the west, and highlands along the coast. You are welcome to join us.'

Gwynn shook his head. 'We must remain. We can't walk away from this.'

The Priestess raised her head to the giant. 'And what of you, Bellurdan? Will you remain?'

The Thelomen nodded ponderously. 'I must. My people have asked it of me.'

She sighed and Blues could almost imagine her looking skyward behind her cloth wrap. 'Well, perhaps you could accompany us a *little* way to the west?'

Gwynn smiled at that and Blues was quite startled to see for the first time ever open warmth in the man's expression. 'Of course,' Gwynn said. 'You must tell me of your adventures these years past.'

'And you must tell me of yours,' she answered, laughing again.

*

That night they were offered poles and hides to fashion a tent of sorts. And as the Jhek did not appear to have much food themselves, they ate a small meal out of their last scavenged dried meat and biscuits. In the morning camp was broken: all the huts and tents were pulled down and piled onto sledges or travois or just heaped onto shoulders, along with all the rest of the people's possessions.

Jhek children ran about, staring at them in open curiosity. The youths were minded by pregnant women, oldsters, both men and women, and walking wounded. Peering up and down the file of march, Blues saw few hale or whole warriors. The battle against the Malazans had obviously been a catastrophe for these people, and now only the young, the old and the sick or maimed were left to struggle on.

Gwynn walked beside the Priestess's litter, conversing. The imposing Ursana lumbered along nearby, perhaps chief of the old woman's guard. Bellurdan had advanced to the fore. Blues, Jacinth and Black slowly fell back towards the rear where they could talk more easily.

'These people have taken a beating,' Blues murmured to Jacinth.

The Talian nodded her agreement. 'Few proper warriors left to defend everyone.'

'No wonder they're retreating,' Black observed.

'No choice,' said Blues. The circumstances of these people reminded him uncomfortably of the situation of the Crimson Guard itself: its scattering and diaspora at the hands of the Malazans, and its own – now official – lack of a homeland. Yet K'azz had promised a return for them one day. And perhaps that day would come. Perhaps when they found him.

So, he and the three others would accompany these people for a few days, but after that they would have to return to shadowing the Malazans. Who knew? Perhaps the damned Malazan mages would somehow manage to master this mountain by themselves.

Then the Guard would really have a fight on its hands.

* * *

Duties for Hessa and her crew were, to say the least, light. So she was bored, frankly, while they waited for the Che'Malle engines to reach

181

full power and efficacy. Therefore she followed Turnagin down the maze of ramps and halls when he said he had something to show her. The mage led her on a wandering route, ever descending, for the better part of a day, until they reached one of what Corbin called 'feeding' halls, or sleeping quarters of the K'Chain Che'Malle. A large opening here looked out over a wasteland of roiling smoke and steam coiling above bare baked rock which sent up heat ripples.

Hessa swept an arm to the forbidding vista. 'Was this what you wanted to show me?'

'Partly.' Leaning against one side of the opening, the mage eased himself down to sit and Hessa was reminded that he was far older than she tended to think – all this privation must have been very hard on the man. He sat regarding the landscape before them, tapping a tall carved stick he used as a staff.

Hessa sat next to him, stared out too for a time. 'Well,' she said, 'at least we won't freeze to death out there.'

Turnagin cracked a small smile. 'Quite the opposite, I'm sure.'

'The twins are supposed to be collecting a cache of food for the run.'

The mage nodded. 'You'll need a fair bit.'

Hessa frowned at that and eyed the fellow. 'You mean *we'll* need a fair bit, right?'

But Turnagin shook his head, his greying, wild and dirty hair hanging down. 'No. I'm staying.'

Hessa surged to her feet. 'Oh, don't do this!' She paced the opening. 'Don't get all noble on us. This isn't worth it.'

'Yes. Yes, it is.'

She threw her hands up. 'Okay, fine. Yes. This is important. That's why we have to get the word out.' She pointed to the Abyss-like landscape. 'We'll have a better chance out there with you.'

The old mage winced at that. 'I'm sorry. But I have to stay.'

'You? *You have to stay.* Why?'

He looked away and tapped the staff. Willing to give him his time she sat next to him once again. He pointed the staff out the opening. 'We're looking more or less south here, you know.'

'Hard to tell,' she drawled.

'Indeed. This is one of their feeding places. Corbin was right in that.'

She grunted, uninterested.

'These Che'Malle are scavengers. Eat anything that's meat. Dead or alive. Doesn't matter to them.'

'Un-huh.'

'So, I came across this among the bones of old corpses and carcasses dragged here.' The mage pulled a dirty rag from the folds of his robes, handed it to her. Beneath the dirt and dried crusted blood the cloth was black. She spread it out to see a portion of a sigil on it – the upright sceptre of the Malazans.

'They're out there somewhere,' Turnagin said.

Hessa let the cloth fall. 'Good. Then it's not our problem any more. We can go.'

'Someone will have to be here when they arrive. Someone who can guide them. Show them how to shut the mechanisms down.'

She looked to the stone ceiling, let out a long hard breath. 'Gods damn it all to the Abyss. They'll just kill you as a collaborator.'

'Not if I help.'

'Maybe even then.'

The mage lifted his shoulders in silent commentary.

Struck by a thought, Hessa let out a snort. 'Hood, Singer might have us killed tomorrow anyway.'

'He still needs us.'

'Yeah . . . but there's somethin' wrong with—' She fell silent as the thumping steps of one of the K'ell Hunters drew near and the monster itself appeared from the mists to lumber in. Its sword-sheathed forearms dangled loose and its heavy head seemed to hang, its eyes dim. The Che'Malle didn't even seem to notice them as it passed.

Turnagin watched it disappear inside. Once it was gone, he said, 'What's being done to these creatures is a crime.'

'A crime? They're beasts. Monsters.'

'No, they're not. They're a race, just like us – or the Jaghut.' The mage grasped hold of the staff and set his chin on his forearms. 'Which is what I can't make any sense of. There's no history of antagonism between the K'Chain Che'Malle and the Jaghut. So why is he doing this? He intends to unleash this mountain – but upon whom? And why?'

'He's mad,' Hessa judged, dismissively.

At this Turnagin nodded, slowly and sombrely. 'Yes. I think you are right. He is mad. And definitely ill. If not dying. An ill, dying, mad Jaghut. And we are in his power . . .' The mage shook his head, appalled.

'The twins won't stay,' Hessa said. 'Nor Corbin.'

'Nor do I expect them to.' He eyed her. 'Or anyone.'

Hessa waved the subject aside. 'We'll see. Like I said – we probably won't live long enough anyway.'

The mage shook his shaggy head again, this time wryly, eyeing her sidelong.

*　　*　　*

The infantry advance was slow and methodical. It had to be: the ground was either a boggy quagmire or a maze of scalding mud and steam, and even naked crackling rock too hot to walk upon. Worse, visibility was limited as the steam and smoke roiled across the landscape in clouds or hung heavy and unbreathable above cracks and holes all about. Many soldiers voiced the opinion that they had somehow stumbled into Hood's own paths.

When contact came Tayschrenn was towards the rear of the centre phalanx. He was walking carefully over the uneven ground as he'd abandoned his useless boots and now wore a pair of standard military issue sandals, tied high in leather strapping up to his knees beneath his trousers.

Heavy blows sounded from the right flank and immediately the phalanx before him halted and hunkered down ready to rebuff any attack. Orders carried through the mists and Tayschrenn strained to see. Some large darker silhouette was there far off to the right where it reared high above the ranks. One of them? Then it was gone, seeming to melt away. He went forward to Dujek.

The commander was at the centre of the phalanx, scanning the fog banks ahead. A staff officer came pushing her way through the press to Dujek's side, saluted. She was panting and her face was wet with sweat. 'Contact with the – them,' she stuttered. To Tayschrenn's eyes the woman appeared half shocked by the encounter.

'How many?'

'Just the one.'

'One? Casualties?'

'Seven dead, seven wounded.'

'Seven! Did you finish it?'

'No. It withdrew.'

The Fist clawed his hand down his face. 'Gods damn the thing. One? Just the one . . . ?'

'Captain Orosé asks for orders.'

Dujek blew out a breath. 'Continue the advance – at the ready.'

The officer saluted and withdrew.

Tayschrenn motioned to the front, saying, 'I assume you will want me to do massive physical damage to our enemies, here, yes?'

'Yeah? So?'

'Then I'll have to be much closer to the front. The effects are, ah, expansive, and indiscriminate.'

The Fist shook his head. 'Not yet. This looks like plain brute force grunt work. Can't risk losing you to that.' Tayschrenn paused, frowning, again troubled by the man presuming to give him orders. Dujek seemed to sense this, for he added, roughly, 'If you will.'

The High Mage nodded his compliance – for now.

Soon orders sounded up and down the lines and with a rasping of armour the phalanxes slowly resumed their advance, this time with shields raised and weapons out, at the ready.

As the ground was becoming less and less passable the lines had to constantly adjust their marching order. The surface gave way in places to reveal pools of liquid rock that then immediately crusted over in hardened black stone. The mists of steaming meltwater thickened, as did the fumes coursing from gaps in the ground – fumes Tayschrenn worried might be poisonous.

The poor visibility was obviously greatly troubling the Fist as he glowered about, scowling his displeasure. He was reaching to a messenger to give an order – probably a halt, Tayschrenn imagined – when yells of warning and the crash of heavy blows rang up and down the front.

The impact of just two of these gigantic creatures ran like a shockwave through the ranks, right to the rear of the phalanx where Tayschrenn stood near Dujek at the command position. Troopers recoiled a step, jostling, and the Fist growled, 'Steady . . .'

The creatures fought in eerie silence – but for their huffed heavy breaths – and so the noise was all of troopers grunting as they sloughed blows, or snarling their pain at savage wounds.

'Definitely an experienced mind here,' Dujek said. Tayschrenn, who had been staring with growing fascination and a strange sort of dread at one of his first close field battles, turned his head and saw that the Fist was addressing him.

'Yes?' he responded, his voice faint.

Dujek was nodding to himself, scratching the greying bristles of his chin. 'First a light probe – almost a test, really. Followed by a solid warning punch.'

Tayschrenn was now feeling oddly dizzy, even nauseous, as the stink of sweat and blood seemed to choke him, while the Fist's guard pressed in closer than he liked, almost jostling against him. 'Yes?' he repeated, distractedly.

'So,' the Fist growled on, 'we can punch too. Go ahead and give whoever's behind this something to think about.'

Tayschrenn found his throat strangely dry. He nodded, not daring to speak. And yet, why the discomfort? He'd fought countless duels against sorcerers, witches and warlocks all across Quon Tali. Or rather, had intimidated most into submission simply by demonstrating his power. He'd never dreamed of actually testing himself against one of the ancient Elders. Surely this was a matter for sword and muscle to decide, not magery.

The ugly suspicion occurred to him then that these K'Chain Che'Malle might not even be affected by a mere human Warren.

He would have to be closer – the mass of soldiers was in the way. And so he nodded, dumbly, and forced his way forward, summoning his powers. With his Warren raised he now saw the various blooms of the minor cadre mages among the phalanx and noted how most were using their powers to defend their fellow troopers by helping to deflect the ferocious blows, or hardening armour. Yet even as he pushed forward further into the ranks he saw more and more of these mages turn to what Denul healing magics they knew.

The tight press of soldiery frankly repelled him. The stench of sweat, blood and even – Gods forfend! – faeces, was offensive. The troopers jostled him; armoured bodies gouged him among the closed ranks until he eased a touch of his power into impelling all away. This cleared a space about him and he could breathe once more.

Unfortunately, through the coiling mist and vapours, the nearest saurian head rearing so far above the ranks now swung his way. He wondered, belatedly, if perhaps he shouldn't have created an opening among the ranks.

186

The enormous beast now heaved itself in his direction, its glistening blood-wet forearm blades swinging, and he stared upwards at the lizard-like form of the fabled K'Chain Che'Malle only two ranks of troopers away. He summoned his full Warren powers, driven by need and, he could admit, damned fear, and sent a coursing burst against the Elder. Incredibly, the creature came on through the onslaught and Tayschrenn stood amazed. He'd never had to unleash such might against any previous challenger – frankly, it would have reduced him or her to motes of ash. Yet now this creature came on. Trailing smoke and brutally scoured, yes, but still advancing.

He wondered again about the efficacy of human Warrens against Elders, or perhaps these K'Chain specifically, as they had their own particular sort of alien energies that they had mastered.

The remaining troopers ahead of him understandably flinched back a step, knocking him backwards, almost stepping on top of him. None, however, panicked or fled, or abandoned the line. They hunched behind their shields, defending themselves and him. Defending *him*.

Grimly, he mustered what potency he had left to send another excoriating surge against the Che'Malle soldier – a K'ell Hunter, he believed to be their name.

The Elder beast swung one heavy curved blade and men and women grunted, falling. Something hot and wet slapped across Tayschrenn's face and he wiped it away to see thick arterial blood smeared all over his hand. He stared, stunned by this unprecedented sight.

Then he let his hand fall, for the K'ell Hunter was throwing back one bladed arm, aiming for him, and he realized he had to act, to do something. He reflexively strengthened the circle of protection he'd raised about himself. The blow hammered down upon his warding and he was knocked flat by the force of the impact. He lay blinking, dazzled, his vision blurred. He heard, rather than saw, the Elder rearing over him and he raised his arm as if that would ward off the coming final blow.

An eruption of power sent the Che'Malle staggering backwards. The might of the blast stunned Tayschrenn. *Who?* he repeated blearily to himself as he fought to clear his vision.

Hands raised and straightened him and he now saw before him

the severe, hatchet face of Nightchill. 'That,' the woman said, 'was very foolish.'

Tayschrenn could only nod his agreement. Then he knew nothing more.

Opening his eyes, he saw the tapered canvas ceiling of his tent. The sounds of the camp reached him. His head ached abominably. He rubbed his forehead and groaned – both from the pain and from the disappointment of what had just occurred.

Someone moved in the tent, cloth rubbing, and a glass hove into view. 'Tea,' Nightchill said. 'Medicinal.'

He took the warm glass, sat up on his cot. 'I suppose I owe you my thanks.'

'Yes, you do.'

'What happened? What's going on?'

'We held, but at an enormous cost. Heavy casualties. We then withdrew a short distance to a better defensive position and we are now digging in – if that is the right term for squatting on bare rock.'

'*We* held? You mean you held.'

'I mean *they* held. The troops. You owe them your thanks. They fell in front of you.'

'They did their job,' he allowed.

Nightchill pursed her already tight lips, eyed him strangely for a moment. 'And you didn't do yours,' she finally said.

He nodded, not offended, as the evaluation was factual. He rubbed his brow once more. 'I don't understand. I summoned all I had and it just kept coming. I'd never thrown that much against any opponent before.'

The woman sighed, paced the tent to the closed flap. 'You've never had to. These are K'Chain Che'Malle. Frankly, you've been wasting your time all these years against hedge-wizards or uncooperative city mages. You haven't been challenged like this before. Or at least not in a long time.' She pulled aside the heavy canvas flap, eyed him thinly again. 'There is more in you – I see it. You could achieve more. I wonder, though, whether you merit it.' She let the flap fall behind her.

He snorted and finished the tea. Strange woman! *Merit?* Who does she think she is? His mind returned to Hairlock's vague warnings and suspicions regarding her. Did she have a 'game'? And he half-laughed, thinking, was the game just to bait him?

Yet she must have some goal. And the only one he could see worthy of someone of her power was the throne itself.

He rose, wincing, his vision darkening for a moment. He must find the Fist and apologize. That would be the principled thing to do. He pushed aside the flap and stood blinking in the smoke and ash. Two figures rose from sitting before the tent: a squat fellow and a young woman, both medium infantry, marines. He frowned at them. 'Yes?'

The man held out Tayschrenn's cape, muddied and bedraggled. 'This was torn from ya.'

He took it from him. 'Well . . . my thanks. But you need not have bothered.'

'It's our job,' the fellow said. 'We're your minders.'

The young woman elbowed him and he rubbed his side. 'That is – your guards.'

'Really? You've been assigned to me, have you? I am in need of guards now, am I?'

The very petite woman looked pained. 'Aides, maybe? Your staff?'

'Ah. So I have staff now.' He eyed them sceptically. 'What are your names then?'

'Ute,' said the fellow, and he gave a rather poor example of a salute.

'Missy,' said the young woman.

'Missy?' Tayschrenn echoed. 'Your name is Missy?'

'That's what they call me.'

Tayschrenn paused for an instant, considering a response, then simply brushed past them, not even caring if they would follow or not. *We will see about this . . .*

He entered the command tent without a pause, found the Fist giving orders to his staffers even as he was being shaved. The Fist nodded to him, waved everyone out. He wiped his face clean, one-handed, using a dirty old cloth. 'Up and about I see. Good.'

'I apologize for my failure, Fist.'

Dujek's brows rose. 'You're apologizing. To me.'

'Yes.'

'Hunh.' He crossed to a brazier, poured out a glass of tea from a kettle hung over it. He offered it to Tayschrenn. 'Tea?'

Tayschrenn waved a demurral. 'Thank you. I've had some.'

The Fist sipped the steaming hot infusion, eyed him. 'Well, firstly it's the troops you really should apologize to. But that's not feasible, is it.' He set down the glass on a table cluttered with scrolls and sheets. 'However, the very fact that you're capable of it shows that there might actually be some humanity somewhere in there after all.'

Tayschrenn cocked his head, a touch confused. 'I'm sorry . . . I don't follow.'

The Fist appeared surprised. He let out a breath and waved the comment aside. 'Never mind. Can't say I didn't try. Interestingly, you're not the first officer in here today offering their apologies. The Sword was in earlier offering his for failing to protect *you*.'

Now Tayschrenn was surprised. 'He was? That is, he did? There's no need for that.'

'Exactly. And that's what I told him.'

'Very good. In any case, I wish you to know that I underestimated our, ah, opponents. And that it will not happen again.'

'Understood.'

From the Fist's tone Tayschrenn understood the topic and the discussion to be closed. He gave the slightest inclination of his head and headed to the opening. Just before exiting, he turned. 'One last thing, Fist.'

'Yes?'

'You've assigned me . . . minders?'

The Fist nodded as he poured more tea. 'You're a battle mage now, High Fist. No more dusty libraries. No more one-on-one sorcery duels across entire valleys. Best to have some troopers with you – to help show you the ropes, so to speak.'

Tayschrenn gave another tilt of his head, this one very tight indeed, and exited. Outside, his minders rose from sitting. Their appearance before him caused him to pause, but he brushed onwards, pacing stiff-legged across camp, headed for the cook tents. Halfway, he turned back to ask, 'By the way; just what was the Sword doing during the engagement?'

'Ah!' Ute responded, throwing his arms wide. 'You shoulda seen him, sor. The entire left flank was near to collapsing then he charges

190

in taking on one o' them horrors hisself. Holds it off, he does!' The marine pressed a hand to his chest. 'S'truth! I swear by Togg's tits.'

Tayschrenn cast a look to the clear sky. 'Wonderful.'

'Yes, sor. He is a wonder.'

Tayschrenn paced onwards for the cook tents – though he felt his hunger draining from him.

Chapter 13

A LIGHT PROBE FROM A WARREN WOKE SIALLE WHERE SHE lay wrapped in her blanket. It was just dawn, though beneath the thick black cloud cover it was difficult to tell. She raised her head and found Hairlock a little way off, eyeing her; he motioned her up. 'Been contact with the main force. They want us back.'

'Good.'

The mage crouched at the fire's low embers to warm his hands. 'First we'll just run off this scum.'

She rose, rolled her blanket thoughtfully. 'Was that the order?'

A hard, toothy grin. 'That's my order.'

'It's a column of families – we've forced them off their land already.'

'Then they won't put up much of a fight.'

Nodding, she walked off to the west, faced away. 'You know I am of the Seti, Hairlock.' He grunted something noncommittal. She motioned to the west. 'I'm from a small clan like that one. One that no longer exists thanks to some over-zealous Malazan irregulars who were never punished for their crimes.' She turned to him.

He rose, his eyes narrowing. 'So?'

'So, I vowed never to let that happen again.'

He shook his hands at his side to loosen them. 'Aw, girl. You ain't gonna . . .'

She nodded. 'Yes, I am.'

'Stupid bitch!' He threw his hands up but she was faster and a coursing blast of power sent him spinning backwards. He jumped up, spitting dirt. Gashes from the mass of gravel sent against him now welled up and he brushed at the blood smearing his face, yelling, 'Fucking whore!' Marines ran to his side. 'Where is she!' he bellowed, blinded by the blood.

'Gone, sir.'

'*Fuck!*'

'Orders, sir?'

'Gimme a rag would you?'

Some cloth was shoved into his hands and he wiped his face. 'Dammit to the Dark Taker. She's gone to warn them. No point now.' He shook off the troopers helping him. 'We're turnin' round. Mister High-and-Mighty wants us back anyway.'

*

The main rambling, rather bedraggled column of the Jhek villagers had set out that dawn. The Priestess, however, remained behind, standing next to her litter, accompanied by a bodyguard of twenty warriors. Blues and the rest of the Guard remained as well, a sort of rearguard, along with Bellurdan.

'What's she doing?' Blues asked of Gwynn.

The mage shrugged. '"Waiting," was all she would tell me.'

Half the morning passed; the column of villagers had advanced out of sight among the gently rolling hills, even the slowest of them. Blues let out yet another breath of impatience. There was a small Malazan force out there, not too distant. Did the Priestess want to confront them? Foolish, and unnecessary.

Out of the many birds constantly circling overhead, four of the largest hunters stooped down to pounce upon something and Blues jumped, startled. The birds, three plains eagles and a red falcon, perched among the grass, wings half-opened, watchful.

Blues exchanged uneasy glances with Jacinth and Black, who had hands upon their weapons.

A pale blur appeared among the grass, growing to a petite young woman in leathers, her hair a thick shock of white. Her expression seemed contrite. Bellurdan suddenly let out a great bout of laughter.

This newcomer called to the Priestess, 'I should've known.' Ullara waved her forward. The bear-warriors stepped between, however, growling.

193

'Let her come,' the Priestess said.

Blues and Gwynn approached as well, warily; this one must be a Malazan cadre mage.

The young woman had the sun-darkened hue and wiry compact build of Seti tribal stock. She bowed to the Priestess. 'I am come to offer my loyalty and my services.'

'Do not trust her,' Blues called.

This newcomer eyed him and Gwynn. 'Mercenaries, I take it?'

'She's burned her bridges,' the Priestess answered. She seemed to regard the woman through the thick cloth wrapped round her eyes. 'There's no going back for her.'

'You were watching.'

'Of course.'

The young woman bowed again. 'I am Sialle.'

'You are welcome, Sialle. Though, be warned, you *will* be watched.'

'Of course.'

'We must go,' Ursana rumbled. 'We have delayed long enough.'

The Priestess nodded her agreement. 'Yes. We are done here.' She climbed back into her litter, her guards surrounded it, and they set out. Blues and the rest of the Guard followed, accompanied by Bellurdan. The newcomer, with her thick mane of snow-like hair, held back discreetly, shadowed by two wolf-warriors.

Blues couldn't help but constantly glance back to her as she followed along, a strange sort of smile at her lips.

* * *

It was the thick of night just before dawn and Dancer stood together with Cartheron Crust at the side of the *Twisted*. He could not stop rubbing his chin, which needed a shave, until he noticed what he was doing and dropped his hand. '*All*, you say?' he asked of Cartheron.

The Admiral gave a sombre nod. 'All. In twenty different groups. Can't chase 'em all.'

Dancer blew out a breath and glanced to the door of the main cabin. 'No. You couldn't. I understand.'

'But will he?' Cartheron asked, also looking to the door.

'Retribution hasn't been his style so far . . .'

'But he was damned insistent we keep them in.'

Dancer offered a reassuring smile. 'We're only one ship, Admiral.'

Cartheron snorted a laugh and shook his head. '*Admiral*,' he said, in scorn.

Dancer headed to the cabin but turned back to ask, 'North, though, yes? They went north?'

'Un-huh. North.'

'Well, that's something at least.'

He unlatched the door and entered into utter darkness. The dim starlight cast a weak glow just past him. Dancer possessed quite good night-vision and so was surprised by the gloom; he suspected something more. He called, 'Kellanved?' a touch wary.

Cloth shifted in the dark. A muffled grunt.

'Kellanved?'

He heard what sounded like shoes scraping the floor, more grunting, then the man emerged from the murk, pulling on a brocaded vest over a black ruffled shirt. It appeared to Dancer for an instant that the mage had coalesced from the shade itself and he rubbed his eyes, frowning.

'What is it now?' Kellanved asked in a sigh.

Dancer decided to just come out with it. 'The ships have all fled.'

The Emperor's eyes now fully widened. 'They have?' The eyes narrowed. 'Which way did they go?'

'North.'

Kellanved appeared to relax; he let out a breath, nodding, and his walking stick appeared in his hand. He brushed past, saying, 'Good.'

Dancer stood blinking. He wasn't sure he'd just heard what he'd heard. '*Good?*'

'Yes, good.'

He followed Kellanved to the side. 'What do you mean by that? I thought you wanted them held back.'

'Exactly. That is exactly what I wanted them to see.'

Dancer looked to the night sky. 'So that they'd want to move on.'

'Exactly.'

'Well, you could've let me know the plan.'

A tiny wave of a hand as if to say: *A piffling matter.*

Kellanved addressed Cartheron, amidships. He pointed the walking stick. 'That is north, yes?'

195

Cartheron nodded. 'Yes, that'll be it.'

The mage squinted into the pinking early dawn horizon. 'They must've finally put their heads together.'

'And that's good too?'

'Yes. It means they're likely to follow the plan.'

'What plan?' Dancer asked, now quite exasperated.

The Emperor's brows rose. 'Why, mine, of course.'

Through clenched teeth, Dancer grated, 'Could you perhaps lay out this plan? *If* you would be so kind?'

Kellanved smiled beatifically. 'With pleasure, my friend.' He planted the walking stick, laid his hands upon its silver hound's-head pommel, and rocked back and forth on his heels. Dancer resisted rolling his eyes, as he knew this would only delay things further. 'I planted it in little kernels here and there during those cabin talks with the captains. Little suggestions. Hints. No doubt they think it theirs.'

'And this plan actually is . . . ?' Dancer cut in.

Kellanved frowned, displeased by the interruption. Dancer sighed and invited him to continue. The mage cleared his throat. 'To divide up into smaller attack groups, flotillas, task forces. Call them what you will. They couldn't possibly defeat the Falarans at sea, so to attack them where they have a better chance – on land.'

'Land? What land?'

'The *islands*, my friend. To take the ports, the cities. To capture the islands. As many as possible. The Falaran navy is perhaps undefeatable. But their army?' Kellanved shrugged. 'Nonexistent.'

'They'll mass the navy, clear them out one by one,' put in a third voice and both Dancer and Kellanved turned to Cartheron who stood a short way off. The Admiral looked sheepish. 'Sorry, couldn't help overhearing.'

Kellanved waved his permission. 'A good point. However, as we discussed, the Falaran navy is made up of all the ships of the many islands. How can it mass when half of those islands are threatened, under attack, or being sacked or captured?'

'They will withdraw,' said Dancer, thinking aloud. 'Each to their own island to defend it.'

The Emperor was nodding. 'Indeed. Or so I hope.'

'Then we can pick *them* off one by one,' Dancer finished.

Kellanved smiled again. 'Eventually.'

'Divide and conquer,' Cartheron put in, crossing his arms. 'But among islands. Except,' and the Admiral was now stroking the greying bristles of his chin, 'this gang o' pirates – this pirate navy – they don't need to answer to you any longer. You'll lose control of 'em. Some may even name themselves king or queen of this or that island. Or try to.'

Kellanved's beatific smile returned. 'I dropped such pearls before them as well.'

Dancer's patience gave way. 'Really? Whatever would you do that for?'

'Deniability, my friend. Deniability.' And Kellanved headed back to the cabin.

Dancer and Cartheron watched him go and the door shut, then they looked to one another, frowning. *Deniability?* Dancer wondered. He was uneasy then, regarding what any deniability might be needed *for*.

* * *

Gianna watched the dark line of shore disappear to the west and frankly did not know what to do next. That had been the third island to refuse them. None would accept the kids. That is, once they realized who and what they were.

She couldn't blame them. No small isle dare risk the ire of the Faith.

Nor any single ship's captain, either, for that matter. She turned to Brevin, and the expression on her face must have said everything for the captain glanced away. The big woman let out a great long breath. 'They're a good crew,' she began, 'loyal and true – but can only be pushed so far. They expect paying work, and my job is to provide it – or I'm the one out of a job, hey? I'm truly sorry, lass.' She gestured to the north. 'I'll let you off at the next isle. Maybe at night. Can't refuse you once you're ashore, hey?'

Gianna crossed to the opposite rail. A youth came up to her, proudly holding a hooked silver. 'Excellent . . . ah . . .'

'Ranat,' provided the lad, nonplussed.

She tousled his already unkempt and quite dirty hair. 'Well done, Ranat. Captain . . .' she called, struck by a thought.

Brevin glanced back. 'Aye?'

'Is that the only objection?'

'Objection? How so?'

'To giving us passage. Payment. Is that the only problem?'

Brevin idly scratched her wide stomach, almost shaking her head. 'Lass . . . last time I looked you weren't carrying any coin.'

'I know. I know. But if I could pay you . . .'

'Lass, we're sympathetic. We don't like the Call any more than you. But I don't see how . . .'

Gianna waved that aside. 'One last passage then. North-east to Lurk.'

'Lurk? Those are treacherous shores, lass. What's on Lurk? You got relations?'

'Not what's on it. What's just east of it.'

Now Brevin's thick brows rose. 'The graveyard of ships?' She shook her head. 'Sorry, lass. But those shoals and currents aren't to be trusted.'

'I know them well. I can guarantee our safety.' She gestured to the children at the sides, all dangling lines and chatting happily – for them the voyage had been nothing but one long fishing expedition. 'Would I risk them? No. If this doesn't pay off then you can let us go on Lurk and be rid of us.' She pressed a hand to her chest. 'I promise.'

Brevin drew a hand over her reddish hair, all pulled back into a long queue. She let out a weary sigh. 'Very well. To Lurk. Mael forfend.' She raised a finger. 'But you'd better know your way through those shoals or I'm swinging us away.'

Gianna gave a fierce nod. 'I'll see us through.'

Passage north-east skirting the edges of Walk Sea took two days, stopping at a small cove overnight. No one voyaged straight across Walk Sea. Though bounded by a ring of isles, the centre was open and free of all landmarks. Falaran sailors relied upon line of sight. Voyaging among a multitude of islands, one had no need of any more sophisticated means of navigation.

Brevin had been keeping them to a scattering of tiny isles off the coast of Walk, one of the largest of the Falaran Isles. She was wary of approaching any larger community; even wretched War Isle possessed a temple to Mael.

Now they were striking out for the wide swath of shallows and shoals that made up Sparrow Pass Cut, a byword for treachery and loss among all Falarans. The graveyard of ships as it was sometimes termed. The cut was deceptive: it appeared to offer the quickest and most direct route east out of Walk Sea. Yet few ever dared its shallows.

It was late in the day when they approached the coast of Flood Isle and so Brevin once again set a heading to a small sheltered cove. In passing, she told Gianna, 'I'll not enter Sparrow Pass Cut at night.'

Despite her desire to finally reach the site, Gianna had to agree.

As soon as the sea-anchors were dropped, so too were numerous fishing lines in numerous small hands.

'An eager crew,' Gianna said to the captain, who laughed.

'Aye. Eager. Quick to follow orders. Even scouring. The *Glimmer* hasn't been so clean in ages.' She squeezed the shoulder of a girl at the side. 'But we're over-crewed, hey? Too many mouths to feed.' She eyed Gianna. 'If that's where this is headed.' She shrugged her meaty shoulders. 'I'd like to – but, sorry. Just not good, for them or me.'

'They're fishing. Feeding themselves,' Gianna pointed out.

'Oh, aye. But no time to lounge about and drop a line during a paying voyage. Have to buy stores for the trip.' She shook her head. 'That drives up costs. Eats into any profit. Not an option as I see it.' She leaned against the side, crossed her thick arms. 'So . . . Sparrow . . . What's the plan?'

Gianna nodded her cooperation and blew out a breath: *Here goes* . . . 'Done any salvaging work?' she asked.

Brevin rolled her eyes in scorn. 'Thought that was where this was headed.' She sighed. 'Lass . . . there're more scavengers' bones in the cut than there are wrecks. This is the Twins' own foolish chance.'

'I can see us through.'

'Why? Why you?'

She shrugged. 'Mage of Ruse.'

'Plenty of Ruse mages around. Why haven't they been out?'

'I have a – well, an *affinity* for finding wrecks.'

Brevin's doubtful expression remained unchanged. 'Is that so?' She shook her head. 'Well, this is your last chance, lass. Sorry, but that's the way it has to be.' She walked off.

Gianna remained at the side. Her last chance. She'd better make it count. And she knew, then, which wreck to seek.

They heard the rocks and shoals before they reached them: waves surging and crashing. Gianna knew there were many theories as to what had created the wide stretch of shallows. A lost isle, was one. The rage of the monstrous Jhistal another. Or both together. It was suggestive, some thought, that the shoals should lie so near to the isle that most agreed was the site of the last known attack of the actual Jhistal itself, hundreds of years ago.

Rubble Isle, some named it, after the scattered ruins of many buildings that lay across it. Ancient and semi-mythical Kayanarle, or Kynarl. Seat of the height of Old Falar's civilization. Destroyed by its own hubris, was one theory. Delving into forbidden knowledge. Or possessing it. In any case, the evidence was plain for all to see. Incontrovertible. Mael might have sent this Jhistal against them for their transgressions – or an earthquake, as either was his to command – or so said the priests of the Faith.

Gianna sat at the ship's prow, her Ruse Warren raised, probing ahead for any hidden obstruction, and sensing for directions to one very particular wreck. Brevin also had crewmen and women dropping weighted and knotted ropes for soundings: she might trust in Gianna's abilities, but wished to have a second opinion in any case.

They proceeded in this manner for the better part of the day, tacking round taller rocks where sea-birds circled and spray misted the air. Whenever the captain crossed near to the bow Gianna could feel her growing impatience.

'Finding anything?' Brevin finally growled, late in the day.

'I'm looking,' Gianna answered, distracted.

'Looking? Can't drop a rock without hitting a wreck here.'

'Most of these have been scavenged.'

'Then what're you looking for?'

'One that hasn't been discovered yet,' she answered, curtly, not looking away from the waves.

'Not discovered? Naw – not the *Emerald*, surely.'

Gianna bit back her own impatience. 'Yes, the *Emerald*. Now . . . if you don't mind?'

'There's no chance, lass . . .'

'Please. This isn't my first search. I've been through here salvaging many times.'

Brevin raised her hands in surrender, and, still shaking her head, walked off.

Gianna, of course, was not certain herself. It had been an early such contract: diving for a rich client out of Walk. One who wished to become much richer, and had the funds to try. Not the *Emerald*; not per se. Still, something worth all his time and expense.

And she'd come through, hadn't she?

Found a prize worth scavenging.

Still, not the *Emerald*. But that last dive she'd sensed something, a flicker amid the murk and sands churned up by the currents. It had been only an instant's image in her Ruse-aided awareness: a flash of piercing, brilliant *emerald*.

North, her senses had told her then. Somewhere due north.

A hint, or vision, she'd put away for future reference, thinking, maybe someday . . .

And so here she was, pursuing that very mad chance.

'We must drop anchor!' Brevin shouted to her.

'Soon!' she called back. Close – it *felt* close. She pointed ahead to where a crowd of sharp rocks pierced the surface like jagged teeth. 'There! Drop anchor there.'

'We'll be dashed to pieces,' Brevin warned.

'Tie off then! Snag a rock.'

Grumbling, the captain shouted out her orders. The *Glimmer* hove-to close to one rock and the sturdy sea-anchors were dropped. Lines also went out to catch amid the steep sides of the tooth-like shoal.

'Tomorrow, then,' Brevin called, giving her a hard warning stare.

Gianna nodded, 'Aye. Tomorrow.'

She hardly slept that night, but then no one did; the contending currents and tides of Walk Sea and Land's End Sea fought and clashed the night through, the winds rose, and a steady cold rain fell.

Gianna rose already sodden. The cooking brazier was still going somewhere in a slim hold belowdecks and a cup of hot tea and hard-bread was her dawn meal. She stripped down to shift and shorts and two men of the crew readied a long line. Brevin watched the preparations closely. As they raised the line she stepped in with,

'Not the chest, fools.' She took the line from them and cinched it tight on Gianna's left wrist.

Though she'd been on countless dives Gianna found her mouth dry, her heart hammering. She nodded her thanks to Brevin.

'Yank three times when you find that chest full of gold, hey?' the captain told her, smiling.

She shared the smile. 'Aye. In no time.'

She swung her legs out over the side, started slowing her breathing – as best she could. The youths all stood at the side, close but not crowding, watching intently, some with knowing looks.

'Ready?' Brevin asked. She nodded.

'Clear the line!' the captain warned.

And she dived.

Few salvagers dared the shoals of Sparrow Pass Cut and Gianna fully knew why. The cross-currents slapped her nearly sideways as she fought to swim straight down. Churned-up sand and muck left the normally clear Falaran waters as opaque as soup. She extended her Ruse Warren as she swam ever downwards, seeking the sandy bottom.

Savage side-currents tugged and buffeted her – these she knew to be the contrary waters rushing through narrow gaps between the rocks that now towered round her. And therein lay her greatest threat: being dashed against one.

If the *Emerald* had gone down among these rocks it was fully obvious why none had discovered it – no diver would voluntarily dare these waters. Only her Ruse Warren kept her from tumbling or spinning helplessly.

Kicking and kicking, she finally found bottom. Here she felt about, blind, amid the sands and broken smaller rocks. If the wreck were here, she assumed the powerful pulling currents must by now have spread it over a swath of shifting sands. She dug down – it might well be buried.

She kept moving, tugging out more line, using handholds among rocks to fight her buoyancy. She kicked and pulled her way round one after another of the rearing black teeth as she searched amid the billowing sand and muck. All she needed was one artefact, one piece of corroded iron or broken crockery. Anything to prove *something* had gone down here.

She'd already been down for much longer than any diver could normally sustain. She now also feared that yank on her line meaning those above were worried for her and meant to pull her up – dead or alive.

She felt her way through one tight cut between jagged coral-encrusted rocks, only to be suddenly pushed down into a deeper rift. She tumbled and kicked yet spun helpless.

Rocks reared before her and she was sucked between, scraping her side viciously. Her arm halted her, yanked back behind her almost out of its socket. She floated there, a cork in a savage dragging current, and reaching back for her arm she found it wedged in a narrowing cleft.

She couldn't reach through the rocks and she almost laughed then, despite her tightening chest. Mael had her now! She had defied him too often, staying down beyond all known endurance again and again. He finally had her now – by the arm!

She pulled out her knife and hacked at the encrusted ledges and edges. *Damn you Mael! I defy you!*

Her vision was narrowing and greying – a bad sign. This was further than she'd pushed herself in a long time. Her chest was afire! The urge to inhale almost overwhelming. Consciousness, she knew, would leave her soon and that would be the end.

Then, small things tugged and pulled at her, almost tickling, and she smiled. Fish? Nibbling her already? She forced open her eyes and jerked, appalled. Four black-haired youths swam about her, probing at the narrow cleft. Furious, she waved them off, pointing up. They ignored her.

Small hands reached in where she could not. From sacks tied at their waists came chisels and hammers and they hacked away at the rock. Each blow released a mass of sand and fragments that the current immediately whisked away.

Suddenly, she was free, wheeling loosely, too weak to fight. The line now pulled her up to shimmering daylight above. And consciousness finally did leave her somewhere during the climb.

Bright daylight stabbing her eyes woke her. She winced, blinking. Numerous small faces crowned by tousled black hair stared down at her.

'Still with us,' Brevin announced, sounding openly amazed.

Gianna raised her head and peered around; she lay on deck,

crowded by the youths, most of whom were just as sodden as she. 'You dived . . .' she murmured.

Eager nods and grins all round.

'Couldn't stop 'em,' said Brevin. 'They grabbed lines and tools and jumped in. Followed your line down, I suppose.'

'You saved my life,' she told them, wonder in her voice.

'Amazed you were still alive to rescue,' Brevin growled. She touched Gianna's hair. 'Favoured of Mael *and* mage of Ruse.' She shook her head. 'A powerful combination.'

Gianna tried to rise and a coughing fit took her. 'I'm sorry for dragging you out here, captain. The cross-currents are too powerful. Maybe something is down there – just no one can reach it.'

The big woman nodded her cheerless agreement. 'I'm sorry too, lass. But it was worth a shot, Oponn willing.'

The smallest of the ones who had dived, a mere stripling, raised his hand. Brevin gave him a gruff, 'Yes? What?'

'Pardon, cap'n,' this one said, 'but I did find this among the ledges and cracks below.' He opened his canvas sack and pulled out a flat round object, like a thin stone.

Brevin took it, dubious. She brushed at it, frowning. Then brushed further, harder, pulled bits of seaweed from the edges, her eyes widening. '*Ye gods* . . .' she whispered, awed, and handed it to Gianna.

Gianna turned it over and over in her hands. A rich deep yellow flashed from the thing – a plate. A plate of gold.

And Brevin laughed, a great belly-heaving chuckle, and she turned to the crew, calling, 'Strengthen the lines, lads and lasses – we're going to be here a while!'

* * *

Tayschrenn did not spend much time in the expeditionary command tent during the march, but now that things had settled into a stationary siege it was hard to avoid stopping in. It was where everyone waited – he wasn't certain what it was they were waiting *for*, but he had to wait along with everyone else. He sat alongside one wall, perusing one of the books he'd brought among his personal possessions. Hairlock sat drinking, rather sullenly, his head still bandaged where he'd been gashed by Sialle's unexpected attack. When the Seven

Cities mage had returned with news of that betrayal Tayschrenn's immediate thought had been to regret being down one mage already while facing their greatest threat to date.

He'd spoken by Warren to A'Karonys, Leathana and Nedurian: all were embroiled in suppressing uprisings or pursuing outright campaigns. Nightchill was in touch with Kellanved, but Tayschrenn didn't think the Emperor would be of much help in this situation; the K'Chain Che'Malle were unlikely to be impressed by flickering shadow hand-puppetry. Or the Hounds – why risk losing them? Again, the Che'Malle were unlikely to be intimidated. As for the Claws – assassin-mages – though impressive, again what use against a monster the height of two men?

The Sword, however, had proved his worth. The camp was abuzz with tales of his prowess in the fight. He was out now, somewhere, serving a watch himself or simply mixing with the troopers.

Which left himself and Nightchill. Or rather, so far, just Nightchill. She stood outside the tent right now, staring steadily out into the night – keeping far closer to camp now that they faced such a dire threat.

As for himself: he'd disappointed. Thinking about it – as he had for every night since – he was coming to the opinion that he'd been unprepared. Too hurried. He would have to ready himself for far greater exertion. Expect stronger resistance; expect more of himself. Yet how? He'd given it all he dared.

Dujek, during these days, paced incessantly, back and forth: to the opening to stare out to the clouded, shrouded north and grumble to himself, and mutter; then away, rubbing furiously at his chin or balding pate, or the stump of his arm.

Finally, Tayschrenn could take the unremitting muttering no longer and asked, 'You are troubled, Fist?'

Dujek snorted. 'Oh, aye. I'm troubled.' He thrust his hand to the north. 'Why haven't they attacked? They should be attacking. They must've seen how close they came to crushing us. Yet they hold back. This doesn't make sense and I don't like it.'

'Their strategy is defensive, then?' Tayschrenn suggested.

'And why?' Dujek asked, not scornfully, but rather inviting a response.

From the rear of the tent, Hairlock offered, 'Maybe because they ain't as strong as they seem. They ain't ready.'

The Fist nodded. 'Exactly. *Maybe*. We don't know, and that's the problem.'

'How so?' Hairlock answered.

Now the Fist fiercely rubbed his neck. 'Because this demands that we find out.'

Tayschrenn raised his brows in appreciation of the thorny problem. 'Ah. I see.'

Dujek continued nodding, unhappily. 'Can't send plain scouts or troopers. They just wouldn't make it back.'

'Don't like where this is going,' Hairlock growled. 'Send one o' them back-stabbing Claws. Skulking around like rats is what they do best.'

'None were assigned to this expeditionary force,' said Dujek, adding, 'that is . . . officially.'

Tayschrenn smiled at the addendum. Yes, he considered, who knew how many had been sent secretly, all to keep an eye on them and report back to Surly. He cleared his throat, offering, 'Are you asking for volunteers?'

'You stepping up?' Dujek answered, a new edge to his voice.

'Well, I don't wish to . . . however, yes. I am.'

The Fist appeared quite startled. 'Really?'

'Yes. Any rational analysis points to my doing so.' And he shrugged. 'Therefore, I shall.'

'And I,' put in Nightchill from the entrance. Tayschrenn dipped his head in acknowledgement of the support – though not certain of the motive for it.

Dujek shook his head. 'Gods,' he murmured, 'I'm about to dare lose the Empire two of its most powerful assets . . . Kellanved will have my head on a platter.'

From the rear, Hairlock put in, 'I notice you're not sending the Sword.'

'There's only one Sword,' the Fist answered reflexively.

At this, Tayschrenn caught Nightchill's eye and raised a brow. *Well, there's us put in our place.*

206

Chapter 14

GLINITH APANAR, ABBESS OF THE SANCTUARY OF CABIL, Guardian of its Inner Holies, sat in her dungeon cell far in the depths of said Sanctuary waiting for her death. She had disappointed the Guiding Council of the Faith one too many times and Ortheal Leneth, Proctor of the Faith, had ordered her arrest.

She paced the tiny cell – four small steps – arms crossed, fingernails biting into her biceps. It was that bitch Giandra, or Gianna, whichever! It was all her doing. Losing the spoiled High Priestess once was one thing. But losing her twice? Gross negligence – in the words of Ortheal.

So she waited, knowing that when death came it would be in the dark, and quick. No ceremony. No one else present. Only her executioner.

She had played the game; risen to heights unimaginable from her wretched beginnings. Abbess! A seat on the Guiding Council of the Faith! But now she had lost. Ortheal had been waiting for an excuse like this. Now he would replace her with one of his dimwitted followers, and with the Celebrant firmly under his sway three of the seats would be in his grasp.

Steps and a key rattling in the lock. Glinith raised her chin, shoulders back. They might smear her – but she would have none question her courage.

The door opened and Glinith blinked, blinded by the bright glare of a lantern. She half-shielded her eyes, squinting, then stared long and hard, confused. There stood not a guard, but the short and paunchy form of Mallick Rel, lantern in hand.

She tried to peer past him, up the hall, stammering, 'Master Rel, Overseer of Coin . . . not whom I was expecting . . .'

He sighed heavily, sat on the cell's bed, which was simply a platform of cut stone blocks slightly higher than the rest of the filthy floor. He patted the space next to him. 'We have, I think, much to talk about.'

She sat, barely daring to hope. 'Am I – that is, is there to be a reprieve?'

He pressed his fingertips together, his fat-ringed eyes half-lidded. 'I *may* have it in my power to spare your life.' She nodded eagerly. 'However . . .' and he frowned, examining his fingertips, 'I would expect certain things in exchange.'

She straightened, still nodding. 'Name them.'

'Loyalty,' he said. 'Your complete loyalty and dependability. I would, after all, own your life.'

She crossed her arms to hug her thin chest tightly. *So. An offer from Rel. Well . . . better this one's creature than Ortheal's.*

She knew the Proctor of the Faith was a fanatic who would stop at nothing to further the creed, but this one – this one struck her as one of those giant bloated jellyfish one sometimes encountered at sea: a monster that slowly enmeshed everyone and everything in its tentacles and before anyone came aware of it they were numbed and trapped in his power. This one, she knew, was far more dangerous than Ortheal.

'You have it,' she said.

He raised a pudgy pale hand. 'Careful. One must not be too hasty here. It seems to me that you must make a choice: you can choose to remain and face a clean death, or, you can leave this cell with me.' The hand clenched. 'But! If you leave with me – there will be no turning back. No change of heart. No questioning.' He now looked to her, blinking heavily. 'Is this clear?'

For the first time Glinith felt the full, dreadful, deathly purpose of this man and she almost faltered. *This one hides the true depths of his frightfulness well,* she realized. *And he has chosen to reveal it to me now because he knows I will either be dead or his.*

She bowed her head. 'I am yours, Mallick Rel.'

A sombre nod in answer. 'Very good. I believe you have chosen well.' He picked up the lantern. 'Come with me then.'

She almost laughed. 'We are to just walk out? Now? The two of us?'

He paused in the hall. 'Yes.' He frowned anew. 'Is this a change of heart I detect? A questioning of your choice?'

She bowed her head once more. 'No. I do not question.'

'Very good. Come, then.'

She followed. They climbed the stairs from the lower prison to a landing that sat halfway up the long route ascending to the upper, main, prison. Here Mallick paused and extended a hand indicating that she should wait.

'What is it?' she whispered. 'Guards? Ortheal's Faith Militant?'

He motioned for her silence, and, remembering his warnings, she clenched her mouth shut.

After a long wait in the dim light of the lantern, plus the two guttering oil lamps on the stone landing, a new light came hurrying onwards down the staircase that circled above.

Glinith tensed, expecting, as she'd warned Mallick, Ortheal's Faith Militant, his fanatical soldier-priests. But she was quite shocked when the figure hurrying down the stairs emerged as Ortheal Leneth himself, the Proctor of the Faith. He was not alone of course, as he never was: accompanying him was his loyal guard, a great hulking mailed lieutenant named Crena.

Ortheal stabbed out a finger. 'What is this? The Purser of the Coin interfering with matters of the Faith? With matters under my authority?'

Mallick bowed to the man. 'The Abbess should not be treated so. She is the Guardian of the Inner Sanctuary. The most extreme mysteries of the Faith.'

Ortheal closed upon Mallick; the finger stabbed out again as if to impale the man's fat chest. 'Do not lecture *me* on the mysteries of the Faith – you mere coin collector! I see what is happening here. You would tempt her to your counsel, to your true demeaning of the Faith!'

Mallick nodded thoughtfully as he walked to the very edge of the winding stone staircase down. 'And when Crena brought word to you of my coming here, of my intent, you rushed over immediately to put an end to this.'

Ortheal laughed. 'Of course! You have gone too far this time,

Mallick. I will have the Celebrant denounce you for this.' He smiled his satisfaction. 'The two of you may even share a cell.'

'I think not.' And Mallick tilted his head towards the descending stone stairs.

Crena surged forwards, and, taking the Proctor of the Faith by the collar and the rear, lifted him and tossed him down the stairs.

Glinith stood frozen, horrified, unable to block out the meaty thumps and cracking of bones as flesh struck stone, as Ortheal rolled and tumbled on and on down the winding staircase, seemingly without end. Finally, the echoing, sickening noises of the descent ceased, and Mallick turned to Crena. 'It seems that the Proctor of the Faith, hurrying to see to important matters in the prison, has taken a fall. Do see to him, won't you, dear Crena?'

The huge fellow grunted and lumbered down the stairs. Mallick tapped his fingertips together, waiting. Glinith simply stared, quite beyond words. And all along she'd thought *she* was the hard one? She shook her head. Gods and daemons! It appeared she'd made the right choice after all.

Presently Crena returned and he growled, 'Ortheal is dead.' He knelt to one knee and Mallick extended his hand. 'Mael welcome the new Proctor of the Faith,' Crena announced, and he kissed the man's limp fingers.

Glinith's own hand went to her throat. *Quite. Welcome to the new Proctor.* She, too, knelt before Mallick and kissed his fingers. 'Mael watch over you,' she blessed.

'Indeed, indeed,' Mallick murmured, sounding almost gratified.

*   *   *

Hessa sat at the lip of one of the southern portals and threw stones over its edge. The mountain floated now – at least in this section of its bulk – some two arm-lengths over blackened rock that steamed, broken here and there by gaps where molten red lava churned sullenly only to cool and blacken itself.

Escaping was frankly moot now. Anyone attempting it would burn to death unless they kept to one of the routes, or roads, kept passable for the K'ell Hunters to come and go. Problem was, they were full of K'ell Hunters.

Their chance had come and gone it seemed. Now they were at the mercy of an insane, sickened Jaghut seemingly at death's door. The best they could hope for, she supposed, was him dropping dead. However, from all the stories and legends she'd heard, these Jaghut had a way of clinging on.

Footsteps behind brought her attention round.

Hyde was sauntering up the hall, kicking rocks and tearing at a piece of dried meat. At least they wouldn't starve to death. The Che'Malle had stores of dried meat for themselves that they could scavenge from. Hyde stopped just behind her, peered over and down. 'Singer wants ya.'

She sighed, levered herself to her feet. 'Fine. About what?'

'How should I know?'

It was the now familiar long walk back up to the main control chamber. Hyde dragged behind, now pulling with both hands and teeth at the shred of dried meat. Hessa hoped it wasn't human.

Inside, she found Turnagin and Ayal waiting with Singer. The Jaghut looked positively ill: leaning back against a metal wall of levers, dabbing at his mouth, his eyes red and sunken. Upon seeing her his animated smile quirked anew. 'Ah!' he exclaimed. 'We're all together now.'

'Not quite,' Ayal growled.

'Yes,' Hessa added, 'I haven't seen Corbin in some time. Do you know where he is?'

'He will join us shortly,' Singer answered. 'I was more worried about you. I thought that perhaps you'd tried to run off.'

'The K'ell Hunters would get me,' Hessa answered.

Singer nodded, grinning, well, crazily. 'Quite true.'

'So what's this all about?' Turnagin asked.

'We are close to full power,' Singer announced. 'Soon we will be able to begin the sequence to fully lift the mountain.'

'How high?' Hessa asked. 'Like the Moon's Spawn?'

A savage coughing fit took Singer for a time, hunching him over, but he rose, nodding and wiping blood from his mouth. 'Well . . . like that, but not in kind. Just a man-height, I believe. The Che'Malle must be able to jump in and out, you understand. It is a different, perhaps far older, mechanism of the K'Chain Che'Malle. Some speculate a precursor to their floating fortresses.'

'And then?' Turnagin asked, warily.

Singer nodded. 'And then you are done. All done. You may go with my thanks – and your collected riches.'

'Just like that,' Hessa put in.

The strange tilted smile remained upon the Jaghut's mouth. 'Indeed. Just like that. Oh!' and he raised a finger. 'I almost forgot. I do have one more thing.' Reaching aside, he drew out a cloth-wrapped object about the size of a small box. 'Your friend, Corbin. He tried to escape.' Singer threw off the folds of rag to reveal a human head – Corbin's severed head.

Ayal jumped to her feet, backing off. 'Hood damn you!'

Hessa's hand went to her sword. 'What have you done?' she demanded.

'It was what he did,' Singer explained. 'He tried to run off. He built a box on top of the sledge, filled it with gemstones, and headed north. He'd even rubbed himself with rotting meat to disguise his scent. But the K'ell Hunters intercepted him of course.' He touched his nose. 'They have your scents and can't be fooled. He was where he shouldn't have been. The head was all I could salvage.'

'And you expect our cooperation?' Turnagin breathed, pale with disgust.

'Or your heads will sit here – yes.'

'You've made your point,' Hessa cut in, her voice under savage control. 'May we go?'

'Of course. Just don't go too far,' and Singer laughed again, which descended into a cough, and he staggered off, hunched, breathing raggedly.

Once the Jaghut was out of sight, Ayal snarled in a low voice, 'We have to get out of here.'

'That was not the intent of his lesson,' Turnagin put in, rather dryly.

'So what do we do then?' Hyde demanded. He looked to Hessa. 'What'cha gonna do about this, cap'n?'

Hessa eased her hand from the silver wired grip of her Daru-jhistani steel sword. 'Corbin made his choices. Paid his price. I intend to get the rest of you out of here alive. *That* is my intent.'

Ayal backed away even further, shook her head. 'Fat lotta good that did Corbin.' She waved Hyde to her. 'C'mon. Singer mentioned the sledge. Maybe they dragged it back.'

Hyde brightened. 'Damn! A sledge fulla gemstones. Holy Burn!'

'Don't go where you shouldn't!' Hessa called after them. 'Dammit.' She looked to Turnagin. 'And you? What of you?'

'I will remain.'

Hessa raised her eyes to the ceiling in utter frustration. 'To what end, Turnagin? What could you possibly hope to accomplish?'

'As I said – to listen, and to learn.'

'Learn what?'

A wintry smile raised the mage's lips. He reached into his robes and drew forth a tube of wood with holes carved down its length. This he put to his lips, set hands to the length, and blew a faint note.

Hessa fought the urge to snatch it from the man's hands. 'Gods, man! Do you really think you could—' She peered round, expecting a K'ell Hunter to come charging in at any moment. 'He would kill you the moment he suspected.'

'I *am* being circumspect.'

'Fine, yes. But do you really think you have a chance?'

A fatalistic shrug. 'Do you have a better idea?'

Take the gemstones and run? she wondered. Like Hyde and Ayal? Or try to fight back – to stop this madness. 'The Malazans are coming. Let them deal with this.'

Turnagin shook a negative. 'We've been over this. They'll need someone on the inside. Someone who knows what to do.'

Hessa turned away, pacing. 'So you say! Fine! We'll see. He still needs us for now.'

'For now,' Turnagin agreed, but as a warning, not assent.

* * *

Blues stood at the edge of the Jhek makeshift camp, facing east. He was not officially on guard duty, but pretty much everyone kept a wary eye out. He was hungry, footsore and dirty. In short, he was in the field again, and felt comfortable once more, thank the gods. It was frankly so much simpler – plain direct problems and goals. Not at all like the periods between where roles were unclear and there seemed nothing, yet at the same time a vague sort of everything, to do.

A presence nearby and he glanced over: Gwynn had come to join him. He felt no irritation – over the course of the garrison duty he'd come to dislike the fellow, but now, in the field, he respected the man's skill and directness.

Both now faced the ice-waste plain to the east 'So, you've met your bird-woman,' Blues said.

'And we know the cause of the disruptions,' Gwynn added.

'So . . . we're done.'

Gwynn did not answer, and Blues remained silent as well; both studied the wastes and the layers of shifting black and white smoke above. In the corner of his eye Blues saw Gwynn tapping a finger to one of his crossed arms. In that silence the two came to an understanding and an agreement regarding what lay beyond and what to do. Blues kicked at the half icy, half boggy moss and grasses. 'Well, let's go give them the bad news,' he told Gwynn.

Back at camp they found Black and Jacinth at their cooking fire; the two looked up eagerly as they approached. Jacinth, in her quilted cloth and leather haubergeon, her long and wild mane of auburn hair loose, straightened and gave a fierce nod. 'We headin' out tomorrow?'

Blues and Gwynn exchanged a glance. 'Yeah . . .' Blues began.

'Good!' Black cut in. 'We ain't even on contract here!'

'We're going to reconnoitre the mountain,' Gwynn said. Blues winced at his bluntness.

Black and Jacinth gaped at them. Finally, Jacinth answered, her voice flat, 'We're gonna what?'

'We can't just walk away,' Blues began – both Black and Jacinth glared their silent commentary. 'We need to know their plans. Their intentions. Yes?'

Black waved a dismissal. 'Let the damned Malazans handle it.'

'Should we?' Gwynn asked.

Jacinth eyed the man warily. 'What do you mean by that?'

'I mean that perhaps we shouldn't stand by and let the Malazans study such power. What if they mastered just a fraction of it? What might that mean for us?'

Now Black and Jacinth exchanged glances; Black exhaled noisily. 'But what about linking up with Shimmer?'

'She can wait,' Blues answered. 'And, by the way, she'd support this.'

'We're still not on contract,' Jacinth pointed out.

'I will pay,' called a woman's voice and they turned to see the

214

Bird Priestess approaching. She wore loose robes, her usual cloth scarf across her eyes, her greying hair wild about her shoulders. Four bear-warriors accompanied her.

Blues smiled his appreciation, yet said, 'Pay us with what, Priestess? I'm sorry to say it, but you have very little.'

She nodded her agreement. 'This is true. However – I offer payment. A king's ransom, in fact.'

Gwynn now eyed her quizzically. 'And where is this proverbial ransom?'

She pointed to the north-east. 'I offer half the legendary fortune of the mountain.'

Black and Jacinth barked out laughter. Blues let out an admiring breath but shook his head. 'We haven't agreed to storming the damned place.'

She tilted her head in a very bird-like manner. 'Perhaps a more subtle approach?'

Gwynn looked up as if struck by a thought. He bowed his head to her. 'You are wise now, little one. Wiser than us all. That is the answer, of course.'

'What is?' Black asked, rather befuddled.

Gwynn opened his hands as if it were obvious. 'If they are all that the legends say then we cannot possibly defeat them in battle. We must look for another way.'

'And you make it sound so damned easy,' Jacinth answered, scoffing. 'Then the treasure will be ours.' She shook her thick mane of reddish hair. 'Skinner wouldn't touch this.'

'But Shimmer would,' Blues answered. He turned to the priestess. 'We accept.'

She inclined her head. 'My thanks. And the thanks of my people.'

Black crouched at the fire. 'Don't like it one bit.'

'Look at the bright side,' Jacinth offered.

He squinted up at her. 'The bright side?'

'Sure. Kill a Che'Malle and you can take the Black the Greater name from your brother.'

He probed the fire. 'That's true. But just so you know – I really am the Greater.'

'Sure,' she grinned back. 'Sure.'

Gwynn and Blues accompanied the Bird Priestess to her tent. On the way Gwynn observed, 'Your timing was rather providential.'

215

She nodded. 'I saw you talking and knew you were discussing whether to leave. I hurried over to make my offer.'

'You intuited all this?' Blues said, quite impressed.

'Yes. And,' she smiled, quite mischievously, 'I am also a very good lip reader.'

* * *

Tayschrenn examined the twenty infantrymen and scouts Dujek had assembled and shook his head. 'No.'

'What d'y'mean, no?' the Fist growled. 'Best we got.'

'I mean no.' He almost continued on to say, *I'll not take these troopers to their deaths*, but caught himself in time. He invited Dujek aside and lowered his voice. 'They'll just get killed.'

'Maybe – so might you.'

'They'll only slow us down.'

The Fist scratched his chin, eyeing him. 'I'm thinkin' maybe the opposite.'

He was fast losing his patience. 'Why? I thought we agreed: just Nightchill and I.'

'I ain't sending either of you in without minimal – *minimal* – protection. Kellanved would toast me alive if he found out.'

'I don't think either of us needs protection.'

Dujek waved his hand. 'Fine. Escort. Call it what you will.'

Tayschrenn realized he would get nowhere with this and so clamped his mouth shut. He gave a curt jerk of assent. 'Fine.' He'd just leave them behind at the first opportunity.

Dujek saluted the party of scouts and tribals, men and women, and marched off. Nightchill, nearby, rose from her crouch. Walking up came Tayschrenn's two minders, Missy and Ute, both wearing rucksacks.

'What's this?' Tayschrenn demanded.

'We're comin' too,' Ute answered – neither looked happy about it.

'No you're not.'

'It's our place,' Ute answered, glowering.

'No.'

'Time's passing,' Missy observed, in a rural drawl.

Tayschrenn turned away – they'd be safe with their fellow troopers.

216

He and Nightchill led, the party following double-file. It was early morning. They had decided that night and day had little difference for the K'Chain Che'Malle who, accounts implied, relied more on sound and scent than sight.

Mists quickly obscured the ordered Malazan lines behind. The ground was rocky. Pools of bubbling water lay here and there. Tayschrenn could already feel the heat penetrating his sandals.

Both he and Nightchill had their Warrens raised – though just which Warren she accessed he didn't know. He knew only she was damned powerful. He used his Thyr magics to shift the heat away from himself as he went. It then occurred to him that perhaps he ought to extend such protection to the entire party, and, grudgingly, he did so.

This gave him an idea and, motioning for Nightchill to follow, he set out towards the nearest open field of crackling, smoking rock. To their credit, the escort followed without balking, or even a murmur. In this fashion, keeping to the hottest, most inhospitable stretches of half-molten rock, he hoped to escape any encounter with the Che'Malle.

Perhaps it worked, or the Che'Malle weren't out patrolling, or even interested in them, but they made good progress. The fields of baked and yielding rock now became open pools of viscous, glowing lava. These he simply had to weave between as best as he could.

Occasionally, Nightchill raised a hand to signal a pause and all stopped. Tayschrenn strained to penetrate the dense sifting clouds of smoke and steam; sometimes he thought he glimpsed the silhouettes or smudge of one of the beasts passing. He didn't know the source of the sorceress's ability to passively sense the monsters, but he had to trust it as he dared not reach out actively with his Warren.

The dark bulk of the mountain reared closer, now filling the entire north. At a larger patch of solid bare rock surrounded by wide pools of churning magma he signalled for a halt. He turned to the huddled escort. 'Who's in charge here?' he asked.

'Ah . . . you are, sir,' a woman whispered back. Her face was smeared near black with soot and glistened in sweat.

Tayschrenn bit back a frustrated retort. 'Fine. We'll spend the night here. Arrange watches.'

217

The woman saluted. 'Yes, sir.'

Aside, Tayschrenn turned to Nightchill. 'I'm surprised we've made it this far.'

'They seem to be few in number.'

'Or we're beneath their notice.'

She nodded. 'There is that. I find it encouraging that you are capable of such a thought,' and she moved off to peer in the other direction.

He stared after her, frowning. What by all the gods and dae-mons did the woman mean by that?

As night deepened a peculiar phenomenon emerged to the north. A line of brightness, a hair's thickness from this distance, glowed a brilliant whitish-blue across what Tayschrenn assumed would be the base of the mountain. It was so intense he couldn't stare dir-ectly at it.

'What is that?' he asked of Nightchill.

The sorceress's own gaze was narrowed. 'We must get a better look.'

'Tomorrow.'

'Yes. A quick glimpse would suffice.'

'Just the two of us.'

She nodded.

In the morning, Tayschrenn waved the huddled escort to him. 'Nightchill and I will reconnoitre ahead, alone. We'll try travel by Warren. Remain here until we return.' A trooper raised a hand. 'Yes?'

'How long?'

'How long what?'

'How long you gonna be gone?'

Tayschrenn allowed himself a nod. 'Good question.' He peered at the dim glow of the rising sun behind clouds. 'Noon. If we're not back by noon, decamp.'

The troopers eyed one another. Clearly, they were wondering just how on earth they would navigate the magma fields without them. Yet a female trooper saluted, 'Very good, sir.'

Strangely, the gesture made Tayschrenn feel vaguely ashamed. He offered Nightchill a nod and she invited him onwards. Almost immediately they entered her Warren, or at least the active effects of wherever it was she drew her powers from. The landscape now had a ghostly, monochromatic look to it, as if it had somehow lost its full dimensionality.

It then occurred to him that perhaps it was *they* who had lost their full dimensionality and were travelling now between realities, or realms. In which case the source of Nightchill's powers might be extremely dangerous indeed, for it might draw upon the miasma, the inchoate chaos that most agreed lay beneath and between the realms.

The effects were unlike anything he'd ever heard reported. Not the swirling darkness of Rashan, nor the blurred smokiness of Meanas, nor the breathless rushing of Serc. They were, however, crossing ground very quickly. He asked, 'Why couldn't we have travelled this way the entire trip?'

His voice had a strange, hollow, echoing quality to it.

'Bringing anyone with me is quite taxing,' she replied, frowning her irritation. 'And there are energies here from these Che'Malle, or the edifice – clawing at me.'

They travelled in silence for some time after that. Finally, Nightchill snarled something, a curse in another language, and threw down her hands. 'This is as close as I dare go. These Che'Malle presences are interfering with all magery – even my own. The emanations from this structure almost overwhelmed me.'

Tayschrenn nodded; he'd been wincing for some time himself and knew he'd be nursing an awful headache on the morrow.

They returned to the plain and now stood upon a small outcropping of solid stone surrounded by black and sullen orange-red fields of heaving, turgid molten rock. The heat beat at them through the protective shielding of Thyr he'd thrown up. Choking smoke wreathed them, steam scalded with every breath.

Then the swirling clouds parted, briefly, and they glimpsed the narrow sword-like blade of brilliance, and that the mountain clearly floated upon it.

Nightchill cursed again.

'Does this mean it will float off?' he asked.

'No. The accounts speak of it . . . hovering. An entire mountain, near weightless. It is its means of movement.'

'Movement! It could really move? I thought that all just . . . poetic.'

'They move. I know this. And the ground they travel over is

reduced to this – to blasted molten rock. They destroy everything in their path.'

'Kellanved must be told.'

'Yes. We must find out if they—' Nightchill silenced herself, squinting to the east.

Tayschrenn saw it as well: four lumbering silhouettes through the mists, heading off at speed.

'Only one thing could provoke an alarm like that.'

'I fear they've been found.'

The sorceress waved him off. 'Go! I will try to delay them!'

Delay them? By the gods, woman, you are either insane or courageous beyond understanding. He swept himself up in his Warren and hurled himself back to the camp with all speed.

He emerged into bedlam. A single towering K'Chain Che'Malle, one of the warriors he understood to be named K'ell Hunters, had discovered the troops and was in the process of slaughtering them. Half lay sprawled dead already, torn apart by ghastly deep eviscerating slashes. The rest huddled behind shields while attempting to hack at the beast's legs.

Strangely, the first thing he felt was outrage: *How dare they! These are my people. They look to me for protection! And I . . . I have failed them.*

His collapse now made sense to him. His earlier confrontations and duels had, for him, frankly been mostly intellectual exercises. Engagements of cool, balanced calculation and measured evaluation of capacity, magnitude and anticipated threat potential.

This was no intellectual exercise. Nor could he count on this opponent breaking off or fleeing to fight another day. This was flesh and blood, life or death. Rage and passion. All the shrieking corporeal demands that he thought beneath him.

It's not about the mind, Nightchill had told him. Now he understood. Hairlock had slapped his stomach – it's in the gut. The sight of these men and women torn apart gave it to him, and, for the first time ever, he surrendered himself to it.

He reached down into blind searing utter power and drew it to him. All without thought for the limitations of his flesh, of his capacity, or the multitude of usual qualifications that go with measured bleeding of the Warrens. The agony pulled his own scream from him to add to those of the scouts falling beneath the creature's scything blade, and he released it all in one detonation that took his consciousness with it.

*

Cloaked in Elder Night, Endest Silann studied the Che'Malle arte-fact. For though an apparent natural object, the mountain was now something sculpted, manufactured. An alien artefact. A brother to the much smaller one his Lord had taken as their cur-rent abode. Yet older – cruder. An early attempt at a transportable hive?

Endest pondered whether to move closer: such a rare opportun-ity for study, after all. And such knowledge to be gained! He tilted his head, deciding. Yes, perhaps the potential reward was worth the risk. His Lord would expect some interesting fact or observa-tion gleaned by him, would he not?

Yes, he—

An eruption of astonishing magnitude staggered him, even here, half-shielded in Galain. He squinted, a hand raised before his face: the source, a mortal Warren? Astounding! Such depth of power. Such an unleashing! He retreated further into Galain, considering: an Elder; a mortal mage of such prowess; and the K'Chain Che'Malle . . . He shook his head. *No.* He was no warrior mage. He was a scholar – powerful in his own way, of course, but not one for fighting.

No, someone else would be needed here. Someone not unsettled by such odds. Comfortable in battle. An Andii willing to walk into a very hive of K'Chain Che'Malle.

Endest smiled and nodded to himself. Yes, he believed he knew the very person. Yes, she would not be deterred by such odds. She would do very nicely indeed.

He withdrew completely into Elder Night to begin his journey. Shreds of utter lightlessness swirled, faded, and he was gone.

221

Chapter 15

Blues crouched with Gwynn, Jacinth and Black on the plain of barren burned-over black rock that surrounded the Che'Malle mountain and he winced in searing, burning pain. He winced, pained, not only from the scale of the threat they faced, but from the strange alien energies streaming constantly from the object. It was like a rasp being drawn across his mind, over and over.

Yet he gritted his teeth and kept to his D'riss Warren, the magery of stone and earth, to deflect the roasting heat surrounding them. Meanwhile, Gwynn cloaked them in shifting shades of darkness, obscuring them even more within the mists and vapours. Apparently, the scholar-mage had read that the Che'Malle could somehow see light humans could not. Blues glanced to him and saw by his pinched brows and tight slit lips that he, too, was feeling the tearing and clawing at his mind.

'What use can we be here?' Black complained under his breath.

'We don't know yet,' Blues answered, his voice taut with hurt.

'What d'y'mean we don't know yet?'

'That's why we're here,' Gwynn put in. 'We're reconnoitring to find out.'

The contrary winds gusted then, momentarily clearing the air between them and the still distant bulk of the mountain itself. A brilliant whitish-blue light glowed across its base, like a sword-blade. Blues squinted hard. 'Am I wrong,' he murmured, 'or is that thing floating?'

'It is indeed,' Gwynn affirmed.

'Floating? Bullshit,' Black put in.

'Will you all shut up?' Jacinth snarled.

All knew not to answer back when Jacinth used that tone.

Gwynn nodded ahead. 'Movement.'

Several of the enormous beasts, vague mist-wrapped shapes, were hurrying southwards.

'We been sniffed out?' Black grumbled.

'Doesn't look like us,' Gwynn said, 'but something's stirred them up.'

'We wait it out,' Blues said.

'Quiet,' Jacinth warned again.

Everyone was silent. Blues's legs became cramped from crouching. He tried stretching them out, one at a time.

'How long—' Black began when an eruption from the south made him wince. 'What the—'

Blues fell over. The power of the magical blast numbed him for an instant. Unbelievable! He held his head almost as if to assure himself that it was still in one piece. 'Some kind of Che'Malle weapon?' he gasped.

'No,' Gwynn answered, his voice cracking. 'Human. Purest Thyr I've ever seen.'

'Gods! Whoever that is I don't want to face them.'

'Agreed.'

'We should withdraw,' Jacinth said. 'So much for a quiet look-see.'

The four turned and began carefully inching their way back west. Blues now struggled to keep hold of D'riss to drive the heat from them. Black hissed his pain and Jacinth almost yelped when to steady herself she touched a rock with her bare hand. '*Blues . . .*' she snarled.

'Working on it,' he gasped.

Stones and gravel clattered ahead as a shape reared before them: twice their height, bulking more than all of them combined. A long, snouted, saurian head turned their way. Twin blasts of air from wide nostrils sent the mists curling.

Oh, yes, Blues remembered, *their sense of smell is far better than ours too.*

Black unlimbered his wide, rectangular shield. Jacinth drew her longsword in both hands. 'Get us out of here!' she yelled to Gwynn.

The pale mage backed away. Night-dark shreds of Rashan guttered before him as he struggled to re-grasp his Warren.

The creature's man-length scimitar blade of pitted iron swung to crash against Black's shield. Metal grated and screeched. Black grunted, yielding a step. Jacinth went for a leg but the K'ell Hunter warded her off with a swing of its tail.

Blues stepped in to take the next attack on his stave, attempting to shift the blow aside. The impact numbed his arms and the length of hardened wood snapped from the strain. Black got a cut in with his bastard sword.

'*Gwynn . . .*' Blues warned, backing off.

Filaments of darkness now spread about them – even half-obscuring Blues's vision. Black took another crashing blow on his shield and was driven to one knee.

Jacinth moved to flank the beast, but Gwynn yelled, his voice hoarse with strain, '*No! Stay close!*'

The shreds coalesced. They thickened into wrapping winding sheets. Jacinth howled her blunted rage. Blues couldn't see a thing. The crash of another punishing blow sounded, then the ground shifted under his feet and he staggered, almost falling.

They now stood further west. Gwynn was on his knees, panting and gasping. Blues sympathized; he felt as if he would vomit.

Black examined the deformed and battered piece of metal on his arm then tossed it aside. Jacinth angrily slammed her sword home. 'We could've taken it,' she snarled.

'Not our mission,' Blues supplied.

Black took Gwynn's arm and helped him up then half-supported him as they started walking west. 'So what was the point of that?' he asked conversationally, almost cheerful. 'Did we learn anything?'

'Yes,' Gwynn responded, now back to his usual dry and sombre self. 'We learned that Tayschrenn *can* deliver destruction – if pressed sufficiently.'

'The High Mage?' Blues answered. 'You think that was him? I've never seen anything like that from him. That kind of ferocity.'

The pale mage, now even more ghostly ashen, nodded. 'Oh, yes. That was him.'

'So we're done then,' Black said, waving everything off.

'No. Not necessarily. We also learned that Blues can get us in and that, theoretically, I can get us out. Therefore, we have our approach.'

'We're going back?' Black said, his voice rising.

'Good!' Jacinth affirmed from the rear.

Gwynn rubbed his head as he half staggered. 'We just have to, ah, recover.'

Blues nodded his hearty agreement then wished he hadn't. Just moving his head induced jabbing needle stabs in his brain.

* * *

'Pirates!' the ragged youths shouted. 'Pirates!'

At the path leading down to the shore, Imanaj eyed the pack of youths with affection. Well did he remember similar street games of his childhood, save that the enemies were always invading soldiers from another of the Seven Holies.

They jumped about him and waved their driftwood swords. 'Pirates?' he said, wonderingly. 'I am a stranger, I admit. But I understand that Falar prides itself upon the absence of pirates.'

A tall boy, sand-covered, in a torn tunic, peered up at him. 'Real pirates,' he said, breathlessly. 'People from Belid's seen 'em 'n everything!'

Imanaj tilted his head. 'You've heard this? How?'

''Cause they're here! People fled the pirates. They landed on the east shore.'

'People? With boats?'

A girl chimed in: 'Fishin' boats, rowboats ... whatever they could flee with. Them pirates burned all the galleys – strange, hey? Who would do that?'

'Leaving them with the only battle-ready boats?' Imanaj mused aloud. 'I'd call that a distinct tactical and strategic advantage.'

The children gaped at him. 'Foreigners are weird,' the girl solemnly announced, then they all ran off in a pack, yelling and screaming.

Imanaj carried on down the track. He came to a group of locals, mostly fishermen and women, all clustered close together in heated conversation. 'What is this news I hear of pirates?' he asked.

All jumped as if scalded, then hunched, embarrassed. 'Sorry,' one fisherwoman said. 'We're a bit on the hook – you could say.'

'Understandably,' Imanaj offered. He added, 'Just who are they, do you think?'

'Probably those damned Seven Cities scum,' one fisherman growled.

All eyes turned to him, then to Imanaj. The fellow paled, mouth working – rather like a gaffed fish, Imanaj thought. 'I mean,' he said, 'you're from Aren, yes?'

Imanaj nodded.

'Then some uncivilized Seven Cities scum from Ehrlitan . . . or Ubaryd . . . obviously.'

'Of course,' Imanaj soothed.

All the fisherfolk nodded, letting out held breaths. Imanaj gave a bob of the head in farewell and continued on.

At the shore he headed round the narrowing edge of the strand to where his boat lay on its side, its ribs exposed where repairs remained ongoing. Imanaj was no nautical man, but the vessel lay there rather like a large, dead sea-beast. Hands on hips, he stood for a time searching for the shipwright. Then loud and wet snoring led him round the vessel to the shade where the fellow lay propped up against a pile of timber, an earthenware jug hugged to his chest.

Imanaj leaned forward and slowly, very gently, eased the jug from the fellow's grip. He took a delicate sniff of the open spout then pulled his face away, grimacing. He set it aside and returned his attention to the shipwright. He kicked the fellow's foot; tapped it again.

The shipwright snorted and smacked his lips. His hands searched for something at his chest, patting and feeling about. Rather like two blind questing crabs? Imanaj thought to himself.

The eyes, deep in their wells of fat, opened, only to narrow quickly, pained. The fellow shaded his face, peered round, raised puzzled eyes to Imanaj. 'Yes?' he croaked.

'How is the work proceeding?' Imanaj asked, as mildly as he could.

The shipwright slipped a hand under his soiled shirt to scratch his wide belly. He smacked his lips. 'Fine. Just fine. Making good progress.'

'I see. Excellent. And this wood here. Timbers for the hull and such, I assume?'

'Un-huh.'

'Again,' Imanaj said, 'I am no builder of boats – but I notice the wood is not in fact *on* the boat.'

226

The man's eyes had found the jug and he was staring at it where it sat just out of reach in the sand, and licking his lips.

'Good craftsperson? Shipwright?'

'Hmmm?'

'The timbers?'

The fellow roused himself. He strained to rise, failed, fell back. 'Hunh? The timbers? Ah! Each has to be sized and shaped, y'know. Individually.' He raised a hand that shook; he quickly tucked it down to his side. 'Delicate exacting work that.'

'I see. Then I should leave you to it I suppose.'

'I'll get right on it,' the fellow assured him.

'Good.' Imanaj turned and walked off a few steps then stopped to turn back. The shipwright had dragged himself to the jug and now froze, one hand on it, his eyes wide on Imanaj. 'A thought, sir. Perhaps you'd best hurry with your work . . . what with the pirates and all.'

The fellow peered round – as if the aforementioned criminals were sneaking up on them now, intent upon stealing his jug – then he snorted a laugh. The laugh grew to belly-shaking jollity. He slapped his side repeatedly. 'Pirates!' he guffawed, shaking his head. 'Everyone knows there ain't no pirates in Falar!' He waved Imanaj onwards. 'Foreigners,' he chortled to himself, 'don't know nothing.'

Imanaj felt his lips pursing, his jaws tightening ever so slightly, but he dipped his head in farewell instead and made his way back to the inn.

That evening, after a meal of boiled crab and scallops, he ordered a glass of what passed as the local wine and returned to studying the view over the bay in the sunset, as was his habit. He watched for a time only to frown and turn in his chair to where a group of what could only be described as island elders was standing, behind him. He returned to the view. 'Yes?'

The five crowded round to the opposite side of his small table. One, the most bearded of the lot, pulled over a chair and sat.

'May I help you?' Imanaj asked.

'We hope so,' this elder answered – though, elder may be too broad a category, Imanaj reflected, as being a young man he tended to regard anyone older than himself as an elder.

'You are the island priest, are you not?'

The man inclined his head. 'Rendren. Priest of Mael.'

'Of course you are.'

'We were wondering, good sir. If we could hire you.'

'Hire me? Whatever for?'

Rendren raised a helpless gaze to his companions; they glared at him to continue. He cleared his throat. 'Well . . . you are a fighter, sir. Are you not?'

'I was. Now I am a sailor. A traveller.'

'A traveller? Really? Well, sir . . . if I may . . . you have not done much travelling of late. You've been on our isle for near a month.'

'I'm waiting for my boat to be repaired.'

Three of the four fisherpersons snorted and raised hands to cover smirks. The priest peered back at them and frowned his disapproval. 'I see, sir. If I may, then. It would seem you are of two minds over your travelling.'

Imanaj shifted his gaze from the darkening horizon to the priest. He saw there very keen and penetrating eyes and he realized he'd made a beginner's mistake – he'd underestimated the person opposite. Luckily, he wasn't on the duelling sands, else it might have spelled a very deep cut indeed. He waved away the other four folk. 'Your friends can leave us.'

Rendren nodded his agreement and urged them off. They went, grumbling and shuffling.

'A glass for my guest,' Imanaj called to the host.

'I really shouldn't,' Rendren protested – weakly.

The glass arrived and Imanaj poured him a drink of the local red. The priest took a sip and shuddered. 'I knew I shouldn't have,' he said.

'So, I am of two minds regarding my travel?' Imanaj prompted.

Rendren nodded again, cleared his throat. 'I have been watching you. You have what some might call a sensitive spirit. One may even say the spirit of an artist.' Imanaj half-smiled at that. Indeed, in Aren he was considered an artist. An artist of the sword. 'Therefore,' the priest continued, 'you say you wish to journey to see the wide world, but at the same time you worry that perhaps you shouldn't depart. Being content to remain here is your resolution to this conflict.'

228

Imanaj tilted his head, considering. He returned his gaze to the purpling night. 'Perhaps. Perhaps this is so . . .'

Rendren leaned forward, cleared his throat once more. 'And since you *are* here . . . perhaps you could help defend us?'

Now Imanaj frowned, his contemplative mood ruined. 'No.'

'No? Just like that? We are fisherfolk here. How can we defend ourselves against these pirates?'

'Don't.'

'Don't? Please explain yourself.'

Imanaj shrugged. 'Do not fight them. Let them land, search about, take what they will, and go.'

Rendren shook his head wonderingly. 'Just like that? Let them do what they will? How can you – a fighting man – advocate such a philosophy?'

Imanaj shrugged again. 'I am no longer a fighting man. I have forsaken violence. It is . . . only destructive. It is no way of life.'

Rendren nodded his agreement. 'I understand that. And I approve. However, what if these pirates have come to kill? What then?'

'A good point. What to do in the face of violence? Moot, however, I believe. Pirates are just thieves – thieves with boats. They are rarely killers. No profit in it.'

Rendren sat back frowning his disappointment. 'Then what would you suggest we do?'

Imanaj sipped his wine. 'I suggest you do not provoke them.'

The priest pushed himself from the table. 'The islanders will not like to hear that.'

'It is a pragmatic and practical solution. And these folk strike me as a pragmatic and practical people.' Imanaj nodded farewell to him. 'It has been good speaking with you, priest. Perhaps we can talk again.'

The fellow eyed the night-dark waters of the bay, his expression worried. 'I hope we shall never have the need.'

*   *   *

Abbess Glinith had always cared nothing for these council meets. They had never been anything more than a pantomime act. And now that Mallick had control of every seat – excluding the

Celebrant, of course, as he was oblivious to all manoeuvrings – the theatre of it had, in her eyes, turned to ridiculous parody.

They sat in silence, she, Nuraj and Mallick, awaiting the arrival of the Celebrant. There was really nothing for them to say; they would merely listen to Mallick.

The door opened and the Celebrant's aides helped the frail old man into the chamber and to his seat. He peered round with his red rheumy eyes, his gaze going to Ortheal's seat, but, finding the squat toad-like shape of Mallick there, he blinked, perhaps confused, and lowered his gaze.

'Brother Ortheal will be missed,' Mallick began, in a conciliatory note.

The Celebrant nodded ponderously and slowly. 'He will indeed! To be shorn of his wisdom in this, such a perilous time, is a great tragedy. If anything, the man was too dedicated to his calling.'

Mallick was tapping his thumbs together on his stomach, eyes downcast. 'Quite,' he murmured. 'Now, on to the pressing business of these pirates.'

'Pirates!' the Celebrant snorted. 'To think of that! In this day and age.' He shook his head and Glinith had to admit that the man's great mane of white hair lent the gesture much gravity. 'Some Seven Cities natives getting ahold of a few boats and managing to figure out how they work, no doubt.'

'I believe the matter far more grave than that,' Mallick offered.

'Oh? How so?'

'Reports from my – that is, the Faith's – network of agents suggest these raiders represent far more of a threat.'

The Celebrant's thick white brows clenched together as he eyed Mallick. 'Well? Out with it, man. You know I have little time for such games.'

'These pirates are not behaving as pirates, or raiders,' Nuraj Senull, Guardian of the Faith, put in. 'They're behaving like invaders.'

'Invaders! Invade us? That's absurd! Impossible. These islands are ours!'

'They were someone else's once,' Mallick murmured, eyes downcast.

The Celebrant waved impatiently. 'Well, what are you waiting for? Send out the fleet! Crush them!'

230

Nuraj opened his mouth to answer, but Mallick interjected, 'Of course, Celebrant. Our next order of business.'

Rentil nodded again, rising. 'Very good.' He waved a blessing over them. 'I leave you to it, then. Sweep them from our seas!'

'It shall be done,' Mallick murmured.

The Celebrant's aides helped the old man from the chamber and the door closed behind them. Nuraj turned a sceptical eye on Mallick. 'And just how is this to be done?' he asked, brow arched.

'One way or another,' Mallick answered, his murmur now more of a clenched-lip hiss.

Glinith started at that comment, eyeing the rotund fellow much more sharply. Mallick raised his gaze and met hers – she looked away from his dead flat eyes.

'Plans are afoot to retake the High Priestess, Abbess. I trust that once we have her under our control once again there will be no repeat of her previous escapes, yes?' Glinith nodded fiercely and Mallick leaned back, his eyes sliding away. 'Good. Because should she slip from your grasp once more I will have to test the edge of the Blade of Offering on your neck. Am I clear?'

Glinith swallowed hard, nodding again. She'd made the right choice in following this creature, but now she knew she must sail lashed to him – all the way to Mael's Deep, if need be.

* * *

They kept the *Glimmer* in place as a platform for their salvage operations through sea-anchors and lines tied to nearby rocks. There was plenty to eat: all the shellfish, octopus and squid one could want. Fuel for cooking and fresh water were the shortages. When necessary, Brevin sent two crew members out in the *Glimmer*'s tiny rowboat to head to the isle of Lurk for firewood and to collect water from streams.

Most of the youths were eager to dive, but Gianna only allowed the older, more experienced boys and girls down. Yet to date they had little to show for all their efforts. A few plates and cups, corroded iron and bronze fittings. No great chest brimming with coins as in legends and stories; which didn't surprise Gianna as she knew those particular items could only be found in such fanciful tales.

What she hoped to accomplish was to find the debris field – the direction and terrain the wreckage had spilled over as it was tossed about by the currents on its way to finally settling amid the silt and sand. Then she could focus their efforts.

Nearly two weeks passed in this fashion. Ships went by, but always far off; everyone avoided the dangers of the Cut. It was a surprise then when a shout went up from the watch of a vessel approaching.

Gianna had just come up from a recent dive and was drying in the sun. She went to captain Brevin's side where she stood watching, her eyes shaded. 'A galley,' Brevin said. 'Sails luffed. In the grip of the currents.' She shouted up to the lookout: 'Any sign of crew?'

'None,' came the answer.

'She came unmoored, maybe?' Gianna asked.

'Unlikely,' Brevin growled. 'Boats are not something you just lose.'

'Derelict?'

'Unlikely as well. Looks like she'll be passing our bows.'

'Will you try to salvage it?'

The captain shook her head. 'We have our hands full just staying in place. She's on her way out to sea, Land's End Ocean.'

'A shame.'

'Is there nothing you could do . . . ?' Brevin asked her.

Gianna knew she meant with her Ruse Warren. 'It's possible,' she allowed. 'But it would take an awful effort to drag that in.'

'Ah. I see.'

'I wonder—' Gianna never finished her comment as at that instant an arm closed about her neck and a dagger point pricked her throat.

'*Do not move!*' a voice hissed in her ear. 'No tricks from you, mage of Ruse.'

Gianna peered about the deck: men and women in the blue robes of Mael now held curved blades to the necks of Brevin and several of the youths. To port, the derelict vessel shimmered, blurring, to reveal a crewed galley, under rudder, and well oared.

'Ruse is not the only Warren practised in Falar,' the one holding her laughed in her ear.

'Damned Mockra filth,' she snarled.

232

Another low laugh. 'Try anything and these little ones will pay the price . . . understood?'

Gianna gave a fierce, stiff nod. 'Understood.'

'Good.' The fellow released her, but kept the knife point pressed to her back. 'Now we go.' A gesture and whipping winds rose about Gianna.

'Wait!' she called, but to no effect as the winds lifted her from her feet. Her surroundings blurred. The air moved so violently about her that her breath seemed pulled from her lungs. Her vision darkened. *Serc!* Didn't they realize she wasn't used to this?

Then a thumping landing on wood where she lay dazed. The winds relented and she fought for breath. 'Tie her in chains and weights,' she heard the fellow order and her hands were taken and manacled at her front. The iron manacles were yanked to pull her to her feet.

She now stood on the deck of the other vessel, as did six of the youths.

'Full sail!' the fellow who'd grabbed her ordered. 'Deese, work the sails.'

A heavy-set woman in the blue of Mael grunted her answer. Gianna turned to the fellow to see that he was actually quite short and strikingly skinny. 'Who *are* you?' she asked. 'Faith Militant?'

Mocking laughter from the men and women. Sailors were now locking similar manacles and weights to the youths. Gianna realized that if she tried messing with the boat she and they would likely drown – as was the intent. 'Bounty hunters?' she offered. More laughter. The sails boomed and Gianna was nearly pulled from her feet as the bows dug into the water. The woman, then, was the mage of Serc and she was now using that Warren to hurry them on their way – their return trip to Cabil, no doubt. 'Who are you then?'

The fellow leaned back against coiled line and heaped canvas. He offered her a wink. 'We are with the Faith Militant – you're right in that. Each of us has particular, ah, *talents*, that put us in a special corps. A special corps for special jobs. Ortheal had no time for us. Not, ah, *orthodox* enough for him. But Mallick! Much more practical, he is.'

'Mallick? The Master of Coin?'

'Master of the Faith now. Ortheal's dead. Met with an accident.'

She'd seen the greasy fellow now and then. Even been introduced. Hadn't ever talked at length with him, not that she'd wanted to. She'd heard enough rumours of the fellow though – they seemed to swirl around him like whirlpools. A man to avoid, was the recurring message.

This fellow slapped his thighs, rising. 'So, sit back and enjoy the voyage. Don't try any Ruse trickery. I've heard you can hold your breath for an astonishingly long time . . .' he jerked a thumb to the file of chained youths, '. . . but can they?'

Gianna sat back against the galley's low rail. Damn them all to Mael. Then she almost laughed: kidnapped again! It was almost embarrassing. And thinking of it, this lot reminded her of those foreign siblings – mages also. Operatives of some kind. Working for whom? She never did find out. Should she warn this crew of them? She was, after all, of Falar in the end.

She shook her head. No. Why should she do this gang any favours?

* * *

Tayschrenn awoke to a stunning, lancing headache and the noises of camp: men and women talking, barked laughter, the hammering of a portable anvil. His head, he was sure, was that anvil. Closer, however, came a steady shush such as of stone on iron. Carefully, he raised his head – his vision starring and temples throbbing – to peer about his tent. The girl, one of his minders, Missy, sat nearby, honing a rather large knife.

'What time of day is it?' he croaked, his voice hoarse, throat dry.

The girl started, surprised, nearly dropping the stone. 'Oh! You're awake! I'll tell the commander, sor.' She charged from the tent before he could ask for a glass of water.

Gingerly, he sat up and lowered his feet to the ground. Then, wary of splitting his head, he rose and crossed to a table holding a jug of water and a brass washbasin. He drank from the jug, emptying it.

'Back with us I see,' came a growl from the tent flap and Tayschrenn turned to acknowledge Fist Dujek.

'Indeed.' He made an effort to straighten his dirtied, torn and singed shirt and vest.

Dujek touched his fist to his chest. 'From all the reports – well done, High Mage.'

Tayschrenn cocked a brow. 'Oh?'

The Fist tilted his head, studying him. 'You don't remember?'

'No.' He held out the jug. 'Could I have more water, please? I am quite dehydrated. The heat and exertion, you understand.'

Dujek leaned out the open flap. 'More water for the High Mage!' He returned his attention to Tayschrenn. 'You saved the lives of the escort. Those that survived the initial attack, that is. All agree you appeared and blasted the K'ell Hunter to ashes and charred bones.' He cleared his throat into his fist. 'Then you fainted – from the effort, I suppose.'

Tayschrenn's other minder Ute entered, a waterskin in hand that he offered to Tayschrenn, murmuring, 'High Mage.'

Tayschrenn took the waterskin. 'Ute, yes? Good to see you survived.'

Ute bowed. 'Thanks to you, High Mage.' He backed away then hurried out.

Tayschrenn eyed Dujek. 'And then . . . ?'

'Then, apparently, even unconscious you still kept up your protection from the deadly heat for the escort while they carried you out. And on the way you blasted another of the Che'Malle to burnt bones.'

Tayschrenn drank a long pull from the waterskin then wiped his mouth. 'I did, did I?'

'All the patrol agrees.'

'I don't remember a thing.'

Dujek shrugged. 'Maybe it'll come back to you.' He gestured to the entrance, inviting Tayschrenn out. 'In any case, I'm pleased – you've made my job much easier.'

'Oh? How so?'

'The old saying is that an army marches on its stomach, which is true. It also holds as firmly as its morale – and you just secured that. So . . . my thanks, as the commander of these troops.'

Tayschrenn ducked out the opening. 'That was not my intent, commander.'

'I didn't ask you what your damned intent was,' Dujek growled, tight-lipped.

Just outside the opening a squad of soldiers straightened, saluting, Missy and Ute among them. Tayschrenn answered the salute.

As he passed each trooper the man or woman half-bowed, murmuring, 'High Mage.'

Only then did he recognize them as the survivors of the escort who'd accompanied him to the mountain. He answered each with a nod.

Dujek urged him onwards to the command tent.

'What is it?' he asked. 'I am not quite recovered, you know.'

'A briefing,' the Fist answered. 'The Sword has news for us.'

'Indeed? News?' Personally, Tayschrenn didn't think the Sword could possibly have anything of interest to say, but he would be politic and indulge the fellow.

Within the command tent awaited the captains, Ullen and Orosé, Hairlock, Nightchill and, of course, the Sword.

When Tayschrenn entered, the Sword straightened, brushed back his long night-black hair and saluted him, saying, 'Well done, High Mage.'

For an instant Tayschrenn wondered if he was being mocked, but discarded the idea as this swordsman, Dassem, struck him as incapable of sarcasm. So he nodded, allowing, 'I did what was necessary.'

'You did more than that, High Mage,' the Sword answered, with odd emphasis.

'Indeed,' Nightchill added.

Tayschrenn nodded to the sorceress. He had things to say to her as well – but they would wait.

Dujek went to a table and poured himself a glass of watered wine. 'You have a report?' he prompted Dassem.

'I do. I was out with my best scouts, four Wickan youths, when we spotted another party approaching the mountain. From the west.'

Hairlock spat to the ground. 'Damned Jhek!' He pointed to Dujek. 'I warned you!'

'Not the Jhek,' Dassem cut in. 'Others.'

'Who?' Dujek asked.

'A party of four,' Dassem continued. 'Three men and one woman. One fellow a very big, heavy-set fighter; the woman equally big, with a mane of red hair; the second fellow pale and slim, dark-haired. A mage. The fourth was a mage as well, but has the broad build of a swordsman. He carried a stave and two fighting sticks. They communicated by hand-signs. And I know those signs.'

'Yeah?' Hairlock asked. 'Our troopers use signs as well.'

'Not our signs,' Dassem said. 'The hand-signs of the Crimson Guard.'

Dujek coughed on his wine. 'The Hood-damned Guard? What're they doing here?'

Hairlock pointed north. 'I'd say they're after what we're after – the mountain.'

Tayschrenn nodded at that. 'Makes sense. There are secrets there. If they could master some of it . . .' He eyed Dujek. 'We can't let them grasp such power.'

Dujek answered the nod. 'Understood. You'll have to go back. Make certain that doesn't happen.'

'I will accompany him,' Dassem put in. 'If it is the Guard, I will face them.'

'I will return as well,' Nightchill said.

'Very well,' answered Dujek, rather unhappily. 'I suppose if you three can't manage it, I don't know who can.'

The tall sorceress appeared to take this as the end of the meeting for she stood and crossed to the entrance. Tayschrenn headed after her. Ullen and Orosé bowed to them both.

He found he had to hurry to match the sorceress's pace. 'What was your meaning?'

'Meaning?'

'Regarding fighting the K'Chain.'

'I think my meaning should be obvious enough.'

'And it is?'

She regarded him sidelong, her lips quirked. 'It has been some-thing of a standing debate as to whether humans could ever face down any of the Elders. Kellanved has somehow managed it – by trickery, no doubt. And now you have as well. It took its toll, I know, but your body will get used to it. Few have ever managed it anywhere. You Malazans will have to be careful now; you're enter-ing into a larger world.'

She tilted her head then, in farewell, and walked off. Tayschrenn watched her go. 'You Malazans', she'd said. The wizard Hairlock's words and warnings returned to him then. What was this strange woman's game? Yet she had encouraged him, hadn't she? Was this outcome what she'd wanted all along? Why? He shook his head; frankly, he had enough to concern himself with. Such as how to do what he'd somehow managed to do . . . more than once.

Chapter 16

Hessa and Turnagin were dozing, stupefied really, in the punishing heat and steam of the central chamber when Singer came limping in. 'Now is the time!' he called. 'Rouse yourselves!'

Hessa blinked heavily, rising. 'What?'

'Time to begin the final commands!'

She pulled Turnagin up. 'Now? Why the rush after all this time?'

The Jaghut's features, scar-twisted and uneven, twitched madly, then he dismissed the question with a wave and turned away. 'Come. Your friends have arrived – few in number but great in magery. I am surprised. We must finish our work while we can!'

'And Hyde and Ayal?' Hessa called, following.

'They have been briefed in their duties! Now it is your turn.'

She eyed Turnagin. He shrugged, then called: 'So after this we can leave?'

'Yes, yes!' Singer pointed to a large panel supporting numerous levers and toggles. 'You, captain, here. This is your station. Mage, follow me.'

Hessa studied her 'station'. She was dubious. Many of the controls were far beyond her reach. She dragged over a heavy box they used as a stool and found that by stretching she could just reach the highest. She brushed the strange metal of the panel and hissed, pulling away. 'It's hot!' she called. 'Singer? Hello?'

'*Wait!*' came the shouted, impatient answer.

She heard the murmur of Singer giving instructions to Turnagin.

After a while the dragging, limping brush of Singer's uneven footsteps approached. He emerged from round the corner of a central station. Hessa waited, arms crossed.

The Jaghut eyed her stool then nodded his approval. 'Good. Now, I will mark the instruments as before – numbered one and onwards for the sequence, yes?' She gave a curt nod. 'And I will mark the up and down changes in charcoal as well, yes?' He dotted the panel-face in scratches from a burnt stick.

She gave a curt bob. 'And the sound cues?'

He shook his head, the tangled and matted mess that was his greying hair falling all about. 'No. This time I will call out your name as your cue – yes?'

She frowned, 'So . . . the first call will be one,' and she pointed to the lever.

He nodded, then coughed, the cough becoming a racking, shuddering, body-spasming gasping, and he half collapsed upon the panel, swallowing and dragging in great gulps of air. Blood wet his lips and chin, that he wiped away, panting.

Hessa eyed the fellow narrowly – just how ill was he now? Was this the end of him? Was he weakened enough? Her hand strayed to the silver wire-wrapped grip of her sword.

She saw his uneven, wild eyes upon her hand and he quirked a lopsided smile. 'I could still squash you like a mouse, child,' he growled. 'And your remaining crew . . . think of that.' She let her hand stray away from the weapon. He grunted at that. 'Mind your instructions,' and he banged a clawed hand to the panel. 'Now we commence!' and he hurried off.

Hessa watched him go, then, thinking of the searing hot metal, pulled out an old scarf, tore it and tied the pieces round her hands.

Shortly, the eerie, inhuman tones and notes of the Jaghut's instrument sounded out, loud and jarring. The hooting and droning continued on for some time. Between notes she heard Singer urging Turnagin to his tasks.

Then she heard a barked: 'Captain!' and she yanked on the first lever.

It did not budge.

She yanked again, but to no effect. The metal burned her palm. '*Captain!*' Singer called again, urgent. '*The lever, damn you!*'

'It won't move!'

'Pull harder!'

240

She raised both her feet up onto the panel face and pulled. She yanked with both hands, her back arching. The massive metal piece ground downwards and she released it, panting and waving her seared hands in the air. *Gods! There are seventeen more!* He made it sound so easy – but then, he was about as strong as a Che'Malle, wasn't he.

She waited, recovering, while Singer droned on and hooted long low notes. Her next turn came as he shouted once more – she bunched even more cloth round her hands and set a foot up on the panel, pushing up with all her might. This lever creaked like rusty iron as it ground its way up and she wondered what to do should one seize? The machines certainly seemed ancient and abused enough for that.

So much for Singer's ambitions perhaps.

Then yelling – Singer abusing Turnagin; seems the man made some error.

'Captain!' the Jaghut called. 'Put that switch back to its original position!'

Hessa groaned, but complied. By the Lad's luck, the mechanism did not seize.

More blasts of alien notes, and Hessa, waving her hands to cool them, realized she'd heard nothing from or of Hyde or Ayal, and was struck by a sudden nasty suspicion.

'Now move that switch again!' Singer called.

'Where are Hyde and Ayal?' she answered defiantly.

'The lever, captain . . .'

'*Where?*'

Silence, then a curse in some guttural language. 'Faugh! Damn this! They are far below, with the engines. Overheating is our greatest danger now and they are in place for that.'

Hessa considered; it did seem plausible. She took hold of the lever. 'Very well. But if I find they are dead nothing will stop me from drawing on you.'

'As you choose – the lever, now, please.'

Grudgingly, she strong-armed the switch up.

The rest of the series proceeded without incident. Hessa now had all her spare rags and clothes wound round her hands. The heat even increased and sweat stung her eyes. Steam burst into the chamber and the ringing and clanging of machinery – or alarms, she did not know which – assaulted her ears.

241

Finally, she reached what appeared to be the end of her marked duties and she slumped down, leaned back against the tall station, yelped at the biting heat, and rolled away.

Rising, she staggered to where she believed Turnagin and Singer had operated. Clouds of scalding steam billowed and she waved her hands, squinting. The entire structure shuddered then and she fell against another of the tall stations.

And where were these damned K'Chain Che'Malle anyway? she wondered.

Eventually, after some searching, she found Turnagin amid the clouds of steam. He was peering down at a dark heap at his feet: Singer.

She approached and saw that the Jaghut still wasn't dead – as she'd hoped. He was prone, his chest labouring, one eye rolling wildly, one edge of his mouth crooked and limp. 'We're done,' she told him. *As are you.*

He grinned his toothy lopsided smirk, croaked, 'For now.'

'What do you mean "*For now*"?' She drew her sword and pressed the point to his side. 'Perhaps I should kill you now.'

Turnagin gently pushed the blade aside. 'He's dying without our help.'

Singer chuckled weakly. 'And you'll never get out of here without my say-so. The K'ell guard every opening. No one enters or leaves – unless I order it.'

'Then order it!'

A shake of the head. 'Not yet. Not *quite* yet. But soon. Very soon.'

'Stop playing your damned games – what more is there to be done?'

A sly smile now crept up the Jaghut's ravaged features. 'The final commands. I simply must decipher the last series to engage all the mechanisms and systems.'

She and Turnagin exchanged uneasy glances. 'Final?' Hessa asked.

'Well,' Singer said, 'I believe so. I've never done this before.' And he laughed, coughing.

With a wave of disgust Hessa dismissed the madman. She urged Turnagin to follow her. 'Come. We're wasting our time here. Let's find the twins and make certain they're safe.'

Singer's wet laughter followed them down the hall for an eerie length of time.

* * *

Gianna spent her time manacled to the side of the Mael Faith Militant vessel. The youths were chained belowdecks. The second day they saw smoke to the north, perhaps over Walk. The sailors and these Faith Militant mages all watched it, uneasy.

They also sighted two obviously foreign vessels. Both of these passed them by without so much as a cursory look. Gianna peered about for the short, skinny mage, and caught his eye. 'Don't they see us?' she asked.

He nodded, his gaze returning to the second vessel.

High it was, and broad across the beam. Gianna knew it would be slow and sluggish. No threat to a nimble Falaran galley. A modified merchant ship, perhaps, now bristling with armed crew.

'Making an entire ship invisible?' the mage answered. 'And maintaining the illusion? That would be quite the achievement. No, they just see a smoking derelict, looted and listing, of no interest.'

Before this Gianna had seen only a handful of foreign vessels in all her life. 'Where are they from?'

'The south. Malaz,' he answered, distractedly.

Gianna straightened, fascinated; she'd heard so much of that distant land. 'They say the wars there have been terribly fierce.'

'They have been,' the fellow answered. 'We may be looking at the losing side.' He rubbed the knife-edge of his nose, his gaze slitting even further. 'Or the winning . . .

'Deese!' he shouted. 'We must make Cabil in all haste!'

'I'm working on it,' she called back in irritation.

The skinny fellow now regarded Gianna. 'You may have chosen the worst possible time to flee the temple, priestess.'

'What do you mean?'

He raised his chin to the now distant foreign vessel. 'I mean we may be facing an invasion.'

Gianna couldn't help herself; she burst out in laughter. 'I'm sorry, but that's absurd.' She waved to the ship. 'Those fat scows? They're no threat to our navy.'

'I said an invasion – not a naval dance.'

She frowned at him, puzzled. 'What's your name, anyway?'

He shrugged. 'Call me Lee.'

'Well, Lee, I think you're getting a little carried away.'

He ambled off. 'We'll see.'

Later that day their galley was travelling along the coast of one of the hundreds of tiny, unnamed isles of the archipelago, when they rounded a headland to the open water of a small bay. Within the bay several local fishing boats were under attack by two more of these foreign vessels.

The foreigners – huge, broad merchantmen – had the fishing flotilla trapped within the bay and were in the process of methodically setting them aflame with a hail of fire-arrows.

Gianna stared for a time, horrified. Who would be so vicious? Fishing craft weren't war ships. 'Do something!' she yelled to Lee. But the small fellow just watched, arms crossed, rubbing his chin. 'Do something!' she yelled again.

He shook his head. 'Not our worry.'

She turned to the bay and summoned her Warren.

'Ware!' Deese yelled.

Instantly Lee was there at her back, his knife at her neck. 'Don't reveal our presence,' he hissed. 'My job is to get you to Cabil – and I intend to succeed. Mallick does not accept failure.'

'*Bastard*,' she grated.

She felt him shrug.

He held her there until the curve of the shore had hidden the ugly scene from sight. She angrily shook him off. 'You disgust me.'

Again, he appeared indifferent. 'Looks like this is war, girl. No time for niceties.'

The next night they approached Cabil Isle. To Gianna's surprise there was no sign of this invading naval force. Surely they'd target Cabil, wouldn't they? The near capital of the region? Yet none were here; they seemed to be all spread out, striking everywhere. Everywhere except any stronghold, such as Cabil.

She sensed various Warrens now raised about her. The mage group that was holding her communicating with the fortress, no doubt.

They slowly edged up closer. So close, the tall sea-walls now

244

reared over them like dark cliffs. She eyed Lee, uncertain. He just grinned back. The other three of the Faith Militant mages emerged from belowdecks, the chained youths in tow.

Stone grated from somewhere nearby and now a dark opening was visible in the sea-wall. Gianna glared at Lee. Of course! A secret way for their secret coming and going.

Deese, the mage of Serc, manipulated the winds to bring them still nearer the narrow opening. Two tall and burly priestesses waited there. Gianna recognized them as proctors of the Sanctuary, her old minders.

Lee knelt to her shackles, then hesitated, eyeing her. 'Now would be your last chance. And you might try to take it. But remember,' and he pointed down, 'the boys and girls are still chained – what will be their fate?'

'You are a bastard,' she grated, and he laughed again.

Knife at her neck, he straightened her there, at the side. Her chains remained, her weight, a large stone, dragging over the deck. While the vessel rose and fell, bumping the sea-wall, the priestesses beckoned. Lee, with a knife jab to her back, urged her to step out to the stone platform.

She went, snarling curses against the fellow and wishing she could drown him. The proctors took her arms and yanked her along a narrow tunnel to stairs. Here they told her to take up the stone weight, which she did, cradling it in her arms. She was exhausted by the time they reached the end of the long ascending stairs, her arms numb.

The Abbess herself, Glinith, met her at the top, looking as severe as ever, her long greying hair pulled back tight, her thin arms crossed at her equally thin chest. 'Giandra! How pleased we are to see you again.'

Gianna just stared – long past the usual insulting banter. She let the stone fall with a crash that echoed through the halls. Glinith winced at the noise. 'Your dogs brought several children along too. Black-haired, as the Faith desires. What will become of them?'

The Abbess lifted her bony shoulders. 'They will serve the temple, of course.'

Gianna considered that a banality that covered any number of crimes, but let it pass without comment – she was finished with this woman.

Seeing her dismissal in Gianna's eyes, the Abbess curtly gestured her forward, along with the proctors. Gianna, however, refused to move; she pointed to the stone at her feet. Glinith angrily waved for one of the proctors to carry the thing. Gianna followed along, her chains rattling.

She was escorted back to her old cell. The proctor set the stone down just inside the threshold. Gianna held out her manacled wrists but the Abbess shook her head. 'A new regime, my dear. You're going nowhere.'

The Abbess swung the door shut and locked it from the outside. 'May Mael curse you!' Gianna yelled.

'Oh, you recognize him now, do you?' came the mocking answer.

Gianna kicked the door, then stood still, fuming, her arms heavy at her sides. Sighing, she knelt to pick up the stone and crossed to her bed. She set the weight down next to it and lay back to stare at the ceiling while she frantically tried to think of new schemes of escape. Finally, exhausted, her eyes fell shut and she slept.

* * *

Charts of the Falaran Isles were extremely rare in Quon Tali, and the ones imperial agents had managed to borrow from private libraries or temples, or confiscate if necessary, were all in extreme disagreement on many features of the region. The official Imperial map had been stitched together from these various sources – and not without serious debate. Still, some version was necessary. Even if it was compiled by clerks who'd never set foot in the region. As a result, Cartheron held the *Twisted* back while comparing the few original sources he'd managed to acquire.

Occasionally, Kellanved came below to squint at the vellum sheets, make knowing sounds and point here or there, at this feature or that piece of coastline, to shake his head and sigh. But quite quickly he would become bored and amble off, tapping the boards of the lower deck with his walking stick.

Cartheron knew they had navigated the eastern coast of Quon Tali, up the icy waters off the shore of the Great Wastes, and onwards to an apparently uninhabited coast of rocky cliffs and forest. This was Fenn on some of the Falaran charts, the northern half of the Quon Talian continent. But distorted – rather disgracefully so, for a seafaring people. Yet perhaps here was the clue: as navigators they were only interested in coastlines, and so those were recorded in great detail and accuracy; as for what might lie inland out of sight, its size or shape, or width or breadth, they could not care less.

He sighed himself and squeezed his grainy eyes. Fenn, therefore, or the Wastes, was often portrayed as small because it was unimportant to the Falarans, while the nearby island of Delanss was apparently significant, and therefore featured correspondingly large.

Cartheron rather suspected the opposite for their true respective sizes.

And mountains! These Falaran cartographers seemed inordinately fond of mountains. They were everywhere – even completely encircling the Northern Wastes on some charts.

He shook his head. They must think them visually impressive or something.

However, and he moved an ink-stained finger to Delanss island, mountains were shown here and the island was now just east of them, in plain sight. And where were these mountains? Highlands, yes, and some pointy hills, but true mountains?

He rather suspected these Falarans wouldn't know a real mountain if one fell on them.

He sighed again and tapped his quill to the vellum stack, leaning forward on his crossed forearms. All in all, a true mess. He was also beginning to think these Falaran cartographers had filled their boring evenings indulging that universal excuse: artistic licence.

Footsteps on the steep stairs and he straightened. Dancer ducked within, nodded a greeting. 'How goes it?'

Cartheron made a face and went to a side-table, growling, 'I need a drink.'

'That bad, hey?'

He tossed back a glass of watered wine, gestured to the cluttered table. 'Problem is, all these Falarans are sailors, so *they* know where everything is – why bother drawing it? Who needs a map if it's here?' and he pointed to his temple.

'So?'

Cartheron cleared his throat. 'So, we hang back. Avoid getting ourselves hemmed in somewhere.'

Dancer nodded as he eyed the heap of vellum charts. At that

moment, to Cartheron, he appeared a young man – a so very serious and grave youth with his hacked-short hair, thin face and wiry build. And Cartheron thought to himself: *This is who we, I, follow. Not the other one. The crazy one.* The one who he suspected would throw them all over a cliff to realize his ambitions.

But not this one. At least, that was the opinion he clung to.

'That's fine,' Dancer said. 'Kellanved wants us in open water. He wants them to come to us.'

'But what about this Jhistal thing?'

'It may just be a legend.'

Cartheron grunted, unconvinced. He'd encountered a few of those so-called legends in his lifetime, such as the T'lan Imass. 'Then we're close to a good spot,' he said, crossing to the table. He jabbed a finger to one chart.

Dancer closed to study it in the yellow lamplight. 'Between the Fenn coast and this other isle?'

'Yes. The added attraction is that we also close off the main line of retreat for our freebooter friends.'

Dancer quirked a smile and Cartheron, who saw little of him, once again had the impression of the youth the lad must have been. Lad? He was old now – they all were. 'Why the smile?' Cartheron asked.

'I think Kellanved will be pleased.' He gestured upwards. 'Let's go give him the news.'

'Very well.' Cartheron rolled up the sheets and tucked them away.

It was night, the sky clear. A sailor's treasure, Cartheron thought, eyeing all the stars. The deck deserted but for the night watch and the short and dark figure of the Emperor, humming to himself and rocking back and forth on his heels.

'Our Admiral suggests we hold near here,' Dancer announced.

Kellanved gave them a glance then nodded, thoughtfully. 'Very good. This should do fine.'

'You expect them to attack?' Cartheron ventured.

A mischievous smile flitted across the old man's wrinkled features. 'You could say that. I expect them to send their fiend here against us.'

Cartheron frowned his scepticism. 'Why should they do that? Against one ship? Makes no sense.'

The Emperor nodded. 'Oh yes. You do have a point, my friend. However, I count on the duplicity, mendacity, and plain turncoat dishonesty of our fellow men and women to take care of that detail.'

Cartheron sent a raised questioning eyebrow to Dancer, who only shook his head. 'I gave up long ago,' Dancer murmured.

Kellanved tapped his walking stick to the deck. 'Quite. If we are all done then, I will retire.'

Cartheron offered a half-salute and the Emperor ambled off towards the vessel's only stateroom, humming to himself.

'How long do we wait?' Cartheron asked of Dancer.

'As long as it takes.'

'You know our sea-bandit friends are probably setting up tinpot kingdoms and robber-baronies all over these damned islands.'

'I know.'

'And they won't want to give them up.'

A nod.

'So . . . what does our esteemed leader have in mind?'

A wince and a shake of the head. 'I'm still trying to work that out.'

Cartheron winced as well, and sighed. *What a damned way to run an invasion.*

* * *

Ullara stood wrapped in an old blanket at the edge of camp. She watched the mercenaries going through their preparations for their return to the mountain. This time Bellurdan would be joining them – against their own objections – and thinking of that Ullara bit her lip.

What would the Fenn say if their representative was killed? Would they blame the Jhek? It was a worry. She wanted the accord between the two peoples to stand. It was imperative for the future she planned for her adopted kind.

A future that would only work if she could maintain a sort of peace with the Malazans as well. At least, if not a peace, then a basic mutual grudging disregard would do – if she could arrange it.

And she believed she could; theoretically. If she dared reach out to . . . him.

But would he answer? Would he even remember her?

That silly little child-witch he knew so long ago in Heng?

Footsteps and the heat of someone close; she turned to see her newly recruited tribal mage Sialle next to her. And with her, the huge bulking shadow of her she-bear minder, Ursana.

Sialle crossed her arms, her wild mane of white hair tossing in the winds, her gaze on the mercenaries. She appeared unimpressed.

'I never thought I'd ever see or meet them,' the Seti shamaness said.

'The Crimson Guard?'

'Yes.' Sialle slowly shook her head. 'All those stories. The battles. If they're so good – why do they look like they've been dragged behind horses?'

'Because they hold nothing back and save nothing for themselves?' Ullara answered, studying the shamaness sidelong.

The girl flinched at that. She waved a hand. 'Hardly. They're mercenaries. They fight for pay. Not ideals.'

'Some,' Ullara agreed.

'In any case – I don't trust them. Perhaps I should follow along. Keep an eye on them.'

Ullara shook a negative. 'Not necessary. Stay with us and keep watch here, yes?'

The young shamaness gave a half-bow of assent. 'Very well. If that is your wish,' and she departed.

The she-bear commander, Ursana, watched her go, her expression sour. Once the shamaness was far enough off, she growled, 'I do not trust *her*.'

'I do – for now, in any case.'

Ursana grunted her scepticism. 'Why?'

'I suspect she's following her true loyalty – her blood. And she shares so much with the Jhek.'

'She is of these invading Malazans. She may be here to spy upon us.'

Ullara laughed, but affectionately. 'Believe me, Ursana, the Malazans do not need to plant a spy here among us to know what we are doing.'

The great hulking she-bear just rumbled wordlessly, then growled, 'And these invaders? What of them?'

'I suspect they are no invaders, Ursana.'

'You suspect? Why?'

'They do not behave like invaders. They are behaving like a people who do not wish to be where they are. They build no fortresses of occupation. No supply depots. Have established no routes of resupply. And, lastly, they do not have enough troops to occupy all this wide land.'

The tall and shaggy commander now lowered her gaze to the petite old woman at her side. 'You may be a priestess – but you talk like a true warrior.'

Ullara gestured to the sky. 'I've been watching for a long time.'

*

At their camp, Blues sat with Gwynn while Black and Jacinth checked their gear. 'Extra water,' he warned.

'I know,' Jacinth answered, huffing. 'That's the tenth time you've said that.'

Black rested his arms on his knees, his long night-black hair blowing about. 'Are we really gonna take this damned Thelomen with us?'

'Don't see how we can stop him,' Blues answered.

'He'll just stand out like a . . . like a damned giant.'

'You just don't like being the runt,' Jacinth observed, grinning wickedly.

'You just keep out of my way while I take down one o' these Che'Malle.'

'More like I'll hack one to bits then you'll come runnin' in and stab it in the foot and claim you did all the work.'

'Now that's not fair. Since when would I do somethin' like that?'

'Since north Tali.'

Black looked affronted. 'I held those heavies off!'

Jacinth laughed. 'After I took out most.'

Blues shared a glance with Gwynn and strove to keep his face flat. It was good to hear the banter again. They were about to walk into Hood's own threshold and needed to work themselves up to it.

Gwynn gestured aside and Blues glanced over to see the tall, unmistakable form of Bellurdan approaching. He waved everyone up. Jacinth stopped honing her captured Malazan longsword and thrust it home.

'Got that extra water?' Blues asked.

Jacinth rolled her eyes. Black patted the fat skins hanging at his side.

Gwynn nodded a greeting to the huge Thelomen. 'Ready then?'

Bellurdan nodded gravely. 'Yes. We should go.'

Gwynn turned and waved to where the Priestess stood watching. The woman waved back. 'I will keep watch!' she called.

'I'm all relieved,' Jacinth murmured, and started off.

* * *

Endest Silann found that tracking down the certain Tiste warrior he had in mind was not the difficult part. Approaching her was. For some unknown or possibly abstruse reason the woman haunted the very uttermost far-flung verge of Kurald Galain. A locale where few dared or even desired to travel. It took all Endest's dedication, and a measure of courage that surprised him, even to make the journey.

He came upon her at the Cliffs of Night, a storied, legendary location in itself. Here Night – the very Realm, plane, or Hold, call it what you will – ends, and is bordered, or circumscribed, or constrained, one may choose one's image, by the emptiness that surrounds all: Utter Void.

Not Chaos, mind you. That raw stuff of creation and all that may or can be. Void, rather. Nothingness. Emptiness. The place beyond.

Reasonably, then, he held back from that dreadful edge. She, however, stood upon the very crumbling cliff lip, hands at her back, peering down into the unfathomable emptiness. Pensive, perhaps.

He cleared his throat.

'I sensed your approach, Endest,' she answered, then turned. 'What in all creation would bring you so far from home?'

'You, Feral, as a matter of fact.'

Her familiar narrow and hard features twisted even more harshly in disbelief. 'Really?' She crossed her arms. 'Rather, I believe you are on some errand for your master.'

'Our master – surely.'

Feral raised one brow in dubious comment. Endest cleared his throat. 'Yes, well. Anomandaris knows nothing of this, truth be told. I have been given full autonomy in a certain investigation.'

Feral looked to the night-dark vault above and turned away. 'Spare me your academic investigations, Endest. I care not where this or that rare plant grows – or when some insignificant tribal chieftain lived.'

'This is a matter of some greater consequence, I assure you.'

He waited for Feral to ask after this matter, but she remained silent, obstinately so, it seemed to him. He continued, 'A hive of K'Chain Che'Malle have awakened.'

He saw her shoulders rise in a shrug. 'So? What is that to us?'

'You are aware, despite your voluntary exile, of the stirring of the Imass?'

'Yes. They say that sullen and unreasonably stubborn race walk the earth once more. But again, what is that to us Andii?'

'The selfsame human mage responsible for the wakening of the Imass is even now meddling among the K'Chain Che'Malle. And it is said he also has somehow gained command, or the allegiance, of the Hounds of Shadow.'

Now Feral turned, her head tilted and sharp eyes slit. 'The Hounds? In truth? A fell gathering of power.'

'A very potent Elder also has enlisted with him. Which, I do not know as yet. And a very formidable human mage of Thyr – one strong enough to face the Che'Malle.'

She was nodding, her gaze aside, thinking, then her raptor-like eyes fixed upon him. 'Why bring this to me?'

'My fear, Feral, is that should they be allowed to continue this pattern of meddling, this new power may constitute a threat.'

Now she laughed, throatily. 'A threat? You mean to us? Really, Endest. You think too much of these human wretches.'

'No, Feral. You have been away for a very long time. Think of what we see now.' He raised a finger. 'The Elder kind, the Hounds of Shadow, compelled – or somehow suborned.' He raised another finger. 'The Elder Imass commanded, somehow.' He raised a third. 'Now, the Elder race of the K'Chain Che'Malle awakened and this same meddler involved.' He raised his shoulders. 'Which Elder kind may be next?'

She snorted. 'Very well, Endest. I see your point. I will look into this – if only to measure these *so-called* powerful entities you so worry about.'

Endest felt his shoulders easing. 'Thank you, Feral.' Yet his words were lost in a rush of air as the woman had thrown her arms upwards and down, and in a surge of wind was airborne, changing, swelling, transforming in mid-flight into a sinuous winged dragon as black as the Void itself.

He watched her travel till he lost sight, and he sighed. Ever fond of her Soletaken form was Feral. A dragon few could match in ferocity and in might.

Chapter 17

IMANAJ SAT AT HIS USUAL SEAT OVERLOOKING THE COVE THAT held the main hamlet of War Isle. In the morning he watched the few battered open fishing boats head out. And, in the evening, he watched them return. He told himself he wasn't waiting for the inevitable; that it wasn't even inevitable. But, eventually, war did come to War Isle.

It arrived as a single foreign ship under oar easing into the cove. Even to his unsailorly eye the vessel's design appeared strange: fat and broad, high-sided, two-masted, yet fitted with oar-ports. Some strange variety of merchant or coastal cargo hauler he thought it. Only now it hauled crew, a large crew, male and female, and all quite obviously armed.

He remained seated even as the islanders first gaped at the vessel as it came, then hurried left and right scooping up children and their most precious possessions, running up and down the dirt streets of the hamlet. He sat even as the inn emptied in a crashing of chairs and general panicked yelling. And he was still seated when a clatter of booted footsteps came up the stone-flagged stairs to the inn and a gang of the armed foreigners arrived, to throw down a handful of gathered island residents. These islanders, hostages, Imanaj assumed, included Rendren, the priest of Mael, dishevelled, lips bloodied and cheeks bruised.

One of the raiders stepped up before Imanaj – the one who presumed himself their leader, he assumed. You could almost always tell which one of these shabby gangs thought him or herself a leader: the swagger, the posturing.

Imanaj sighed and looked away to the sea.

The raider gestured to Rendren. 'The priest here says you're some kinda dangerous man from up north. Is that so? You gonna give us trouble?'

Imanaj struggled with the fellow's barbaric accent and strange words, but made his way through to the man's meaning. He edged his head in a slow negative. 'No. No trouble.'

The fellow threw his hands wide and looked to Rendren. 'There! You see? This one's got sense. Unlike others I could mention.'

Imanaj now looked to this raider chief: the rings on his fingers were bloodied, the short but wickedly sharp and curved weapon shoved through his sash was also bloodied. He was lean and wiry: a hungry wolf of the sea, murderous and hard. Imanaj grudgingly re-evaluated his estimate of the fellow. *Not* just a bandit with a boat. 'Your accent is strange,' he said. 'Where are you from?'

'The south,' the bandit leader answered, easily enough. He pointed to the inn's central hearth. 'Stoke that fire up. Get it nice 'n hot.' He waved to one of his crew. 'Drag one o' these fine upstanding citizens over to the fire there, Gaff.'

'What is your name – may I ask?' Imanaj enquired.

The raider eyed him up and down, his gaze hardening; but then he shrugged. 'Rollo. Captain Rollo they call me.' He leaned over to take the drink that sat in front of Imanaj and downed it, only to cough. 'Hood's bones! That's fine spirits. What's it called?'

'Ikkor.'

'Ah yes. The famous ikkor of Falar. Heard of it.' He examined the stoneware jug. 'Lives up to its reputation.' He motioned towards the inn's rear. 'Collect all the kegs and barrels in there for the journey, lads and lasses.'

Seven of the gang headed back to ransack the inn. Captain Rollo sat at Imanaj's table as though they were old companions. Imanaj studied him sidelong: worn and much-mended leather hauberk over a tattered shirt, unkempt black hair hacked at all lengths, a sun-darkened and lined face given to frowning. Imanaj had no idea how well he might wield that short blade at his side, but the fellow appeared used to violence – and, it followed, killing.

'How's that fire going, Gaff?' Rollo called.

The raider working the embers responded, 'Gettin' nice 'n hot.'

'Good. Stuff that citizen's left hand in there would you?'

Imanaj's brows rose; he'd seen much in his days as a city champion, but never plain torture.

The priest, Rendren, lunged forward. 'No!'

He was kicked down by a raider. Rollo strode over and pressed a foot to his back. 'You have something to say, priest?'

Rendren shook his head. 'Please . . . we have very little.'

'Ah! Then this fellow *does* have something.' Rollo waved for his mate to continue. The raider grabbed the fellow's wrist and pushed his hand towards the glowing embers.

'Tell them,' Imanaj called out.

The mate paused, looking to him. As did Rollo. The captain gave him a nod. 'There, you see?' He kicked the priest. 'A man with sense.'

The villager, perhaps the local hetman or an official, Imanaj didn't know, was sweating and gulping in air, but he said nothing. He appeared more dazed and stunned in disbelief than afraid.

Rollo sighed, motioning, 'Get on with it.'

The moment the man's hand entered the hearth he cried out his agony and Imanaj shouted even louder, 'Your bag of coins or baubles aren't worth your hand, fool!'

The mate released the villager who slumped, weeping, gripping his seared hand. The stink of burnt flesh wafted through the inn.

'Show them, Barnow,' Rendren said, almost begging.

The villager, Barnow, jerked a pained nod. The mate pulled him to his feet and pushed him into the arms of two others of the crew who dragged him off into the darkness.

Rollo now peered down at Rendren. He stroked the stubble at his chin. 'And what of you, priest? What of Mael's tribute?'

'Sapphires!' a raider called out.

'Emeralds!' another added.

Rollo nodded to this. 'Yes. So the stories go. Falar's many isles' annual tribute to Mael.' He prompted the supine priest with a kick. 'And pearls, too. Especially pearls – so I've heard. Question is . . . where?'

'I will give you what you want,' the priest answered, his head hanging.

'Now?' Rollo demanded.

'Yes,' Rendren panted.

The captain gestured to his crew and many hands yanked the

priest to his feet. Crew members pulled him off towards the path, but the priest held back, digging in his feet, as he glared down at Imanaj.

'I thought you a wise man,' he ground out, 'but I see now I was mistaken . . . you are just a coward. A coward hiding behind words.'

Imanaj's jaws tightened, and he refused to look to the man. Rollo barked a laugh and waved the priest off. Two of his crew dragged him away. Rollo sat again at Imanaj's table. He poured himself another drink from the stoneware jug of ikkor.

After downing the drink and smacking his lips, Rollo told Imanaj, 'You're smart. That's what you are. Why risk yourself for these peasants?' He waved dismissively. 'You're right. They're not worth it. How about joining up? I could always use another sword.'

Imanaj edged his head in a negative. 'No . . . as I said, just passing through.'

Rollo lost his half-smile, set his glass down. 'Too bad. If you're not one of the wolves then you're sheep. Sheep get sheared.' He held out a hand – his other going to the grip of the shortsword shoved through his sash.

Sighing, Imanaj slowly, and carefully, edged back his chair and rose. Nearby crew shifted into ready stances, hands at weapons. He reached into his shirt and pulled out his coin bag. This he dropped to the table in a loud clink of metal, then he turned to go.

'He was right,' Rollo called after him, 'the priest.' Imanaj paused to glance back. 'You are one of the sheep.' Imanaj's jaws worked, but he kept on.

Out in the cool dark of the night, he paused and stood staring out over the glimmering waters of the bay. Was he running away after all, he wondered? Nothing more than that in truth? Not a rejection, but an evasion? Perhaps he was wrong to think he could escape – it seemed that no matter where one went, people and human nature were the same.

Letting out a long breath, he walked on down the path to the room he'd rented. Behind, the night grew loud as the raiders occupied the inn and began to drink.

In the morning, Imanaj headed to his favourite spot to look out over the nearby coast and the hamlet. No smoke hung over the collection of huts and shacks and that was good. The raiders appeared satisfied with what they'd managed to shake out of the islanders. He saw that they were loading their two launches with barrels and bundles of supplies and commandeered goods.

He'd half turned away when he glimpsed out of the corner of his eye lumber being carried out to one of the launches. He froze for that instant, then looked to the brightening sky and pressed a hand to his forehead. *By all the demon-gods of the Great Jhag Odhan – I should've anticipated this.* He headed down the path to the shore.

At the surf, he strode out knee-deep in the waves and gestured to the crew loading the planks. 'That is my timber,' he called.

These raiders, three men and one woman, paused to eye one another. The biggest of the lot laughed. 'No. This is our wood.'

'Really . . . I am very sorry. But I need that to repair my boat.'

'Well, *we* need it for *our* repairs,' the crewwoman snarled.

The big fellow, armed with a wide shortsword, wore tattered pantaloons that might once have been blue, and a leather hauberk too small for him. He scratched his beard, bemused. 'We was told you weren't gonna make any trouble. Don't make me run you through.'

Imanaj sighed at the inevitability of what was taking shape. 'I am sorry,' he stressed, 'but I must insist you return it.'

The fellow barked another laugh.

'Oh, just get rid of him, Durkhan,' the woman said.

Sadly shaking his head, Durkhan sloshed over while drawing his shortsword. 'I'd run now if I was you, little man,' he warned.

Imanaj stood his ground, though he shifted sidelong, his rear foot digging into the loose gravel and wet sands.

'Fool!' Durkhan ground out while thrusting.

Imanaj shifted just slightly, took the man's wrist in his hands and bent it back, snapping it, and yanked the sword from the limp hand. He smacked the iron pommel to Durkhan's head, knocking him unconscious.

The other three gaped at him for an instant, then all cursed as one, drawing their own various weapons and charging.

Imanaj had time for just two experimental swings of the cumbersome shortsword to get a feel for it before they were all upon him at once – no fair fighting among raiders, apparently.

He took these three down with crippling thrusts to their upper thighs.

'Keep pressure on the wounds and you may live,' he told them where they lay grasping their legs in the now red-streaked surf. 'Use rags for tight tourniquets.'

'Oh, go to Hood, you asshole,' the woman snarled.

He tossed away the heavy shortsword and picked up two of the lightest, longest weapons dropped: two long-knives. These he hefted as he turned to meet the crowd of raiders charging down the path towards him.

Instinct told him to wait in the deeper waters where, presumably, his opponents would find their movement limited and encumbered – this should favour him. And so he waited while they came pushing through the deepening waves, slowed and hampered. He kept edging sideways to keep them clumping and impeding one another and met them as they came. He parried and countered, slicing upper arms, flensing muscle and ligaments, leaving men and women to fall aside clutching at their crippled limbs. This saddened him as he swung, but at least they had a good chance of living.

As they came on – with admirable ferocity – he turned his thoughts to the end game. How to extract himself from this debacle? He saw their captain, Rollo, now entering the surf; unfortunately, the man carried a crossbow that he was now loading.

Imanaj cursed. Yet another complication to bear in mind. He shifted to keep a raider between him and Rollo.

So the fight surged on. Imanaj found himself admiring the blades he'd chanced upon: wickedly sharp, more like kitchen tools for dismembering carcasses, which, in a sad way, was close to the work he'd sunk himself into here.

Imanaj pressed inwards, towards the raider captain, now impatient and slicing throats. Rollo looked up, and, in the widening of his eyes, Imanaj saw his reading of the fact that few of his command stood between him and his opponent. He raised the crossbow.

Imanaj took a raider woman in the torso then held her before him while she sagged onto him. Rollo took his shot and the quarrel hammered them – the point penetrated through the woman and broke the flesh of his chest, but that was all. He dropped the woman and surged forwards.

Six of the crew remained; two of these peered round at the blood-red surf, the wounded and bodies rolling with the waves all about them, and ran off. The remaining four charged. Rollo reloaded while backing away up the gravel shingle.

Imanaj duelled carefully, one eye on Rollo. He chose the largest – well, the fattest – of those remaining to keep between them – this one would be last. Pushing forward, ever forward, parrying and countering, he steadily closed the gap. The two remaining crew members, the fat fellow and a woman, backpedalled, now on the defensive.

He slashed the woman across the front – shallow, yet incapacitating – and faced the last crew member.

'*Get down, Tun!*' Rollo bellowed.

The fat fellow dropped into the surf. Imanaj cursed and dived himself. He searched through the murky bloodied water and found what he was looking for: a corpse. He rose with it held before him. He was still blinking away the stinging salt water when something punched him in the shoulder and spun him around. He dropped the corpse to clutch his shoulder, turned, and found Rollo now backing away as he frantically reloaded. Imanaj charged.

The water hampered him; he saw that he wouldn't make it. At the last possible moment, he drew back his remaining long-knife and threw while surging onwards.

A hissed curse and a snap of release – without the dreaded hit – was his reward. He closed upon the captain who now struggled with his off-hand to draw his blade. Imanaj yanked it free and jammed the weapon into Rollo's chest. The captain staggered backwards, stunned disbelief in his eyes. He fell onto his back, clutching the blade where it stood from his chest.

Lying sprawled on the gravel strand, the man laughed wetly, coughing up blood. 'Looks like you finally found the will to fight,' he managed.

Imanaj crouched next to him. 'Yes. Seems some things you just can't run away from.'

'Was that what you were doing? Bloody running away?'

'I suppose so. I didn't think so at the time. But yes . . . I suppose so.'

The captain didn't answer. Imanaj glanced down; he was dead.

He stood to peer down at the corpse, then turned, taking in all the rest of the bodies gently rocking in the surf. He shook his head: to think he'd left to avoid all the bloodshed. He continued shaking his head at the absurdity of it.

'Are they all dead?' someone asked from nearby.

Imanaj raised his gaze; it was the priest, Rendren. 'Some are wounded. A few ran away.'

'You said you were done with violence.'

'Yes, I said that.'

'They will kill us all for this.'

Imanaj gestured to the anchored vessel. 'Tow that off and sink it. Hide all the evidence. I suggest you bury everything. Another ship might not even visit here.'

The priest was nodding. 'Yes, I see. That is possible.'

'Send the boatwright to me,' Imanaj told him.

The priest limped off.

More of the villagers came edging down to the strand. They began dragging bodies off to where, Imanaj imagined, a pit was being dug. He tried not to look when fishing knives flashed and those raiders who remained alive gasped. He remained where he was, and waited.

Eventually, the boatwright approached, white-faced as he eyed all the blood in the waves. 'Yes, sor?' he asked. 'You wanted me?'

'Yes.' He pointed to the lumber. 'Retrieve all this and fix my damned boat. Immediately.'

The man swallowed, paling even further. He bobbed his head like a puppet. 'Yes, sor. Certainly. Immediately. Yes.' He backed away, still bobbing his head.

Imanaj rolled his head to loosen his neck then headed for the path up to the inn. He would return to Aren after all. The fates, it seemed, had decided things for him.

*　*　*

Glinith Apanar, Abbess of Cabil and Keeper of the Inner Mysteries of the Sanctuary, hurried through the bustling halls of the Basilica of Mael to a full meeting of the Guiding Council of the Faith. These chill stone halls were usually never so busy, the council

262

rarely met so often, and Glinith had certainly never before hurried to attend any one such meeting. Times, however, were remarkable – if not stunning.

Foreign invaders had boiled up from the south, striking everywhere, making landings, burning, raiding, even occupying towns and ports all across the archipelago! It was unprecedented, unimaginable. The entire populace clamoured for the Faith to eliminate these pirates. To sweep them from the waters. For her part, though, Glinith suspected it would not be so easy. There were reports that some of these gangs were actually busy fortifying their new island possessions.

She was beginning to dread that this was no simple hit and run raid. That these were no mere bandit thieves bent upon scooping up all the coin and rich goods they could hold in their arms to flee back south.

For now, however, she kept her suspicions to herself. From all the discussions she'd heard to date around the council table she deduced that such an opinion might not be welcome. And seeing as she was by far the least powerful member of said council, discretion dictated that she not make waves.

Guards – armed priest-soldiers of the Faith Militant – opened the doors of the chamber and allowed her entrance. This, too, was something new. Although Falar found itself at a disadvantage in possessing no formal army, what it did have was a very large body of rather fanatical armed faithful.

Nuraj and Mallick were already at the table. Glinith offered a curt bow and sat. The council was short one member in that no new Overseer of Coin had yet been elected from the ranks. Mallick appeared in no hurry to select anyone and, prudently, neither Nuraj nor she ventured any comment on the matter. 'The Celebrant is on his way?' she asked.

Looking rather like a turtle, Mallick cleared his throat and murmured, 'The Celebrant shall not be joining us today. These difficult times have been hard on his nerves. I encourage him to rest. We shall have need of his . . . reassuring presence . . . in the future.'

With Mallick's words Glinith felt a visceral thrill course through her. *We three guide Falar!* She had done it! She had come to a true seat of power.

She dipped her head in acknowledgement of the Proctor of the Faith's wisdom. 'We are a quorum, then.'

'Indeed,' Mallick observed, quite dryly. His dead, sea-creature gaze slid to Nuraj, the Guardian of the Faith. 'Your report?'

Nuraj nodded his lean head; the man appeared exhausted, his eyes sunken, face grey and seamed. He leaned forward, clasped his hands on the tabletop. 'These invaders have split up into disparate groups, attacking multiple islands. Many have stopped raiding and are now fortifying cities and ports they've captured. I believe they mean to set themselves up as minor despots – even petty kings – and negotiate with us.' He opened his hands. 'Frankly, it doesn't seem organized at all. It's simply complete and utter chaos.'

'They fear our final resort,' Mallick answered. Nuraj and Glinith shared an almost furtive glance. 'They know we will not use it against one of our own isles.' He tapped a plump finger to an equally plump lower lip. 'Unless we could lure them together all on one isle . . .' He seemed to consider the possibility, then shook his head, rejecting it. 'Whether or not, we still need to ascertain whether we can count on this, ah, weapon.'

His unblinking gaze now slid to Glinith. 'You have the priestess in hand? Know the required invocations?'

Though she knew the dreaded question was coming, Glinith still jumped, startled. She opened her mouth but no sound emerged, cleared her throat. 'Yes, Proctor. However, not in many hundreds of years has the Ritual of Summoning been invoked. We cannot even be sure—'

Mallick cut her off with a curt wave. 'Yes, yes. Yet you could, in principle, satisfy every step.'

She nodded, not trusting her voice.

Mallick tilted his head as if evaluating her anew. 'Very good. We shall proceed with the summoning.'

'And the target?' Nuraj enquired. 'They have scattered themselves, like a kicked nest of roaches. Where would this . . . thing . . . strike?'

Mallick leaned back, nodding, appearing smugly self-satisfied, and Glinith knew they had now reached the point he had been guiding them towards. 'It just so happens that a target of a kind has presented itself.'

Nuraj and she shared another uneasy glance. 'And it is?' Glinith obediently prompted.

'This invasion's erstwhile commander.'

The Guardian of the Faith blew out a scornful breath. 'You do not believe these ridiculous reports, surely?'

Mallick nodded, his expression quite serious. 'Oh, yes, I do. Were they one or two sources, no. But my agents have collected many such reports – by bribery and by pain – and all concur. A powerful archmage, perhaps even this purported *Emperor* of the southern continent, leads this invasion fleet. And he waits anchored west of Delanss Isle. We will set this thing against him there.'

'A risk,' Nuraj observed.

Mallick's grey eyes flashed, suddenly icy. 'Of course it is a risk! Every choice we make from this point onwards shall carry risk.'

Glinith let out a breath, for she had been about to say the same thing. *What an awful risk! A gamble. A calculated risk. But something this man has built his climb to power upon.*

'More specifically,' Mallick continued, settling back in his chair, 'he is anchored in an isolated location. Therefore, we will not announce the unleashing, nor the target.' He pulled at his plump lower lip. 'And if nothing comes to pass . . .' He shrugged. 'We can say nothing and still have the threat of this ultimate resort to hold over everyone.'

Glinith could not stop her brows from rising. *The breath-taking mendacity! He would hang on to it – even if it were false!* She shook her head in admiration.

His dead-eye gaze moved to her. 'Begin the preparations.'

She bowed her head. 'Immediately, Proctor.'

*

Gianna was at one of the barred windows of her quarters when she heard the lock of the door rattle, and open. She assumed it was, as usual, a meal being delivered, and, her back turned, said wearily, 'Just leave it on the table.'

'Not today, Giandra,' answered a familiar, hated voice.

She turned; there stood the Abbess Glinith with four heavy priestesses.

Feeling a knot of sudden apprehension, she asked, 'What is it?'

'Just checking on you,' said the Abbess. Yet there was a strange tone to her voice, and an unsettling silky smile played about her colourless lips. 'Can't take the chance of you running off. Not now.'

'Oh? May I ask why?' Gianna worked to keep her voice scornful, though her heart now pounded.

'You'll see. Soon . . . very soon.' Glinith gestured to the four guards, who advanced upon Gianna. 'Tie her down – there, on the bed.'

Two grasped Gianna's arms before she could react. She stared at the Abbess in utter disbelief. 'What is this? Have you lost your mind?'

Glinith raised a hand. 'Just a precaution. Your time is coming. Soon. Can't take any risks.' She was smiling now, openly.

The priestesses secured her arms outspread, one to either post, then tied her legs together. Glinith eyed their work critically and nodded to herself. 'That should do for now. If you become hungry, or need to empty your bladder, just call.'

'I'd rather starve.'

The priestess tilted her head in thought, then opined, 'I don't believe you'll have the time.' She lowered her head in a mockery of a bow. 'Good night, High Priestess.'

Gianna cursed them on their way out; having spent a lot of time sailing and around sailors, she was not very ladylike at all in her language.

*　*　*

Hessa dragged herself, footsore, weary and hungry, to find Turnagin at the outlook where he usually kept watch. The mage nodded her a greeting and lowered the pipe he'd been blowing notes upon.

'I wish you wouldn't play that damned thing,' Hessa growled, her voice hoarse and faint.

'I have to practise,' the mage explained reasonably.

'Damn I'm thirsty. Have you anything to drink?'

Turnagin drew a waterskin from his shirt and offered it. 'I suspect we'll expire of thirst before anything else. Did you find them?'

Drinking, she shook her head, swallowed, and gasped, 'No.

266

They're hunting after that sledge and its box of gemstones. Gods alone know where it is – if it hasn't been smashed or burned.'

'They'll make a run for it if they find it.'

Hessa shook her head, sighed. 'I expect so.' She pushed past the mage to peer out the slim crack amid the naked stone that opened to a bare rock face high up on the mountain. Winds buffeted her and blown grit slashed her face. She squinted at the blackened, shadowed plain below. She imagined this could be what Hood's demesnes might resemble, and decided she wouldn't be surprised to spot all the dead staggering about wringing their hands and bemoaning their fate. 'Anything?'

'Nothing.'

She grunted her bewilderment. 'They sure are taking their damned time . . .'

'Perhaps elsewhere they—' A tremor far stronger than usual silenced Turnagin. Both peered warily about. Rocks tumbled and clattered down the cliff face.

'That didn't feel right . . .' Hessa murmured, then both staggered as the solid stone floor beneath them lurched. 'Singer!' Hessa snarled, and she ran for the main chamber.

It took some time, as distances within the mountain were large. Occasionally, tremors threw her side to side within the broad halls. Cracks were even gaping that she couldn't remember seeing before, in walls and floors. Eventually, she reached the high chamber and searched among the banks and rows of towering machines.

She found him slouched before a broad and tall panel of toggles and crystal controls. She crouched next to his bent form. 'Singer? You alive?'

A faint smile cracked the Jaghut's lips. He peered up from under his brows, grinned his familiar manic leer. 'As yet. As you see . . . I am victorious.'

'Victorious? Whatever do you mean?'

A weak wave to the panel above. 'I have succeeded. I have parsed the commands. We are finally in motion.'

'In motion?' Hessa breathed, barely able to accept it. 'The entire mountain?'

Turnagin arrived, panting, red-faced. 'There are collapses everywhere!'

A nod. 'Indeed.' Struggling, gripping the panel, Singer dragged himself upright. He leaned over the machine for support. 'It halted for good reason, I imagine . . .' He regarded the panel's glittering controls, frowned. 'Wait. This cannot be right.' He gripped levers and pushed at them, grunting his effort. 'North! No – wait. South-east. The route I outlined was south-east!'

'Perhaps it is following its older, original commands,' Turnagin suggested.

The Jaghut snarled and spat something in his own language.

'Why south-east?' Hessa now asked. Then, lower and fiercer, 'What is it you intend?'

Singer gave one more yank on a toggle only to groan and slouch to his knees, fighting for breath. He turned to set his back against the machine and began to laugh. It was painful to hear, hoarse and racking, and it went on and on while he shook his head.

Hessa leaned over him, demanded, 'Why south-east?'

Singer swallowed heavily, peering up. 'An eye for an eye, good captain. You should understand that.'

'No. I don't understand. What do you mean?'

The Jaghut gave a weak wave. 'What to me was only yesterday, but which was before you were born, I was insulted and much abused in the lands south of us.'

'Quon Tali,' Hessa breathed.

'Call it whatever. Now, the ruler of said lands has the impertinence to meddle in the affairs of the ancients.' Singer coughed anew, bloodying his lips, and sighed heavily. He waggled a finger. 'One should not play with fire.'

'Ancient wars,' Turnagin breathed in wonder.

Singer laughed anew. 'Indeed. The Imass have been stirred awake. Did he not imagine there would be repercussions?' And his head slowly sank.

Hessa backed away from the Jaghut. She raised her gaze to the mage. 'What does this mean?'

'He intended to send this machine south-east, round the Fenn Range, to rampage across Quon Tali.' Turnagin looked to the broad panel of multiple controls before them. 'But all that is academic now. It is moving north – towards Falar. Who knows what destruction it will wreak there? We must get to the Malazans.'

'The Malazans? Let's just find the twins and flee, dammit!'

'No! This thing must be stopped.' He ran off.

Hessa reached out after the mage as if she could grasp his dirty, tattered robes, only to snarl, impotent. She yanked free her sword and pressed the point to the Jaghut's chest, moved to thrust, but stopped herself, unable to complete the attack. Snarling again, she slammed the blade home in its sheath and ran after Turnagin.

*

On the steaming, melting bog and marshlands of what once was the Ice Wastes, a blot of complete and utter darkness emerged into the night then dwindled, coalescing into a tall and slim figure, her skin and hair black, her leather armour black as well. She crossed her arms and stood regarding the K'Chain Che'Malle mountain in the mid-distance, where it belched out its great clouds of black and grey smoke and ash.

Another, smaller blot of darkness emerged just behind. It collapsed, spinning, to reveal Endest Silann. The Tiste Andii mage grimaced as his sandals sank into the wet peaty ground. He gingerly approached the woman.

'Ah, no trouble finding it then, Feral. Good.'

The woman cast him a sharp, disparaging glance. 'Of course! Their stink is unmistakable.' She gestured to the plain. 'Yet I see no battle-magics. No sky-cracking eruptions or daemonic Galain summonings.' She eyed him, her gaze slit. 'If you have disturbed me for no good reason . . .'

He raised his hands defensively. 'Really, Feral, I spoke truly. All we need do is keep watch—'

'*We?*' she interrupted. '*You* may do as you like – meaning meekly keep watch. I, on the other hand, regret having listened to you.' She tilted her head, examining him up and down. 'Endest,' she sighed. 'I do not understand you. Really, I do not. There are depths to you – even power. I respect that. Yet you seem to shy away from it. I have always wondered why.'

'Well, to me, violence is—' He broke off as the ground beneath them both shuddered, and both staggered to remain upright.

'What in the name of Mother?' Feral growled.

Endest pointed to the mountain. 'Look!'

Feral shaded her gaze against the blazing energies emanating from the titanic object, and swore. 'Is it . . . ?'

269

Endest nodded, his gaze also shaded. 'Yes, it most certainly is.'

'It has been ages since a K'Chain Che'Malle mountain prowled the world,' Feral breathed, almost reverently. 'This I must see.'

'Do be careful!' Endest called even as the Andii woman's shape disappeared within an enmeshing shroud of utter darkness. And then he was alone. He shuddered, and pulled his robes more tightly about his shoulders.

Chapter 18

THE RETURN TO THE SEARED AND BLACKENED PLAIN OF THE Wasteland was no improvement on the first journey. Nightchill, Dassem and Tayschrenn walked in no particular order. It was early morning, though it was hard to tell as the sun was a mere sullen glow behind the thick black clouds above. Mists and banners of vapour obscured the landscape and the three walked a wandering route, avoiding bubbling mud-pits and open pools where crimson lava churned and coursed before disappearing once more beneath a surrounding hardened crust of porous and brittle rock.

As before, Tayschrenn shielded the party from the worst of the pummelling heat. But even he couldn't block it out entirely and he found himself walking on his toes, and saw the Sword's leather sandals actually smoking. Nightchill lent him no sorcerous aid in his efforts as she was saving her resources for the trial to come: somehow stealing the three of them into the mountain itself.

The Sword, Dassem, was, as usual, lightly armoured in a mail and leather hauberk, long-sleeved, with greaves, but without helmet. In the beating heat the man's long black hair now hung wet with sweat. He carried at his side just one weapon – a rather large two-handed blade. Tayschrenn knew him to fight sometimes with two swords and supposed the man had chosen this particular weapon in view of the disproportionate size of his opponents.

They made good time despite circling the worst of the hazards and avoiding the open routes, or roads, the Che'Malle used for travel. Yet even as they closed upon the mountain, Tayschrenn was more and more uneasy that so far he'd seen none of the creatures.

Where were the beasts? Was he missing something obvious? Some change or shift in behaviour? It was quite worrying.

Even Nightchill appeared concerned, for she paused now and then to peer about, her brow wrinkled.

'Where are they?' Tayschrenn whispered to her.

'I do not know. This is not like any of the accounts I have heard. They may be—' She cut herself off as the ground suddenly shook beneath them. Dassem weaved, struggling to remain upright. Then, thunder rolled over them – a deafening, ongoing roar as of . . . well, hundreds of continuous avalanches.

'What is this?' he called to Nightchill.

She was studying the mountain where it reared in the middle distance. Dust, or debris of some sort, now obscured its base in roiling clouds. 'Elders, no,' she breathed.

'What is it?' Dassem asked, joining them.

'It moves,' she answered, flatly.

Tayschrenn stared at the gigantic edifice of rock. A mountain. A literal mountain. Such a thing was almost beyond comprehension. 'It is moving, now?'

'Yes. We must hurry. I will take us.'

'We've yet far to go,' Tayschrenn observed, a touch worried for her.

'We may have waited too long as it is,' she answered, and he wondered just what she meant by that.

He did not ask, however, as at that moment the world went strangely monochrome once more, and the distances flattened in an eye-watering manner. He felt himself swept up and along with the sorceress. He knew he was moving, yet everything was a distorted blur and he could not be certain exactly *where* he was. Again, the experience was unlike any Warren phenomena of which he'd heard or read, and again he wondered just who, or what, this woman was.

Cessation came as a jolt. He was released to run up against a stone wall and painfully clout his head. He held it, wincing, his eyes watering anew.

The sound of someone dry-heaving eased his pain – somewhat.

He blinked away the tears to see the Sword leaning against a wall of natural stone, shaking his head and spitting to clear his throat. 'Not used to Warren travel?' Tayschrenn asked.

'Yes. But this is different,' the man answered.

Tayschrenn had to agree. Now the intense heat bit at him and so, as before, he quickly raised his Thyr Warren to shield them from the worst of its effects. Also distressing to him was the yammering and thundering clamour; rock was crashing all about as in an avalanche, and mechanisms hammered and boomed: it was as if he were inside an immense smithy with hundreds of armourers beating on anvils.

He looked to where the sorceress Nightchill stood aside. She was hugging herself, her face far more pale than usual.

'The energies are even worse now,' she whispered, her voice hoarse, and she pressed a hand to her brow.

Tayschrenn noted that whereas travelling within the fields of this artefact had laid him prostrate, this woman merely appeared to be experiencing a severe headache. He raised his voice to ask, 'Where are we?'

She shrugged her thin shoulders. 'Somewhere within.'

'Which way?' Dassem asked, straightening and clearing his throat.

'Upwards and inwards I believe,' Nightchill answered.

'I will take the fore,' the Sword announced, and he pushed past them, still unsteady.

Tayschrenn shared a raised brow with Nightchill.

As he went, Dassem drew the heavy, two-handed blade and carried it readied, point raised before him.

They traversed wide and empty halls. Dust and wind-blown ash and soot revealed the passage of the K'Chain in broad, taloned prints.

'This could take days . . .' Tayschrenn whispered to Nightchill.

She nodded her answer then gestured ahead. 'I believe we may be approaching a node of some sort. We may find more options.'

He gave an answering bob of his head. They rounded a curve in the hall of natural stone and Dassem suddenly stopped short to face aside.

A massive K'Chain Che'Malle lumbered from a side alcove. It reared twice the man's height and lashed out with deceptive speed; Tayschrenn flinched backwards.

The Sword, however, slashed as well, and one forearm with its

273

curved blade flew aside. The beast screamed its pain and rage and reached for the swordsman with its remaining forearm; this, too, was severed. Next went the beast's left lower leg and it crashed to the stone floor, where Dassem finished it.

Tayschrenn had to cast Nightchill another glance, this time with both brows raised.

Indeed, the Sword would take the fore.

Beyond the curve they did come to a major series of intersections and here they found a ramp leading upwards. They increased their pace up the slope.

*

As he had done before, through the use of his D'riss Warren Blues blunted the worst of the searing heat. The party ran across fields of hissing, crackling and undulating rock crust, hopped from blackened outcropping to jutting boulder, and skirted wide expanses of churning, turgid lava. With Blues were Gwynn, Black the Lesser, Jacinth, and the Fenn giant, Bellurdan.

'Stands out like a walking menhir,' Black complained to Blues as they jogged along, nodding to the giant.

'These mists obscure everything,' he murmured in answer.

The swordsman merely grunted, sour and unconvinced.

No Che'Malle pickets or guards challenged them, however. Which frankly made Blues uneasy. *Where were they all? Preparing an ambush?*

Maintaining his D'riss Warren within the energies of the Che'Malle mountain was also now taking its toll upon him. He rubbed his sweat-slick brow, winced as the alien fields grated against his mind like shards of broken glass. Gwynn, he noted, was watching him with sympathy in his glance.

Yet they kept up their pace, hunching occasionally behind boulders, scanning the banners of shifting steam and mists. Then darting onwards across the open ground.

They were close to the mountain when that ground suddenly bucked and rocked, nearly knocking them all over. Blues staggered, his feet wide apart. Open to his D'riss Warren he knew immediately what had occurred; it struck like a stunning dislocating blow to his mind.

The other Avowed of the Guard looked to him expectantly. He

274

nodded while struggling to recover from the shock and find his breath. 'It's moving,' he gasped.

'Moving?' Jacinth scoffed.

Gwynn, however, now faced the east. 'Yes,' he answered. 'Just as the ancient sources attest.'

Black frowned, scratching his chin. 'What . . . the whole damned thing?'

Jacinth mimicked clouting him across his helmet. 'Yeah. Try to keep up, man.'

The Fenn giant Bellurdan emerged from the mists. 'Why have you halted? We must hurry.'

'The thing's moving,' Black answered, gesturing to the east.

The giant's craggy features wrinkled, bemused. 'Of course. It is what they do. Now come.'

They continued onwards across the blasted and burnt landscape. The ground continuously shuddered beneath their feet and, distantly, avalanches of rock roared. It seemed as if the mountain were tearing itself apart. It towered now through the smoke plumes as a cliff before and above them. And it *was* moving – ever so slightly.

To Blues, it was as if they faced an immense cave, its base a scene perhaps out of Elder Light itself: a blazing white-hot field of roiling and frothing lava. Though pushing his D'riss Warren to deflect most of the heat, Blues still felt as if he were roasting. A blacksmith's bellows of searing air pushed him back.

While above, a roof of stone glided past and enormous rockfalls tumbled down its sides continuously.

Black raised his open hands, helpless. 'How're we ever supposed to . . .'

Bellurdan pointed to the north and shouted over the cacophony, 'There – a great pile or boulder.'

Blues saw it too: a titanic block, a fallen shard of the mountain, that the main body now grated and scraped against. Bellurdan led the way. Reaching it, he bounded up the steep cliff face. Blues aided Gwynn, who lagged. Together they were the last to reach a jumping-off point.

Ahead, from up on the passing cliff face, Jacinth and Black beckoned.

'You'll have to jump!' Blues bellowed.

The scholar-mage smiled wanly. Sweat coursed down his ash-blackened cheeks. 'So I see.'

'Tell you what – I will go first and help you! Yes?' Gwynn nodded. 'Very well.'

With that, Blues took two running steps from rock to rock and leapt. Maintaining a grip was easy for him: the moment he touched upon the steep cliff face he anchored himself to the stone using his D'riss Warren – he hoped to do the same for Gwynn. Turning round, he beckoned.

The mage of Rashan nodded, warily, Blues thought, then took a few tentative steps and jumped.

Blues cursed: too hesitant. He let himself fall, caught a handful of the man's shirt and slapped the rock face to affix himself with D'riss.

Gwynn scrabbled for foot- and handholds, even paler than usual beneath the soot, then nodded his thanks.

Movement upon the mountain slope caught Blues's eye: Black far ahead, gesturing them onwards. Blues motioned that way and set off – but pointing to each hold, gap and ledge for Gwynn to follow along.

Eventually they came to the others, who were waiting, clinging to the rock face, just short of the lip of what appeared to be a broad cave, or portal, into the mountain. Bellurdan was at the fore. He leaned out to catch Blues's eye then pointed to himself. Blues nodded his approval.

The Thelomen giant clambered to the lip. As he did so, a strange vision came to Blues: to his Warren-lensed sight the giant suddenly blossomed and took on a shimmer of power. Blues felt almost foolish then: of course! Weren't the Thelomen an Elder race? Possessing their own sort of racial powers or Warren?

No sooner had the giant disappeared round the lip of coarse stone than a roaring and crashing shook the rock. Black and Jacinth surged forward and Blues followed.

Over the edge and in the portal, Blues met his fellow Avowed standing with weapons lowered, peering at the spectacle of Bellurdan atop a fallen K'Chain Che'Malle warrior, disengaging his arms from its broken neck.

'Wouldn't have thought it possible . . .' Black breathed, awed.

The Thelomen straightened, panting to catch his breath, yet continued studying the fallen monster.

'What is it?' Blues asked.

'This Che'Malle warrior. It moved too slowly. Something seemed wrong. As if it were sick . . . or half-awake.'

'We have to hurry,' Jacinth cut in. She asked of the giant, 'Which way?'

'I know not,' Bellurdan admitted, and shrugged as if indifferent.

'What in the Abyss?' the swordswoman swore. 'Aren't you supposed to know this Elder stuff?'

'No one asked.'

'Gods damn it!' and she almost raised her sword. 'This place is enormous! It'll take days to find anything!'

From behind Blues, Gwynn called, 'Calm yourself, Jacinth. My readings spoke of the Matrons leading and commanding from the peaks of these artefacts. So, we must go up.'

'Fine,' the woman ground out, 'then let's *go*.'

The mage of Rashan looked to Blues. 'Can you sense anything?'

But Blues's D'riss Warren, the very magery of stone and rock, now freed from shielding them from the lethal heat, was already probing and spreading out through the walls and long corridors. He found vast caverns great enough to hold entire towns, league upon league of halls, galleries, storerooms and what appeared to be endless workshops of some kind. He pointed up the hall. 'This way.'

* * *

When they woke her it was night. Four burly priestesses of Ortheal's Faith Militant – yet Ortheal's fanatics no longer, that creature Mallick's now. They untied her bonds and yanked her upright to march her out and down the hall.

She was guided to the main worship precincts of the Basilica, which she found empty, echoing and strangely dark. They urged her onwards to the rear doors that allowed access to the halls of the Inner Sanctum and that was when realization struck her. This was it. Her time had come – as they say.

Indeed the priestesses marched her on, ever inwards, climbing staircases that narrowed as they went, until they emerged at a hall rough-hewn from naked rock, lined with priests and priestesses of the Faith Militant, all murmuring a low chant, heads downcast. The two priestesses at her arms urged her forward. The hallway ended at a narrow landing and walkway, lined by officials of the Faith, and the yawning circular pit containing the Holy of Holies: the Sacred Pool of Mael, some twenty fathoms below their feet.

Here the Abbess Glinith met her, a thin silk-wrapped object in her hands, and with her, Rentil Orodrin, Celebrant of the Faith, his great mass of grey hair and beard blowing in the gusting winds, looking so very severe as always.

'Child of Mael . . .' he greeted her. His voice quavered with age, yet was still powerful enough to echo across the pit. 'We are thankful to you, in this, our time of need. Thankful for your sacrifice . . . and your devotion.'

Gianna threw her head back and yelled, 'If you think I'm going to—'

A leather gag was slapped from behind into her open jaws and yanked tight. She growled and snarled the rest of her curses and writhed in the strong grips restraining her.

The elderly Celebrant flinched from her rage, his thick brows rising. He turned away, to another priest nearby, the squat potbellied form of Mallick Rel. 'This does not seem . . . appropriate, nor becoming to the sacredness of these proceedings . . . good Proctor.'

Mallick raised one pale and limp hand. 'My apologies, Celebrant. We could not convince her as to the, ah, munificence of the gesture – and so had to bring stronger methods to bear.'

Rentil huffed, his brows knit and he shook his head. 'This will not do, Proctor. I am displeased. The ritual clearly calls for a volunteer. A vessel of purest self-sacrifice.'

'With the Celebrant's permission I will handle these final stages – I believe I will be able to bring her around.'

Rentil studied her, blinking his rheumy eyes. 'Well . . . if you believe so, Mallick. I leave it to you. Child,' he said, now addressing her, 'I shall pray for your soul that you shall come to see the blessing that is your service to Mael.'

From behind her gag Gianna screamed where the old man could shove his *service* and Rentil flinched from her once more. He withdrew, aided and guided by his servants.

Mallick now turned to her; he motioned that the gag should be withdrawn.

Gianna drew in a deep breath, snarled, 'You piece of worm-shit.'

The short priest just smiled thinly, revealing his sickly grey-green teeth. He pointed past himself, to a stone spar that jutted out over the black water of the pool far below. 'What is required, High Priestess, is that you voluntarily draw the Blade of Offering across your stomach then walk out upon that ledge and stand there until you faint away from loss of blood.'

'Go to the Abyss.'

Again the thin and unsettling smile from the man. He gestured behind her, waving someone forward. 'I thought as much. And so we must do what you are forcing us to do.'

Two of the priests-militant pushed up to her. They held a youth between them – a black-haired girl that Gianna recognized. One who had saved her life that day in Sparrow Pass Cut. The child stared up at her, frightened and confused.

Mallick now gestured impatiently to the Abbess who handed over the long and slim object in her hands. He raised the curved and glistening white Blade of Offering up under the girl's chin. 'Now, High Priestess,' he began, 'must we play out this pantomime of threats and capitulations? Must we walk through the entire useless charade? Or will you cooperate?'

At the sight of the blade tucked to the child's chin, the girl's eyes now so wide in mute terror, Gianna felt all her strength and resistance drop from her as if knifed herself. She nodded her submission.

Mallick answered with his own smug nod of satisfaction. He pulled the blade away. 'Good. I am glad you see reason. After all, blood is blood . . . yes?'

He held the blade out to her, but pulled it away at the last second, gave her a warning look. 'Now, should the thought of plunging this into my chest cross your mind – remember, these children here will pay the price. Understood?'

The thought had in fact crossed her mind, but the creature was right: the youths would be killed in retaliation. One by one their stomachs would be slit open and their blood allowed to drain down to stain the water of the Sacred Pool below. All to summon this . . . Jhistal . . . whatever the thing might prove to be.

I see your true colour now, Mael. It is the colour of innocent blood. And I reject it.

Mutely, she held out a hand for the blade. Mallick reversed it and slapped the carved grip to her palm, then gestured invitingly to the stone wedge that extended out over the crater pool so very far below. Black and gritty the rock was, the very stone of the mountain itself.

Gianna slid one foot forward.

'If you experience any hesitation in the cut,' Mallick offered from behind, 'I am certain we can offer our help.'

'It would be my pleasure,' the Abbess added.

Gianna turned round on the narrow ledge. First, she directed her gaze to the manacled youths. 'Don't worry,' she called to them; then she turned to Mallick, who eyed her now, uncertain. She raised her chin and shouted over the winds out far above the pool, 'Hood must hold a special path for filth like you! You too, Abbess. This is my answer to you!'

And she threw herself backwards off the stone platform. The last thing she heard over the roaring winds was a panicked scream from Glinith.

The Abbess clapped a hand over her mouth. Below, so very far below, the High Priestess hit the water like a dart. The smallest of ringed ripples arose to widen across the dark waters, then all was still. She raised her horrified gaze to Mallick and she thought to herself – *Disaster! Will I be next?*

But the Proctor of Faith was staring down musingly, pulling at his fleshy lower lip, appearing mildly puzzled. He sighed and shook his head, raised his gaze to her. 'Well,' he announced, 'that's *one* way to sacrifice oneself . . . is it not?' He tilted his head and tapped a finger to his lips. 'How soon shall we know?'

Glinith shook herself and squeezed her hands together. 'Ah. The accounts say it is supposed to take a full turn of the world – next dawn, then. We should know then.'

Mallick nodded. 'Very well. We will give it until then. And how should we know, in any case?'

She cleared her throat. 'Yes. Well, the tides. There should be the lowest tide of any records. The waters should practically disappear from all the shallowest coastline.'

Mallick continued nodding, thoughtfully. He gestured to the youths. 'Until then keep these close. We may yet have need of them.'

She bowed from the waist. 'Yes, Proctor.'

*

Impact with the surface should have killed her – crushed the vertebrae of her neck. But she projected her Ruse Warren before her, easing her entry through the water, until her speed slowed. Then she kicked onwards, ever lower, seeking the depths. She could hold her breath for longer than any account she'd ever heard tell of – every such legendary feat – even longer than the most accomplished Ruse adept, yet she knew she would have to push herself further than she'd ever dared before.

They would be watching for her to resurface. Alive or dead, no matter. This pool, this crater lake, it had no outlet. She had nowhere to go; she would have to wait them out.

She sculled her hands and kicked lightly, maintaining her depth just where the faint daylight could reach no further. Unknown depths lay below, as cold and black as night. The impact with the water had torn the Blade of Offering from her grip. Frankly, she was lucky it hadn't been driven into her skull. She should've thrown it aside as she fell; but panic has a way of driving clear thought aside. It must lie below now, amid the silts and . . . other things she did not want to think about.

She was also frankly rather surprised to still be alive. Since she was, she knew what she had to do: she'd glide over to where the shadows were deepest – this being morning the sun's rays would be a long time slithering down the walls. Directly below the ledge would probably be the best place.

She'd climb up and hide among the rocks. Wait for night. Rescue the youths. Somehow. She really didn't have any idea how but she had to try. Wild schemes of disguise and stealth flew through her thoughts. Anything. She could— Wait, she was sinking. Why was she sinking?

She kicked harder to maintain her position, failed. Something was drawing her down. Perhaps a current, yet the waters appeared calm. She threw her Ruse powers against it yet failed again to slow her descent. It was as if she were powerless before whatever it was that had her.

The waters darkened above her and she now floated in utter night, unable to know even whether she was moving at all. Onwards she drifted, sinking – or thought she was. How deep could this lake possibly be?

She was now so far down she knew she no longer had time enough to reach the surface when her breath gave out. Somehow, she no longer cared about that. There was no longer any need for panic or fighting. It was oddly relaxing, really. Floating. She even felt her eyes becoming heavy.

The last thing she noted was a strange blueish light far below. She seemed to be falling towards it through ink-like Abyss – as if it were a star drawing her in. Then she knew nothing more.

* * *

Dancer was used to Kellanved testing his patience, but this was now beyond even his – admittedly frayed – limits. For more than a week they had waited, anchored, here in this channel in Falaran waters . . . waiting. And for what? Even this simplest piece of information was not forthcoming from the squat little Dal Hon mage, who stood day after day at the *Twisted*'s side, tapping his walking stick on the deck, humming tunelessly to himself.

Finally, one late afternoon, as the sun passed behind the coast of the mainland to their west, Dancer approached his erstwhile partner and, reluctantly, cleared his throat. He was reluctant because he knew the man would consider this surrender to impatience a personal victory for him. Dancer, of course, did not.

Kellanved's brows rose expectantly.

'The crew were wondering—'

'The crew?' Kellanved cut in.

Dancer gritted his teeth. 'The crew – and I – were wondering just how much longer all this might take.'

The little fellow shrugged. 'I really have no idea. I am not conversant with our enemy's plans.'

Dancer resisted snarling, *I know this!* He drew a deep breath instead. 'And do you really not have any idea what form this response might take?'

Still looking out across the darkening waters, the mage nodded thoughtfully, as if acknowledging the justice of the question. 'Some accounts have it as a great towering figure of a man – Mael himself – armed with spear and net. Others have it as a great squirming nest of tentacles, eager to pull down all ships. A number mention an accompanying mound of water. As if it were pushing up a great monstrous wave.' The little fellow shrugged again. 'There you have it. Who is to say? We shall see.'

'And what do you intend to *do*? How could you possibly answer such a creature or manifestation?'

Kellanved threw his hands in the air, the stick waving. 'I am quite fed up with these constant interruptions! If you need me – I shall be in my cabin.' And the mage scuttled off, hunched, slamming the door behind him.

Dancer caught Cartheron's eye where he stood across the deck, and the Admiral blew out a long breath, slowly shaking his head.

It was dawn the next day when Dancer awoke on deck; stretching, he took a drink of water from a ladle. He surveyed the now familiar vista of the channel between island and mainland and had to admit that the region had its attractions. The heat of the day was not too hot; the cool of night not too chill; the waters were beautiful, clear and turquoise; the islands rugged and picturesque. In all – a worthy prize.

Too bad he had such doubts regarding the taking.

The door to the captain's cabin opened and Kellanved emerged. He stood blinking and squinting in the light as if stunned momentarily. The fellow's black silk shirt and vest were askew, his hands now stained in ink, a parchment scroll in one. Clearly he had been up all night catching up on reports from all across the lands. His squinted gaze scanned the deck and found Dancer; he crossed hurriedly to join him.

He tapped the scroll. 'One of our lads and lasses brought this to me. Apparently, Surly has targeted the leader of these wasteland Jhek for elimination.'

Dancer was inspecting a small wooden keg of dried fruits. He nodded. 'They could prove a danger with good leadership.' Were there no dried peaches left? Were they out? It wasn't going to be the damned prunes, was it?

Kellanved coughed into his fist. 'Well . . . yes. Apparently, this Priestess can communicate with animals. Birds, especially.'

Dancer nodded absently. Sadly, prunes it would have to be.

'And, according to our intelligence, this Priestess who talks with birds happens to be blind – and wears a cloth tied across her eyes . . .'

Dancer dropped the keg. '*What?*'

Kellanved backed away, his hands raised. 'Now, we can't know for certain—'

Dancer's hands reflexively checked for all his weapons. 'Send me. Now!'

Kellanved continued backing away, his hands open. 'You know that's not how Shadow works . . .'

Dancer stalked forward. '*Do it!*'

'I can't guarantee . . .'

Dancer did not think about it – he simply drew on Kellanved. He pointed the blade. 'Send . . . me . . . now.'

The mage looked to the brightening sky. His shoulders fell. He adjusted his silk shirt. 'I'll do my best . . .'

'Now.'

'Very well!' He tucked the scroll into his shirt and raised his hands, gesturing. 'As I said – I can't guarantee where—'

Dancer ground out, 'For the love of all the gods, just shut up and do it.'

Kellanved raised a brow. 'Well, if you're going to be that way about it – fine.'

Ribbons of shadow gathered about Dancer. Sailors on deck shouted their alarm. The shadows coalesced into a dense adumbration that obscured the figure of the assassin. Then they faded away, like smoke, revealing nothing. He was gone.

Cartheron hurried over. 'What in the Abyss was that, damn it all to Hood!'

Kellanved was eyeing the spot where the man had disappeared. Oddly, to Cartheron, the little fellow's gaze appeared sad, even touched in regret. The Emperor murmured, 'Our friend has a pressing engagement.'

Chapter 19

GIANNA WOKE SLOWLY. SHE FELT AS IF HER CONSCIOUSNESS were a swimmer surfacing from a very deep dive. She dreamed she was salvaging once more, searching among sands and wafting fan corals for something . . . a lost treasure . . . ridiculously enough, a chest of bronze. One lying amid certain formations that looked strangely familiar.

She jolted fully awake, gulping in air.

Someone, a shadowy figure, recoiled from her, sandals scraping over stones.

She lay in some kind of cave, a grotto, half in lapping water. Flickering gold light danced from one end of the cavern.

'You are awake then,' observed a gruff, deep voice.

Raising her head, she found a short, pot-bellied bald fellow peering down at her, hands at the knots of a dirty loincloth that was his only covering. 'Where am I?' she managed, weakly.

The fellow gestured around. 'The Sanctuary of Mael. The Holy of Holies. His very home.'

'Wonderful. This is some sort of cavern then, connected to the pool?'

'Indeed.' He gestured her to follow. 'Come, come. I will show you . . .'

Unsteady, Gianna forced herself to her feet. Her linen trousers and long shirt clung to her, sodden, yet she was not chilled, as the grotto seemed quite unaccountably warm.

The pot-bellied fellow urged her onwards, now pointing towards the light. 'See? See him?'

She staggered over the cavern's uneven rocky floor. A field of guttering and flickering candles lit what appeared to be two enormous stone feet. Her gaze rose, up naked thick legs, equally enormous, to the kilted torso of a bearded, powerfully muscled man, his stony gaze severe and stern, a gigantic spear and net in hand.

'Mael,' the squat fellow announced, sounding very proprietorial.

'Impressive,' Gianna allowed, and she turned away, searching for an exit from the cave. 'And who are you?'

He appeared surprised by the question, and pressed a hand to his bare hairless chest. 'Me? I serve the sanctuary. I keep the candles lit and make the requisite offerings.'

'I mean your name. What's your name?'

Again the surprise. He peered about as if panicked. 'Name? I am nothing. Less than nothing. An insect. A bug. Just a bug.'

'I see.' She was beginning to suspect that the fellow wasn't quite all present. 'And is there a way out of here?'

'A way out?' He shook his head. 'No. There is no way out.'

Gianna bit back a curse and rubbed her brow, sighing. 'Surely there must be. How do you receive food? How did you get in?'

He nodded now, all eager. 'Oh, yes. Once a month the tides are low enough that one narrow tunnel clears. They come then, in a small punt, and leave supplies.'

'Why don't you leave then? Don't you want to?'

He lowered his head. 'I cannot swim. I never learned how.'

Gianna eyed him, quite amazed. A Falaran who couldn't swim? There had to be a first time for everything, she supposed. 'Well I can. Where's this tunnel?'

'I will show you. But first, I must know . . . did he speak to you?'

'Who? Did who speak to me?'

'Mael, of course. Did he speak – or did you *see* something? Did he grant you a vision?'

Suddenly, Gianna felt a strong fear of the short, unimpressive fellow. She almost backed away. 'A vision? I was half drowned!'

'Exactly.'

That silenced her for a time. She remembered her dream of swimming then, and the chest. A bronze box, corroded and half-buried in sands. Peering off into the darkness, she admitted, whispering, 'I saw an old chest of bronze, long submerged.'

He nodded at that. 'Ah. Jhistal's Bane.'

'Jhistal's Bane?'

'A legend. Ancient accounts say that the last attack of the Jhistal was for a certain reason – and that reason was locked in a strong chest that is rumoured to have survived the attack.'

'Ridiculous. I know of no such legend.'

'The cult keeps such things to itself.'

'Then how could you know of it?'

The fellow shrugged his meaty shoulders and dropped his gaze as if embarrassed. 'I was once high in the Faith. I, however, spent years warning them against this use of the Jhistal. I warned of Mael's displeasure. Until finally I was imprisoned here. I have been down here a very long time.' He glanced about at the dark as if about to confide a secret and lowered his voice. 'I fear that I may have become peculiar.'

Gianna cleared her throat, managed, 'Not so as I'd noticed.'

He brightened. 'Thank you. You are most kind.'

'The way out?'

'Ah!' He started off. 'This way.' At one extreme edge of the cavern he pointed to where water barred the way. 'Under there.'

Gianna nodded and carefully began feeling her way down among the rocks.

'I should wait until noon,' the priest offered.

'Oh? Why?'

'It is completely dark in the tunnel. Impossible to find your way. But sometimes I see light streaming down. Noon, I presume.'

She paused among the cold slimy rocks. She could hold her breath – but she couldn't see in the dark.

'And it is dangerous now.'

'Dangerous? How so?'

He hung his head. 'The Jhistal has been called.'

Gianna surged from the shallows. 'The Jhistal!' She yanked the priest's elbow. 'How do you know this?'

He blinked up at her. 'It has been summoned. I felt it.'

'Yes. And? What is it?'

'A terrible, destructive force.'

Half-snarling her frustration, Gianna threw herself aside. She stumbled to a larger boulder to sit, hunched, her sodden shirt still dripping. Well, she told herself, if this were true, at least the children were safe now – no need for any further blood. It seemed her sacrifice had been accepted by the hoary old god. 'Is that all you know of it?'

The priest sat as well, clasped his meaty hands. 'What I know,' he began, 'is that long ago Mael wandered all the waters of the world and that here, in Falar, he found a people living very much as a part of the seas. He – that is, it is said that they became dear to him and he gifted them the secret of the Jhistal so that they could protect themselves.'

'Protect themselves?' Gianna echoed. 'From whom?'

A shrug. 'From others. Outsiders. Invaders. However,' and the priest sighed, 'it did not work. Centuries later others came. At first, no more than a few traders. A few small temporary settlements. But more came. And more.'

'The *newcomers*,' Gianna murmured, remembering her mother's cursed name for them – those who now had the gall to name themselves Falarans.

'Indeed. Red-haired colonists and settlers. The first peoples were loath to unleash the Jhistal against them – and soon enough it was too late. These newcomers, however, seized upon it and, well . . . you know the rest.'

Gianna nodded as he sat for a time, brooding, then she noted a growing hunger. 'Do you have anything to eat?'

The man raised his head, blinking, seemingly surprised. 'Food?'

'Yes. Anything? I haven't eaten all day.'

He rubbed his blunt hands together. 'Food . . . oh dear. I'll have a look.' He padded over to the altar and its enormous looming statue. After rummaging about for a time, he returned with what looked like a loaf of bread. He offered it.

She took it and noted immediately that it was as hard as stone. She brushed the dust from it, eyed the fellow curiously. 'This is ancient. Like a rock.'

'Oh? I'm sorry.'

'What do you eat then?'

He rubbed his chin. 'I, ah, ate all of it. Just out. Apologies.'

She held her head in both hands. Gods! Would she have the strength for another challenging swim?

The priest cleared his throat. 'Well . . . there are fish in the tidepools here . . .'

She rose, eyed the dark water. Of course. 'Make a fire, would you?'

288

Now the priest backed away from her, his brows climbing. 'A fire!' He peered about, almost panicked. 'Really? Must we?'

'To cook the fish – yes.' She stepped down among the wet rocks; he wandered off, wringing his hands and muttering unhappily to himself.

She soon had her fish and returned to the light of the altar. Here she found the fellow had piled together a bunch of dry driftwood. She eyed the heap, then him. 'Couldn't you have lit it?'

He stood wringing his hands and shifting from foot to foot. 'I don't think I've ever done it before. Lit a fire, that is.'

She cocked a brow. 'Really? It's not that hard.'

'For you perhaps.'

She gestured to the altar. 'Bring me one of those candles. You light them, don't you?'

He padded to the altar. 'Oh, yes. *Those* I can light.' Returning, he offered a candle, which she used to light the fire. She then drove a stick through the fish and set it high over the flames. Once it was hot she tore into the cooked flesh; her hands greasy, she extended the rest to the priest.

He eyed the remains. 'You are offering me this fish?'

She urged him to take it. 'Of course. Go ahead.'

With an odd reverence, and with both hands, he took it and walked over to the altar and set it there.

'Aren't you going to eat it?'

'I'm, ah, not hungry right now. I'll have it later.'

He was, she decided, *very* peculiar indeed.

'You must be tired,' he said. 'Sleep. I will wake you when I see daylight.'

The last thing on her mind was sleep – despite her exhaustion – yet a wave of drowsiness did wash over her then. She decided it must be from having just eaten.

The priest held out a bundle of old, dusty cloths. 'Lie upon these. I will wake you – do not fear.'

'I really shouldn't . . .'

'Rest. You will need your strength for the trial ahead.'

She took the bundle. 'You will wake me?'

'Yes. Assuredly.'

'Very well. At first light?'

'Yes. At first light.'

She was hesitant, but she was so very tired. She spread out the cloths as best she could and lay down.

It seemed as if that very same instant she was woken, the priest withdrawing his hand from her shoulder.

'You are awake? Good. It is time.'

She blinked at him, puzzled. 'But I'd only just . . .'

'No. You slept long and well. How do you feel?'

She considered the question. Indeed, she must have slept for she felt refreshed; in fact, she felt excellent – strong and relaxed – as after a rest on the most comfortable of beds. 'I feel . . . at ease.'

'Good, good.' The priest motioned her to the cave's edge where the waters lapped. 'Here. See? The light playing in the depths?'

She crossed to the edge, peered into the waters. Beams danced and flickered there, far off – the sun must be directly overhead. 'I should hurry.'

The priest was smiling at her. 'Yes. Go. Good luck in all your tasks. And,' he raised a hand in benediction, 'go with my blessings.'

For some reason the gesture gave her pause; she almost told the disgraced priest what she thought of any blessing from Mael, but the poor fellow truly seemed to mean it, and so she nodded her acceptance then stepped down among the wet and slimy rocks. She slowly submerged herself until only her head remained above the surface, took one last long breath, and dived, kicking.

*

The pot-bellied fellow watched her rippling form go, then padded in his flat-footed walk to the altar. He peered up for a time at the gigantic and heroic figure looming above in the shadows, net and spear in hand, then shook his head and crossed to the opposite side of the cavern where he searched among the rocks.

He returned to the altar with an object in hand: a slim, curved, cream-hued blade that shone opalescent in the candlelight. He laid one hand palm up upon the thick black basalt rock of the altar then pressed the tip of the blade to the centre of the palm. He pressed harder.

He leaned over the blade, put his full weight onto it. The shell-dagger quivered, almost singing with the forces being exerted.

The blade's keening grew louder, ringing, almost shrieking, until in an explosion of forces it burst into dust and fragments.

The fellow lurched, grunting, then raised his hand: a single pearl-like drop of blood gleamed there upon his palm. He shook the hand over the altar until the single drop reached the edge of the palm and fell onto the stone.

The drop touched the immense slab of basalt in a sledgehammer explosion of force that echoed throughout the cavern. The four-foot-thick block was now split in half. Cracks slithered up the statue. Dust and rocks pelted down as the grotto shook. The fellow steadied his footing, then let out a long and satisfied breath. Peering up to the ceiling, he nodded to himself with a lopsided grin. 'Almost free . . .' he murmured.

He looked to the tunnel pool and inclined his head in salute. 'Thank you for *your* blessing, High Priestess.'

* * *

Anticipating a rocky arrival, Dancer landed rolling. He came up instantly, blades ready – then let his arms fall – he was alone in a pre-dawn dimness standing in a flat wilderness of rock and bog dotted by dirty fields of snow and ice.

He cursed Kellanved heartily.

Where was he? Where was Ullara? Which way?

Near frantic, he scanned all about to spot, in the west, thin greyish plumes of smoke. It was all he had, so he took off, arms pumping.

He was nearing what appeared to be an encampment of rough tents when he saw to one side the slumped form of a huge beast. Swerving, he ran over and knelt next to the mound of pale fur. A dead snow-bear. Yet not a beast, for it wore a harness of leather. He slid a hand over it to find it still warm, and its neck wet with blood.

A guard – he might be too late . . . *no!*

He ran for the tents.

A distant strangled snarl of pain snapped his attention to the north and he swerved, doubling his pace.

*

Sialle was meditating, her senses cast wide about the camp, as was her practice each night. The bear- and wolf-warriors stood guard of course, and were completely loyal and dedicated, but she knew what was coming and these warriors – though fierce and fearless – stood no chance against an Imperial Claw.

These last few nights she'd been even more vigilant, as the Priestess's allies, these Crimson Guard, were no longer at her side. Meeting them, these Guardsmen and woman, had been rather a shock for her and she'd even played with the possibility of approaching them as a recruit.

After all, her goal had always been to hurt these Malazans. Somehow. In some way. To make them pay for what they had done, and were doing. Even as she endured their brutal training and indoctrination.

Becoming a good little Claw herself.

She smiled then, in recollection of all those years of training and bowing and serving – all the while staring back at them and maintaining her inner core, her true identity . . . her mission.

The small smile of satisfaction froze on her lips.

She sprang to her feet.

Someone was coming . . .

She ran and raised her Beast Warren to its fullest extent. *No need for hiding now.*

Moving through the Warren, she stormed right past the lumbering bear guards, straight to the Priestess's tent and pallet where she lay asleep.

She shook her. 'Awake, Priestess. Assassins come. We must flee.'

The woman fumbled with a cloth that she drew over the dark pits of her eyes. 'Assassins?'

'Yes. Get up. Please.' She helped the aged woman stand. 'I will take you with me now into my Warren to hide, yes?'

'Hide?' the Priestess asked, bleary, but sceptical. 'From ones such as these?'

'We shall see.' Sialle opened a way and took the frail woman's arm. She stepped forward only to snarl and stumble as searing pain slashed down her back and she – with the Priestess – tumbled out of the Warren onto boggy ground and night.

She jumped up once more, this time with twin knives bared, to stand over the Priestess and face the Claw. Only to despair – as she recognized who it was she faced.

This one, male, dark-skinned, wore the usual black gauzy

uniform, yet the eyes were bared, and these, odd and elongated, together with the vanity of rings at his fingers, gave the man's identity away. Topper. Surly's favourite operative.

Seeing the recognition in her gaze, he nodded, murmuring, 'Sialle.' He waved one blade in warning. 'You were foolish to have remained. Word of your, ah, desertion has reached us – your name is now on our list. And really, you were to merely have spied upon the cadre and this expedition. Truly, how difficult could that have been?'

Her back burned like fire, but she adjusted her footing while the Priestess, behind, stirred and groaned awake. 'I found a real calling.'

The Claw mock-frowned. 'Truly? What in Treach's name could that possibly be?'

'Something to protect.'

Topper saluted her with the narrow blade. 'Well, then, you shall have the privilege of dying for it.'

'So it's true,' she answered.

He frowned anew. 'Is what true?'

'What everyone says – that you talk your victims to death.' She swore she could hear his teeth grinding as his jaws clenched.

Snarling, he lunged.

She held her ground, parrying frantically, but knew she was overmatched; she took three cuts to her front and barely avoided a killing thrust as something smashed into the man, disrupting his rhythm – and saving her life.

The assassin slid back a step and wiped the back of his hand across his face, coming away with blood. His enraged gaze focused behind Sialle and she knew the Priestess was now awake.

Topper immediately closed in again, slashing in a blur. She parried desperately, all the while knowing she was done – even as cold iron punched into her stomach and she sagged.

A shape and thumping wings struck Topper once more, but the man swung overhead and the beast – a huge owl – tumbled to the ground in a ruin of broken feathers.

Panting against the numbing pain, Sialle fought to straighten one final time.

Topper stood over her; he shook his head in regret. 'A shame and a waste. You were a valuable asset. Now you die for nothing.'

Through clenched teeth she managed, 'Not for nothing.'

He shrugged nonchalantly. 'Whichever.'

A voice called then from the night: '*Stand down!*' and Topper stiffened. He turned to face this new arrival.

Through dimming eyes Sialle watched this newcomer approach; commonplace he seemed, in worn leathers, of medium height and slim, but he moved with a smooth, deceptive grace.

Topper actually backed off a pace. 'What are you doing here?' he demanded, openly surprised.

'This order is withdrawn.'

Topper shook a blade. 'Not within your authority, Dancer. This is an internal matter of the Claw.'

Sialle stared, utterly shocked. *Dancer?* In truth? Hands moved her – the Priestess binding her wounds.

Dancer crooked a brow. 'The Claw, I think, lies within the Emperor's and my authority.'

Topper's gaze slid to the Priestess where she leaned over Sialle. 'You've never interfered before. What will Surly think to have her will cast aside like this?'

'She'll survive.'

The Claw shrugged again, now affecting indifference. He saluted Dancer. 'Very well. But one day we shall have to settle this between us, don't you think?'

Dancer merely stared; his features steady, expressionless.

Topper grinned anew and slowly backed away, one step at a time. With each step he faded, becoming less distinct in the night, until his form disappeared entirely.

Dancer – if indeed it was the Master Assassin himself – knelt at Sialle's side to help the Priestess bind her wounds. 'Can you stand?' he asked of the Priestess, who nodded. She stared at the man though her eyes remained covered. He picked Sialle up and offered an arm to the Priestess, who took it, still staring, amazement plain upon her features.

As they walked the Bird Priestess murmured, 'You came.'

'Yes,' Dancer answered. 'I came.'

That was the last Sialle heard before unconsciousness took her.

* * *

They walked halls clearly not designed for the human scale; they climbed wide sloping ramps; crossed chambers choked by tall machinery that hummed and spun and whose purpose mystified Blues.

Bellurdan and Black led the way, ever watchful for more Che'Malle. Yet – also mystifying to Blues – so far they'd only come upon one other in the many halls, and this one they defeated by attacking all at once, taking only terrifyingly deep gashes in Black's shield.

This absence gnawed at his thoughts almost as much as the brain-cracking aura generated by the K'Chain Che'Malle energies. Each time he raised his D'riss Warren to tease out a path through the maze of chambers and caverns he felt as if knives were flensing his skull.

Gwynn winced in sympathy each time he saw him questing ahead.

'Where are they all?' he murmured to his fellow mage.

'Perhaps they are all guarding the lower ways. Or operating these mechanisms.'

'Well, I don't like it. Feels like a trap.'

Gwynn lifted his shoulders as if to say: *What can we do?*

Jacinth joined them. Her scavenged Malazan scale armour rustled as she moved and her hair hung lank with sweat from the punishing heat. 'How much further?' she demanded under her breath.

'A full day of travel perhaps?' Gwynn offered.

The swordswoman snarled her impatience.

The Thelomen giant, Bellurdan, gestured from the fore and Blues came to his side. A corner ahead opened onto a broad hallway, or gallery.

'This way?' Bellurdan asked.

Blues was unhappy about it, but nodded. 'I believe so.'

The Thelomen appeared equally displeased and let out a long rumbling breath, yet stepped out and advanced. Black and Jacinth flanked him. Blues and Gwynn followed.

They were far along the gallery when figures appeared ahead – not Che'Malle but human. A party of three: one swordsman who led; followed by an obvious mage in fine, dark clothes with a cape, his long black hair pulled back in a queue; and a tall and thin woman with short mousy hair, in plain linen shirting and pantaloons.

Both parties stared at one another for a time, stunned.

Then Gwynn whispered aside to Blues, '*That's Tayschrenn.*'

'And that's Dassem,' Black added.

Blues stared anew. *Hood's Blood.* 'We're overmatched – Gwynn, get us out of here!'

'I'll try . . .' Gwynn answered through clenched teeth. Blues sensed the man's Rashan Warren rising.

'Hold!' the distant mage – Tayschrenn – shouted out. He gestured and Gwynn grunted as if punched; Blues felt the man's Warren disperse like leaves in a strong wind.

Nothing for it then, he sighed, and drew his fighting knives. 'All of us on Dassem – now!'

Black and Jacinth drew as well and all charged, Bellurdan at the fore.

Dassem answered by raising his longsword two-handed crossways, and stepping up to meet their advance.

Then the giant suddenly skittered to a halt and threw out his arms, nearly knocking Blues flat. '*Wait!*' the Thelomen bellowed. Black, Jacinth and Blues all eyed the giant, all tensed yet uncertain.

Dassem crouched, ready for any rush.

Bellurdan squinted at the Malazans then threw his hands into the air, shouting, 'Sister—'

'Nightchill!' the woman cut in, her voice like a whip.

'Ah,' Bellurdan answered. 'Of course. But – is it really you?'

The woman casually pushed past a blinking Dassem and the two, the giant and she, embraced; she, tall for a woman, reaching just to his stomach.

Mystified, Blues felt his arms falling. Dassem, the Sword of the Empire, straightened, frowning his confusion.

The giant held her out now before him, looking her up and down. 'It has been so long!'

Blues saw Gwynn cock an eye to Tayschrenn, the High Mage, who answered with a raised brow.

'Looks like a truce . . .' Blues announced to the hall at large, and the Sword nodded his consent.

*

The woman, whom Blues now recognized as *the* Nightchill – a Malazan mage just as fearsome as Tayschrenn himself, had tugged Bellurdan aside and the two were now engrossed in a low conversation. Tayschrenn was approaching, while Black and Jacinth watched the Sword – quite warily.

The High Mage eyed them, and Blues thought he saw disapproval in his gaze – though it was hard to tell as the man appeared to disapprove of everything he saw.

'And you are . . . ?' Tayschrenn asked of Blues.

After staring for a time, Blues managed to stammer, 'Ah, Grief.'

'Andar,' Gwynn put in. 'And you?'

'We choose not to divulge our names for now. Rude, I know. But there you are.' The High Mage gestured to their gear. 'You are wearing Malazan-issue armour and leathers. How did you come by it?'

Blues shrugged. 'Bought it here and there.'

Tayschrenn's mouth puckered even more sourly. 'Indeed. And how did you come to join up with a Thelomen giant?'

'We were hired together to look into this place.'

'By whom?'

'That's our business.'

Blues enjoyed the man's clenched jaws.

'I hope you realize that we cannot let you take away any of these secrets,' the mage pronounced.

'No one should,' Gwynn answered.

Again the lifted brow. '*We* are here to shut this installation down.'

Blues nodded. 'That would be our preference as well.'

The High Mage gave a sceptical snort.

Nightchill and Bellurdan rejoined them. 'We shall travel together,' the woman announced. 'Our chances of success are manifestly improved if we do so.'

Over everyone's heads, the giant sent Blues a wink. For his part Blues was not pleased by the proposal, but it beat a running battle through the halls, so he nodded his consent.

'We agree,' the Sword added, and he offered a strange sort of amused half-smile.

Tayschrenn blew out an impatient breath. 'Very well.'

Nightchill gestured up the gallery. 'This way.'

*

While they walked, Tayschrenn fell in with Dassem. He whispered, 'Do you think they know we know who they are?'

'Perhaps. They choose to pretend, for now. An unusual alliance for us – don't you think?'

Tayschrenn let out a choked breath. 'It is *not* an alliance. I quite assure you of that. In fact, I worry we may have lost our best chance to cut them down.' He examined Dassem. 'You could have, yes?'

The Sword cocked his head, thinking. 'Blues is the Guard's weapon-master. Jacinth and Black are both formidable champions, no less strong than Skinner himself. Throw in a giant Thelomen and I wonder. It would have been close. Very close.'

Tayschrenn said nothing further as he paced along, hands behind his back, but this was sobering news indeed. He did not inform the Sword that here, within the alien energies of these mechanisms, the best he could muster was to merely interfere with Gwynn summoning his Warren. Yes, sobering news.

It appeared that, at least for the meantime, they were stuck with each other.

Chapter 20

WHEN KELLANVED SAID HE'D SENT DANCER OFF ON SOME unknown errand Cartheron was furious. Now the man's safety was his responsibility! How would it look if the Emperor was killed during his watch? Surly would absolutely crucify him.

He managed little sleep that night, or the following. He was further infuriated when he found that the *Twisted* carried almost no other talent. He questioned every sailor and marine and the best he could roust was one elderly deckhand whom everyone *swore* was a talent.

Cartheron now looked the grey-haired fellow up and down, and he wasn't impressed: lacking rather too many teeth for anyone with any talent – in his opinion. 'I need you to keep an eye on our, ah, *passenger*, hey?' he asked of the emaciated fellow. 'You can do that?'

The old sailor shook his head. 'Nope. Can't help you there.'

'Why the Abyss not?'

'Not my strength, if you know what I mean.'

Further irritated, Cartheron snapped, 'So what can you do then?'

The fellow peered round, smoothed his scraggy beard. 'Oh . . . have a nose for the wind I do, the waves . . . that sort of thing.'

Cartheron looked to the bright blue sky. 'Fine. Thank you so very much. Keep your nose poised, would you?'

The veteran sailor tapped the great, canted object of discussion, and winked knowingly. 'Oh, that I can do.'

Cartheron pressed a hand to his brow. Gods – where were all

these mages 'n such that were always coming and going? Where under the sun were they? Defeated, he set guards on the man's cabin and doubled the standard watch.

He reassured himself with the knowledge that at least they were anchored in the middle of a wide channel, in the middle of nowhere, with no other ships in sight. He didn't think they had much to worry about in that regard.

Two days later he was on the mid-deck going over the stores situation with the ship's quartermaster Teal – she would not let him forget that the sweet-water was nearly all gone, as were most perishables – he knew he'd have to talk to Kellanved about putting in somewhere, anywhere, for supplies. During the discussion the grey-haired old veteran sailor, The Nose, as Cartheron thought of him, approached and knuckled his brow.

Cartheron dismissed Teal, who grumbled her displeasure, but departed, then he eyed their so-called mage. 'Yes . . . ' – he realized he didn't know the man's proper name – '. . . what is it?'

'Well, sor,' the fellow began, 'been keeping an eye on the winds and the waves – as you ordered, sor.'

'Nose. I thought it was your nose.'

The sailor nodded sombrely. 'Oh, yes. That too.'

'And?'

'Well, sor. Something's coming.'

'Really? Something. Something's coming.'

The veteran nodded very gravely. 'Oh, yes. Definitely. I'd say something's definitely coming.'

'Can you perhaps be more specific?'

The fellow screwed up an eye and cocked his grizzled head. 'Well, I'd say it's something more to do with the water and the waves rather than the winds – if you know what I mean. And I'd have to say it's something pretty big, too. An' it be coming from the north-west, and fast. An' be here soon, too.'

'Fast? Is it a ship?'

'Ah, no, sor.' The fellow pointed. 'I'm thinkin' maybe that be it.'

Cartheron squinted up the channel – north-west. The waters did look strange across the horizon. Looked like a large wave, which was unusual for the region, as the relative calmness of Falaran waters was well known.

The strange phenomenon seemed to grow, or swell, even as he

watched: was it approaching quickly, or truly enlarging? All that came to mind was a wave, an aberrant large wave . . .

He spun, yelling, 'Cut anchor! Raise sails! Bring us round bearing south-east!' Then ran for the cabin.

He banged on the door until an annoyed answer came, 'Yes, by all the gods, what?'

'A problem here, ah, sir. Looks like a rogue wave. Coming fast.'

The door opened and out stepped an unkempt Kellanved; he blinked in the light rather like a startled mole. 'Ah! Our legendary Jhistal, no doubt.'

'I don't think so, sir,' and Cartheron turned to the north-west – only to stare himself, shocked.

This was far worse than any rogue wave that might drive the *Twisted* onto rocks or shore: a veritable wall of green was now surging upon them – and rising ever higher as he watched.

'Oh dear,' Kellanved managed. 'This isn't what I was expecting. No, not at all.'

Cartheron was surprised by the calmness in his voice as he observed, 'This will obliterate us. There's nothing we can do.'

'Not you, perhaps,' Kellanved answered. 'But there is *one* thing I can try. Not with all of you, though,' and he raised his hands, gesturing.

Cartheron had time for one warning shout of, '*Don't you*—' before the world turned an odd sort of monochrome of shadowy greys and he stumbled, falling among rocks and brush. The flat, colourless light faded away, rather like the eclipses he'd experienced over the years, and he found himself close to an island shore. Nearby, crewmen and women rose as well, cursing and grumbling, from the thorny brush. Cartheron saw Creel, the mate, Geddin, the old steersman, the quartermaster Teal, even The Nose – it looked like Kellanved had transported the entire crew to safety. But where? He fought through the thick brush to Creel. 'Where are we?'

'Don't know, cap'n.'

Cartheron raised a hand to the sun – looked like no time had passed.

The Nose approached and knuckled his brow once more.

'Yes?' Cartheron answered.

The old fellow smoothed his uneven beard. 'Well, sor. That was rather a *lot* of water. And I'm thinking that if we're still nearby, it could be headed our way – if you know what I mean . . .'

Cartheron offered an obliged nod. Of course. He pointed uphill. 'Everyone! Head to higher ground. Now!'

*

On board the *Twisted*, Kellanved regarded the advancing mountain of water. Already it towered four or five times higher than the masts of the vessel. A thump upon the decking announced the arrival of the nacht and he now eyed it sceptically.

'And will you be of any help, pray tell?'

The beast yawned, exposing oversized fangs and a pink tongue, then shoved an entire walnut into its mouth and gagged upon it, gasping for air.

Kellanved sighed. He began rolling up a sleeve. 'Oh, you think so, do you? Too much? Very well. Typical! It all comes down to me in the end. As usual! But not like me to complain, though! Not at all. Quite used to it, I am.' He started on his other sleeve. 'I will show you something here, my friend! I swear. I will not hold back – I assure you!' He glanced over to see the beast urinating a great stream to the deck.

His gaze narrowed to slits. 'Oh, so you think so? In the wind? We'll see. Ready yourself!'

He turned to the mounting, foam-webbed cliff of water poised above the vessel. It towered so high it now blocked the sun, throwing him into shade, and he faltered momentarily – but gathered himself, throwing his arms wide, to announce:

'*Welcome to Shadow!*'

* * *

Dujek was shaving when scouts returned from watching the mountain. He was peering into a small mirror of polished bronze and drawing a straight blade over the lathered pate of his head – not an easy task for a one-armed man. A knock on the pole next to the door-flap made him flinch slightly, and cut the top of his head. Pressing a rag to the wound, he shouted, 'Enter!'

Three scouts ducked within, saluting. Dujek glowered at them. 'Yes? News?'

'It's definitely moving, sir.'

Dujek stared at the three, almost unable to process this news. His hand remained pressed to the top of his head. Something that immense moving? 'Really? The entire fucking thing?'

'Yes sir. Definitely. Picking up speed too – though slowly.'

'Which direction?'

'North, more or less.'

He peeled his hand and the rag from his head. 'Well that's just great. North is Falar! What's it doing going north?' He waved his hand. 'Never mind. Just thinking aloud.' He gestured them out. 'Send Captain Ullen to me.'

They saluted and departed. Dujek wiped his head clean of any remaining lather. A knock announced the captain's arrival. 'Enter,' Dujek called. Captain Ullen ducked within, saluted. Dujek poured himself a glass of watered wine. 'I understand this Hood-damned mountain thing is actually moving.'

'So I hear, Fist.'

'Well, we'd better tag along – don't you think? Relay the orders to break camp. We move out tomorrow dawn.'

The captain saluted. 'At once.'

Dujek waved him out, but called after him, 'Oh, and have Hairlock sent to me.'

Ullen nodded, then frowned, pointing to him. 'Fist, sir. You are, ah, bleeding.'

Dujek slapped the rag to his head. 'Dammit.'

It was after the evening meal when the cadre mage Hairlock came thumping into the tent that served as both Dujek's private quarters and command gathering place. The mage searched about, found the wine carafe and poured himself a drink. He sat with a sigh of ease.

'You wanted to see me?'

Dujek was unenthusiastically eyeing the clutter of paperwork on the one table. 'Yes. Still no word from Tayschrenn or Nightchill?'

'Not a word. Nothing. They went in and nothing since.'

'But the thing's moving now – related?'

The mage shrugged, threw back the drink. 'Who knows? Can't say.'

It occurred to Dujek that Tayschrenn's and Nightchill's

disappearance would be quite the career advancement for this fellow. 'Well, keep trying.'

Hairlock ran a hand over his own bald scalp and gestured to Dujek. 'Missed a spot there.'

The Fist grimaced. 'Got interrupted.' He glanced significantly to the open door-flap.

The mage pushed himself from the camp chair. 'Yeah. What do you think I *was* doin'?'

'Let me know if you sense anything at all.'

The squat mage padded to the entryway in his flat-footed, side to side gait. 'Course,' he muttered as he disappeared into the night.

Dujek leaned over the table and for a time sorted through orders, reports, and other logistics. It was close to midnight when he crossed to the sideboard to pour himself another glass of the watered wine. Turning, he threw the glass across the tent directly at the same camp chair. Something deflected the glass to one side, the chair flew backwards, and a curse sounded.

The air about the chair rippled, revealing a dark-skinned man in a green silk shirt, silk sash and pantaloons. This figure gestured to himself. 'Do you know how hard it is to clean silk?'

'Don't sneak into my tent, Topper. You're lucky it wasn't a dagger.'

The Claw straightened his stained shirt. 'You lot and your tents. *You're* the lucky one.'

Dujek poured himself another drink. 'What do you want?'

'Surly is concerned. Things are not going as planned.'

Dujek snorted. 'When have they ever?'

'And Dancer has interfered with her orders.'

The Fist froze for an instant then set down the glass. 'How so?'

'The leader of these Jhek was sanctioned. He forestalled it.'

Dujek grunted at the news, nodding. 'Well, he may have his reasons. And it lies within his prerogative – don't you think?'

'He shouldn't step on her authority like this.'

The Fist raised a brow. 'Or *yours*, you mean, perhaps?'

'Immaterial. They get along because they keep to their own fields.'

'Well,' Dujek downed the drink, 'perhaps it was done for the Empire's good, hmm? Does your wounded pride allow you to consider that possibility?'

The Claw snarled something under his breath, stalked to the tent-flap. He paused here, pointing. 'For some unknown reason you are something of a favourite of hers. Do not count too much upon this to protect you,' and he swept out.

'Or *you*,' Dujek called after him. 'A night for visitors,' he murmured to himself, and hunched in front of the bronze mirror to examine his scalp.

*　*　*

The vessel was an ancient, dilapidated merchant coaster out of Jook. Given the general fear of these invader raids and pirating, and the shut-down of almost all sea-trade, the captain considered himself lucky to take on an obvious veteran hand for the crossing to Belade.

For her part, it tore Gianna's heart to leave the youths behind in Cabil. But the Jhistal had been sent and so they should be safe – for the meantime. Once a moon was the Faith's legend regarding the summoning of the Jhistal – though she didn't know for certain. No one in the priesthood did. These were uncharted waters for everyone.

She'd scavenged an oversized leather cap and frayed shirt and trousers and kept herself busy on board the *Irene*, hoping the captain would be unwilling to risk losing such a good hand by asking any annoying questions regarding her background, or her rush to leave Cabil waters.

Her goal was to return to the shoals of Sparrow Pass Cut, where she hoped to find Brevin, captain of the *Glimmer*, still salvaging – there was a month of the season left before the choppier waters of winter. And then, she had a hunch about just where she'd find this chest, this so-called Jhistal's Bane.

They reached Belade harbour without incident. The crew spotted a few foreign raiders in the distance, yet the invaders appeared reluctant to approach Cabil itself, and seemed content with their looting and securing of new bases among the islands.

Belade itself was intact – it was a large enough city to fend off any raids. Gianna was surprised, however, by a line of damage across the entire waterfront: docks canted, vessels half-sunk, buildings knocked aslant.

Captain Jensk of the *Irene* tried to lure her into hiring on for the return run, but she begged off, making excuses about relatives in Belade, and set off up the damaged and uneven wharf. The first person she came to – a labourer hanging about piled cargo – she asked, 'What happened here?'

He snorted at her ignorance. 'Tidal bore is what – at least that's what the city council says.' He peered around, touched his temple, 'But everyone knows otherwise. Was the Jhistal itself. The crest-wave of its passing through the waters.'

'Passing? Where? Did you *see* it?'

The fellow appeared uncomfortable. 'Not m'self, no. Others did, though. Say it was as tall as a mountain o' water.'

'Where did it strike?'

The labourer nodded to the east. 'The channel to the Ice Sea is what they say. Rose up there, some saw. Probably 'gainst these invaders.'

She gave him a nod and walked on. The waterfront was a wreck and empty, and this worried her. How would she get to Belid, or Flood? Sea-traffic looked to have thinned to nothing; everyone shut behind doors and walls. Hoping to wait out these raiders, perhaps. Hoping someone else would deal with them.

As she walked, she considered: just who *did* she know here in Belade? Anyone?

Well, there was old Torva – if he was still alive. Gods, the old smuggler captain had been ancient all those years ago when she'd been a young first mate on board his low-slung galley, the *Sea Snake*. She snorted to herself: those early years had been among the happiest and most carefree of her life.

Thinking of Torva, she peered round to spot the nearest water-front tavern. A few questions and she was directed up a lane that led towards the poorest, lowest-lying section of the city, where ramshackle shacks leaned sadly against one another and near-naked children played in pools of muddy water.

A few more questions and she found herself before a tiny hut of scavenged planks, and she felt her heart sink. Here lived the one-time greatest smuggler of the isles? Perhaps she had the wrong fellow, though.

A deep rumble of distant thunder drew her attention to the south then, and she frowned. Not the season for storms – and

306

certainly not out of the south. Yet a line of dark clouds obscured the southern horizon, peeking out there beyond the low coastal range.

She knocked on the lashed planks that served as a door.

A gruff, dismissive, 'Who's there?' answered and she knew she had her man.

'Permission to come aboard,' she called.

Shuffling within and the door opened a crack. An elderly, sun-darkened face peered out, all deep seams and grey stubble. 'Who'sat? Thought I heard a voice of m'old days.'

'You did. It's me, Gianna.'

The face brightened in a toothless half-smile. 'Why, so 'tis. Gianna. Best first mate ever sailed the clear seas.'

'May we talk?'

''Course! Come in. Just don't mind the mess. Been meanin' to brush the place up.'

The door creaked open and Gianna slipped inside. It was dim, the only light being beams slanting through two boarded windows. A table stood crowded with empty stoneware bottles. A grey dog, perhaps as old as Torva himself, lay next to a hearth of dead ashes.

The ancient smuggler sat with a sigh. 'So, Gianna. Me old mate. What you been up to all these years?' He gestured to another chair – full of more empty bottles. She set them aside and sat.

'Salvaging . . . mostly.'

Torva grunted. 'An' what can old Torva do for you?'

Gianna peered about the run-down tiny hut and felt her heart ache at the condition of her old captain. 'Torva . . . I'm sorry, but I have to ask . . . what happened? You were the most successful smuggler of your age – or so everyone said.'

The old man nodded. 'Ach. Had a run of bad luck. Ran up debts. Had to sell the good ol' *Sea Snake*. After that, no one was interested in listening to my tales of the better days.' He waved a crooked hand in dismissal. 'So it goes if you live too long in our line o' work. I ain't sour. Just miss me old friends and companions.'

She blew out a breath. 'I need to get to Belid, or Flood, but no one's sailing. Any ideas on where I can find passage? Or a boat?'

His grey bushy brows knotted as he frowned in thought. 'Well . . .' he began, 'there's me fishing punt. We can take that out.'

She stared at him. 'A punt – a rowboat? To Belid?'

''S gotta steppable mast an' a square sail. It could make it. 'Specially in the hands of two canny sailors like us.'

She was shaking her head at the outrageousness of it. A crossing of that length in a tiny rowboat? Ridiculous.

'All we need is some potable water,' the old man continued, screwing up his face, 'some stores . . . a spare sail wouldn't hurt neither.'

Gianna was now waving her hand. 'No. Torva – thanks, but no thanks. I'll find another way.'

A scoff of disbelief. 'Oh? Got another boat hidden somewheres?' He rose, gesturing, 'C'mon, let's take a look.'

'Torva . . . please . . .' but the old man pushed past her. At the door he collected a cane that was nothing more than a cut tree-limb, polished with use. He turned back to her. 'Well? What's the hold-up? You used to be the one at the fore – as I remember.'

Defeated, she shook her head. 'Fine. We'll have a look. But I'll go alone if it comes to that.'

'Not in *my* boat,' he muttered. Then he pointed to the dog. 'You – stay!'

The ancient grey-muzzled beast hadn't moved a muscle the entire time, as far as Gianna could tell, and it didn't even raise its head as they pulled the door shut.

It was a punt – a small ship's launch – in fairly good shape, pulled high up the shore. Keeled, with oarlocks and a steppable mast.

Gianna straightened from examining the hull timbers. 'She was high up enough, then, when the tidal bore swept through?'

Torva gave a hoarse laugh. 'Tidal bore? That pittance? Ha! Why, in m'youth, in the year Mount Lessen erupted, why, there was such a wave as none o' these blowhards have ever even imagined. Three chains high it was if it was anything at all! Swept all o' Clump off the shore.' He thoughtfully scratched the stubble of his chin. 'Which was an improvement to my way of thinking, by the by.'

Gianna had raised a hand. 'Yes – thank you.'

With her Ruse skills, she imagined she'd probably have the best chance of anyone. She thought aloud, 'I have some pay for stores . . .'

'I'll get us waterskins.'

308

'For one. I should go alone.'

He pulled his chin in, offended. 'Now listen here, lass. My boat, an' I'll kindly take you to Belid, or Flood, but only if you sink such nonsense.'

'It's too dangerous. What if something should happen to you? I'd never forgive myself.'

He smiled crookedly, shook his head. 'Ah, lass, me headin' out there,' and he pointed his cane to the bay, 'is where I belong. You be doing me a favour.'

She didn't say it aloud – but she agreed. He being at sea, doing what he loved, was far better than the lonely, impoverished fate that being unlucky enough to have outlived all his contemporaries, and his usefulness, had doomed him to.

* * *

Glinith Apanar, Abbess of Cabil, knew it was foolish – perhaps even weak – to stare out one of the narrow windows of the council chamber overlooking the Bay of Cabil, but she couldn't help it. What was happening this very instant so far away in the strait between the mainland and the isle of Delanss?

What, she wondered, had they unleashed in the name of their desperation, and, yes, perhaps even hubris? A monstrosity which would terrorize them all? Would her name go down as one of the greatest villains of the region – or one of its saviours?

The next few hours would tell.

She turned from the slit window, deliberately put her back to it, and faced the long main table. Reports and other minutiae of logistics cluttered it. Nuraj Senull, Guardian of the Faith, sat at the centre of it, surrounded by messengers coming and going, delivering a never-ending stream of demands, pleas, lists, affronted denials, and not so thinly veiled insults.

The poor man was practically pulling out what little hair he had left on his pate.

Mallick Rel, Proctor of the Faith, meanwhile, sat immobile, fingers entwined over his round stomach, his fat-cupped eyes half-lidded, seemingly asleep despite the turmoil.

Sitting at the table, she asked, 'When will we know?' and immediately regretted it.

309

Rel's gaze slid to her and she read contempt in its depths. He did not deign to answer for a time, then sighed wearily. 'We have agents watching from the surrounding coasts. And our priests-militant are monitoring from Rashan. We should know soon.'

The doors to the chamber opened and one of the said priests-militant entered. The woman handed Mallick a scroll, bowed, and exited.

The Proctor of the Faith, and for all practical purposes the true power of the Jhistal, read slowly, deliberately. His thick lips drew down.

Both she and Nuraj wordlessly eyed the man, waiting.

He cocked one brow, as if mildly surprised, and lowered the sheet. Clearing his throat, he began hesitantly, 'Well . . . it seems the Jhistal has struck. However, all witnesses agree that none saw the *thing* itself – if indeed there ever were such a thing.'

'What do you mean, man?' Nuraj demanded. 'What is the report?'

'The report – verified by multiple witnesses – is of a titanic wave. Estimates place its height perhaps as great as ten chains.'

'That's impossible!' Glinith blurted, then bit her lip.

Nuraj let out an awed breath. 'That should be destructive enough – don't you think?'

Mallick nodded. He tapped the sheet. 'No sign of the vessel remains behind. However,' and he frowned anew, 'there are conflicting reports of the aftermath. Some sources recount the wave seemingly disappearing utterly. Or immediately withdrawing, or some such odd thing.'

'Mael may do as he wishes,' Nuraj mused, rubbing a stubbled cheek.

Mallick offered a nod of assent. 'Indeed. That is *one* answer.'

'So that is it, then,' Glinith said. 'The leader of this invasion is destroyed – whoever he may have been.'

Mallick re-twined his fingers over his paunch. 'Yes. Quite. We have convincingly demonstrated the powers at our command. Now we must wait and see how these invading captains respond. Will some open negotiations? Will some withdraw? Will some turn on their fellows? We shall see.'

'But we may not be able to summon the thing again – perhaps for a full moon.'

Again Mallick's dismissive gaze slid to Glinith. '*They* do not know that, do they?' and he smiled, revealing his sickly grey teeth.

* * *

Janul stood peering out at the gathering twilight from the open back door of the lowest kitchens of the Basilica. 'Looks like it might rain,' he told his sister Janelle. She nodded, her eyes on the door leading to the narrow stairs up. 'Even the rain here is warm,' he continued. 'I could get used to that.'

'Quiet,' she murmured, and pushed back her straggly greying hair.

Janul's gaze slid to the inner door as well, and he quickly stepped outside.

The door creaked open and a plump priest, Brother Lethor, edged in. Janelle crossed to him, bowing. 'Welcome, sor. What a surprise.'

The brother peered about the dim chamber. 'We are alone?'

'We are.'

'I have news.'

Janelle carefully closed the door behind the priest. 'Oh? News?' She led the man further into the low-ceilinged kitchen. The priest ran a finger over counters dirty with flour and grease and his wide face wrinkled in distaste.

'I want . . . a pledge of consideration from you – from your, ah, masters.'

'Oh? Consideration?'

'Yes.' He crossed his thick arms. 'I travelled in my youth. Many lands. Including Quon Tali. I have seen the Malazan military might. If they want Falar, they will have it. We cannot forestall them.'

Janelle, too, crossed her arms; her hands, hidden in the wide sleeves, found the grips of the knives sheathed there. 'Your information has been of help,' she admitted.

Brother Lethor inclined his head in acknowledgement. 'And I have not asked for silver as I hope you have noted. It is not coin I wish for, it is . . .' He trailed off, searching for the word.

'Immunity?' Janelle supplied.

'Yes. And a place in the new, ah, administration. There will be need for people with local knowledge. Liaisons, and such. Even

311

priests. The Malazans, wisely, do not interfere with local religious practices.'

Janelle nodded. 'True. But such special consideration would require a demonstration of trust. Of proper intent.'

Brother Lethor edged closer, eager. 'Yes! And I have it. Important news. The Jhistal has been summoned and dispatched.'

Janelle nodded, coolly. 'We have heard.'

'Ah! But do you know upon whom it has been loosed?'

Janelle edged her head in a slow negative.

'The putative leader of this first wave of invasion – if that is what it is. The ship far to the south-east, in the channel to the Ice Sea.'

Janelle's hands convulsed upon the grips of her daggers and she clenched her teeth to keep from cursing. 'You are certain of this?' she asked, her voice hoarse and faint.

'Indeed!' Brother Lethor answered, his voice rising, almost in pride.

Janelle winced and motioned for quiet. 'You expect much for little. This is all too late, is it not?'

The heavy-set priest hunched, put thick fingers to his mouth. 'This is true,' he stage-whispered. 'However, there is more.'

'Oh? More? Pray tell to Mael, what more could there be?'

Brother Lethor peered side to side, lowered his head even closer. 'The Faith had eyes upon the event. Multiple witnesses, watching.'

'And?' Janelle nearly gasped, almost faint with dread.

'Complete destruction,' the man breathed. 'Utter annihilation. Not a scrap of wood left. Nothing left behind.'

Janelle flinched from the priest's hot breath, swallowed her now near panic. 'Thank you, Brother. Your information will be passed along. Your, ah, cooperation will be noted.'

The fellow nodded knowingly and backed away. He inclined his head in farewell, then turned to open the flimsy wood-panelled door and pulled it shut behind him.

Janelle turned to see that Janul had already entered.

'I will go,' he told her.

She gave a curt nod. 'Go. Though they probably already know.'

'We mustn't assume. We must pass this along.'

She waved him off. 'Yes, yes. Go.'

He dashed from the kitchen. Alone, Janelle leaned against a

counter, crossed her arms once more. Nothing left, this informant had said. Not one timber – no wreckage . . .

She tapped a finger to her lips. He might have fled to Shadow. But taking an entire ship with him? The entire thing? Was that even possible?

She shook her head. Who was to say? Perhaps the witnesses were all fooled. *That* sounded more like the Magister she knew.

* * *

The tent was dark, smoky, hot and crowded. Dancer stood close to the single entrance while multiple figures crowded the girl on the straw cot. At his side, the Bird Priestess, whom he now knew in truth as Ullara, motioned him out.

Straightening, he drew a breath of the clean, cool night air. 'I hope she will recover,' he said. 'The girl showed true courage.'

'All our best wolf-matron healers are treating her. They will bring her through.'

Dancer motioned to the woman's arm, wrapped in a sling. 'What of you?'

She laughed – and echoes of a much younger woman's laughter lingered in Dancer's ears. 'It is nothing. A bruise, perhaps. When I fell.'

'I hope so.'

Tiny birds came careering down to settle on the woman's shoulders – even amid her grey hair. Dancer felt many eyes upon him.

She motioned to another, larger tent. 'Here. Come. Let us talk.'

Before they reached the tent, a huge bear-warrior female with a great thick mane of grey and white hair came lumbering up to Ullara and knelt before her. 'I failed you,' she said, her voice a low growl.

Ullara waved it all aside. 'There was nothing you could have done. You would be dead, like poor Kai.'

'Still . . .'

'No matter. Think no more of it, Ursana.'

The woman rose, reluctantly. She eyed Dancer up and down.

'An old friend. He saved my life.'

The woman, Ursana, grunted at this and gave a curt nod. 'Then I am in your debt.'

313

Dancer answered the nod.

'I would speak privately,' Ullara told her. 'Please keep watch.'

Within, Ullara sat in a wide chair of leather and wood, and sighed, cradling her arm. Small birds came and went through a central opening in the canopy of sewn hides. They perched all about on the tent's framework of poles.

Dancer pulled over a stool to sit next to her. 'So many times over the years I've wondered – what became of you? Where did you end up? How were you faring? And now . . . look at you.'

She self-consciously smoothed her mussed and greying hair. 'Yes – look at me.'

'I mean what you have accomplished.'

'I? What of you and your companion? Look at what you have accomplished.'

He drew her hand down from her hair. 'I see that you have given much to these people.'

She nodded, smiling. 'Yes. I have given everything. Held back nothing.' She reached out to brush his cheek. 'No High Denul healing to be had here in these wastes.'

He took her hand, thin and frail. 'I would stay for a time – if you wish. We have much to talk about.'

'I would not keep you from your responsibilities.'

'My main responsibility can take care of himself.'

She laughed, then winced when her lashed arm knocked against the chair's back. 'Those are not the rumours I hear. I hear you have your hands full keeping him alive.'

He sat back, smiling crookedly. 'Well, that is true. He is a handful.' Then he regarded her critically. 'But tell me – what of your travels? How did you get here? How did you find these people?'

'Tell you my tale?' she answered with a rueful smile. 'Very well. It is no doubt not as eventful as yours, but it will take some telling. I will send for food.'

Chapter 21

T HEY WALKED TALL CORRIDORS, SEEMINGLY WITHOUT END. Occasionally, a sharp jolt shook the entire party and Blues winced anew at the mental slashing these eruptions, failings and concatenations of falling cracking rock tore through D'riss. Gwynn even steadied him, from time to time, and he nodded his gratitude.

The Sword led, though no further K'ell Hunters had appeared.

Bellurdan and the sorceress Nightchill walked side by side just behind Tayschrenn.

The Guard brought up the rear.

By now Blues was beginning to wonder whether all the K'Chain Che'Malle had deserted this rather obviously sinking land-vessel. 'Perhaps it will blow itself up,' he called ahead to Tayschrenn.

The mage peered back, scornful. 'We must make certain.'

'You, halt!' Dassem shouted, pointing his blade.

Blues squinted ahead, wiped sweat from his eyes; far up the hall two figures had appeared. Instead of fleeing, however, they were now running towards them.

'What are you doing here?' Tayschrenn demanded of them.

'Thank goodness,' one panted – the elder, in sweat-damp, worn and tattered robes. 'You are here to stop this, yes?'

'Indeed,' Tayschrenn answered. 'We seek the main chamber.'

Both nodded their obvious relief. The other, a woman in salt-stained leathers, was armed with a duelling blade that Blues recognized as rare Darujhistani steel. She pointed ahead. 'We can show you the way.'

'Good,' Tayschrenn said. 'But again – account for yourselves.'

315

The woman said, gesturing them on, 'I don't know how much time we have.'

As they walked, the older man explained, 'We were captured and forced to help manage the controls.'

'Why would the Che'Malle have need of your help?' Nightchill asked.

'Not the K'Chain,' the woman answered. 'They aren't responsible for this – it was a Jaghut.'

'A Jaghut!' Nightchill exclaimed. 'Impossible. None would do such a thing. It is not in their nature.'

The woman shrugged. 'Well, this one wasn't right, I'll tell you that. He was sick with something. Dying. Probably dead now.'

Blues exchanged glances with Black and Jacinth. Could they take a Jaghut? Even a sick one? None appeared eager to find out.

This woman, and the fellow with her, probably a mage, Blues thought, fell in with him and Gwynn. Blues eyed her sidelong. 'Captured, hey? Come for the legend no doubt.'

'Whatever,' she growled.

'What's your name?'

'Hessa. This is Turnagin.'

Blues gave his name as Grief.

'Straight on!' Hessa shouted ahead to Dassem, gesturing.

'Is it far?' Tayschrenn asked of her.

'Everything's far in this damned place,' she grumbled.

It was very far – at least Blues thought so. The route steepened now: long curved ramps and rising floors. He could march all day with the best of them, but uphill all the time? It was killing his legs. That, plus the enervating heat, left him panting and nearly dizzy.

The woman, Hessa, caught his eye. 'You wouldn't have any stores, would you? We're dying for anything other than dried meat.'

'We have some dried fruit.'

She held out a dirty, soot-stained hand. 'Please. It's been weeks.'

Blues handed over a small sack of dried fruits. Hessa and Turnagin tore into the meagre supplies like famished wolves.

'Water?' Hessa asked.

Gwynn extended a goatskin flask. This they upended, gulping, until Jacinth snatched it from the mage, snarling, 'Hey! We're short too, you know.'

They nodded their thanks. Turnagin wiped his mouth then peered ahead, pointing. 'We're close now.'

Thank the gods, Blues silently added.

Hessa now eyed Blues and asked, 'You didn't happen to see any-one else on your way, did you?'

He shook his head. 'No. No one.' Her wide mouth drew down, twisting. 'Missing someone?'

She nodded.

'Well, sorry. We saw no one.'

'Thanks, anyway.'

Nightchill approached. 'Show us where you last saw this Jag-hut,' she demanded.

Hessa gestured ahead. 'This way. Like I said – he's probably dead by now.'

'They are rather hard to kill,' the sorceress answered, one brow raised.

Hessa stepped up but Dassem extended an arm to hold her back. 'I will lead the way.'

She pointed and the Sword nodded, advancing, blade ready.

They were now edging through some sort of collection of machin-ery: tall banks of instruments, large metal gears, and hanging, clanging lengths of massive chains. Hessa pointed ahead.

They rounded one tall bank of levers and what looked like large, platter-sized dials, and Dassem halted to sign back to everyone that he'd made contact.

Nightchill simply continued on – followed closely by Bellurdan – though Dassem hissed for them to stop. Blues shrugged and followed.

It was a Jaghut, as the woman claimed. The giant figure – huge, though not as large as Bellurdan – lay prostrate, apparently dead. Just as Hessa had said.

Nightchill knelt by the figure. She laid a hand upon his chest, felt his neck, announced, 'He lives yet.' She shook her head. 'Oh, Juage. You poor fool . . . what has become of you?'

'Fucking bastard,' Hessa breathed, her hand going to her blade.

Dassem raised a hand to her and she snarled something under her breath, and released her grip.

The creature coughed then, wetly, and drew in a heavy breath.

He blinked up at Nightchill, stared, then laughed – or tried to, but coughed instead, convulsing.

'So . . .' he gasped, 'you again.'

'Yes. Seems we've danced this dance before. Tell me – what happened? What happened to you?'

He nodded, swallowing. 'Something broke. Something broke in me.' He struggled to raise his hand, touched a finger to his temple. 'I feel it inside. A sliver in my mind. Driving me mad.'

'We can stop this. Tell us how. Now, before it is too late.'

He shook his head. 'No. It is too late. Already far too late. I am gone. And so, my parting gift to you . . .' and the creature threw back its head and let loose a shockingly loud call that made Blues jump with its piercing, keen ululation.

Nightchill flinched from the sprawled Jaghut, breathed, warily, 'What was that?'

But the form lay immobile now, somehow diminished, and Blues knew he was dead.

'What was that shout?' Tayschrenn demanded of Nightchill.

The sorceress turned to him, her odd almond eyes widening. 'I do not know for certain, but I fear—'

'Movement!' Dassem called, pointing.

Halfway across the chamber lay an opening where a broad ramp led upwards. One wall of the opening appeared to be bulging, stretching. A large shape could be seen moving behind the wall, which was now semi-translucent and seemingly malleable.

A tear in the material and a clawed foot and armoured leg emerged.

Nightchill's hand went to her throat. 'By all the Ancients . . . A Shi'gal Assassin. We must go now – while we can.'

'There's eight of us!' Black complained, unlimbering his shield.

Bellurdan gestured them all away. 'Not even a Soletaken would dare challenge such a one.'

'But what of the commands?' the mage, Turnagin, sputtered. 'Shutting down the machines?'

'We will try below, among the engines,' Nightchill answered, her voice hushed.

The Sword crossed to the woman, eyed her closely. 'Best to take it now rather than to let it hunt us down.'

Nightchill beckoned him to move. 'No. Their duty is to guard the Matron. It should ignore us if we keep to the lower levels.'

318

'You are certain of this?'

She nodded stiffly. 'We must go – before it gets our scent too strongly and decides to chase us anyway.'

Blues could almost hear the Champion's teeth grate as he considered, then gave a grunted, 'Very well.' He waved everyone away. The ex-captive, Hessa, grasped a handful of her companion's robes and dragged him along with them as they fled.

Behind them something large and heavy thumped to the stone floor and a jarring, keen bellow, an answering call to the summoning, echoed among the stone walls.

Blues hurried a touch faster – even as he shook his head: Gods, after climbing all this way, only to have to descend to the very bottom? His poor damned legs!

*

Retreating from the command chamber, Tayschrenn was torn. So many secrets! Such knowledge! Yet it would take years to decipher and understand – if that were possible at all. And they had no such time; he accepted Nightchill's warning. In his researches he'd come across accounts of these creatures, the Shi'gal.

Guardians of the Matron, many named them. In records of the wars among the Elder races, the so-called Founding Races, these Shi'gal were held in dread. Perhaps such stories were fictions, semi-mythical. Yet all agreed these monsters slew the dragons themselves. Dragons of Starvald Demelain!

He shook his head as he half-limped back down the halls – too much of a risk. Far too much.

And in any case, all this while he'd been preparing himself for a possible confrontation with a Matron – not a physical threat from a bodyguard, one that even Bellurdan, of the Elders himself, dared not pursue.

So he limped along, panting, wiping the sweat from his eyes as he went, teeth clenched against the burning agony of exhausted muscles. He caught Dassem's – the Sword's – eye as they half-jogged, asked, 'Would you have remained?'

A chagrined half-smile. 'Only if you had.'

'I thought you came to test yourself.'

'Our mission is reconnaissance.'

'Ah. Of course.'

Now the Sword eyed him sidelong. Searching for mockery, no doubt. But he meant no disrespect. In fact he was relieved by such a rational attitude from the Champion.

Perhaps the man was not so glory-driven as he might have supposed.

Thinking of it now, rubbing his slick forehead, he could admit that between the two of them, perhaps it was *he* who had the more to prove to himself.

* * *

The fortress city of Jick, on the north-west shore of Walk Sea, built into the cliffs of the rugged Walk mountains, rightly considered itself one of the most secure of all the Falaran settlements. It fell in one night, however, when five of the foreign raiders' ships glided into the narrow harbour under oar, and promptly set alight all other vessels. In the chaos that followed, the raiders secured the fortress main tower and disposed of the prior ruler and family by tossing them off said tower to the paved courtyard below.

Since then, the inhabitants of Jick, the fisherfolk, the petty merchants and shopkeepers, the coopers, carpenters and smiths and other tradesfolk and burghers, had found themselves at the mercy of crews of drunken raiders who took or abused what or who they wished and answered any refusal or complaint with the sword.

Gaddeth, the ranking priest of Mael of the local temple, found himself presiding over far more funerals than ever before. He also found himself thrust – unwillingly – into the role of representative of the local inhabitants, after the erstwhile mayor had likewise been thrown from the tower roof.

Imagine, then, his elation, when during his weekly communion with his fellow priests of Mael via his – rather thin – grasp of Ruse, he learned that the Jhistal had been unleashed upon these invaders and their leader had been obliterated!

He hiked up the rope belt round his wide waist and set out at once for the keep to inform these sea-wolves that their tenure would soon be at an end!

He found them carousing as usual: drinking and mock-duelling in the main reception chamber where tables had been set up and straw lay thick upon the flagged floor. They hailed him, laughing, and one captain, Balethen, rose unsteadily to his feet to salute him.

'Ho! What complaint now, priest of Mael? Seduction of your favourite sheep?'

Gaddeth raised his hands. 'Your time has come, invaders! The Faith has unleashed its mighty Fist upon your leader and he has been destroyed. You should all flee now while you are able!'

Balethen lost his mocking smile. 'Whatever are you blathering on about, you fool? Don't think those robes protect you.'

The revellers pelted bones and apples at him. 'Be gone, dog!'

He drew himself up as straight as he could in an effort to maintain his dignity under a barrage of half-eaten food. 'I am saying your leader has been crushed by the Jhistal!'

Balethen now blinked at him, weaving, half-drunk. 'What's that? Our leader?'

'Yes. Anchored in the strait off Delanss. The Admiral, or Archmage, or whatever he was. His ship has been destroyed!'

The barrage stopped. All faces now stared at Gaddeth.

Balethen pointed the eating-knife in his hand. 'If you lie I will drop you off this tower myself – relations with the town be damned. Do you lie?'

He raised his chin, defiant. 'This is our god's own truth from my own Faith. I swear.'

The captain scooped up a metal cup at hand, raising it. All present surged to their feet; Gaddeth flinched, thinking himself about to be torn to a thousand pieces.

Instead, the hall echoed in a roaring cheer as these foreign invaders smashed cups together, slapped one another, guzzled the ale and wine and howled with laughter. Gaddeth gaped, stunned.

'*The Ogre's dead!*' Balethen yelled to an answering cheer.

Gaddeth backed away from the insanity. Who were these monsters? How could they celebrate? Why were they not fearful?

He ran from the hall where the cheering and merriment only grew louder and more raucous – with calls for more wine and ikkor.

He shook his head. These foreigners were mad!

* * *

A voice that was more of a growl from outside his tent woke Dancer: 'Outlander . . .'

'Yes?'

'There is a person at the edge of camp. She says she has a message for you.'

Dancer blinked in the dark. Of course – they *would* find him, wouldn't they? He rose. 'I'll be out.'

Ducking through the flap, he straightened. It was a very dark night, the cloud cover thick. Idly, he wondered how much was natural and how much could be attributed to the mountain-artefact to the east.

The guard, a wolf-warrior, gestured him south. He nodded his thanks and half-jogged off.

Standing a respectful distance outside of the encampment waited a lean woman dressed in functional dark-stained leathers; twinned knives hung sheathed across her chest, at her hips, and on her thighs. As Dancer approached, she knelt to one knee, murmuring, 'Master.'

Uncomfortable with these observances, Dancer waved her up. 'Yes?'

When her dark eyes met his he clenched his teeth; she was obviously anxious, fearful even. 'What is it?'

She swallowed, bowing her head. 'News, Master of the Rope. Terrible news.'

'Yes?'

'He is gone.'

'Gone? Who is gone?'

'The . . . Magister.'

His first reaction was a snort. 'I've heard that before.'

She shook her head, so very slowly. 'No. Truly. Gone. We none of us can reach him, nor know his whereabouts.'

'It's happened before.'

'True. But never so . . . abruptly. And it coincides with the news that the priests of Mael sent their curse, this Jhistal, against him.'

Now he growled under his breath: Of course – the moment he leaves the man's side, they strike. The timing was too perfect. 'What was it . . . this *thing*?'

'None know. None of ours saw. Some say it was hidden in any case. Hidden within a gigantic wave.'

Or it was a gigantic wave. That would probably be enough. 'Can you bring me to the ship – the *Twisted*?'

She shook her head again. Her jaws worked with suppressed emotion. 'No. It is gone as well. Destroyed utterly.'

The Twisted *as well?* He didn't think that possible. It seemed so, well . . . indestructible.

'Can you take me to the expeditionary force? Dujek's command?'

She bowed. 'Of course.'

'Very good. Wait here. I will return.'

'As you command.'

He jogged for the central tent, Ullara's. The two bear-warrior guards stood aside for him to enter. Within, he found the central hearth burning high, birds fluttering about, and Ullara in her chair. He crossed to her. 'You are awake.'

'I find I sleep less and less these days.'

'I must go now.'

She nodded. 'Yes. Of course you must. You have your responsibilities, as do I.'

'Your people – these people – have my protection now.'

'They – we – have managed well enough on our own for some time.'

He smiled, warmly. 'I know. But they took you in, and for that they have my gratitude.'

'And mine.'

'How is the girl?'

'Her strength returns.'

He nodded. 'Good, good. She will have nothing to fear any longer.'

'Thank you.'

He took her aged hand and pressed his lips to it. 'I hope to see you again . . . some time.'

'I hope so too.'

'Until then – farewell.'

She dipped her head. 'Yes. Farewell.'

'Yes.' He cleared his throat, bowed as well, and turned to the exit.

Outside, he paused and drew a long breath of the chill night air, then let it pass over his teeth, and jogged south.

He found the Talon waiting, a wolf-warrior nearby, keeping an eye on her. 'Dujek's camp,' he told her. 'Now.'

She bowed. 'Of course, Master.'

Darkness thickened about them, blotting them out. When it dispersed, the two were gone.

The wolf-warrior crossed to this spot, sniffed the air, then loped off for the main tent. Within, he bowed low on all fours before the Bird Priestess.

'The outlanders are gone,' he announced.

She nodded. 'Yes. I watched them go. Thank you.'

'What orders?'

'Send your fastest and most cunning to keep an eye on the mountain and our Malazan guests. I am watching, but I cannot see everything. My pets do not like the mountain.'

He bowed again. 'Yes, Priestess. It will be done.' He loped off.

Alone once more, Ullara raised a finger and a tiny yellow songbird alighted upon it. She touched its head, gently, and sighed.

* * *

Temporary camp had broken and Dujek marched as he dealt with messages that runners brought. A shortage of stores – of course. A shortage of potable water – naturally. A shortage of any leather to repair rotting footwear – constant, that. Too many sick from all the cold and damp. How to transport them? Carts were bogged down, and the squad medicers and Denul talents were now reduced to having them carried in litters. Two troopers per litter. That's three swords out of action!

If he had any hair he'd be pulling it out! Fully a fifth of his force were now the walking sick.

Mulling on this, he trudged along, rubbing his hand over his pate and grumbling to himself. Then a familiar voice spoke next to him:

'Where are your bodyguards, Fist?'

Despite being a battle-hardened veteran, Dujek couldn't help but flinch. He glared at Dancer now walking along beside him. 'Gods, man! Do *not* do that.'

'Well?'

A shrug. 'I'm among my force – safe as home.'

The lean fellow shook his head, still sceptical, then his mouth drew down. 'I need to see Tayschrenn and Dassem right away.'

Dujek cleared his throat. 'Ah ... well. They and Nightchill entered the artefact. Haven't heard from them since.'

Dancer eyed him sidelong. 'You let the Sword and our two best High Mages enter a K'Chain Che'Malle hive all alone?'

Dujek drew his wide paw down his jowls. 'Well . . . really couldn't stop them – could I?'

Dancer blew out a breath. 'Suppose not.'

Dujek peered round. 'Is the Old Man with you?'

Now Dancer rubbed his cheeks and was silent for a time. Obviously uncomfortable, he allowed, 'He's missing too.'

Dujek gaped, then let out a belly-laugh. 'Fine pair of commanders we are, hey?'

'He'll turn up,' Dancer growled. 'He always does. What's the situation?'

'The artefact's actually moving – just like the myths. Imagine that, hunh? We're following along. Keeping our distance. Hard to miss, though. Thing leaves behind a trail of steaming semi-molten rock leagues wide.'

'Any encounters?'

'No. None. We think maybe they've withdrawn to guard the thing.'

'North, then?' A nod from Dujek. 'How long do you think till it reaches Falar?'

Dujek rubbed his jowls once more, screwed up his eyes. 'Well . . . don't really know the lands north of us. Our maps are shit. Some say there's mountains ahead, others say an open plain. Still, it's moving night and day, continuously. We're thinking maybe a month, at least. And anything could happen in that time. Could slow up. Could break down. Abyss, could blow itself up! Just hoping on getting some good guidance from Tayschrenn and the others – when they return.'

Dancer nodded his agreement. 'Mind if I hang around till then?'

'Not at all. Not at all.' He eyed the slim fellow sidelong. 'Just don't you go in there hunting after 'em, all right?'

Dancer looked to the northern horizon dominated by the dark silhouette, its peak disappearing behind a dense cover of heavy black roiling clouds. He shook his head. 'No. Enough of us have disappeared into that thing.'

Dujek grunted, 'Lady, yes.'

* * *

325

At first, sailing with Torva was nothing near the trial Gianna had dreaded. The old salt was full of entertaining stories, and the two soon fell into a rhythm reminiscent of their old days together.

The third night she was all for seeking shelter in some narrow bay to sleep as they'd been pushing themselves hard. Torva scoffed at the idea, calling her fainthearted, and vowed to man the rudder through the night – just as he used to. Gianna was dubious, but, not wanting to directly challenge the old man, she acquiesced, and late into the evening lay down to rest.

She woke being tossed about to find the boat wallowing side-long to the waves. Torva lay insensate in the bottom, snoring. The night was near moonless. She groped about for the sheets, found them, and steadied the square sail.

She directed them towards the nearest shore. Sheltered, she allowed herself to sit back and relax then turned her gaze to the still snoring oldster. She shook her head. No more night watches for you, old man. Sighing, she let fall the anchor – a heavy rock on a line – and lay down to try to get a little more sleep.

She woke again to the scent of hot tea. Torva sat hunched over a small iron brazier. He held out a stoneware cup. 'Tea, gal?'

She sat up. 'Thank you.' Smiling, she watched the old fellow as he squinted at the forested shore, scratched his grey bristled chin, frowning. 'What is it?' she asked.

He flinched, vexed. 'Nothing. Just wondering which isle this was, is all.'

'Just another rock near the coast of Delanss.'

He nodded, absently. 'Told ya I'd get us here.'

'Of course.' She pulled up the anchor. 'Take the rudder. I'd like to pass far out from Delanss proper, if you don't mind.'

'I know the shore,' he growled. 'Them pirates probably patrolling, hey?'

'Probably occupying,' she answered, darkly.

After a small meal of hard bread and dried meat she lay down to try to steal a few more hours of sleep before night. It was their fourth day now, and she figured they were near a third of the way. So, another eight days – not enough stores for that. They'd have to put in somewhere. Perhaps near the north headlands of this, one of the two largest of the Falaran Isles. A small fishing village close by, ideally. She'd prefer to avoid Belikan for the same reason she was passing well out from Delanss port; she didn't know which, if any or all, were in the hands of these invaders.

Noon heat woke her. She took the rudder. Torva lay down to try to steal some sleep as well.

They passed a cove and a slim galley came charging out, surprising Gianna. She relaxed, however, recognizing the tree and shield sigil on its prow as Delanssian. She collapsed the sail to await them.

Once the galley came alongside a sailor shouted, sounding a touch puzzled, 'What are you doing out here?'

'We are for Belikan,' Torva answered – having awoken.

'The waters aren't safe for anyone! You should follow us in.'

'Then Delanss is safe?'

'Aye,' the fellow called back. 'We drove them off.'

Gianna stood. 'That is excellent news! What of Iguan or Belid? When will you free them?'

'We guard our own – now follow us in.'

She set her fists to her hips. 'So you guard your own harbour then? While others suffer this plague? Band together. Drive them off!'

'There's no one to band with!' the Delanssian shouted back, angered. 'We'll not leave our city defenceless. Now follow us.'

'No. We have business elsewhere.'

'Do not make us tow you in.'

'We are free citizens! You cannot coerce us.' She raised her chin. 'Have you a mage of Ruse with you?'

'Of course.'

'Ask the mage if you should interfere with us,' and she raised her Warren.

Rather exasperated, the fellow – the captain, Gianna assumed – turned and called, 'Halan! Get over here! Who is this damned woman?'

A fat and bearded man appeared at the side. He stared at her for some time while stroking his beard, then grunted, surprised. He turned to the captain. 'Can't say *who* she is – but we best let her go her way. In fact, I rather doubt we could stop her.'

The captain gaped at his mage, then shook his head. 'Falar has gone insane. It really has.' He turned to Gianna. 'Fine! Go your way – but these foreign pirates will take you! You're warned.' And he waved them off.

Torva set the sail. The galley back-oared away then darted off in a broad curve.

Gianna watched them go and shook her own head in turn at the incomprehensibility of it. How could this have happened? These isles were accounted among the paramount sea-powers of all peoples! Mentioned in the same breath as the lethal galleys of Mare, and the great sea-castles of the Blight.

She found herself wiping her eyes, and she cursed. Of course she knew how it had happened. These neighbours had abandoned all shared defence. Fled to their own islands when they were threatened. She was frankly ashamed.

And then these ruthless invaders did the unthinkable – the outright wicked – they burned the galleys. Destroyed Falar's greatest works of art. It was an unanswerable crime.

Her grip on the gunwale tightened. She would make them pay. First, she would rid everyone of the Jhistal and then these damned pirate scum!

Though she knew that – in theory – any talent can detect an active Warren, she considered herself isolated enough to risk it, and power surged through her hand to the vessel and surrounding waters. The boat lurched forward.

*　*　*

Young Learnan, their best scout, popped up from the brush ahead of Cartheron where he and the crew crouched in cover, startling him. 'Don't do that,' he growled, kneeling once more behind the thick undergrowth. All around it was quiet, night-time. The island had proved a small one, bearing a tiny population of fisherfolk and woodcutters.

'The boats?' Creel asked, his voice low.

Learnan nodded enthusiastically. 'Yeah. Fishing boats. Mostly all damned beat up. But there's one really nice new boat up on the strand. Freshly rebuilt.'

'Size?' Cartheron asked.

'Six-crewer, I'd say.'

Cartheron grunted. It would be crowded – but what choice did they have? 'Any guards?'

'A bunch a fisherfolk? Naw.'

Peering round, Cartheron saw only eager nodding faces. He let out a breath. 'Fine. We'll push it out, double-time.'

Two crew members lurched forward but Cartheron threw out an arm, halting them. '*Quietly*. Damn it to Hood!'

They nodded – still grinning – and everyone started edging downslope through the brush to the shore.

On the strand he found that it was indeed a fine boat. Newly cleaned and repaired. You could still smell the fresh pitch. The crew set to pushing it down its log rollers to the surf. Four jumped in and began oaring against the waves while the remaining hands – Cartheron included – kept pushing even up to their chests in the water then grasped hold of the gunwales and heaved themselves up and over. The main square sail was quickly raised and a bow-wave rose.

Now grinning himself, Cartheron gazed back at the receding shore and there he believed he could just make out the single upright figure of a person watching them, motionless, arms crossed.

Feeling that there was enough safe distance between them, Cartheron dared give the fellow a cheeky wave farewell.

*

For a very long time Imanaj remained standing alone on shore. Long after his boat disappeared from sight. Long after that mischievous last farewell wave. He stood with crossed arms, tapping a forefinger to one biceps. *One day*, he thought to himself with regret. *I waited just one day too long . . .*

Too much temptation for the universe at large – by way of the Twins' laughing intervention no doubt.

The sky brightened pink and golden in the east and he sighed.

Gravel crunched at his side and he turned to see the priest, Rendren, his face still bruised from the beating he'd received at the hands of the recent pirate incursion. 'Who were they?' he asked of the man.

Rendren cleared his throat. 'The villagers have been poking around. Everyone's accounted for. No one's missing. Looks like one of these foreigner Malazan crews. Marooned or shipwrecked. Needed a boat – took yours.'

Imanaj sighed again, looked to the paling sky. 'They owe me a boat, then.'

Rendren cleared his throat into his fist once more. 'About that . . .'

Imanaj glanced to him, 'Yes?'

'Well . . . we, that is, the village as a whole, we're agreed that we'll take you home.'

He crooked a one-sided smile. 'Now you volunteer to take me? You mean you've finally all decided you're better off without me.'

Rendren clawed his beard, looking away. 'Something like that.'

'I understand.' Imanaj offered a reassuring nod. 'And I accept the offer.'

The priest of Mael let out a long breath, answered the nod. 'Very good. That is . . . my thanks. I'll select the best hands at once.' He sloshed away through the surf, his robes sodden up to his thighs.

Imanaj remained, arms crossed, regarding the glimmering waves. These Malazans – they had interfered twice in his plans . . . He frowned then, regarded the cliff-top village behind and let his arms fall. But then, what was that compared to what these local Falarans were suffering now? His troubles were as nothing compared to the anguish inflicted among these islands. These Malazans seemed to spread chaos and suffering wherever they went.

Chapter 22

FINNEK-SHORTARM, ONE OF THE LEAST OF THE TRIBE, WAS given the honour of watching the slumbering god. Frankly, he did not know whether to be honoured or terrified. First he asked Renoch-Longseer, one of the Great Elders, 'Why does it lie insensate like this?'

The elder gnashed his long mandibles together, rumbling, 'It has worked a mighty act of creation for our benefit and now it rests, regaining its strength.'

Finnek nodded, 'Ah, I see. And elder, why does it look so . . . strange? It has only four limbs.'

The elder chuckled, irritating Finnek. 'Little one, this is a god. It may appear however it wishes.'

'Ah. I see.'

'Any further questions, young quester?'

'No. Not for now.'

The elder lumbered away. 'Very good. Tell us when it wakes.'

So Finnek sat and watched. He twitched his four forelimbs impatiently, trained his multifaceted eyes upon the rather ugly and malformed entity and wondered, why was there a slim trail of fluids dribbling from its mouth as it lay there? More mysterious god-like behaviour?

He noted, once or twice, that the being seemed to flicker and fade, and that he could see right through it on a few occasions as if it were the thinnest shade or shadow. Should he report such things to the elders? But then Renoch's mocking chuckle came to mind and he decided against revealing any further ignorance.

Finally, the god's tiny little eyes popped open and darted

about – almost as if it was in terror itself – but how could a god experience fear?

Finnek bowed to the being, murmured, 'Welcome, ah, Great One.'

The being gaped at him; had he displeased it? He bowed even lower. 'Abide. I shall summon the elders.'

Finnek backed from the mud cave in which they had placed the entity then turned and hurried off – rather relieved, frankly, at the chance to pass all this responsibility along to the ancients.

Renoch answered his calls. 'Ah! It has awakened, has it?'

'Yes, elder.' Finnek pointed the way with one forelimb.

'Good! Let us offer our gratitude for its great gift.'

When they returned, they found the short being had emerged from the cave and was standing, peering about, blinking in the half-light. Finnek thought it appeared rather lost – but again, how could a god appear so?

Renoch crossed his forelimbs and bowed low. 'Greetings, Magnificent One! On behalf of us, the People, I offer our eternal gratitude for your answer to our prayers!' And he spread his limbs to indicate the immense body of water beneath the slate-grey sky.

The being blinked at the lake, the hair above its eyes rose and it said something short and clipped.

'We do not understand your tongue, Great One,' Renoch said. 'Do you comprehend ours?'

The entity waved its limbs before its face and Finnek recognized the manipulation of Shadow itself – something beyond his own kind.

'Can you understand this?' the being asked.

'Indeed,' Renoch answered. He bowed once more. 'I was thanking you for your Great Blessing.'

It waved its limbs at the waters. 'You mean that?'

'Yes.'

'That? Oh, that's just . . . ah, what do you think it is?'

The elder Renoch crossed his forelimbs in recitation mode and began, 'Ages ago our people, the People, fled unending war and persecution. We came to this realm. This refuge. Here we have survived, and we are thankful. However, we had but one problem. One lack. We were fishers once, but the bounty that sustained us dried up ages ago. Since then we have prayed for a return of the waters . . . and you have delivered!' The elder bowed once more.

The god scratched its head. 'Hunh. Well, let's take a look.' And he started down towards the lake.

Finnek noted that it now had a stick in its limb that it swung about.

Reaching the shore, it poked the stick into the water. It addressed Renoch: 'It won't last. Already it's fading away.'

The elder crossed his forelimbs in agreement. 'Yes, it shall fade. As all things do. But in the meantime we are glad, and grateful. If you would grant us your name, we would know who to send our prayers of thanks to . . .'

But the god was peering off into the distance, towards the gigantic construct of wood that had arrived with the waters.

'Ah! Your conveyance. I assure you, we have not approached it.'

'Why not?'

'Why, because your mighty servant guards it, of course.'

The being muttered to itself, 'Mighty servant?' and headed off in that direction.

Finnek sidled up to Renoch, whispered, 'This one does not seem very god-like.'

'Their ways cannot be understood by the likes of us.'

'Perhaps we are mistaken.'

Renoch raised all forelimbs in agitation. 'Shush, little one. Its patience may not be infinite.'

As they neared the conveyance the Guardian could be seen curled up asleep in the slightly deeper shade of the structure. The god laughed and shook its head then kicked sand over its servant. 'Get aboard, you! We're leaving.'

Finnek winced, expecting an explosion of rage. However, the Guardian merely yawned, stretched, then made a show of taking its time climbing up the side of the structure.

Renoch turned to Finnek, crossed his forelimbs in vindication. 'There, you see? Who else could command a demon lord?'

Young Finnek's chest was still too tight from his fright and so he merely nodded.

The god turned to them, planted its stick. 'My thanks for watching over me – and for not trying to eat me.'

Finnek and Renoch shared uncertain looks.

It waved to the great body of water, grey and black beneath the flat pewter sky. 'Enjoy my munificence. It is yours. Fare well! I must be going.'

It then, with great difficulty, climbed up the side of the conveyance.

Finnek and Renoch backed away some distance.

The huge structure began to lose its definition, to become hazy, almost translucent, then faded away to nothing.

The elder tapped his forelimbs together. 'Control of the very stuff of Shadow itself. It may be that this realm possesses a new master.'

'But the Guardian of the Borders has said nothing of this.'

'Perhaps he does not know yet. Perhaps he cannot catch him. This one appears to come and go as it pleases.'

Finnek scratched the bristles of his head. 'So, just like that, this one leaves – without saying anything further?'

Renoch peered down at him. 'Little one, you desire more? That is an expectation.' He waved a forelimb. 'You must abandon all expectations when dealing with such beings.' He urged Finnek round with a push. 'Now come. Let us swim – and fish!'

Finnek hung his head. 'I cannot get the hang of it.'

Renoch rubbed his mandibles together in laughter. 'You will! It takes practice.'

* * *

The endless corridors, causeways and halls of the Che'Malle mountain now seemed so hot Blues thought he would faint. The exertion of his long jogging descent didn't help either. Sweat bathed him yet his lungs burned and his throat gagged, dry and cracked. Glancing about, he noted Black panting, near stumbling, while Jacinth marched on grimly, her face set in a rictus of pain.

If one of those K'ell Hunters were to jump them now he frankly doubted he could lift his sword.

Their new guides said they knew the swiftest way and so led – the Sword guarding them. Bellurdan and the sorceress Nightchill also held to the fore, unflagging, the heat and exertion seeming to have no effect upon either.

Interestingly it was the High Mage Tayschrenn who lagged, his breath ragged, his long black hair plastered in sweat.

Their guides led them ever onwards, down sloping ramps and halls. They came to a region of multiple side-portals, and, peeking in, Blues saw the walls appeared bulging and translucent here, as they had above, past the control chamber. And within each kind of 'cell' lay, half-visible, the recumbent shape of a K'Chain Che'Malle.

Alarmed, he surged ahead to take the arm of the Malazan captain, Hessa. 'These are some sort of quarters!' he whispered, hoarse. 'You've brought us into the middle of them!'

She nodded, gestured for silence. 'I know. A short-cut to the lower levels.'

'But what if—'

The Sword came to their side. He gave a curt gesture to move on, and Blues reluctantly released the woman's arm.

Black and Jacinth came abreast of him; the swordswoman sent a questioning look. Blues just signed for quiet and started jogging once more.

These 'quarters', if indeed they were such, went on for what seemed a good league and over multiple levels. Gallery after gallery of slumbering giants; and Blues felt himself very small indeed among them.

After hours of descent their party had become rather bedraggled and stretched out. And into the middle of it, stepping out from a side-portal, emerged a tall and thin woman, all in black leathers, her hair long and black, and even her complexion as dark as midnight. She was in the act of shaking gore from a rather long and narrow blade.

Everyone halted in consternation.

She peered round at them all then raised a brow in bemusement.

Blues stared, amazed. One of the legendary Tiste Andii? Here? Why?

'What are you doing . . .' Nightchill breathed, dread in her voice.

'Killing them all,' the woman replied, matter-of-factly.

'But they are dormant! Helpless. No threat to anyone!'

The Andii woman shrugged her indifference. 'They may be in the future. And when an enemy is helpless, that is the best time to kill them – is it not?'

'Who—' began Tayschrenn, but the woman ignored him, addressing Nightchill and extending her sword.

'And I see another weak enemy before me . . .'

335

Bellurdan surged forward. '*No!*'

Ferocious biting cold suddenly filled the hall, numbing Blues's hands and face, and he hunched away. Breathing was almost impossible; he felt crystals of ice in his throat.

'That won't—' Nightchill began, only to grunt as something flew from the Andii's hand to strike her and she fell.

The dark wood grip of a dagger now stood from her chest. Bellurdan stooped to cradle her.

All charged forward but a wall of vicious iciness billowed up to choke the hall. The biting cold and dark intensified and all flinched away, snarling their pain, even the First Sword. All save Tayschrenn, who remained unmoved. 'I cannot allow this to continue,' he told the woman. Gold flames of his raised Warren rose flickering about him.

Shielding his face, Blues looked to Gwynn. 'Do something!'

'That is Elder Night,' he answered, awed. 'Kurald Galain! It is beyond me.'

The Andii woman faced Tayschrenn and she nodded to herself. 'The mortal mage I was warned of. I would urge you to flee – but I think I will just crush you instead.'

The freezing cold became yet more intense. A rime of ice crawled like mould on the walls, floor and ceiling. Just inhaling the air was near impossible for Blues and all retreated down the hall. Bellurdan carried Nightchill in his arms, unconscious, or dead.

All except for the High Mage, who remained facing the Andii woman. A pool of liquid gold surrounded him, repelling the cold and darkness.

The Andii woman snarled something and threw both hands out at him.

Utter night blossomed. Blues was blind within it. Distantly, he heard stone cracking as the freezing became so extreme it shattered the rock. Gwynn, at his side, murmured something and suddenly Blues could see once more, but only in blurry glowing shapes.

He glanced back up the hall and winced, looking away: the High Mage blazed so bright it hurt his eyes. In that glance he saw that the stone floor round Tayschrenn now boiled, molten and bubbling.

A shape came to his side, yelled through the cacophony of

tortured rock, 'We must withdraw!' Blues recognized the Sword's voice. He nodded his assent.

Retreating, they emerged from the intense dark. Black and Jacinth, together with their two guides, awaited them here, further up the corridor.

Behind, an unsurvivable clash of elemental forces grew, swelled, writhed, and fought. Even as the party paused, it consumed more of the stone hallway.

He came level with Turnagin, who was staring his awe. 'How can they maintain their magery here within these fields?' the mage asked of him. 'It must be tearing their minds apart!'

'It's all or die,' Blues shouted back. 'Which way?'

Turnagin waved everyone to him. 'We must go around!'

Blues urged him onwards and everyone followed.

Eruptions staggered them as they once more descended through broad causeways, ramps and corridors. Blues would sometimes be thrown to a wall; he had to pick up Gwynn more than once. When they came to sections of way blocked by fallen rock, Turnagin would lead them back upwards to another branch or turn in the maze of wide passageways and then onwards again.

Blues now recognized that they must be getting closer to ground level as heat began to suffocate him. Wearily, he raised his Warren to do his best to blunt the worst. They came across a K'ell Hunter, yet this one was no threat to them as it lay broken and spasming beneath the gigantic blocks of a collapsed hall. Turnagin guiding, they crawled over the fallen wreckage and shards as far as possible from the crippled beast.

It was an exhausted, gasping party that jumped down from the lip of an opening and backed away from the crawling edifice as it edged along. It was dusk – of which day Blues had no idea. Great gouts of smoke and eruptions obscured the mountain's heights.

He exchanged a look of awe with Gwynn: it seemed the High Mage and the Andii still duelled.

The Sword pointed to a nearby hillock and led the way. Blues staggered along, supported by Gwynn. Everyone followed save the giant Bellurdan, who still carried the unconscious, or dead, sorceress. Dassem urged him onwards but he shook a negative. 'I must go to my people. We will heal her.'

337

'She'll die in that time,' Gwynn answered. 'Let me see to her.'

'No. She is mortal, yes. Yet she remains very difficult to kill.' And he started off southwards.

'Bring her back!' Dassem shouted, but already the Thelomen's great strides had taken him far.

'He seemed to know much of her,' Gwynn offered to Dassem. 'Perhaps he knows best.'

The Sword rubbed his sweaty face, sighed. 'Let's hope so. If not – Surly will not let me forget this.'

They fell atop the hill and sat gazing up at the black silhouette of the artefact as it crawled onwards. Billowing smoke still hid its heights and occasional muted explosions and blasts sent house-sized shards crashing down its flanks. Blues, still fighting to maintain his powers, could only shake his head at the magnitude of the battle – a contest that would have wiped out any standing army in the field.

Eventually, though the heat bit at him, he rested his forehead against his drawn-up knees and fell into an uneasy slumber.

A kick woke him. He blinked heavily, rubbed his eyes. It was after dawn. Black and Jacinth were standing, peering off at the now more distant mountain. Black gestured him up.

In the growing daylight, when the winds blew hard enough to disperse the clouds around the upper reaches of the mountain, Blues could see that an enormous bite had been gouged from one shoulder of the edifice. Smoke billowed there as from a wound.

The artefact also appeared to be listing somewhat now – or so it seemed to him – and one edge was dragging along the ground to leave behind a wide gouge in the earth, like a village-wide furrow.

Dassem came to him, asked, 'Can you sense anything?'

Blues nodded. 'Yes.' Though his Warren was not raised, he easily sensed a presence, a massive power approaching. 'Someone's coming.'

The Sword nodded and his hand went to his sword grip.

The air shimmered before them and for an instant Blues had to turn his face away from an argent brilliance that stabbed at his eyes. Then it disappeared, or was reined in, and he glanced back to see Tayschrenn.

The man's robes smoked and Blues noted that his feet were now bare and that each footprint he left behind smoked and crackled, the rock glowing. He stood for a moment, then collapsed.

The Sword charged in, reached to pick him up, then snatched his hands away, hissing in surprise and pain. He wrapped torn cloth round his hands then raised the High Mage and carried him to higher ground.

Blues saw how the moss and grasses smoked where the Sword lowered him down. Dassem peered about then gestured Blues and Gwynn to him. 'Can you do anything for him?'

Blues had to share a raised brow with his fellow Guardsman. Here, indeed, was a rare chance. The High Mage prostrate before them . . . But of course neither of them would take advantage: the man had fought defending them against a common enemy who probably wouldn't have hesitated to murder them all. He knelt with Gwynn at the Malazan's side. Both examined him with what Denul they knew.

'He'll live,' Gwynn announced. 'Pushed himself beyond all endurance. He'll need time to recover – and he may not recover fully. His mind, I mean.'

'We shall see,' Dassem answered, rather grimly, and Blues was reminded then, just *who* was this man's patron god.

'He was victorious, I take it,' Gwynn mused.

'Or managed to hold her off,' Blues supplied.

The two rose, and the Sword gave them a nod to dismiss them.

A distance off, Gwynn murmured, 'I know of no other who could manage such a feat. To hold off an Elder, a Tiste Andii.' He shook his head, amazed. 'High Mage in truth. The Guard must be informed.'

Blues nodded at that. Yes, Shimmer would have to hear of this. The Malazans possessed a High Mage indeed.

Jacinth signed to Blues: *We should go.*

Blues signed his assent and turned to see the Sword eyeing him, a knowing half-smile at his lips. 'You kept your side of our . . . agreement,' Dassem said. 'Our army is coming. You should go while you can.'

Blues shared an uneasy glance with Gwynn. 'Oh, why?'

Again, the half-smile. 'Until we meet again . . . Blues.'

'You've known?'

339

'Of course. I have seen you fight. I know how you move.'

A touch irked, Blues offered the Sword a salute then waved everyone off.

Coming to his side as they walked, Black asked, 'Where to?'

'North, I think. That thing is still a threat.'

'There's nothing *we* can do about it,' Jacinth complained.

'We'll keep an eye on it until someone does, then. Shimmer would want a complete report.'

The swordswoman just shook her head in mute dissatisfaction.

*

'Looks like the party's breaking up,' Hessa murmured aside to Turnagin, and she nodded her head to the east. 'Let's just be on our way. If I were the twins, I'd a' headed north.'

They hadn't got very far when a voice called, 'You two! Don't wander off.'

She turned; the dark-skinned Malazan swordsman was approaching. Hessa eyed him warily. 'We've done nothing wrong. You can't order us about.'

'Perhaps I can,' the fellow answered.

She put her hand on the grip of her blade. 'You're some kinda officer, aren't you.' She pointed to the prostrate mage. 'You his bodyguard?'

'You could say so.'

A snorted chuckle from Turnagin; she glanced to him. 'What?'

'This is Dassem Ultor, Sword of the Empire.'

'Oh.' Hessa let out a long breath and slipped her hand from her grip. 'Are we under arrest, then?'

The Sword shook his head, pushed back his long, sweat-heavy hair. 'No. You are now our official experts on the Elder artefact. You will draw salary equal to that of captains. You will advise Fist Dujek who commands the expeditionary force.' He raised his chin to the south. 'I am expecting him shortly.'

Hessa eyed the south: distant movement. Small parties. Advance scouts, no doubt. She felt her lips tighten in distaste, glanced to Turnagin. 'What say you?'

'We should be happy to advise.'

Now she felt all the tension leave her shoulders and she looked to the monstrous edifice dragging itself northwards, gouting great

340

masses of roiling smoke to obscure the sky, and she nodded to herself. 'Very well. For a time.'

*   *   *

It was dawn, and they were off the coast of Flood, when they spotted a strange foreign vessel. At first Gianna thought it derelict. It certainly looked the part: sails torn, listing, no movement amid the tattered rigging or the high deck that she could see.

Yet it was moving. Against the winds and current, it was moving.

She looked to Torva: the old man had a finger to his eye – warding off evil.

'Cursed, lass,' he said. 'I swear. Best not go near it.'

'Looks to be headed . . . westerly.'

'Good. Away from us.' He nodded to the east. 'Have troubles enough ourselves.'

She sighed. Yes, Sparrow Pass Cut. The launch was shallow enough – but it was still a maze of clashing currents and standing rocks emerging from the waves. One brush or glancing blow and they'd sink and be cast against the rocks themselves.

'Your friend is in there, you say?'

She gave an uneasy nod. 'Should be. There's plenty to salvage.'

'Right, well then. Need a steady hand to get us through that,' and he straightened at the tiller-arm.

She eyed him, half wary. 'I thought we agreed – I'll use Ruse to get us through.'

He growled and huffed and muttered to himself, but rose, relinquishing the arm. 'Hunh! I don't care what you think, I still call it cheating. Time was it took skill and hard-won knowledge to navigate! Not just a snap of yer fingers.'

She hid her smile, looking away. 'Yes, Torva. Just a snap of the fingers. That's all it takes . . .'

He took the bow, reversed an oar, sat ready to stave off any rocks.

Gianna readied herself then raised her Warren and sent power down through the tiller-arm to the waters surrounding the boat and swung them harder east towards the distant roar and clash of the rocks.

341

Something pulled at her then, from behind, and she glanced back. What she saw there dazzled her Warren-aided vision: the vessel, nearly out of sight now, glowed with ferocious power. Whatever it was, the potency that saturated it was appalling. An apparition straight out of Hood's own demesnes? A curse sent upon them by these invaders?

She deliberately turned her back. Something for the Faith to deal with. She had her own hands full. Spray already cooled her face and the fiendishly light boat jolted and jumped beneath her with every contrary wave.

Threading the tiny boat through the rocks felt like manoeuvring a feather in a wind-storm. The lightest touch from her sent it careering about. Waves batted it like a kite. Torva cursed ferociously at every jolt and turn.

Such responsiveness was a blessing, however, as she easily avoided onrushing rocks. After some time weaving deeper into the shoals she glimpsed what she hoped to see: a vessel, the *Glimmer*, lashed firmly among a crowd of towering seaweed-skirted spars.

She manoeuvred the rowboat to its side. Sailors now stared in open-mouthed amazement. A line was thrown and Torva secured the boat.

Brevin's ruddy face appeared glaring down at them. 'By Mael's balls, lass. Whatever are you doing here?'

'Come for some salvaging.'

Brevin turned, ordered, 'Lower a rope ladder, there.'

Torva held it firm from the bottom while Gianna climbed up and aboard.

Brevin looked her up and down. 'The youths?'

Gianna lost her smile, shook her head. 'Still at Cabil. But safe for now.'

'I'm sorry, lass.'

Unable to climb, Torva was hauled aboard. Brevin looked him up and down. 'And you are?'

'Torva, of Belade.'

'Torva? I know that name. Welcome aboard.'

The old sea-smuggler peered about. 'The *Sea Glimmer*, hey? A good vessel. Stout vessel.'

Brevin glanced over the side. 'You came through the shoals in that? Quite the accomplishment.'

'She's the *Sea Sprite*,' Gianna supplied, smiling, and Torva's brows rose, but he nodded his assent.

'Light as a sprite, she is,' he agreed.

Brevin now eyed Gianna, and crossed her arms. 'So ... more salvaging?'

'You've kept at it, I see. Any luck?'

The captain dropped her arms. 'Faugh. None. Tried grapnels – but no luck.'

'I have something in mind. Help me find it and you can keep any other treasure.'

'Oh? *Everything* else?'

'Yes.'

'And what is this amazing thing?'

'A chest, if you can believe it.'

Brevin laughed. 'A chest? As in – a treasure chest?' She shook her head. 'Lass ... really?'

Gianna smiled, quite understanding the captain's doubt. 'I mean it. I'll find it and bring it up. All else is yours.'

Torva spoke up, 'Now, child, don't go giving everything away so easily ...'

Brevin snorted. 'We've hardly anything right now. The Faith confiscated all we had. Everyone gets equal shares, as shares in nothing remain nothing.'

Though eager to move on and search for the vision she'd had in Mael's grotto, Gianna knew the captain's practicality, and so understood she'd have to offer up something tangible. 'I'll dive here for a few days, bring up what I can first.'

Brevin gave a curt nod. 'Fine. Show me something worth it and the *Glimmer*'s your charter.'

'Agreed.'

* * *

Endest Silann spent his time studying the fascinating flora and fauna of these so-called 'Wastes'. He found immediately that the region was in fact far from deserving such a dismissive appellation. The spongy thick moss housed numerous tiny animals. Blue and yellow wild-flowers, as minute as they were beautiful, blossomed right at ground level. Foxes and birds of prey hunted the many mice and voles.

343

A night-time eruption of energies snapped his attention away from wondering, idly, what the human terms for the constellations he found overhead might be – a dog, perhaps? A sword?

His brows rose as the powers being unleashed within the mountain grew and grew, burgeoning, swelling, then blasting their way free to send enormous shards of rock crashing down the high slopes of the artefact.

Well, he mused, wincing, *it would appear Feral has met someone worthy of her attention.*

The duel surged onwards, powers lashing one another, shattering the naked rock. Endest watched, appalled by the scale. Like the old days, he thought it. The old confrontations he thought he'd never see again – nor wanted to.

Finally, with one last monumental concatenation, the powers parted, snapping out of existence. Rocks came pelting down all about the Che'Malle mountain as if from a true volcanic eruption. Smoke billowed and churned, smothering all.

Something smashed to the ground nearby and he ran to the smoking thing.

It was Feral, of course, as he'd known. She surged to her feet, snarling, wiped her face of soot and sweat. Endest was dismayed by her condition: her fine leathers were scorched, crackling, falling away in ash and cinders. She held the melted stump of something that might have once been her sword. Glancing at it, she snarled again and tossed it away.

'Feral – by the Great Mother – you are whole?'

She glared at him so ferociously he backed away a step.

'Yes, I am fine,' she snapped. 'Dammit to the Abyss! Shut up about my condition. In fact, you will not speak of this to anyone!'

'Ah, yes, Feral. As you wish, of course. But our Lord must be informed.'

She glared again. 'Oh, yes. I will give him a report all right! He will be informed! I will return to the Spawn, get cleaned up, and *I* will report of this. Yes? We are agreed?'

Endest nodded again, fervently. 'If you so wish. Of course. It will be good for you to return. You have been gone for so long.'

She waved him silent. 'Yes, yes.' She noted her gloves, torn and burnt. She yanked the tatters off and threw them aside. 'We will go now.' She started away, running. Night gathered about her. Endest saw her leap and transform in mid-jump, her shape swelling. Enmeshed in her obscuring darkness, great wings beat, lurching her higher, ever higher.

He watched her go until the distances hid her from his sight, then he started walking and as he walked darkness gathered about him, and he stepped into the Elder Hold of Kurald Galain.

Behind him, the thick moss of the Wastes slowly sprang back from where his naked feet had stepped; mice and voles tentatively emerged to sniff the air, and hunting birds of prey swung lower.

Chapter 23

THEY DREW THEIR 'LIBERATED' BOAT HIGH UP AN ISOLATED piece of strand hidden between headlands of tall rocks. Just in case they needed to make a quick getaway, Cartheron explained.

He then had the crew take cover in thick brush while he sent scouts out to take a measure of any immediate threats.

While they waited, hungry and weary, the mate, Creel, eyed Cartheron then asked, 'Why here? On the mainland. There ain't nothing here. No food, nothing.'

Cartheron scratched his thickening beard, nodding. 'Exactly. We got enemies on both sides, don't we? The Falarans would have our guts for fishing lines and the damned pirates would take our heads. This is the mainland, so, according to plan, Dujek should be marching up here any time now with an entire damned army. Right?'

Creel just looked sour. He stretched out his long and wiry form and leaned back on his elbows. 'Well, we're all hungry now.'

But Cartheron's gaze was on the high banners of smoke covering the southern sky and he frowned to himself, muttering, 'We'll see what the scouts scare up.'

Jill, the ship's cook – and best hunter – returned first. She appeared unaccountably grim and motioned Cartheron to the coast. 'You need to have a look at this.'

'What is it?'

She looked away. 'You'll see. Plenty of game all over though, so that's a plus.'

Cartheron motioned for everyone to move out.

346

They crossed a tall and narrow ridge and descended into the next valley. It was late afternoon, the sun was now low behind the mountains westwards. They came to a small fishing village – one of the countless tiny settlements that dotted the region.

One glimpse from high on the slope as they made their way down was all Cartheron needed. Pale wisps of smoke still rose from blackened skeletal remains of huts. The beach was empty, nothing moved. Not even dogs.

He shook his head as they descended. Work of the damned pirate scum no doubt. A raid and the villagers must've put up a fight. A lesson left behind for everyone.

They found half-burnt corpses lying among the remains. Dogs slain. All dead, but very few bodies in total. Where was everyone?

At the narrow beach part of the mystery was solved. The remains of ten men and women staked out at the low-tide mark; little of them left now that the crabs had been at them.

Cartheron turned away. He was hardened – a veteran of war – but this was useless, malicious. What was Kellanved thinking here? This was no way to win over any people. He'd have a word or two for the man . . . should he ever see him again.

Creel came to him, shaking his head. 'Cruel – but ya gotta rule by force, hey? Gotta show 'em they're a conquered people. The rule of strength.'

'This is strength, is it?' Cartheron muttered, looking to the highlands in the south.

The Nose walked up, pointed out to sea. 'Tracks here on the strand. Most were rounded up and taken away.'

Cartheron nodded. 'Impressed servitude. Perhaps even sale into slavery.'

'Sale? Where?' The Nose asked.

Cartheron gestured northwards. 'Seven Cities region, maybe.' He looked to Creel. 'Search the remains. I want anything capable of carrying water. Kegs, skins. Any overlooked stores would be a plus too.'

'We headin' out to sea?'

Cartheron smiled stiffly. 'No. Heading south. Maps call these highlands here along the coast mountains. Hardly worth the name, but we'll head up and have a look round. See all that smoke there?'

As to all that smoke, Cartheron couldn't make sense of it. What was going on? Dujek burning everything? A scorched-earth policy? If Kellanved really was gone then him an' the Fist had some important decisions to make.

Creel peered towards the south, dubious, pulled a hand down his narrow cheeks. 'A march? Like, overland? I hate marching. That's specifically why I joined the navy.'

Cartheron just rolled his eyes to the sky. 'First, let's give these poor souls a burial. At least we can provide that. Prayers to Mael, I imagine. Right? Let's get this done before nightfall.'

*　*　*

Tayschrenn awoke to find himself once more on his cot in his tent, and he groaned. *Again. Getting to be an unwelcome habit.*

So, he must have won. Mustn't he? He couldn't remember; in the end all he recalled was the power. Raw, naked puissance coursing through him – a far greater deluge than he'd ever imagined, let alone ever considered summoning. And the Andii mage had answered it. They were then locked together. Neither daring – perhaps even unable at that point – to withdraw, to tamp down the release of energies that could consume them instantly.

He slowly raised a hand to touch his head – yes, still there, thank the gods. To have opened up to Thyr in the mind-cracking fields of that alien artefact . . . He shook his head, instantly regretted it, and gasped his pain.

The tent flap opened and Ute stepped in. His brows rose. 'High Mage! How are you?'

'Fragile,' Tayschrenn allowed in a croak.

'Can you stand? That is, there is a briefing now, with the Fist.'

'Then I should be present.' He tried to rise, snarled as a spike drove in behind his right eye, fell back again.

'I will help you.'

Hands took him, slowly pulled him upright, steadied him. 'Thank you,' he gasped.

He tentatively tried standing on his own, wove slightly, but managed. He made his way to the flap. Ute hovered close at his side.

Crossing the camp, he was also a touch bemused at the way

every soldier, man and woman, who walked by saluted him, murmuring quite respectfully, 'High Mage.'

Missy stopped before him, saluted as well, announcing, 'High Mage.'

He answered the salute then peered down at his ragged, seared and tattered clothes. 'I have need—'

'Of a change of clothes, sor?' Missy cut in. 'We have your trunk.'

'Thank you.'

'Certainly, High Mage.' She eyed him sidelong. 'Sor, if I may – they say the top of that damned thing was nearly blown off. Was that you?'

He cleared his throat. 'Ah, yes. I encountered . . . someone . . . very powerful.'

Ute and she eyed one another. 'Did you kill them then,' Ute asked, 'these Che'Malle?'

'No.'

The two frowned, somewhat confused, and seeing this it occurred to Tayschrenn that sometimes people required some sort of explanation, or reassurance. 'But those that remain are no longer a threat. I'm fairly certain of that. I believe they are actually all asleep now.'

The two nodded at this. Ute, though, pointed to the dark silhouette of the mountain to the north. 'So who's captaining the damned thing, then?'

Tayschrenn brushed at his seared shirt and vest. 'Well, that *is* the question, isn't it.'

He lifted the heavy tent flaps and all conversation within halted. Blinking in the dim light, he saw that the meeting was something of an impromptu affair by any measure: stools and other make-do seating – casks and small crates – lay scattered about. The Fist himself stood at the one and only table, which consisted of two planks side by side over kegs. 'High Mage!' Dujek exclaimed, coming over to look him up and down. 'Well done. The Sword has told me of your duel. Glad you are recovered.'

'Somewhat,' Tayschrenn managed.

He found the Fist's seconds, the captains Ullen and Orosé, both standing respectfully to one side; Hairlock, sitting, the Sword, and,

349

of course, the lean unprepossessing figure of Dancer, half in shadow. He inclined his head to the second in command of the Empire.

Dancer greeted him, extending a glass. 'Wine, High Mage?'

Still rather uncertain, Tayschrenn took the small glass, adding, belatedly, 'My thanks.'

The Fist eyed him, then shook his head. 'So, a Tiste Andii. And the woman nearly killed Nightchill.'

'Ah, yes, Fist.'

Dujek poured himself a glass, still shaking his head. 'Amazing. The Children of Night. I've never seen the Moon's Spawn, but I suppose it must be out there somewhere.' He waved the glass through the air to demonstrate. 'I suppose we were going to run into them sometime.'

'The K'Chain Che'Malle artefact drew us all, of course.'

The Fist nodded. 'Yes, the, ah, damned thing. So – what do we do? What is your recommendation?'

Tayschrenn glanced to Dancer who obviously judged this Dujek's show and was not going to charge in and take over – as would be his right by rank, but which would be insulting to the Fist. 'Well,' he began, 'continued monitoring of course. And continuing denial of access to it. It may actually simply break down of its own accord. However, I personally doubt that. These creatures obviously built to last.'

He paced, hands behind his back, and spoke while walking. 'Two options then. One, we re-enter and attempt to shut it down – a course of action I personally believe unlikely to succeed. Or, two, if it halts, I seal the artefact by destroying all entryways and place a sealing ward upon it.'

Hairlock guffawed. 'That's impossible. It would take a dozen mages and a month-long ritual to ward that entire Hood-damned mountain.'

Tayschrenn paused and eyed the fellow, blinking. 'I would not propose such a thing if I did not think I could do it.'

Dancer raised a hand. 'Thank you, High Mage. For your evaluation.'

Hairlock half swallowed a snort.

Dujek looked to Dancer. 'So, these Jhek. A truce? We can trust them?' Dancer nodded. 'And Kellanved? What of him?'

A shrug. 'We do not know. Reports are he's disappeared. But that's nothing new.'

Now Dujek half-guffawed. 'That's for certain.' He crooked his hand to Captain Ullen. 'So, you have the maps? What's this thing's route?'

The young officer opened a scrolled sheet of vellum on the table. Everyone crowded round – even Tayschrenn, though he felt dizzy. 'This map shows mountains north of us along the coast. But we can see now that these Falarans don't know what real mountains are. Scouts report that the artefact appears to be headed to what might be a broad valley.'

'I've seen some maps showing an interior mountain range,' the Fist said, pointing. 'What about that feature?'

Tayschrenn rubbed his brow. 'Could be an interpretation of the legends of *some* sort of mountain in the interior of the Wastes.'

'Hunh. Well, how could the thing know to head there?' Dujek mused, sounding frustrated.

'No doubt this route was chosen hundreds, if not thousands, of years ago,' Tayschrenn answered.

The Fist glanced up. 'So, you're saying it's unpiloted? A runaway wagon barrelling down on the archipelago?'

Tayschrenn nodded his agreement. 'Yes. I believe so.'

'Perhaps that is the best we could hope for,' Ullen put in, then nearly blushed as all eyes turned to him. 'I mean – perhaps the waters will extinguish it.'

'Or perhaps not,' Tayschrenn responded. He took a breath to steady himself. 'The waters of Falar are very shallow. The mountain may be taller than most of the sea is deep. It may burn and boil its way across to the next lands – Seven Cities.' Straightening, he crossed his arms and raised his gaze to the tent ceiling, musing, 'We will be blamed for the catastrophe. We Malazans. They will say we sent it. We will lose the regions entirely. Our name will become a curse to everyone.'

'We cannot let that happen,' Dancer commented into the silence that followed that grim prediction. 'Options?'

Tayschrenn gently lifted his shoulders at the obviousness of it. 'In that case, we return and attempt to shut it down.'

Dujek gave a sour growl. 'Without Nightchill our chances are even poorer.'

'We have no choice.'

Dancer nodded his agreement. 'Yes. Once it becomes clear it will reach the coast we will have to try. I will accompany the High Mage.'

'As will I,' put in Dassem.

Dujek shook his head. 'No. I can't allow that.'

Dancer just smiled. 'Apologies, Fist. But you are outranked.'

Sighing unhappily, Dujek rubbed his hand over his scalp. 'I know . . . I know.'

* * *

Janelle found her brother Janul in the yards behind the back kitchens. It was dusk and he was staring out across the intervening fortifying walls and the harbour mast-tops, to the east beyond.

'You sense him?' he asked as she joined him.

'*Something*,' she murmured, tilting her head. 'Comes and goes.'

'Yet it *is* him. He's alive – and has returned.'

'We have to be certain before reporting this.' She gave a deciding jerk of her head. 'I will try to reach him.'

Her brother eyed her narrowly, answered with his own curt nod. 'Be careful.'

'Yes.' She crossed the yard to an entrance to a sunken larder. Steps led down into a chill and damp dark. Kegs cluttered the stone floor.

Here, she raised her Meanas Warren and began reaching out into the darkness, searching.

'Magister?' she murmured aloud – more as an aid to herself as no speaking was necessary. She felt him then within Shadow: strong but distant. She moved through Meanas towards his presence.

The ground beneath her began to rock and shift. She heard the creaking of wood and cordage.

Blinking, she found herself on board a ship at sea. A vessel she knew, the *Twisted*, though in even worse shape than usual, its shrouds hanging in shreds, railings torn away, fittings missing. She crossed to the cabin door, which swung, loose and creaking.

Within was all swirling shadows, confusing even to her Meanas-aided vision.

'Magister? You are here?'

'Yes?' a familiar voice answered from the dense, sifting shadows.

'I cannot see you.'

'Ah . . .'

The tatters of shadows coalesced then, thickening, somehow taking on density, to resolve into the form of Kellanved, seated behind the one table.

Janelle blinked anew at this very odd . . . vision. More of the man's infamous deceit and deception? But why bother for her? Mere habit, perhaps? She bowed to him. 'Magister. Have you orders?'

'Orders?' The arch-mage appeared to be staring off into the distance, almost dreamily.

'Yes. Orders?'

He shook his head. 'No. No orders.'

She cleared her throat. 'Then . . . what is your intent? That is – what intelligence shall I pass along?'

'Ah!' The Emperor set his chin on the silver hound's-head grip of his walking stick, crooked a lopsided smile. 'I am awaiting reinforcements.'

Janelle bowed again. 'Very good. Reinforcements.'

The dark walls of the cabin flickered then, seeming to disappear, to reveal the dark glimmering of a seascape at night.

'You should go,' Kellanved told her.

'Yes, I—'

The vessel melted away around and beneath her then and she plummeted even as she grasped at her Warren.

Janul kept watch through the dusk. Shortly into the evening, sooner than he'd expected, he felt her return. He peered about, making certain there were no prying eyes, and waited for her to emerge.

She came across the yard, her hair plastered down, her clothes dark and sodden, leaving a trail of puddles across the cobblestones.

'What happened to you?'

She shot him a hot glare. 'I don't want to talk about it.'

* * *

They manoeuvred the *Sea Glimmer* most carefully among the jutting spars of stone, using poles, oars and ropes. Once Gianna was happy with a location, she let Brevin know and they secured the ship in place. While the crew saw to the vessel, Gianna checked her own rigging in preparation for another dive.

So it went, day after day. At least so far Brevin had no cause to complain as Gianna's talents had led her to rich debris fields among the sands and corals below.

Yet no hint had come her way as to the location of this one hidden treasure. And now, deep beneath the surface, holding an anchor rope against the pulling current, she was beginning to doubt herself. Was it just a delusion? A dream? Yet that priest had accepted it as a vision.

And the damning question: why should Mael offer her a vision of this so-called *Jhistal's Bane*? Yet he had. Or *someone* had.

Shaking her head, she forced away her doubts.

North-west. Just a chain further, she decided. And she vowed, if she found nothing there, then she'd abandon the search.

Kicking, she guided herself up the rope.

At the surface further lines were thrown to her and she snatched the hanging rope ladder to climb back up over the side.

Here Brevin eyed her. 'Anything?' Gianna shook her head. 'We're short on potable water, lass. Need to put in somewhere.'

She nodded her acceptance of this. 'Lurk Isle, I'm thinking.'

'You can guide us through, hey?' Gianna nodded again. 'And . . .' the captain cleared her throat, uncomfortable, steadied herself against the yawing ship, 'then . . . if you come up empty? Then what?'

She shrugged. 'Don't know.' She laughed then, wryly, and asked, 'Care to see the world?'

The big woman just snorted. 'Lass, I took you back aboard because you'd proved you can find treasure. And you have. We're rich now, thanks to you. S'truth. Crew's happy. But they're not interested in any personal crusade. They just want to go home.'

Gianna accepted a dry cloth from a sailor, towelled her hacked-short hair. 'Lurk, then. If we come up empty after that . . . well, maybe back to Cabil. I can't just abandon the youths.' She eyed her bleeding hands, gashed and scraped from digging among the corals and rocks. 'Just can't do it.'

Brevin gave her own long and slow nod, her lips pursed. 'I understand.' She raised her chin, bellowed, 'Northwards! Hands on the lines! Ready all belaying poles!'

*　　*　　*

Glinith no longer enjoyed her place at the council guiding the Faith, and Falar. It was an understatement to say that things were not unfolding as she'd imagined they would. It seemed no sooner had she achieved her most fantastic ambitions than events were undercutting and eroding the very foundations of those dreams.

Sometimes she wondered whether it was deliberate. The gods, she knew, were not without irony. Or cruelty.

So, the Guiding Council met – almost daily now. Only to hear reports of one disaster or setback after another: Strike refused to lend forces to join a planned coordinated attack on Curaca to help free that isle, citing a lack of numbers to both defend their fortress and mount any offensive; Delanss cited a lack of vessels to lend sufficient numbers to transport any such putative force, regardless.

So on and so forth, report after report. It was almost enough to make her want to throw herself into Mael's Pool in the wake of their foolish 'High Priestess'.

And now this: numerous sightings of the invading force's flagship – all in agreement in description – no doubt bearing its Archmagus commander.

How could he have possibly survived the Jhistal? It was frankly rather terrifying.

Throughout the meetings Nuraj, Guardian of the Faith, handled the communiqués and missives, drafted all replies, sorted through the logistics. Rentil Orodrin, Celebrant of the Faith, had permanently withdrawn to his chambers – praying night and day for their deliverance, was the Faith's official line.

Now knowing the full depths of Mallick Rel's ruthlessness, Glinith wondered whether such isolation was voluntary.

Meanwhile Mallick sat tapping the table with his pale, strangely creature-like hands, saying little. Scheming, presumably.

Until finally, this day, after Nuraj related yet another sighting of the invaders' flagship, now even closer to Cabil, a savage smile cracked Mallick's wide mouth and he snorted something like a laugh.

She eyed him, uncertain. 'Yes?'

The frog-smile widened. She looked away from the man's grey rotting teeth. 'This foreign invader commander – Emperor or not – it seems he and I are much alike after all.'

'How so?' Nuraj asked without even looking up from his reports. The man sounded exhausted.

A shrug of fat shoulders. 'First a show of strength, then this slow approach. An obvious strategy. An invitation.'

'An invitation?' Glinith asked. 'To what?'

'To negotiation.'

Nuraj slammed his scraps of scrolls down. 'We will not negotiate with these invaders! We will drive them out!'

A raised pudgy hand. 'Yes, yes. We will. Eventually. In the meantime, however . . . negotiation would seem prudent.'

Nuraj leaned in for another objection, but Mallick spoke again, forestalling him, 'If only as a delaying tactic – purely to buy us more time.'

The Guardian of the Faith released a long breath, his lean jaws working. 'And who will go?' he demanded. 'You?'

Mallick laughed at the suggestion. 'No. That would be imprudent. The Celebrant is of course too . . . frail for such duties. While you are too important to the war effort. Therefore . . .' and the pale little man looked to Glinith.

She felt her brows rise very far indeed. *You cowardly little shit*, was her first thought. Her second was: *I promised not to question – and he made it clear my life depended upon it.* So, she smiled instead, hoping the gesture resembled the baring of a knife blade. 'And what will I negotiate?'

'Ask their intentions. Their goals, plans, and such.'

'What will I be empowered to promise?'

The repulsive fellow waved a hand. 'Promise whatever you wish. It matters not.'

Because you have no intention of honouring anything. If you even had any concept of honour. She inclined her head. 'Well, we will see if there will be any negotiating.'

'Oh, I believe there will be.' The cold smile returned. 'I believe

I'm beginning to understand these Malazans.' He pushed back his chair to rise – the announcement that the meet was done.

Nuraj lifted a scrap of parchment. 'One last thing. We have a deputation waiting downstairs from Muheres and Pull on the mainland. Been waiting for days. They claim all this smoke and ash and such coming out of the south is from a new volcano there. They say they can see it now – and it's growing fast.'

Mallick scowled his impatience. 'Well, what in the name of all the gods are we to do about this?'

Nuraj tapped the note. 'They're talking about possible evacuation.'

Mallick stood from the table. He waved off the request. 'We have important affairs of state to organize. They can pack their bags and head to Belade. Or Old Falar, for all I care.'

Nuraj shrugged and dipped his quill in an inkpot to jot a response.

Glinith remained seated. Nuraj collected his papers and rose, not sparing her a glance. Seemed already the man had written her off. *Dispensable.* Just like Ortheal before her; the Celebrant, confined to quarters and trotted out only when useful; and eventually even you, Nuraj. Pray you remain useful to Mallick, my friend.

She crossed her arms, tilted her head back to the ceiling, and felt her mouth tighten to a slit. *For my part, it seems* my *usefulness may be coming to an end.*

* * *

From what Cartheron could recall from the maps of the region he'd seen, the easiest route south from the coast was a broad valley, perhaps the dried course of an ancient, meandering river. The valley led from the coast, southwards, more or less, to the plains of the Ice Wastes beyond.

He believed this valley was west of them, and so they'd marched, keeping clear of any locals they spotted, until it came into view. In the distance, downslope to the coast, a town lay at the edge of the broad grassy plain – good farming land, Cartheron imagined.

Getting a clear vision of anything was difficult now though as dense clouds of smoke grew increasingly thick and constant here.

This despite the off-shore winds of the warm nights. Ash drifted down as well, and soot. Again Cartheron wondered if Dujek was burning everything in some sort of scorched-earth policy.

The explanation, however, became clear once they made headway up the valley. Through the deck of churning clouds of smoke to the south they spotted the conical silhouette of a mountain. A mountain from which spewed the smokes of a thousand furnaces. A volcano, obviously, right smack in their and Dujek's way.

He stopped dead in his march and exchanged looks of wonderment with his crew.

The Nose rubbed his namesake and opined, 'Well . . . that's just damned inconsiderate.'

'It never rains but it pours,' drawled Creel, and he spat.

'Is Dujek steerin' wide o' that, you think?' Geddin asked.

'Don't know,' Cartheron answered. 'It's in the damned way, though, ain't it.'

'It's more than in the way!' a voice boomed to one side of them and Cartheron jumped, drawing his only weapon, a sailor's knife.

Out of a heap of boulders nearby rose a giant. A real, honest-to-the-gods giant; Cartheron stared, astonished.

'A Fenn!' Creel yelled, drawing his long-knife and wood baton.

Cartheron pulled his first mate back. 'They call themselves Thelomen,' he growled. 'And they ain't murderous – at least as far as I understand.' He lifted his chin to the giant. 'What do you mean jumping out at us like that?'

The Thelomen grinned, unoffended. His wild beard half hid a jagged crisscrossing of tattoos over his face and he wore layers of stitched hides and blankets heaped upon him like a tent. He planted his staff – itself two man-heights tall. 'Saw you coming a way off. Thought I'd wait for you.'

'Why?'

'First just to study you as you passed. But then I recognized your clothes and your accents. 'You are from the south. Quon Tali. Therefore, you are Malazans. Yes?'

Cartheron eyed him narrowly. 'What of it?'

A curt nod of his shaggy head. 'I wish to propose an alliance.'

'An alliance? Against what?'

The staff lifted, pointed southwards. 'Against that.'

Cartheron sorted. 'A volcano?'

'Not a volcano, though a mountain. It is a home. A hive. An awakening presence of a dangerous Elder. The K'Chain Che'Malle.'

Cartheron scratched the bristles of his chin. 'So that's it, hey? I was warned of this.'

The Thelomen nodded, pleased. 'Ah! So you Malazans are not unfamiliar with the situation. Good. This is a grave threat to the region. We must work together.'

Still unconvinced, Cartheron couldn't keep the scepticism from his voice. 'Against a smoking mountain in a wasteland? These Che'Malle can have it.'

The giant shook his great shaggy head. 'It is to the south now, yes. But it is moving. It is headed north. It is, in short, coming this way.'

Creel laughed his scorn outright. 'A mountain moving? Bullshit.'

But The Nose was rubbing his great sniffer, his eyes screwing up. 'I've heard o' stories o' such. Only they was always moving through the sky.'

Cartheron nodded then. 'Right. The Moon's Spawn. Like that. Only along the ground?'

The Thelomen grinned, pleased. 'Yes. Precisely. This one travels on a river of fire. And should it reach the waters here . . .' he shook his head, appalled. 'It will be a catastrophe. The waters will boil. Impenetrable clouds will shroud the region permanently. Nothing will grow. The lands will die.'

Jill, the ship's cook, cleared her throat. 'Well, why should these K'Chain want that?'

The giant nodded thoughtfully at the question, then tilted his head, answering, 'I don't think they do want that. I honestly think they just don't care – or wouldn't even notice, frankly.'

Cartheron peered about at the windswept grassland. 'Fine, for now. There are supposed to be more of us, you know, a lot more. What do you know of that?'

Another smile that twisted the jagged tattoos covering the Thelomen's face. 'Yes. South of us. Shadowing the mountain.'

'Good. Take us to them.'

'Agreed.' And the giant set off shambling southwards.

Cartheron shared a startled glance with his crew then followed.

'Say!' he called after the fellow, who already had established some distance between them, 'Say! What's your name, anyway?'

'It is Koroll,' the giant called back over his shoulder.

Koroll? Cartheron repeated to himself. The name sounded vaguely familiar. He just couldn't quite place it.

Chapter 24

UJEK'S DAILY BRIEFINGS SOON BECAME REPETITIVE: THE artefact continued its steady, slow, laboured advance northwards. Scouts came and went reporting no visible activity around it or at its various portals. Hairlock soon quit showing up. Dancer paced, apparently restless and troubled. Dujek remained his calm stolid self. Tayschrenn, however, was thankful for the time. Every day the mage cadre healers among the squads sent their tea infusions to his tent. Eventually, the splintering head-aches went away and he felt – mostly – recovered.

The one piece of news that came their way was the report that the *Twisted* had returned to Falaran waters, and the Emperor with it. Dancer nodded at the news and Dujek eyed him.

'You gonna return to the *Twisted*?' the Fist asked.

Dancer shook his head, looking grim. 'No. I'm needed here.'

Tayschrenn understood what the man meant: needed should they have to return to the artefact. It was obvious even he, a fighter and killer trained to an exquisite degree, did not look forward to that eventuality. Tayschrenn knew that he himself most certainly did not.

When the estimate came that the Che'Malle artefact was roughly a fortnight short of the coast, scouts reported movement to their south – a large party of the locals, the Jhek, approaching.

'A war party?' the Fist demanded.

'They're coming in the open,' the scout answered.

'I'll meet with them,' Dancer quickly put in, and Dujek frowned to object, but Dancer raised a hand, forestalling any debate.

'May I accompany you?' Tayschrenn asked, rising from his seat.

The lean fellow appeared displeased at first, but then reconsidered and nodded. He headed to the tent's open front.

'I'll send a troop of guards!' Dujek called after them.

Dancer just smiled then, almost affectionately, as they went.

When they reached the edge of camp – a guard contingent falling into step behind them – Tayschrenn eyed Dancer sidelong. 'I understand you know this Bird Priestess of theirs?'

The man's expression had returned to its usual flat impassivity, but it seemed to Tayschrenn that he clenched up momentarily. 'Yes. I knew her . . . long ago.'

'Ah.'

Ahead, a litter of some sort, on the shoulders of four very large and very hirsute men and women, awaited them. A troop of similarly burly Jhek warriors surrounded it.

At a command from within the litter the guards parted. Dancer motioned for his troop to remain behind, and advanced. Tayschrenn noted several birds of prey perched upon the frame of the litter.

'You shouldn't have come,' Dancer announced. 'It's dangerous here.'

'I can be of use,' a woman answered from within, her voice weak and strained. 'I have been watching – closely. And we have an interest here, do we not?'

His mouth tight, Dancer nodded. 'Yes . . . yes, you do. And the girl?'

'She is recovered. She remains behind, guarding. Also, I thought it prudent she not approach – given her past.'

Dancer sent Tayschrenn an amused glance. 'True.' He let out a long breath. 'Very well. I will speak with Dujek. You may remain. But keep your distance from camp, yes?'

'Thank you . . . Dancer.'

He inclined his head in a half-bow.

On the way back to the picket lines they came upon Hairlock, eyeing the Jhek. 'What's that smelly lot doing here?' he demanded of Dancer.

'They offer their help.'

Hairlock snorted his contempt. 'We don't need no help from them.'

'They have my countenance,' Dancer warned. 'Leave them alone.'

Hairlock's wide mouth screwed up in distaste and he rolled his eyes. 'Fine.'

On the way back to Dujek's main tent, Tayschrenn coughed into a fist and observed, reluctantly, 'If we are going to act, we will have to act soon.'

The man's lean, still faintly boyish features hardened then, ever so slightly, and he nodded. 'Yes. I know . . . I know.'

* * *

They worked their way through the shoals rock by rock, using poles and oars, and lines where they could manage. Gianna winced at the punishment the oars endured, some broken and shattered when the waves and currents drove the *Glimmer* against the tall rocks. Neither she nor any sailor bothered to attempt to dry themselves as the constant spray soaked everyone.

Among the jagged teeth of stone something to the east caught her eye and she wiped the salt water away to squint. The line of rocks there – a certain arrangement of heights and profile, as seen from just this angle – was so familiar . . . she realized this was it. That was the site! There, at the base of those tall spurs crowded together.

She ran to Brevin, grasped her elbow, pointing. 'That's it! That's the spot! We have to stop here!'

The woman scowled. 'Nay! Not here. No good moorage. And we have to get sweet-water or I'll have a mutiny on my hands.'

'But we'll lose it!'

'Then remember it!'

Half-snarling, Gianna threw herself to the side, gripped the railing. Dammit! So close. She scanned all the nearby rocks of the shoals, strained to sear them into her memory. The crew kept them moving and soon the spot disappeared behind intervening tall stones. Gianna let go a stream of proper sailorly curses.

Once free of the worst of the shoals and their contrary waves and currents, it was plain sailing to the coast of Lurk Isle, visible as a dark line across the north horizon. Gianna fumed and urged the *Glimmer* onwards.

Torva came to her side. 'I marked it too, lass. We'll make it back.'

She nodded her gratitude. 'Thank you.'

'If I'd been quick enough, I coulda taken the *Sprite* out to tie off there.'

Gianna laughed, but not unkindly. 'You would've been dashed to pieces.'

The old man's tangled brows rose. 'What? In a little chop like that? Pshaw!'

She could only shake her head.

He peered round. 'Well, I know of a few freshwater springs on the coast – I'll guide your friend to them.'

'I'm sure she knows of some, too.'

The old smuggler snorted. 'Not the *best* ones.' And he ambled off. Gianna noted that his gait was rock steady now that he was at sea. She also hoped that Brevin would not bite his head off when he attempted to give *her* directions.

Brevin had them put in deep in a narrow cove. One so sheltered even Torva allowed his grudging approval. Gianna continued to fume as landing parties were organized, the small launch readied – along with the *Sprite* – kegs gathered, and weapons handed out.

She almost yelled her objection when Brevin gave permission for a hunting party to be sent out to scare up some game. Instead, she gripped the railing, knuckles white, her teeth clenched.

The various parties went ashore to take advantage of the remaining daylight. If they encountered no one – and Brevin was quite sure they wouldn't – they would stay the night and spend all the rest of the next day.

Gianna stood at the railing well into the night; finally, she listened to her better self that she would accomplish nothing here, and so curled up among blankets to rest.

The entirety of the next day she spent pacing, muttering, hands working, as she silently urged everyone on to greater speed. With the waning afternoon light, and deep shadows within the cove, the shore parties returned, shuttled back in the two smaller vessels. Full water kegs were loaded aboard, along with gathered citrus fruits, and the flame-seared haunches of two large stags.

After all was done, Gianna came to Brevin's side. 'So we can go now.'

'Go? The day is almost gone. We'll head out with the dawn.'

'I can guide us through the night,' Gianna objected.

The Master of the *Glimmer* eyed her. 'I said – the dawn.'

Gianna clenched her teeth against her further objections, ground out, 'If we must.'

Brevin nodded, still eyeing her, then walked on.

Torva, now at Gianna's side, shot her a glance. 'She's the cap'n, lass. Don't do to question her.'

She pulled a hand down her eyes, trying to rub the ache from them. 'I know . . . I know. We're just so damned close.'

'We'll see, lass,' the old man soothed. 'We'll see.'

With the dawn the crew was quick to respond to their captain's orders. Anchors were raised and the oars stepped. The *Glimmer* turned to the narrow open stretch of water at the mouth of the cove.

Making the headland, they raised the mains'l and the jib.

Then a shout sounded from the lookout atop the mainmast: '*Sails to the west! Foreign!*'

Gianna cursed and scanned the western waters. She spotted it: a large broad-beamed vessel hugging the coast.

'Full sails!' Brevin bellowed.

'Make for the shoals!' Gianna called to her.

The captain paused, eyeing her once more, then gave a savage grin. 'Aye! They'll not follow there.'

The crew of the *Glimmer* took to the oars, but the pirate vessel, despite its blunt hull, was slowly gaining.

'Too much canvas for us,' Torva opined next to Gianna, who nodded her mute agreement. A single arrow came flashing up from the pursuing vessel to fall to the waves just short of them. 'Gettin' the range,' Torva observed.

'Yes! I see that,' Gianna snapped. She caught Brevin's eye and the ship's master lowered her gaze. It was clear to everyone that they weren't going to outrun the much larger ship.

Gianna thought of all she – and they – had been through; all that they had accomplished, and all that could lie before them, and a rage took hold, hot and churning, in her chest.

'*I will not allow this*,' she snarled under her breath. '*Not now. Not when we are so close.*'

'What's that?' Torva asked, distracted. He looked to Brevin, 'Gonna have to give the order soon or they'll fire.'

Gianna found her hair stirring as her Warren rose, almost unbidden, intensifying to a searing concentration. She threw out her arms towards the pursuing vessel and gestured, both hands clenching.

A report echoed across the waters: an explosive shattering of wood, and the ship suddenly wallowed, losing all headway almost immediately.

'Mael's Mercy, lass,' Torva breathed. 'Was that you?'

Even as she watched, half unbelieving herself, the vessel rolled and sank with astonishing speed, leaving bobbing wreckage and splashing figures amid the waves.

'Gutted,' Torva opined. 'Had its bottom torn right off.'

Gianna was quite astonished herself; she'd never managed anything like that before. She turned to see the eyes of all the crew on her, all touched by wonder and not a small measure of fear.

Brevin inclined her head. 'Thank you,' she managed, clearing her throat. 'Mage of Ruse.' She looked to the crew. 'Reef the sails. We don't want to rush into the shoals.'

The crew set about readying the vessel for the tricky entry to the rocks. No one, Gianna noted, suggested they might circle round to pick up the surviving foreign raiders.

* * *

They established a camp high up the slope of a coastal mount that offered a view of the broad valley below, and the advancing Elder artefact. When not hunting for game, Blues spent time sitting on a rock watching the Che'Malle mountain and the dense circle of constantly billowing smoke and soot widening about it.

Gwynn too was content to watch, whereas Jacinth made it obvious she was anxious to leave. Her grumbling and sour mood was constant, but everyone ignored it as it was only slightly worse than her usual scornful self.

After a few days the advancing smoke cover rolled over them, blotting out most of the sun. It darkened the slope and valley into an eerie half-light.

'They will have to act soon,' Gwynn offered.

'And us?' Blues added.

After a long breath, the mage of Rashan shook his head. 'No. It's the Malazans' problem and they remain the enemy.'

'But the Falarans aren't,' Blues observed. 'And it looks like they'll bear the brunt of this.'

'Perhaps they'll blame the Malazans.'

Blues turned to examine the fellow through narrowed eyes. The mage pursed his lips and shrugged, as if to say: *Fortunes of war.*

Blues shook his head. 'They don't deserve this. I don't think I can just sit here and let this happen.'

'Who was in command of your last posting?' Gwynn asked, a touch cutting.

Blues ground his teeth in a growl.

Gwynn shrugged again. 'There's nothing we can do. And in any case,' he pointed to the sky, 'we're not the only ones keeping an eye on things.'

Blues searched the clouds to find the silhouette of a hawk, or falcon, sweeping low above their heads. He grunted. 'What of them, then? Hey, Gwynn?'

'They're far to the south. They should manage.'

Black the Lesser, leaning on his elbow in the grass, spoke up: 'I don't see all the worry here. I mean, won't all that water just put it out? How could it keep on going?'

'The Falaran seas are very shallow,' Gwynn answered. 'The Che'Malle artefact is far taller. And its fires burn underwater.'

Black straightened up, startled. 'Fires that burn underwater? You shitting me?'

Gwynn looked to Blues, who nodded. 'Yes. We know of it in the D'riss teachings. Heat without fire. But we're warned away from it. It's poison to everything.'

'Well, then, why're these Che'Malle using it?'

'Maybe they don't care,' Gwynn offered.

Black lay back down. 'Hood. I half expect to see the Moon's Spawn itself come flying overhead now.' He tucked an arm under his head. 'You know, when I was young, I was out hunting with my Da. It was night. A full moon. I walked into a meadow and saw all these bright white flowers open up under the silvery light of that full moon. Moon flowers. Somethin', hey? They say they're from seeds that drift down from the Moon's Spawn.'

Blues nodded; he'd heard that tale.

'I went back later to try to find them, but in the daylight I couldn't figure out which of them flowers was which . . . Always wanted to go back to that meadow one night under the moon.'

Over Black's head, Blues caught Gwynn's amused gaze and shook his head. Amazing. You think you know someone then they open up and suddenly you see them in a whole new way.

* * *

The daily council meetings continued; frankly, there was little else to do but sit and watch the stream of disheartening news come trickling in. Glinith was thankful at least there had been no recent sightings of this invader flagship. So, no calls to potential negotiation, as yet.

One encouraging report was of a village in northern Jook Isle that had driven off its occupying force of three raider ships. Glinith thought this very inspiring and hoped that perhaps the entire Isle might rise up and free itself.

Two days later, however, the news came that the raiders had returned at night and burned the entire village to the ground, obliterating it.

Nuraj had pressed a hand to his brow at the news, saying, 'An object lesson for any others considering resistance.'

This alone was dismaying enough, but later that afternoon, after the meet had been dismissed, a messenger came to her to say that the invader flagship had been sighted in the waters just north of the capital, and that a swift courier launch was awaiting her – care of Mallick Rel.

She kept her reaction impassive while inwardly raging. She imagined that the slimy fellow hoped this Malazan warlock would save him the trouble of murdering her.

Still, she could at least show him – and everyone – what courage was. She raised her chin in a curt nod. 'Very well. Let us go.'

The launch, with five oars a side, three rowers on each, was tied alongside the small messenger portal within the outer harbour seawall. The crew, all members of the Faith Militant, helped her down into it and they sped off into the gathering dusk.

A short distance up the coast northwards they spotted the tall, bulky vessel, its silhouette so unlike any Falaran ship. Nearing it,

Glinith was rather taken aback by its battered condition. Did they not take care of their vessels? Then it came to her that perhaps this was damage from the Jhistal, and she changed her initial reaction: if reports were to be believed, this thing had survived that confrontation.

A sobering thought indeed.

Near enough now to reach out and touch the barnacled, rotting timbers of the tall hull, she called up, 'Hello!' only to be embarrassed by her weak and shaky voice. She took breath, yelled, *'Hello!'*

She waited, but no answer came.

'Hello?' she called again. This time a rope ladder came crashing down the side.

She tamped down her misgivings, took hold of the wet and slimy ropes and began to climb.

She found the deck cluttered in broken and tossed equipment, but otherwise empty.

Derelict? she wondered. *Adrift?*

'Hello?'

A banging of wood startled her: a cabin door swinging as the vessel rocked in the waves. She crossed to the cabin, peered into its gloom. 'Hello? Is anyone here?'

A figure seated behind a broad desk wavered into view from the shadows. 'Yes?' a voice answered. 'Who are you?'

She straightened her shoulders – but could not bring herself to enter. 'My name is Glinith. I am Abbess of Cabil, Keeper of the Mysteries of the Faith . . . and you are?'

'My name is Kellanved. What can I do for you?'

Glinith frowned into the miasma of shifting shadows; this was not what she'd been expecting at all. 'You are the commander of these bloodthirsty pirates?'

'No.'

'No? Whatever do you mean? You brought them here. You unleashed this plague upon us. Is that not so?'

A shrug from the ancient and very dark-skinned fellow. 'I drove them out of Malazan waters, that is all. What they do here is their business.'

She stared at this creature. *Their business?* What of all the murders, the looting? 'Are you—' she bit her tongue: calling someone insane was not a good negotiating tactic. 'What,' she asked, clearly and slowly, 'do you want?'

The warlock rubbed his brow, sighing. 'I had plans, but all that has gone by the wayside. A much greater problem has appeared from the south. I propose an alliance. I suggest we work together to do what we can to face it.'

Glinith could not help but glance to the south and the black cloud cover burgeoning there. 'A volcano? Whyever would we have to work together against a volcano?'

'It is more than that. Much more. I strongly suggest you look into it. And quickly. Time is running out.' He waved her away.

Frankly, she did not know what to make of all this. An alliance? Against a volcano? What insanity was this? Utterly ridiculous.

He waved her off once again. 'Go. Now.'

She backed away. 'Very well. However, this does not mean we will not act against any invader, or pirate, or foreign occupier who trespasses upon our lands.'

'Yes, yes. Now go!'

She went to the side, climbed over, and down the rope ladder. Her crew helped her down into the launch and pushed away from the hull. The rowers dug into the water and the launch surged off.

Glinith sat peering back at the dark silhouette of the eerie foreign vessel. Insanity. Complete insanity. In one last strange vision, the vessel appeared to flicker, disappearing, just before darkness swallowed it.

She turned away, then her gaze found the even darker and denser clouds to the south and she frowned anew, troubled by misgivings.

Returning to the Inner Chambers of the Abbey, she was surprised to see a light flickering through the open portal of the Abbess's, *her*, private library – the location of all the most sacred and secret of the Faith's records and writings.

Annoyed, she entered, only to quickly tamp down on her anger as there, amid the opened scrolls of the ritual of the Jhistal, sat Mallick Rel. Glinith lowered her head, greeting him: 'Proctor of the Faith.'

He blinked up at her, sitting back. 'Ah. Abbess. You are returned.'

Yes. Imagine that.

'And how went the negotiations?'

Clearing her throat, she went to a sideboard and poured a glass of watered wine – if only to gather her thoughts. Turning, she faced the man. 'It was . . . strange.'

A lifted brow. 'Oh? How so?'

'He actually offered some sort of alliance.'

He laughed throatily. 'An alliance? Really? Whatever for?'

'He claimed the volcano to the south was some sort of threat to everyone. Or some such thing.'

Mallick waved a pallid hand dismissively. 'Mere diversion. A transparent effort to shift our attention.'

Glinith simply raised her shoulders. 'If you say so.'

'Yes. He and his pirate filth remain the true threat.' He tapped the scrolls. 'When will we be able to summon the Jhistal once again?'

Glinith nearly choked on her wine. 'The new moon is in three days,' she allowed, coughing.

'Very good. We will discuss this tomorrow – at council.'

She bowed her head. 'As you say, Proctor of the Faith.'

'In the meantime,' and he rolled up the ancient vellum scrolls, 'I will keep these for further study.'

Now Glinith felt the hair of her neck actually rising, and she laughed, nervously. 'Those are the only copies of the ritual . . . They have been in the Abbey's safe-keeping for thousands of years . . .'

'Yes. And you have done a magnificent job. Currently, however, in this time of crisis, it seems only expedient that we take greater care of our treasures.'

'I don't see how,' she began, but he raised a brow and she clenched her lips.

'You are not questioning me, are you?' he asked. 'Remember our arrangement.'

Yes, I remember. An old saying came to her mind: Never make a deal with a fiend. Well, she'd made hers, and was now paying for it – without end. She laughed again, uneasily. 'Just what are you proposing?'

He tapped the scrolls. 'These have been enlightening, you know. Once one penetrates the dense commentaries and annotations and reaches the bare original texts – the invocations are actually quite short and simple.'

'It was a simpler time,' she allowed, her voice weak.

371

'It would seem to be more about intent and will than any secret wording.'

Glinith nodded – she peered about, searching for a chair, feeling suddenly rather faint. 'Yes. There's no magical wording . . . one only has to be willing. It is all about the personal will.'

The grotesque man actually smiled then, standing. He tucked the scrolls into his shirt. 'Indeed. Tomorrow, then. I will expect your attendance. It will be historic, I assure you.'

Glinith found her chair. As she sat, Mallick exited. She hardly noticed his leaving. Alone, staring into the dark, rather than feeling merely faint she now felt quite ill.

It was an exhausted Abbess of Cabil who showed up for the council meeting the next morning – earning a dark and annoyed glance from Mallick. She'd slept very poorly; vague premonitions of *something*, something approaching, dreadful and terrible, had assaulted her throughout the night.

She sat and braced herself for what was to come.

Nuraj gave his usual opening brief wherein he outlined current efforts to organize resistance upon the various isles, ship numbers, any reported confrontations, killings, or outright skirmishes. Glinith listened, feeling a growing sense of hopelessness and disillusionment. How could this have happened? Why were they so unprepared? And she answered herself, bleakly: they were to blame. Hundreds of years of rule by fear, extortion and intimidation. Hardly conducive to any sense of community or shared cause to fight for.

She noticed the chamber was quiet and both Nuraj and Mallick were eyeing her, rather quizzically.

'Your report?' Nuraj asked. 'You met with this leader, I understand?'

She cleared her throat. 'Yes. However, I doubt he is their leader. This invasion, or whatever it is, doesn't seem to have any real leadership.'

The Guardian of the Faith grunted his agreement. 'This is my impression as well. Yet they claim him to be.'

She nodded. 'After having met him, I believe he may simply be a powerful magus who himself has fled the south. They fear him but owe him no allegiance.'

Nuraj slammed the table, snarling, 'A damned waste of an attack then.'

'We won't waste it again,' Mallick answered, his voice soft and sibilant.

Nuraj sat back, eyeing the man narrowly. 'Oh? Just what are you proposing?'

'In two days' time I propose we summon the Jhistal once more. And that we unleash it again. This time much more publicly. I propose we use it to destroy one of these pirate nests.'

'Destroy one of our own cities or towns?' Nuraj yelled.

'Kill our own citizens?' Glinith demanded.

Mallick raised a pallid hand. 'I propose Jook Isle. As we have heard – these raiders recently inflicted a lesson in retribution for any defiance. I suggest we do the same. Only our lesson will be final.' He waved again. 'Most civilians, I understand, have already fled Jook. Few remain, as a result of all the recent fighting on the isle and these pirates' reprisals. Obviously all these scum understand is the language of violence and intimidation. Well, we shall give them our retribution. And it will be a lesson that will resound throughout the region – yes?' He nodded to Glinith. 'Through the priesthood, give any remaining residents two days' warning. Flee, or die.'

In response, Glinith felt herself sag. So this was it. This was what they'd come to. Murdering their own in a squalid and pathetic effort to grasp at power. She could not raise her gaze.

And yet, a voice within her answered, *what if they were to succeed?* What then? Would they not be lauded universally as deliverers? If they managed to drive off these invaders, would this not ensure the future of the Faith – and their own reputations – for ever?

'Make the preparations,' Mallick ordered.

Without raising her gaze, she nodded. 'As you wish.'

'Yet,' stammered Nuraj, 'isn't the High Priestess gone? That is, who will . . .' He was silent for a time, before continuing, 'That is, who will be the . . .'

Into the silence following the unsaid question, Mallick murmured, 'We have others.'

* * *

In the end it was Torva who spotted the site – much to Gianna's embarrassment. It took a day of slow wandering through the maze of rocks, poling from one to another, searching. She directed them while standing at the bows. Unfortunately for her, as they went from rock to rock, they all started looking alike. She knew the arrangement she was looking for; she just didn't know how to get to it.

Torva had been nearby all day, pointing out tall stones and suggesting turns that she studiously ignored – as she tried to concentrate. Finally, after beginning to suspect she was now leading them in circles, and with Brevin's impatient frowns growing ever deeper, she turned to Torva as a last resort.

'You think you know where it is?' she demanded, far more harshly than she intended.

'I may have a handle on it,' he answered, as laconic as usual.

'Well?'

He nodded to the north. 'Have to double back a touch.'

She bit her lip; Brevin would not like that. However, for her the shoals were now living up to one of their nicknames – the Maze of Stones. 'Back northwards,' she called to the crew, who looked dubious, but began shifting their poling to edge the *Glimmer* around.

It was slow going, and the sun was now low. The slanting amber light came and went as they passed one standing spur after the other. Gianna wiped chill spray from her face as she squinted, scanning the rocks.

'I'm not so sure . . .' she began, but Torva raised a hand for a pause.

'We're gettin' there.'

'How can you know?'

'I know.' Gianna couldn't keep the doubt from her face, but the old smuggler just smiled indulgently. 'You'll see . . .'

Then, in the half-light of the coming sunset, the set of rocks ahead fell into place in her memory and she turned to Torva. 'How did you know?'

He tapped a finger to an eye. 'A lifetime of memorizing handy mooring-spots, hidden caves and coves.'

'A lifetime of smuggling you mean,' Gianna added, with a shake of her head. She turned back to Brevin, gestured ahead. 'That crowded group of tall rocks there.'

The captain blew out a breath. 'You sure know how to pick 'em.'

'As close as you can, please.'

'As close as I dare . . .' Brevin muttered, and turned to ordering the crew.

It was full evening, the night very dark as a new moon was close. By the time the crew had tied off the *Glimmer* with lines to three different rocks, even Gianna had to admit it was far too dark to dive.

The crew dined hugely that night on fresh fruits and cuts of meat seared over the ship's iron brazier. Gianna, however, thinking of tomorrow, ate little. She then threw herself down early to try to get some sleep, although, with her stomach in knots of anxiety and anticipation, she knew it would be slow in coming.

When dawn's light pinked the eastern horizon she was already awake. The routine of her readying to dive was all very familiar for the crew as they'd been through it many times by now. Brevin, however, made a show of checking and rechecking all the rigging, and personally tied the lifeline to Gianna's wrist.

'May Mael guide you,' the captain murmured to her – and she almost flinched.

'Not that, please. Anything but that.'

Brevin appeared surprised, but nodded. 'Very well. Gods look away, then.'

Gianna sat on the ship's side. 'Yes, that. I much prefer *that*.'

And she dived.

Chapter 25

HESSA WAS NOT SURPRISED WHEN MALAZAN TROOPERS opened the canvas flap of her and Turnagin's tent and gestured them out. She eyed the mage, who straightened his newly washed robes, looking grim.

Outside, Fist Dujek stood awaiting them, with a staff of aides and guards standing a respectful distance off. The Fist met them with an easy nod that soothed Hessa's worst suspicions – at least it looked like they weren't about to be executed.

'Cap'n,' Dujek greeted her, and, 'Sage,' to Turnagin. 'You're both civilians,' he began, rubbing the back of his neck, 'so technically you're guests in this camp. An' I can't order you to do anything. But we're facing a damned dangerous situation here—'

Turnagin was staring upwards at the dense deck of smoke clouds churning overhead. 'I'll go,' he interrupted.

The Fist grunted, nodding. 'Ah, good. The Empire thanks you.'

Hessa had to shake her head – almost laughing at the foolishness of it – saying, 'And I.'

The Fist crooked a sideways smile, nodding once more. 'Have to say, that's about what I expected.' He gestured vaguely across the encampment. 'You've permission to draw stores and equipment from the depot. Be ready at dawn.' And he ambled away.

Hessa shared a rueful glance with Turnagin, who began, 'You don't have to . . .'

'I know. But I will. Can't let you go in alone.'

'I'll hardly be alone.'

'You know what I mean.'

'You're hoping maybe to catch sight of the twins?'

She snorted. 'Gods. If I was them, I'd be long gone by now. But . . . yes.'

Turnagin scanned the direction across camp where the Fist had pointed. 'Let us perhaps see what stores they have.'

'You go ahead for now.'

'Very well.'

Hessa faced the north, and the dominating bulk of the mountain. It appeared to be spewing out even more smoke and soot than before. No, gal, she told herself, you're not going to be executed – at least not immediately.

*

Tayschrenn was sipping tea in the command tent when Dujek entered. 'We have our guides,' the Fist announced.

Blowing on the ceramic cup, Tayschrenn nodded, impressed. Frankly, he hadn't expected that level of courage or responsibility from any civilian. But then, he was now beginning to suspect that perhaps he was more wrong than he realized when trying to understand the motivations, and character, of others.

This after being so certain he knew quite well.

Which itself – he now understood – was a mistake.

'When do we leave?' he asked.

'Tomorrow, dawn.' The Fist peered about the tent. 'And where's Hairlock, anyway?'

'Out keeping an eye on the artefact.' Dujek grunted at this. 'And who will be going?'

The Fist blew out a rueful breath, pressed his hand to his forehead. 'Gods! Dancer insists and I can't stop Dassem.' The man almost groaned. 'Surly will skin me alive.'

'An entire company would be of no help in those halls. Any troops would just be killed by these Che'Malle.'

Dujek eyed him anew. 'Is this compassion for the common soldier I'm hearing?'

Tayschrenn tilted his head, considering. He sipped his tea. 'I believe that I am mostly thinking of the waste.'

Dujek slowly shook his head. 'I'll be outside – getting some fresh air.'

Tayschrenn watched him go. An odd choice of words, he

thought. Given that the air beneath these choking clouds was anything but fresh.

At dawn Tayschrenn emerged from his tent to see his two minders waiting outside. He eyed them rather perplexed. 'You are not coming, surely?'

'Of course,' Missy answered. 'It's our assignment.'

Ute added his own fierce nod.

Tayschrenn stalked off. Ridiculous! He found Dancer and the Sword waiting at the edge of camp, together with their two guides. 'Order these two to remain,' he told the Sword.

Dassem looked the two troopers up and down; the ghost of a smile passed his lips. ''Fraid I don't have the authority.'

'You don't—' He looked to Dancer. 'You, then. Tell these two to remain.'

Dancer shared a glance with the Sword; he shook his head. 'I shouldn't meddle in any military orders.'

Tayschrenn looked from one to the other. He was missing something here – he was certain of it. Something involving what many referred to as soldier's humour. A thought struck then, and he found himself wondering: perhaps he was missing something much greater, something even more foundational.

He turned and regarded Ute and Missy, cleared his throat. 'I want you two – that is, I would *like* you two to remain.'

The two exchanged glances. Ute screwed up his face, chagrined. 'Really?'

'Yes.'

Missy frowned, appearing almost hurt. 'Well . . . if you say so.'

Tayschrenn nodded to them. 'Good. We will return shortly.' He did not add: if they were to return at all.

He found Dancer and the Sword eyeing him as they began the march. 'You sent them off,' Dancer observed.

'How?' Dassem asked.

'I asked them.'

Dancer nodded to himself as he walked. 'Ah, I see. Imagine that.'

Now Tayschrenn frowned, uncomfortable. There was certainly something here. Something he was missing.

* * *

'Is it just me,' observed Creel, the first mate, 'or is that mountain getting a lot closer?'

'As I said,' the Thelomen giant Koroll answered, 'it is moving towards us even as we move towards it.'

'Yeah. That was what I thought you said. But I just kinda thought it was an exaggeration. Not the real honest to the gods truth of it – if you know what I mean.'

As they walked along the hillocked grassy plain, Cartheron looked to the thick deck of cloud cover overhead. Then he eyed the great smoking bulk ahead. 'Maybe we *should* give that a wider berth,' he called to Koroll.

Glancing back, the giant nodded as he shambled along. 'Very well.' He struck a more easterly course.

'I see no scouts or hunting parties,' Jill murmured, looking concerned.

'He's there,' Cartheron assured her. 'Just far to the south, no doubt. Giving things a careful margin.' He called ahead to Koroll, 'What of the K'Chain? Seen any? Should we pull away further?'

A shake of the shaggy head. 'No. It seems they have all withdrawn to their home. They may be preparing it.'

'Preparing for what?' Creel asked.

'For the catastrophe ahead. If it keeps advancing, it will strike the waters of Lure Sea. Even onwards towards Cabil Isle.'

'Cabil Isle?' Geddin the steersman called out. 'Isn't that the Falaran capital 'n all?'

The Thelomen gave a long thoughtful nod. 'I believe so.'

'Could that be deliberate?' Jill asked.

Pondering that, Cartheron shook his head. 'Don't think so. This thing's route was probably set out long ago. Anyway, no matter where it strikes or passes, it will be as our friend here says – a catastrophe.'

'You have the right of that,' Koroll rumbled.

'Well,' The Nose opined, chewing on a stalk of grass, 'if ol' one-arm's gonna do anything, it'll have to be real soon. I give this thing another few days at the rate it's goin'.'

Glancing back, Koroll frowned, troubled. 'Yes. Perhaps we should increase our pace.'

The Nose appeared annoyed. 'Well – can't you just magic us over there? Y'know – snap your fingers and such?'

The giant rumbled a laugh. 'I would not be so quick to raise the ire of the K'Chain Che'Malle by using Thelomen magics here on their very doorstep. We have not been visited by them – let us not test the matter.'

The Nose rolled his eyes and grumbled.

Cartheron gestured for everyone to step up their pace – which was quick already as they strove to keep up with Koroll.

* * *

Aided by the few youths left behind on board the *Glimmer*, on her third dive of the day Gianna managed to manoeuvre close to the base of the assemblage of jagged tall rocks. Reaching that relatively sheltered region of the shoal's floor was nearly impossible as the very barrier of the stones intensified the surrounding currents. Yet these selfsame currents also slowed behind the barrier and over the centuries had continuously deposited layers of sand and debris.

She brought lines down with her and tied off a guide-rope to follow back and forth, then set to work feeling about the gathered sediments. The bank here was thick – the deepest she'd ever encountered. Thankfully, the dragging currents surrounding her yanked away the sands as swiftly as she disturbed them.

Digging was slow, and tiring; she found she could stay down only a fraction of her usual time. This meant even more wasted time climbing and descending the guide-ropes.

On her third descent her extended fingertips, pushing down through the layers, encountered something relatively smooth and broad – not a natural feature of the local coral or rock.

It took two further descents to clear away enough of the sand and detritus to reach the object, and her heart leapt when she saw a barnacle-encrusted flat panel beneath her – one side of a manufactured object, whole, and obviously very old. She kicked her way upwards as swiftly as she dared.

She broke surface, a hand firm on her guide-rope against the pulling currents, and took hold of the rope ladder at the side of the *Glimmer*.

'There's definitely something there,' she called up to Brevin and Torva, both anxiously peering over the rail.

'Could be anything,' Torva answered.

Gianna tamped down on her irritation, 'Yes, I know.'

'You want a line?' Brevin asked.

'Yes. I'll rig it as best I can then tug to let you know. I want four crew on it – the currents will pull like Togg himself.'

Brevin nodded, called over her shoulder, 'A strong line here!'

An end was lowered to her. She took it, drew a deep breath, and submerged. She pulled herself down along the guide-rope, ever deeper into the darkening turquoise waters.

It took two more dives to finish the rigging, and daylight was waning. She had to reach under the damned thing to adequately secure it and that took a lot of digging.

Finally, she was satisfied, and pulled strongly on the line. It tautened. The object shifted. Then, in a burst of billowing sands and muck that momentarily blinded her, it rose.

The driving currents snatched at it. The line angled. She ached to help, but if she took hold her own weight would only add to the load. She followed its ascent, kicking lazily.

She broached the surface first, calling, 'Another line! It's damned heavy.'

This second rigging she tied while the crew held the object just beneath the surface waves. And it was a box, she could see that clearly, now that it was free of all the years of clinging sediments.

Heaving, the crew hauled it up the side and over. Gianna quickly followed. Everyone gathered round.

'A damned chest,' were Brevin's bemused first words. 'In all my years treasure-hunting this is the first time it's ever happened this way. Things are usually spread out all across the bottom.'

'It's bronze,' a sailor announced, poking it with his knife blade.

'Have to chisel off them barnacles and such,' Torva opined.

Brevin waved to the crew. 'Get to it. Hammers and chisels – but gentle-like, okay?'

Gianna came staggering over, exhausted, held up by two sailors, hardly able even to speak. She stared at the chest. *This must be it. Jhistal's Bane. Some way to break it. Perhaps a counter-ritual.*

And just in time, too! The new moon must be close. In fact . . .

She grasped at Brevin's arm. 'The moon . . . when . . .'

Torva threw a blanket over her. 'Get some rest, lass.'

'But the moon . . .'

'Don't worry,' Brevin assured her. 'You just lie down.'

She struggled, weakly, but the sailors guided her to the stern.

* * *

As they neared the artefact the heat radiating from the blackened naked rock they were walking upon intensified. Tayschrenn raised a hand for a halt and the party came together, eyeing all directions. Banners of mist and smoke coiled all about – cover for them, but equal cover for any approaching Che'Malle patrol.

He addressed them, 'As before, I shall do my best to protect us from the heat. So stay close, yes?'

One of their guides, the mage Turnagin, spoke up, 'Spare yourself for what lies ahead, High Mage. I will take on that burden.'

Tayschrenn eyed him, dubious. 'You believe yourself capable?'

The man's tangled greying mane of hair already hung lank with sweat. He inclined his head. 'I will serve.'

'Very well.' Tayschrenn motioned to the man's fellow guide, Hessa. 'Proceed.'

The woman cast her friend a very long hard stare before nodding and starting off. Dassem followed next, then Tayschrenn and Turnagin. Dancer brought up the rear – sometimes walking backwards, constantly scanning the banks of mist.

The ground actually softened here. They skirted open pools of hissing, cooling molten rock crusted in black skeins. The immense bulk of the artefact loomed ahead as a sloped cliff. So far they had seen no hint of its inhabitants and guardians, the K'ell Hunters.

Tayschrenn became aware the two ahead had halted, crowded together. He shot a questioning glance to Dassem who motioned him to join them. He tentatively stepped up to find Hessa crouched, examining something. She directed his attention to it.

He looked closely at the blackened rock here and slowly, almost intuitively, a shape emerged: that of a huge skull, half eroded, scorched and ashy, frozen now in cooling, hardening rock.

'One of their own,' Tayschrenn murmured, surprised.

Hessa nodded, grim. 'Wounded, or sickened; they simply ran right over it.'

'As Nightchill said – this is wrong, utterly wrong.'

The ex-captain straightened. 'Regardless, it must be stopped. Somehow.'

'Can you do that?' Tayschrenn asked.

Almost reluctantly, she allowed, 'Turnagin has a chance.'

'Then we shall see.'

They moved on, and reached the hovering slab of an edge without encountering any Che'Malle patrol or guardian. Tayschrenn found himself becoming more and more uneasy. In truth, he gave little for their chances. However, the attempt had to be made. He looked to Turnagin, a mage of Meanas apparently, now staggering, helped along by Hessa, spent by the task of shielding them from the deathly heat.

The Sword gestured ahead to the darkness of an open cave – one the size of a yawning city gate.

A stone wedge, broken and jagged, stretched out before it like a ramp. Dassem reached up to it, pulling himself off the ground. He reached back down for Tayschrenn, while Dancer somehow sprang up and darted within, covering them.

The Sword pulled Tayschrenn up and over, then reached down once more. He and Hessa struggled together to raise Turnagin. Half-stumbling, the ex-captain managed to lift the mage high enough for Dassem to clasp his arms and drag him up. He lay on the gritty stone threshold, panting.

Edging within, Tayschrenn came to where Dancer stood, motionless, daggers low at his sides, studying something. He stared as well. Eventually, all gathered together in silent regard.

A K'Chain Che'Malle warrior, a K'ell Hunter, guarded the entrance – and would perhaps eternally. It stood motionless, slumped against a wall, dead for some time.

'Starved to death at its post,' Turnagin opined, sounding awed – and horrified.

Tayschrenn shook his head almost in disbelief as he observed the sunken dark pits of the eyes, the hollow cavern of the chest where ribs arched the armoured flesh like tent poles.

'Let us find a defensible position and rest for a time,' Dancer said into the heavy silence.

Turnagin nodded his heartfelt thanks.

* * *

Glinith dressed herself slowly the morning of the ritual. Half of her dreaded what she was about to unleash: deaths on a terrifying scale, an island wiped clean! Yet such risk-taking was just what had raised her to the position she held today. From nameless street-child, to acolyte, to priestess. She had used many – and many had used her.

She drew on her best outer robes, thinking, yes, this could destroy her. But it could also make her. She . . . and Mallick . . . would be the unassailable authority among the isles. All would fall into line behind them – after this day.

She had hardly finished when an acolyte burst into her private chambers, breathless, pointing, 'Abbess! The Sanctum – the Pool of Mael!'

'What of it?'

The young priestess stammered, beyond words, could only urge her to come.

Her gaze hard, Glinith secured her robes and followed.

She found the halls empty and a crowd of attendants and lower Abbey functionaries filling the Inner Temple. As she pushed through, the constant low murmuring dwindled away. All stared as she passed. Glinith saw confusion, fear and some hope upon their strained faces as she passed. But mostly fear.

The doors to the Inner Sanctuary were closed. Her guide banged upon them, whispered fiercely. One leaf cracked open just wide enough for them to slip within.

Glinith saw Priestess Lias here, high among those who tended the Pool. 'What is this?' she demanded. The priestess would only mutely point up the narrow hall. Glinith's anger was checked somewhat as she noted how pale the woman was.

She started up the hall. She found a file of priests all kneeling, hoods raised, hands clasped in devotion. She brushed past them to the vantage portal above the pool.

The highest-ranked of her assistants awaited her here, all of the Faith Militant. Two watched over the fettered line of kneeling black-haired children.

All stared down the deep and wide throat of the Inner Sanctum.

Glinith went forward to the edge and peered down – then had to slide forward even farther, and extend her neck even more, to see that the rock sides of the well continued onwards down and down into shadows and darkness, without a sign of any of the waters of Mael.

She raised her gaze in wonder to Hestasia, Keeper of the Pool. 'What is this?'

'It is gone,' the priestess barely whispered, her voice hoarse.

Glinith mouthed the word, not understanding . . . 'Gone?'

'We are renounced,' Hestasia fairly wailed. 'Rejected by Mael!'

Glinith snapped up a hand. 'We do not know that!' She pulled the woman closer. 'Has Mallick been summoned?'

Hestasia nodded.

'Good. Then we wait. And no word of this to anyone! Yes?'

Hestasia continued to nod while wiping tears from her face.

Moments later a stirring and bustle among the gathered priests announced the arrival of Mallick. He, too, had been interrupted in his preparations: he came to her still adjusting his rich blue priestly robes.

'What is this?' he demanded of Glinith.

The Abbess now found herself also at a loss for words. She gestured mutely to the wide mouth of the well before them.

The squat fellow gave her a wary glance, then edged away to peer over. 'The pool appears low.'

'It is gone. All the water is gone.'

'Why?'

'Exactly – why?' She motioned to the huddled priestesses. 'Some already whisper it is because Mael has turned his face from us.'

Mallick stiffened, half-snarling, 'Such dangerous talk must be crushed.'

'Indeed. Question is – what do we do now?'

Nuraj Senull, Guardian of the Faith, arrived as they spoke. His hatchet face was even more severe than usual. He peered about, confused. 'What is all this murmuring in the halls of the Abbey?'

'The pool is empty. The Jhistal cannot be summoned,' Glinith told him.

He gaped, stunned. 'But . . . we have already announced it through the priesthood. Given warning.'

'And have you tested this assumption?' Mallick blandly enquired.

Glinith blinked at him. 'I'm sorry . . . ?'

He nodded to the manacled file of youths. 'Have you tested it?'

'Well . . . no.'

Mallick rolled his eyes and marched over to the closest youth, took her arm. Hestasia unbound the child. Mallick pulled her to the edge of the yawning well and the stone walkway.

'But the Blade of Offering . . .' Glinith objected.

'Any blade would do the job, I imagine,' Mallick answered, and he drew a short, curved knife from his belt.

Glinith didn't think – something within her drove her forward to take the man's arm. 'It's useless,' she told him. 'There's no water to accept the blood. It will just fall on stone.'

Mallick paused, scowling, his lips working his mute frustration. He whipped the blade from the girl's throat to Glinith's. She felt the cold steel bite her neck. 'If you are wrong,' Mallick whispered to her, 'then your blood will be the next to fall. Am I making myself clear?'

She nodded, wordless, not daring to speak.

The blade withdrew.

'It's this bickering that is useless,' Nuraj cut in. 'We've announced the summoning. The priests have warned Jook. What do we do?'

Mallick now turned his lazy, lizard gaze on Nuraj. He nodded then, allowing the point. 'Yes. What to do.' The blade disappeared among the folds of his robes. 'I . . . that is *we*, will send word through the priesthood that everyone's pleas have stayed our hand. For the moment. That we have determined to wait, for a time. Wait for the isles to come together and cooperate in driving these invaders out. That any isle that fails to commit to this effort – *they* will be the ones to feel the wrath of the Jhistal.' He eyed each of them in turn. 'Understood?'

Glinith inclined her head; Nuraj stroked his sharp chin, nodding. 'That might work,' he granted.

'Make it work,' Mallick growled. He turned to Glinith, lowered his gaze.

Startled, she saw that she still had hold of the cloth of his sleeve; she pulled her hand away.

'No word of this must leave these halls,' he told her. 'If any hint of it escapes, I will hold you personally responsible. Understood?'

She nodded fiercely. 'Yes, Mallick. Yes.'

'Very well.' He straightened his robes. 'Let us salvage what we may from this . . . rather disappointing morning.'

* * *

Gianna woke with a start, gasping and jerking upright. A hand urged her back down.

'There, there, lass. Don't worry. You're safe.'

'I dreamed I was drowning.'

Torva nodded reassuringly. 'Yes, that's common among deep divers such as you.'

She started upright once more. 'The chest!'

'Awaiting you,' Torva answered. 'Wouldn't open it without you o' course.'

She struggled to rise. 'Thank you.'

He helped her up, handed her a ceramic cup that steamed in the chill morning air. 'Tea?'

'My thanks.' Straightening, she peered about, almost panicked. 'We've left the shoals.'

Torva nodded. 'Yes, overnight. The cap'n here trusted me to guide us.'

'We're headed south.'

The old man laughed and gestured to the straining sails. 'Almost no choice. The wind came right up and took us. We've passed Flood already. Coming up on Belid.'

She eyed the canvas and felt a stirring of unease. Such winds here at this time of year . . . it wasn't normal. She hobbled over to where the chest lay amid the debris of chiselled scale, shell and shattered barnacle.

Brevin nodded her a greeting. 'We think we're ready to have a go at the sealed lid. Just waiting for you.'

She sipped her tea. 'Go ahead.'

Brevin gave a curt bob of agreement. 'Right, lads and lasses. There you go. Start in.'

The three sailors who stood in for ship's carpenters set to tapping.

'What are they working on?' Gianna asked.

'A thick seal of lead all round the lid.' Brevin shook her head in admiration. 'Whoever did this had their eyes on the ages, I tell you.'

'Good.'

They waited. Gianna broke fast with a crust of bread dipped in the tea. Then the sailors inspected the cut and gave Brevin a nod. She turned to Gianna. 'Okay. Here we go, yes?'

Gianna gave her own nod.

The sailors tapped bars into the cut and levered. The lid grated and arched, the lead seam tore away. Brevin stepped in and lifted, straining against all remaining resistance. The lid ground open.

Gianna pressed forward to peer in.

Water filled it, of course. No seal could possibly prove impervious over so many years. She reached in and felt about. Tubes met her hand. Long and slim. She drew one out.

It was horn, sealed by a thick layer of what looked like beeswax. *What in the name of cursed Mael?*

She studied the thing, frowning. Brevin made a snapping gesture with her hands. Gianna took hold of the wax seal and bent it. After some effort, the seal came away and she shook out a scroll.

A scroll of finest vellum. She opened it and read the first few lines.

'What is it?' Brevin asked.

She let it roll up and slid it back into its horn tube. She shook her head. 'History. Ancient writings of the cult of Mael.'

'And,' the captain asked, 'is that all? Nothing else?'

Gianna waved helplessly at the chest. 'Have a look.'

Brevin nodded to the carpenters who then fished about the murky water. They drew out horn and bone tubes, one after the other.

Gianna walked to the ship's side, peered at the churning waters. *You damned bastard. You've had your jest, haven't you? All at my expense.*

She took hold of the railings with both hands and was frankly tempted to throw herself over.

'Ship ho!' a call sounded from above.

She blinked, peering about. 'I see no – ah.' A small vessel was bumping and wallowing among the waters, more or less in their path.

Brevin came to her side. 'What in the name of Beru . . .'

The rowboat – for it was just that, a tiny one-man rowboat – struggling through the tall waves. Its occupant was waving his arms, hailing them.

'Heave to!' Brevin ordered. 'Throw a line!'

The occupant of the rowboat – and Gianna groaned within, recognizing the half-naked potbellied fellow in a loincloth – watched while the *Glimmer* circled, slowing.

A line was thrown and he took hold and began heaving his tiny vessel closer.

Brevin simply stared, amazed. 'How in the name of Beru did this fellow manage such a thing?' She nodded to the crew. 'Raise sails!'

'He's a priest of Mael. Well,' Gianna corrected herself, 'an ex-priest of Mael.'

Showing amazing agility, the lone sailor secured his boat then drew himself up the line to climb the side of the *Glimmer* and step down onto the deck.

'Welcome!' Brevin greeted him. 'Any sailor such as yourself is most welcome on board my vessel.'

Gianna thrust a finger at the short, bandy-legged fellow. '*You! You little shit! What in the name of – well, of – Fanderay*, are you doing here? How – *how did you find me?*'

The ex-priest of Mael bowed. 'Your example gave me the courage, High Priestess. And, I was gifted a vision.'

'*High Priestess?*' Brevin echoed, starting away from Gianna.

She waved that aside, pointed to the chest. 'What in the name of the Abyss is this? Histories? What of—' She caught herself in time, eyed Captain Brevin, then drew the ex-priest aside. '*Jhistal's Bane, you said!*' she hissed, her voice low.

He was nodding and raised his hands in reassurance. 'Yes. I understand.'

'And how in the name of – well – of Togg! – are you here just now?'

The fellow, shorter than she, bobbed his head in agreement. 'Yes. How.' He took a deep breath. 'After you escaped, I was gifted with a vision from Mael. Like yours. Only mine was that I could . . .' He struggled then, lowering his gaze. '. . . That I could *redeem* myself if I helped you discover the truth of the Jhistal.'

'Truth?' she snarled. 'What in the name of—' She bit down on her tongue. 'What do these histories have to do with that?'

He straightened, eager. 'These are the truth! They contain the true purpose of the Jhistal.'

Gianna threw herself from him. 'What does this have to do with anything! How can this possibly help us now?'

She crossed to the ship's side, pointed west. 'They could be summoning one now!' The truth of that struck then, as a knife to her stomach, and she gasped, 'With blood . . .'

The ex-priest came to her, stood before her. 'Do not worry. Please, do not torture yourself. In this vision I saw that the Jhistal has been taken from them. That it is theirs no longer.' He wrung his hands, frowning. 'That Mael . . . ah, yes, that Mael has with-drawn it.'

She stared at the pot-bellied fellow, shook her head, almost weeping. 'How can I possibly believe that?'

'Please do. You can. You must. Mael—'

She threw herself from him. 'Speak not of *him* to me!'

He let his hands fall. 'Yes. Why should you listen. After all this time.' He sighed. 'All I can do is give you my vision. I suppose that is all anyone can do.'

Facing away, arms crossed, she answered gruffly, 'What of it?'

'Yes, well. My vision is that the Jhistal has been given to you.'

Gianna choked back an almost manic laugh. She faced him. '*Me?* Given to me?'

'Yes. It is yours. Yours to use—'

'I would not touch such a disgusting thing!'

The ex-priest took a breath, nodding. 'Yours to use in the man-ner in which it was given. To defend. To protect. To save lives.'

She laughed then, openly in the man's face. 'Hypocrisy. Spare me all those self-serving lies.'

'That you have known and seen all this time, yes. But a threat is approaching. A very great danger. One that the Jhistal was exactly meant to answer.'

She turned away, shaking her head. 'No. No more. I'll not listen to you any more.' She gestured to his rowboat. 'Go. Leave. Goodbye.'

The fellow stood silent for a time. He examined his wide work-man's hands. 'Yes. I suppose I deserve this. Very well. I will go. The threat comes from the south, by the way. A moving mountain of fire. You can see its smoke now.'

'Just go.'

The fellow went to the side, threw a leg over. 'I'm sorry. It seems I've failed you – and I'm sorry.'

He clambered down the rope ladder to his tiny rowboat where it bounced along next to the *Glimmer*'s side. He threw off the line and set the oars in their docks. Gianna watched the boat quickly fall behind.

390

Brevin came to her side. 'What was all that about, lass?'

She let out a hard breath. 'I suppose you could call it a religious dispute.'

Brevin set her hands on the railing. 'High Priestess, is it?' she asked, eyeing her narrowly.

She snorted. 'Once, perhaps. No longer.'

'Well, you have your chest, and the crew are eager to cash in their shares of the salvage. No holding them back now.'

She gave a wry laugh. 'They want to get a move on, hey?'

'Yes, lass. Apologies.' She glanced back to the chest. 'Not what you were hoping for, I understand. I have contacts in Gravid. Cousins. They'll help us move all this. Then it's north for us, I think. Plenty foreign ports up north where no one knows us.'

'They hate Falarans. They won't let you dock.'

Brevin offered a grin, rubbed her fingertips together. 'Silver and gold smooths away so many obstacles.'

Gianna raised a hand, almost in surrender. 'Yes. I understand.' She sighed anew so heavily she felt her shoulders falling. 'So, west it is.'

Brevin gave a curt half-bow, turned away. 'Raise all sail!'

Gianna glanced aside to see Torva at the side, a slight distance off, eyeing her edgeways. 'What do you have to say?' she demanded.

The old smuggler shrugged. 'Not for me to comment, hey? That's all between you and your faith, I'm thinking.'

She nodded. 'Yes. I suppose so. A faith I should've lost a long time ago.'

'That's not for no one to say. Not even you.'

She raised a brow. 'Oh? You a religious man, Torva?'

He appeared uncomfortable, hunched his shoulders. 'Age does things to a person. Some harden into their old ideas, shut their eyes. But others see things different when they look back. There's those who say they have no regrets for anything – I say that's complete stubborn ass-headedness. *All* I see are regrets.' He drew a hand down his greying stubble. 'All the things I wish I'd had the courage to say or to do at the time. All those lost chances . . .' He shook his head.

'Is that wisdom speaking there, Torva?'

'Hunh. Age ain't no guarantee of wisdom, lass. There's plenty of stupid old people out there. Believe you me.'

She laughed then, unreservedly, hurting her stomach. 'Thank you, Torva. For that bit of wholesome folk wisdom.'

He raised a greying beetle brow back at her. 'Oh – was *that* what that was, lass?'

The winds remained strong and favourable. They stormed past Delanss and by late that day were already heading towards Ictor. Gianna looked up from her reading of the scrolls to scowl at the billowing sails.

Following her gaze, Brevin, from the stern, laughed her pleasure. 'We're fortunate! Such winds at this time of year? This keeps up we'll set a new record for such a crossing.'

Gianna's scowl deepened. *Yes, unheard of . . .*

She returned to her reading. Every scroll she opened only amazed her further. No wonder these records were sealed away! The very cult of Mael criminalizing the open and free worship of their own god? Stunning truths. She returned her latest scroll and sat back. Yet who would listen? How would she escape censure and arrest should she whisper one word of this?

'Boats abows!' came the shout from above.

She stood, peered ahead. Numerous small craft crowded the waters to the west. Having made such excellent time, she judged the *Glimmer* to be nearing the Strait of Lure.

Brevin called to lower canvas. The *Glimmer* slowed.

They found themselves amidst a rag-tag flotilla, or convoy, of fishing boats and other small family craft.

'Ahoy!' Brevin called from the prow. 'What's this? What news?'

'Don't go west!' came an answering shout. 'Head off with us – north!'

'Why?' Brevin answered, almost laughing.

'The gods' own retribution is upon us!' someone else yelled back. 'From the south! We are doomed!'

Gianna let the bone and horn tubes fall. She threw herself to the rail.

Brevin now eyed her, almost warily.

'What do you mean – retribution?' Gianna shouted back.

As one craft passed, the fellow at the side-tiller answered, 'A great mountain of fire! A walking volcano! All will burn! Where do you think all this smoke is from, fool!'

Gianna thumped back down to her seat.

'Where?' Brevin called to another passing boat.

'The mainland coast of Lure Sea! South of Cabil.'

Gianna pressed her hands to her mouth. Brevin came to her, stood before her.

'What is this?' the captain breathed, her eyes on the passing craft.

Gianna stifled a near-manic giggle. *The true purpose of the Jhistal,* he'd said.

She lowered her hands. 'Set sail for Lure Sea.'

Brevin pressed a hand to her heavy jowls. 'I was planning a more northern crossing, lass.'

Gianna snorted a laugh. She noted the strong gusting winds. 'I have a feeling the seas would be against that, captain.'

Chapter 26

Blues and Gwynn busied themselves drying and smoking any game brought back by Black and Jacinth – while keeping an eye on the limping mountain as it laboured northwards like a wounded god. Blues estimated two days were left at the most before they'd know the fate of it or the region: drowning in the sea, or a cataclysm of eternal smoke, mists and poisonous fumes.

'We're not alone,' Gwynn announced late that afternoon, and nodded to the tall, windswept grasses of the slope. Blues scanned them, seeing nothing, but feeling . . . something. A presence.

Gwynn urged whoever or whatever it was up from cover.

A figure rose from the waving grasses: slim, female, bearing a thick shock of white hair. She approached.

Blues nodded to himself. 'Ah. The Beast Hold. Always hard to detect.'

'How did you know?' the young woman asked of Gwynn, looking irked, the nostrils of her narrow and sharp nose flaring.

'Just a feeling. And I've learned to trust my feelings.'

She brushed a hand through the tall grass. 'Should've known. Crimson Guard 'n all. I considered joining, you know.'

Blues invited her forward. 'We could use you.'

Gwynn shot him a look. 'Blues, no poaching. I understand our friend here is spoken for.'

She actually almost blushed. 'Yes. The last thing I expected to find – a home.'

Blues nodded his understanding. 'Yes. Congratulations. Finding such a thing is rare in this world.'

She inclined her head in acknowledgement, cleared her throat, looking away. 'Then on to business. My mistress could not help but notice that you have not yet departed the region.'

'This is so,' Gwynn answered.

'May she ask, then, your intentions?'

Blues eyed Gwynn. 'Regarding . . . ?'

The young woman appeared embarrassed. 'Gwynn . . . despite m'lady's great friendship and gratitude, she must let you know that she is considering a treaty with the Malazans.'

Blues raised his brows. 'Ah . . .' He noted then that the girl – a Beast Hold mage – remained a good ten paces distant from them.

'We are too few to cause any trouble,' Gwynn supplied. 'In any case, our main interest is the artefact and its fate.'

The young woman could not help but glance behind her to the great bulk, its smoke-obscured top just below their altitude on the coastal mountainside. 'Indeed. And once we all witness this you will withdraw?'

'I expect so,' Gwynn admitted.

She nodded. 'Very well. I will inform my mistress. And remember,' she pointed to the sky, 'she is always watching.'

She turned and leapt, sembling in mid-air into a white furry beast, an ermine perhaps, and disappeared among the grass.

Two other figures then arose from the tall grasses, Black and Jacinth, some way off to either side. Both looked a touch surprised. 'She's damned fast,' Black observed, scratching his beard.

Blues looked to Gwynn. 'I'm sorry . . .'

The mage of Rashan raised a hand. 'It's fine. Ullara is right to pursue such a course. She is thinking of her people, their welfare.' He clasped his hands at his back, nodding to himself. 'I would expect no less from her.'

'And those people, should all Chaos be unleashed here?'

Gwynn turned to regard him, blinking. 'Well, I imagine they would withdraw to the south. Wait it out. The Jhek are an ancient kind. No strangers to isolation.'

Blues was shaking his head. 'Well, let's hope they will be safe in the south.'

* * *

395

It was a very footsore and winded Cartheron Crust who came limping in to join Dujek's expeditionary force. His crew followed, straggled-out, escorted by scouts, and he found the commander, Dujek himself, awaiting his arrival, with the mage Hairlock, and flanked by two staff: a tall Dal Hon female officer, and a young, bookish-looking fellow.

Dujek cuffed his shoulder as Cartheron halted, puffing and blowing. 'Good to see you, Crust.'

Unable to speak, Cartheron nodded his own heartfelt relief.

'Scouts report there was a Thelomen with you,' Hairlock put in.

Cartheron continued his nodding until he got his breath. 'Yes. He pulled away – wasn't sure of his reception.'

'Ah,' nodded Dujek. 'Well, he'd be welcome. But what of you? Who's with the *Twisted*?'

'The *Twisted*? You have word?'

'Yes. It's reappeared.'

Cartheron snorted. 'Hunh. Thought as much. And you?' He jerked his chin to the distant shadowed bulk of the artefact. 'What's the plan?'

'We found some civilians, captured raiders we think, who know their way around that thing. They're guiding a small party to try 'n shut it down.'

'Who? Who went?'

Dujek rubbed the stump of his arm and grimaced his discomfort. 'Well, was the High Mage, Dancer, and the Sword.'

Cartheron let out a long whistle, eyed the mountain. 'Gods, man. How could you allow that?'

'Couldn't very well stop 'em, could I?'

Hairlock chuckled, as if at the image of that.

Cartheron blew out a long breath, almost thinking, *Better him than me!* 'Well, no. I suppose not. How long do you think we have?'

Dujek looked to the young officer. 'Ullen?'

'Scouts say tomorrow or the next day, sir. That's it.'

Crust examined the encampment lines. 'Gonna follow?'

'Don't know. Don't want to be too close when that thing hits the water.'

'I agree.'

The Fist next turned to the Dal Hon officer. 'Orosé, any mounted messengers left?'

396

'A bare few.'

'Send one out to invite that Thelomen into camp.'

'Aye, sir.' She jogged off.

Both commanders stood for a time eyeing the towering artefact. Dujek cleared his throat and spat aside. 'What's the report I hear of this Jhistal? A giant wave? You saw it, hey?'

'Yes. Enormous.'

'Those are the legends,' Hairlock added.

'Well, if I was these Falarans, I'd use it against this thing.'

'Maybe they plan to,' the mage growled. 'Maybe it has to be in the water.'

Dujek nodded thoughtfully, pulled his hand down his chin. He eyed the coastal mountain slopes to either side of the river valley. 'Maybe we should hold back even farther – just in case.'

Cartheron added his sober assent. 'I think maybe so. But, for now,' and he studied the camp, 'is that cooking I'm smelling? Me 'n the crew could eat old canvas.'

The Fist chuckled and invited him onwards. 'Apologies – not much of a host, am I. This way.'

Cartheron pointed the crew to cooking fires then followed Dujek to his tent. Hairlock inclined his head and padded off northwards to resume his watch. Inside, Crust fell on sliced meats and old preserves. While he ate a knock came on the post of the tent and a voice announced, 'The Thelomen is arrived.'

Dujek grunted and motioned for Crust to follow.

The giant waited outside the tent. Crust did the honours: 'Thelomen Koroll, this is Dujek, commander of the Malazan expeditionary force.'

Koroll inclined his shaggy head in acknowledgement. 'Greetings. I am here on behalf of my kind to offer an agreement of mutual tolerance – if not a working treaty – eventually.'

Dujek gave a slight bow from the waist. 'We'd be honoured to accept such an offer. I can speak for Malaz.'

'Excellent!' Koroll gestured his tall staff towards the artefact. 'I see that you are keeping your distance. This is wise.'

'Do your people have any knowledge of this thing?' Dujek asked. 'Anything that might help?'

'Sadly no. We try to have very little to do with the K'Chain Che'Malle.'

Crust gave a dry laugh. 'That's wise.'

'Also,' Dujek said, 'one of your people took a mage of ours for healing. Do you know anything of this?'

'Yes. I heard. She is recovering, I assure you.'

'Thank you.'

'And may I ask of your plans – regarding the Hive?'

Dujek snorted. 'Abyss. What can we do? Wait 'n see once this thing hits the water. Maybe it will be snuffed out. Though, we do have a few people inside trying to turn it off, or whatever.'

Koroll lowered his head, appearing troubled. 'That is unfortunate. I think little of their chances.'

Cartheron shared an uneasy glance with the Fist, then asked, 'What do your people know of this Falaran weapon. This Jhistal?'

'Ah! Mael's Gift, we know it as. We have never actually seen it. You are perhaps counting on this?'

Crust raised his hands in a shrug. 'Who knows? It's their land – shouldn't they protect it?'

'I suppose we shall see.'

'Tomorrow, or day after,' Dujek added.

The giant now pointed his staff southwards. 'Is that a Jhek encampment there?'

'Yes. Their Bird Priestess is with us. She's concerned as well.'

'And rightly so! I would speak with her – if you do not mind.'

'Oh, of course.' Dujek invited him onwards. 'We can talk later.'

Bowing, the giant shambled off. Dujek and Crust watched him go, the Fist rubbing the back of his neck. 'I don't like what he said 'bout Dancer and the rest.'

'Well, if anyone can manage, it'll be them.'

'That's damned true. You finished eating?'

'Gods no! What kind of wine you got?'

'The lousy kind.'

Crust headed for the tent. 'Why did I even ask?'

* * *

On the waterfront wharf of the enclosed and walled Cabil harbour, two ageing servants of the Abbey sat together watching the sunset and perhaps taking comfort from each other's company.

The woman, known locally as Jan, a lowly scullery maid of the kitchens, angrily filled her pipe and whispered, fierce, to her companion, 'This is taking too long – we have lost the initiative. I heard an enclave has been cleared out! Soon they'll manage to band together against all the rest.'

'Reinforcements,' her companion, Janul, answered. 'Wasn't that what he said?'

'Yes. But they've been held up, haven't they?'

'The capriciousness of the gods . . .'

'And what is he waiting for? Why doesn't he just sweep in?'

Janul peered about, uncomfortable. 'There are a *lot* of mages of Ruse hereabouts.'

Janelle snorted her dismissal of the mages of Ruse.

The fellow lifted his fishing pole, examined its line. 'Don't be impatient. So this gambit is pushed aside? We'll try again next summer.'

'That's not what happened down south,' she answered through clenched teeth.

He just pursed his lips.

After a time, she drew breath to speak again, but stopped herself, coughed into a fist.

Footsteps scraped the grit of the stone wharf. A portly figure came to stand near them, apparently regarding the harbour waters: a priest of Mael.

'What news, Brother Lethor?' Janul whispered.

The priest nervously glanced about, murmured, 'News worthy of immunity for anyone who dares breathe it.'

'And you are most daring, are you not?' soothed Janelle.

A choked laugh that the priest tried to disguise by hawking up catarrh that he then spat over the edge of the wharf. 'Or most foolish,' he murmured.

'Talk or move on,' Janul hissed, and let out more line on the pole.

'Do not rush our friend,' Janelle scolded him out of the side of her mouth. 'What he is doing is difficult.'

'Yes, difficult,' the priest answered. He drew out a small cloth and mopped his glistening forehead. He swallowed then, steeling himself, blurting, 'There will be no more Jhistal.'

Janelle and Janul shared startled glances.

'You are certain of this?' she whispered.

'Yes. It is gone. Can never be summoned again.'

Janul peered about, warned, 'Best move on now.'

Brother Lethor jerked, fearful, and turned to go. '*Immunity*,' was his parting hissed word.

The two remained quiet for a time. Then Janul spoke. 'Knew *something* was up the way everyone was so jumpy.'

'Yes, they say they chose to withhold it … but one did wonder …'

'This'll have to go up the main channel.'

'Your turn.'

He looked surprised. 'What d'y'mean, my turn?'

'I spoke to the Magister.'

'Yes – but who talked to the you-know-who last? *Me*, that's who.'

'Oh, really? You're going to hold to that …'

'I mean it. You go.'

'Gods above and below!' Grunting, she straightened. 'I'll be on my way then.'

'See you tomorrow.'

Nodding, she ambled off.

The harbour and waterfront of Cabil were of course famously walled and defended. The city's rear, however, facing inland, was another matter. Here, multiple means of egress lay available, from tiny servant's portals to larger gates – usually left open – to a few crumbling, easily climbable, blind lengths of wall.

None of the farmers or labourers coming and going inland gave the old woman a second glance. She walked south-west, crossed the tall ridge of the island, and as the night went on, headed downslope once again to the shore.

She noted the thick bank of clouds to the south across Lure Sea, blotting out the stars like a wall of Elder Dark. She'd heard talk of it of course: a volcanic eruption on the southern mainland, was everyone's opinion.

Still, to her, those clouds looked mighty close.

Nearing the shore, amid woods, she searched about for a secluded grove or meadow, off the main trail and angled aside. As physically alone as she could ascertain, and as far from the monitoring of any active magics by the Ruse mages, she raised her powers, gestured, then stepped through the wavering cut of darkness that appeared, and entered the Imperial Warren.

Here she found herself amid barren and dusty hillocks. A weak anaemic wind moaned about her ankles. She shuddered; this place was a great asset to the Imperium, but she was never comfortable amid its paths. She felt as if some great crime had been committed here and echoes of it reverberated still.

Movement far off drew her attention: a figure approaching, dust trailing behind.

She waited.

As the figure neared, Janelle felt her mood sour even further as she recognized the man: rich green silks, dark complexion, rings at his fingers – Topper, Surly's favourite errand boy.

'What are you doing here?' she called.

He stopped a good few paces off. 'I'm here in case you lot fail.'

'And wouldn't Surly just hate that, hmm?'

An answering smile that was more a baring of teeth. 'You are here for a reason, yes?'

'Yes. We have an asset, a priest high in the Faith here. He says the Jhistal cannot be raised ever again.'

The Claw arched a distrustful brow. 'Really? Quite the claim. You have a second source? Confirmation?'

'The priests threatened to summon it, then said they'd changed their mind. Sounds like they're covering the truth.'

'That's not confirmation. That's speculation.'

'It's good enough.'

'No, it's not.' He waved her off in a lazy gesture. 'Come back with actual independent confirmation, or actual proof.'

She clenched her teeth against cursing the man out. 'You know that's not how it works . . .'

He urged her away as if flicking an insect.

Damned Claws. She gave him her best evil-eye and turned away, snapping out a sign and opening a portal for her return.

Stepping back into night on Cabil Isle, Janelle set her shoulders and began the meandering trek back north.

*   *   *

With the loss of their weapon, the Jhistal, Abbess Glinith saw almost no further purpose in the daily council meetings, but of course she continued to attend. She knew that this was where power was wielded, impotent or not, and to be absent could mean exclusion from such access – permanent exclusion.

So, she sat through a meeting she viewed as little more than absurd pantomime, saying little, reflecting mostly upon what her informants and spies had passed along to her the night before: that the aged Rentil Orodrin, Celebrant of the Faith, was in fact still alive though not seen publicly for the last month. That his health, however, was in decline, while his mind was certainly far gone. He was, as she'd assumed, kept imprisoned in his quarters by servants and aides who were all suborned or in the pay of Mallick Rel.

She also assumed that the Proctor of the Faith was keeping him alive long enough to find the time to have himself anointed as the man's successor in some public ceremony. At least, this was what she used to think – now she was not so certain. Time was passing, yet Mallick was making no moves to prepare for any such *official* handing over of the reins of power.

In any case, it was something to think about to pass the boring hours of useless talk here at the council meeting.

Nuraj opened with talk of the volcano to the south. Indeed, smoke from the eruption could clearly be seen over Cabil. Local inhabitants had, apparently, evacuated themselves.

Mallick, eyes half lidded, murmured, 'We can blame it on these foreigners. Their meddling, and the righteous anger of the gods.' He glanced to Glinith. 'Yes?'

She nodded. 'I will spread the word.'

Then Nuraj caught her interest when he raised a note and cleared his throat, looking uncharacteristically pleased. He tapped the scrap of parchment. 'It is confirmed, Mallick. *Three* of these invader nests have been retaken.'

Mallick tilted his head. 'Excellent news indeed, Guardian of the Faith. Though, I understand these were three of the *smaller* ones.'

Nuraj's long face drew down in offence. 'That's not the point. The point is that the initiative is with us. We can assemble these and other forces to strike a larger target.'

'Such as?'

Nuraj surged forward, eagerly unrolled a map. Glinith and Mallick edged closer to peer at it.

'You are right about these being smaller enclaves, Mallick. Two were merely unwalled hamlets. The number of remaining nests among the isles is now about eleven. Most are small, unimportant. Of them all, in my analysis, five are strategic. We should strike at these, one at a time, ignore the rest.' He pressed a finger to the map over Walk. 'Starting here. If we can retake the main stronghold of Walk then we can split their enclaves to the east and west, and possibly – possibly – retake control of the seas between.'

Mallick tapped a finger to his greying, greenish teeth. 'An admirable plan, Guardian of the Faith. But with what soldiers, what ships, will you accomplish such a feat?'

Nuraj sat back, nodding, rolled the map. 'We have been cajoling all the isles to resist. These successes will be our spark. Through the priesthood,' and he nodded to Mallick, 'word can be spread everywhere to assemble for the strike.'

'But our ships—' Glinith could not help but say aloud.

Nuraj inclined his head to acknowledge the point. 'Yes, we have precious few war galleys left. All spread out between the isles. However, hard lesson learned . . . we do not need them for this. Any boat will do: grain-haulers, fishing craft, cargo vessels, anything that can carry troops.' He let out a hard breath. 'We can learn from our enemies in this, at least. I tell you, Mallick, it has been hard having to wait for these pieces to fall into place.'

'Patience, Nuraj. In this time is on our side.' He raised a finger. 'And, it also just so happens that, through various secret channels, I – that is, we – have received a formal communication from one of your five main invader strongholds.'

'Which?'

'Curaca.'

'What do they want?'

Mallick waved a pallid hand. 'Oh, the usual. Official recognition of its ruler as sovereign king. King Tereth, he calls himself, I believe. Cessation of hostilities. Formal trade agreements.'

Nuraj snorted his scorn. 'There's no need to negotiate.'

'On the contrary, friend Nuraj, there is every need to negotiate. We may have lost a powerful weapon, but the weapons of statecraft are many. Creative negotiation is one. Through the priesthood I will have a sealed answer sent to this self-styled king. We will agree to his requests – but only if he agrees *not* to come to the aid of any of the other invaders. Such will be the terms of our mutual non-aggression pact. We will then also send similar letters to the other four strongholds.'

'Even Walk?' Nuraj asked.

'Indeed. We mustn't treat it any differently.'

Nuraj simply raised his hands. 'Very well, Mallick. This is your warfare, not mine.'

Glinith frowned. 'But the others will simply band together once the first falls, surely.'

'Dear Abbess,' Mallick observed and smiled – his expression reminding Glinith of a sea-snake, 'falsehoods are so very easy to believe if you craft them to say exactly what the listener *wants* to hear in the first place.'

Glinith inclined her head, granting the argument. Somehow, though, the man's point made her so very profoundly uneasy.

* * *

After a long climb, the mage Turnagin announced that they were nearing the upper chambers. Dancer then padded ahead to scout the way.

Despite keeping a wary eye out, Tayschrenn was once again startled by the assassin's return. How could the man be so silent? he wondered. Still, it was the man's job, he reflected. He rubbed his pained brow – and he was rather distracted at the moment.

The assassin crossed to him and Turnagin. 'The upper floors?' the mage of Meanas asked.

'Yes. As you said.'

'We'll have to be very careful now,' Turnagin went on. 'This Shi'gal could strike at any time.'

Hessa whispered, 'You said it just guards the Matron.'

'We may be too close already.'

Dassem nodded at this. 'Yes. If it is worried for her safety it may strike first.' He drew his blade, and Hessa followed suit.

Dancer moved to return ahead, but Dassem murmured, 'No. Best we stay together from now on.'

The assassin frowned at this, but gave his curt assent.

They advanced, Dassem and Hessa at the fore, followed by Tayschrenn and Turnagin, with Dancer now guarding the rear.

An ascending ramp, narrower here in the upper levels, led

onwards. Dassem brushed along one wall as he advanced, his blade extended.

They came to a large chamber filled with rows of squarish machines, the purposes of which were a mystery to Tayschrenn. 'Is this it?' Dassem whispered.

'Further on,' Hessa answered, just as low. She pointed her sword, 'This way.'

They passed between rows of the gargantuan instruments. The intensifying heat hammered at Tayschrenn and he wiped the sweat from his brow, all the while working to keep his Warren at his fingertips.

'We're too exposed here,' Dancer murmured.

Tayschrenn nodded his agreement.

A far wall held another arched portal. The captain appeared to be making for it.

Beyond the arch a very steep ramp rose in a tight spiral. Dassem led, sword at the ready.

'This should bring us to a larger control deck,' Turnagin said softly.

'Can you shut it down there?'

'No. Beyond is the main command deck, or centre, call it what you will. From there you can control all the mechanisms.'

'The Matron's post, yes?' Tayschrenn asked.

Turnagin's pale and anxious features were eloquent enough answer.

They came to another large chamber full of mechanisms and banks of tall instruments. Hessa pointed her sword down a row and the party turned. This way led past a series of what looked like wells, or channels up and down. Heat and steam billowed here, buffeting them all. Tayschrenn found it even difficult to breathe. He noted that the Sword was no longer walking in the wary, crouched manner he had been; he now stood sideways, slid his right foot forward, just brushing the stone floor, then brought his rear leg up before moving his forward leg once more. The sight made Tayschrenn think of a dance.

A narrow arched portal came into view. It opened onto a hall; Hessa indicated it.

As they advanced to enter, a number of things seemed to Tayschrenn to happen all at once.

He had a glimpse of something large dropping down upon them from above. Hessa and Dassem grunted, blades flickering and flashing to meet a thing almost impossible to see since its lithe and long shape mirrored the shades and coloration of the stone about it.

Thrown knives flashed past him only to be deflected from the thing's armoured torso, then Hessa, gasping, was falling backwards; Dassem, grunting, was tossed aside to the wall; Turnagin gestured and a shadow emerged directly behind the thing – the Shi'gal Assassin – marking its position, and Tayschrenn instantly threw everything he had in one concatenating explosion that filled the hall with white light – a writhing reptilian shape caught within, flying backwards – and a booming backdraught of flame and echoing explosion.

Tayschrenn staggered backwards into someone's – Dancer's – arms.

The Shi'gal reappeared at the far end of the hall, betrayed there by the streamers of smoke rising from its form. It worked controls and levers nearby, four arms moving? And the roof of the hall began descending amid the grinding of stone.

Turnagin lurched forward to the fallen captain's motionless body, calling, '*Hessa!*'

Cradling his chest, Dassem staggered to him and the two began dragging the woman back from the hall. Dancer set Tayschrenn against the wall and leapt forward to aid them.

The entire roof of the long hall crashed down in a detonation that shook the stone floor.

On his knees, Turnagin worked at the woman's body, undoing armour, but Tayschrenn could tell from the thick stream and smear of blood marking that grisly trail that it was too late.

Dassem, panting, still cradled his chest, where blood covered his hand and dripped to the stone floor. Smoke wafted from the man's clothes and he gestured to it, shaking his head. 'We're in confined quarters here, High Mage . . . not the battlefield. Don't take us *all* out.'

Blinking, almost blacked out from the agony in his skull, Tayschrenn steadied himself at the wall. 'Apologies. I panicked.'

A wry smile. 'Well, if any situation called for panic – this would be it.'

Dancer set a hand to the mage Turnagin's shoulder, murmured, 'She's gone.'

He nodded, wordlessly. Together, they sat the captain up against the wall. Dancer searched about. 'Her blade?' The mage glanced to the sealed hall. 'Ah . . . a shame that.'

'Now what?' Tayschrenn asked of the ship's mage. The man did not answer; he was staring off at the blocked hall. 'Turnagin?'

The man turned to him, unseeing for a moment. He clawed a hand across his face, pushed back his tangled greying hair. 'We make for the engines – try to sabotage them there.'

'But aren't those areas poisoned?' Dancer asked.

The mage merely pushed past them all, his shoulders hunched.

Dassem straightened and limped after the man. Dancer took Tayschrenn's arm to help him along.

*   *   *

They crossed the strait between Delanss Isle and the mainland swiftly. The seas drove them, and even Brevin had stopped expressing her wonder at it all. Gianna spent the time with her back pointedly turned to the water. She read the scrolls – those she could decipher, for many were badly damaged, or rotten.

What she found only saddened her further; she saw no mention of a blood sacrifice – just that those of the ancient people's blood could invoke the ritual summoning. It seemed that over the centuries things had become lost, or misinterpreted. Or deliberately distorted.

'Coming up on Belade, lass,' Torva announced.

They rounded the point here – the East Reach – and the old smuggler grunted his surprise. 'Burn's Blood, look at those clouds!'

Gianna glanced to the coast and stared. A thick wall of black and grey clouds massed ahead, pushing up from the south, where the skies were completely dark. 'A volcano,' she murmured.

'Ain't no active volcanoes in the coastal range,' Torva growled.

A moving mountain of fire, the ex-priest had said. Gianna shook her head at the preposterousness of it.

Holding a good distance out from the coast, they eventually passed Belade.

'Harbour's damned empty,' Torva remarked.

A hand from the lookout shouted down, 'Very few chimney fires.'

'Any boats?' Brevin called up.

'Seas are clear.'

Brevin grimaced her disquiet. 'Lure is always full of shipping.'

Torva looked to Gianna. 'Everyone's fled. Like those we passed.'

'We don't know that,' she growled back.

The deck darkened then as they passed under the churning clouds and the sun was blotted out. No one spoke for a time. Cordage and timber creaked as the prow jolted into a wave. 'Should reach Muheres by evening,' Brevin said into the silence.

Gianna sat back down next to the chest.

Brevin kept them a good distance clear of the coast. They passed Muheres, finding the town completely dark in the gloom – not one lamp or fire shone anywhere.

Torva pulled at his scraggy beard, murmuring, 'Damnedest thing . . .'

Brevin came to Gianna. 'Gettin' too dark to go on, 'specially under these clouds. No moon, no stars. Should put in for the night.'

'Yes, as you say.'

'Very good.' Brevin nodded to Realt at the side-tiller and he angled them closer to the coast.

As they travelled west a strange glow blossomed in the utter dark. It seemed to come from the south. Gianna went to the side to squint into the murk. Torva and sailors gathered as well.

'What in the name of the Dark Taker . . . ?' Torva murmured.

A mountain came into view along the coast. A mountain where no mountain had ever reared. Gianna and Torva shared a silent glance – both knew this coast well, and both knew no mountain had ever stood in that valley. The unearthly whitish glow shone about it. Fire, perhaps, but a light unlike any fire Gianna knew.

Brevin came over to them. 'That *thing* shouldn't be there – whatever it is.'

'I know,' Gianna said. 'A volcano. It must've grown swiftly. I've heard they can.'

'Grown?' Torva mocked. 'Moved, you mean. Travelled here – like that priest said.'

'That's nonsense.'

''Tisn't. We've all heard o' mountains that fly. Moon's Spawn.'

'No one's even seen that.'

'Not here maybe,' Torva argued, 'but it's a wide world out there. Travellers say—'

'Travellers' tales,' Gianna answered, scornfully.

'Whatever it may be,' Brevin cut in, 'I don't want to get any closer.' She turned to the crew, ordered, 'Drop anchor as soon as you can.'

'Aye, aye,' Realt answered.

'We'll see in the morning – if there's enough light.'

Gianna pursed her lips, nodding. She returned to the chest and sat against it, pulled her knees up tight against her torso, crossed her arms over them and rested her head there. There were too many things to think about; things the ex-priest had said. But she refused to think about them. Did not want to even consider them. And so she rocked herself and hoped sleep would come.

Chapter 27

GIANNA WOKE BEFORE DAWN. SHE WAS NOT SURPRISED TO BE startled awake by vague threatening nightmares. She rose and went to the side to study the coast. The night was far gloomier than the norm, as the heavy, turgid cloud cover blotted out the crescent moon and all the stars.

All was not dark, however. The volcano's glow was unmissable inland to the south. Yet a far brighter, bluish-white light dominated over the orange – not what she expected. And neither luminosity shone from the mountain's dark bulk. Both seemed to lie at its base.

To unleash the Jhistal against this thing – even if she could, and that ex-priest wasn't just a madman! – to what end? One could not extinguish an eruption! Impossible. Yet her visions had been accurate up to this point. And the seas had swept her here. Was this the will of Mael?

And if it was, should she even respect it? So much ill had been done in his name already. Would she merely add to it? Or perhaps not. The ex-priest said it had been shorn from the priests and was in her hands now. It was for her to decide how to use it, none other.

Then to use it – would she, too, be yielding to the allure of power? No better than them?

She pressed a hand to her brow; how hot she felt. Fevered? Was she insane even to contemplate that any of this was real?

Dawn's first light was creeping in from the east when Torva came to her side. He eyed her sidelong. 'Couldn't sleep, hey? Understandable. I'll go if you want to be alone.'

'No. It's fine.'

He looked to the mountain. 'I swear that thing's closer now than it was. Nearer to the shore.'

She nodded, hugged herself.

He cleared his throat, spat over the side. 'You're thinking you don't want to be like them cultists of Mael.'

'Yes.'

'Well, don't worry, lass. That you can even ask y'rself such a question means you ain't. You're usin' it for protection. For what it's meant for – ain't that what that priest said?'

'Others have claimed that.'

'Ah, but you know it's true.' He pressed a finger to his temple then to his chest. 'You know it here and here.'

'Others—'

He waved a hand. 'Faugh. Never mind what all them others have or will say or think. They'll do that no matter what you do. This is up to you. Your heart.'

She gave a wry smile. 'All my fault, you mean?'

He scratched his beard. 'Well, that's the way it always should be, I'm thinkin'.'

She regarded the dark waves rolling and surging about the vessel. The sea was remarkably calm, considering what was about to be unleashed.

She really wasn't certain what to do, or if she was about to look very ridiculous, but she extended her hands out over the side and called upon the waters. For good measure she also raised her Ruse Warren. She invoked all that the scrolls appeared to claim was necessary – the simplest of things.

She merely requested . . . *Come.*

Then she waited . . . and of course nothing happened.

She let her hands fall. She turned to Torva, let out a snort. 'Well, don't I look the fool.'

He screwed up his face. 'Is that it? You done it? Thought maybe it involved more'n that.'

'That's it. I'm quite sure.'

'Hunh. Well, sorry, lass. Was worth a shot though.'

'Maybe I should—'

Both stumbled as the *Glimmer* rocked. Brevin burst from the stern. 'What in the name of Beru!'

The three staggered anew as the *Glimmer* began to rise. Gianna peered over the side: yes, definitely rising.

'What have you done!' Brevin called over a buffeting wind.

'I summoned it!' she shouted back.

'Gods, give us some notice next time.'

'I didn't think it would work!'

The *Glimmer* rocked now atop an enormous plateau of water that extended hugely far in all directions. Gianna took hold of a line as did all the crew. Torva called something to her but she couldn't make it out over the howling winds. They were now so high Gianna could see far inland.

Then the deck began to tilt – definitely tilt – backwards towards the stern. Brevin lurched to the tiller-arm and there struggled alongside Realt to bring it under control.

Gianna realized they were doomed if they slid backwards and she threw her Ruse Warren into turning the *Glimmer*.

The boat slowly began to come about, even as a wash now over-topped the stern.

*

'This is it!' Jacinth called to Blues. 'The big show.'

He sat up, blinked in the pre-dawn light. 'What do you mean?'

The swordswoman bit into a tiny crabapple taken from the dwarf trees they'd found on the slope. She gestured to the north. 'I mean looks like the mountain's entered the dunes 'n such there in the old delta. Could reach the sea any time now.'

Blues almost winced. 'Have some compassion, would you? This could be a catastrophe for the region.'

Jacinth shrugged. 'Not my problem.'

Gwynn was standing, his gaze to the north-east. 'Yes. Very close to the shore. Made good time overnight. The ground must slope.'

'What do we do?' Black asked.

Gwynn looked to him. 'We observe. This will be invaluable intelligence.'

'Then we damned well head out,' Jacinth put in.

Gwynn nodded. 'Yes. We join Skinner.'

Blues rose, looked to Black who appeared equally surprised by the announcement. He affected a laugh. 'No, we join Shimmer.'

412

Jacinth turned to him, frowning. 'Skinner is clearly the future of the Guard.'

Blues shook his head. 'Skinner was supposed to relieve us. He failed in his obligation. We go to Shimmer.'

Gwynn turned to them. He let his arms fall free at his sides. 'I'm sorry, Blues. But I must insist we travel to join Skinner's company.'

Black faced Jacinth. 'Blues and I signed with Shimmer's company.'

'Don't be a fool, Black the Lesser,' she ground out.

Black picked up his scavenged Malazan-issue helmet. 'That's Black the Greater, as maybe you'd like to see.'

Gwynn raised his hands for a pause. Blues was careful to note that no Warren was in evidence. 'I was the last commander of the Red Fort,' he began, 'and thus your most recent commander, Blues. Therefore—'

But Blues was shaking his head. 'Too thin, Gwynn. Too thin.'

'Not thin, obvious. Chain of command is clear—'

Black was now peering off to the north, a puzzled look on his face. 'What is that?'

Everyone turned. Blues shaded his gaze. 'Looks like—'

'A wave?' Gwynn finished. 'A large wave?'

'And it's growing,' Jacinth observed.

*

With the dawn Ullara woke as the day-hunters and song birds began to stir. She switched from gaze to gaze until she rode a shore-bird high above the north coast. As it scanned the beaches and seas beneath, Ullara caught sight of the towering lone mountain that was the Che'Malle artefact, together with the remaining coast before it – a tussock and dune stretch of old dried-up delta.

The shore-hunter shied away from the smoke of the artefact to swing further out to sea, gliding on contrary winds. She was about to move away from the bird as it appeared to be heading too far out over the Lure Sea when she saw something – or thought she saw something – very odd.

The cloth covering of her litter moved then, edged aside, and Ursana loomed in to ask her a question, but she raised a hand for quiet, frowning, concentrating.

After searching for a time, she found a closer set of eyes – a larger hunter – perhaps an osprey, high up. She saw the something again – even larger now – and could not believe it. Then the bird veered aside, alarmed perhaps, and flew off to the east.

She grasped Ursana's shoulder. 'Take me to the Malazan command, immediately.'

*

Cartheron stepped out of his tent, small steaming stoneware cup of tea in hand, and looked to the north. As usual thick clouds obscured the sky, but the Che'Malle artefact could still be seen, out past intervening hillocks and sand dunes.

The young captain, Ullen, approached and saluted.

Cartheron gave a sloppy half-salute response. 'Yes?'

'Compliments of Fist Dujek, sir. You are welcome in the command tent.'

Cartheron grunted and followed along with the captain. 'What news?'

'Scouts say the artefact will enter the sea today.'

'Hunh. And what are his orders?'

'We're to break camp and be ready to move.'

Cartheron nodded at that. 'Sound advice.'

He found the entire front of the command tent open to the north. Ullen headed off – no doubt to further duties. Dujek stood at the one table where he was receiving runners and scouts, coming and going. The mage Hairlock sat aside, eating a morning meal from a wooden plate.

'No news from inside?' Cartheron asked of the commander.

Dujek shook his head in disgust. 'Nothing. Got scouts watching on three sides. No one's exited.'

'Tayschrenn or the other mage could get them out by Warren, possibly,' Cartheron offered.

The Fist just looked sour, but turned to Hairlock. 'Maybe you could keep a watch.'

The mage pushed the last of his meat into his mouth and licked his fingers. Grunting, he rose. 'Near impossible to use magics inside that damned thing.'

'Well, keep a watch anyway,' Dujek answered, his voice taut.

The squat fellow wiped his hands on his robes and padded out.

Dujek watched him go then shook his head anew. 'First time I'm sent out with an expeditionary force and this happens. Bloody fiasco. I'll be busted down to latrine-digger.'

'Surly likes you, Dujek. She likes your strong vein of pragmatism.'

The Fist grunted a sour laugh, poured himself a cup of steaming tea, faced the north. 'Sometime today, they say,' he told Cartheron.

'So I heard. And perhaps, inside, they'll be protected . . .'

Dujek just blew on his tea.

Sudden movement in the skies drew Cartheron's eye. Flocks of birds darted apart in flurries of quick motion, together with further birds rising from all about and rushing off in all directions – all save the north. 'See that . . .' he began, turning to Dujek. But the Fist had seen as well and had stepped out of the cover of the canvas for a better look. He peered about, his gaze shaded. 'What in the name of Togg . . . ?'

The Fist's bodyguard of twenty troopers positioned around the tent straightened to attention and readied their shields. They backed inwards towards Dujek. 'What's this?' the Fist complained.

A guard drew his sword, pointing to the south.

The Bird Priestess's litter was approaching, carried by four sturdy bear-warriors. They were moving in some hurry. With them came the Thelomen giant, Koroll.

'Lower your weapons,' Dujek commanded.

The bear-warriors came to a halt a few paces off. Their breath plumed in the morning air. 'Greetings,' Dujek called. 'What is the meaning—'

'Commander,' the Bird Priestess called from within the litter, 'a wave is swelling to the north. You must move your troops.'

'A wave?' Cartheron interrupted, startled.

'Yes,' she answered. 'A very large wave, growing larger. You must move – now.'

Dujek eyed Cartheron. 'Sound familiar?'

'If it is . . . you'd better do what she says.'

'Hairlock!' the Fist called to the mage, who stood a way off. 'Sense anything?'

The mage approached, scowling and rubbing his jowls. 'I ain't no Ruse mage, but yes. I sense something. Something big – and growing.'

The Fist gave a curt jerk of his head. 'Very well.' He turned to

415

his staff and messengers who waited in the tent. 'Break camp, immediately.'

'Seek high ground,' the Bird Priestess called, then the bear-warriors straightened and the litter bobbed away, headed west, to that steep slope of the valley side.

Dujek waved the messengers off. 'You heard the Priestess – the order is to head for high ground.' He then looked to Koroll, who had remained. 'Yes?'

The Thelomen planted his tall staff. 'I offer what help I may.'

A nod from Dujek. 'My thanks.' He turned to Cartheron. 'You think it's this Jhistal thing?'

'I suppose so.'

'Was it big?'

'It was damned big.'

The Fist pulled his hand over his pate, grimacing. 'Dammit.' He looked to the staffers packing paperwork into boxes and satchels. 'Leave it,' he called. 'Essentials only.' He waved them off. 'Get moving – now!' He started walking west. His bodyguard fell in behind. Cartheron and Hairlock joined him.

'High ground!' the Fist shouted to everyone, waving and urging them along.

'This wave better be as big as you say or you'll look the fool,' Hairlock told Cartheron as they went.

Cartheron eyed him, then answered, 'In case you haven't noticed – we're in a damned valley.'

*

Tayschrenn nodded his thanks as Dancer eased him down in a side-chamber. Dassem brought up the rear, a hand and arm still pressed to his chest, now crusted in drying blood. He leaned against a wall, grimacing his pain.

Turnagin went to the Sword's side. 'May I take a look?'

Dassem nodded then grunted his effort as he peeled his hand away. Turnagin began unlacing the man's torn leather jerkin. 'It's shallow,' the Sword said.

'But is it clean?'

'That was the fastest thing I've ever faced.'

'So all sources say.'

'What I'm trying to say is that she was a brave woman, your captain.'

The mage was pouring water onto a rag. He ducked his head. 'She was that.'

Tayschrenn straightened and, though still dizzy, forced himself to walk to the chamber's opening. 'Now what?' he asked of Turnagin.

'Down. Ever downwards.'

Tayschrenn eyed the Sword. 'Can you manage?'

Dassem bared his teeth in a grin. 'Can you?'

After cleaning the wound, Turnagin pressed a hand to the gashed flesh and murmured a simple Denul invocation to help stop bleeding and to ward off any infection.

Then the mage slumped from the effort of summoning even that most basic of magics.

Dassem eyed Tayschrenn. 'We should rest for a time.'

Tayschrenn nodded. 'This will do.'

From the rear of the chamber Dancer called, 'Someone's been here before us.'

They retreated inwards to find a fire had been set here, the ceiling blackened in soot. Abandoned rags of bedding lay about. Dancer looked to Turnagin. 'Your party?'

The mage shrugged. 'I suppose so. Sometime. Can't remember.' He sat heavily against a wall.

Tayschrenn eased himself down, as did Dassem.

'I'll take watch,' Dancer said, and moved off to the entrance.

Closing his eyes, Tayschrenn attempted to ease the muscles of his neck and shoulders and relax. His head throbbed sickeningly, as if broken shards of glass were crashing about inside. Yet he maintained his Warren at his fingertips – just in case.

He'd almost dozed off when he felt something tugging, or pressing, upon his Warren. It was either something very small and nearby, or very large and far away; he couldn't tell which. Hissing his effort, he pushed himself up and crossed to where Turnagin sat slumped. The scholar's tangled hair hung forward, obscuring his face.

'I sense something strange,' he said. 'Do you?'

The mage of Meanas raised his head, blinking. He frowned,

obviously consulting his Warren. 'Something new. Very power-ful . . . approaching, quickly.'

Tayschrenn turned to the Sword. 'Something's coming – don't know what.'

Nodding, Dassem straightened, drew his sword, and headed to the wide portal opening.

Though it felt as if he were pushing his mind through the broken glass now slicing about in his skull, Tayschrenn attempted to probe this new presence.

It was either burgeoning swiftly, or approaching with great speed, or both. As it came onwards he found it easier to penetrate the jarring energies masking it and his breath caught.

He looked to Turnagin, who now shared his astonishment. 'Like Ruse, but more profound.'

'Elder magics.' Turnagin rose. 'By all the ancient gods . . .'

They both hobbled to the chamber's wide entrance. Tayschrenn waved to Dancer and the Sword. 'Get back!'

'What is it?' Dancer called.

Tayschrenn threw himself against the wall next to the opening – in part to help him stay on his feet. 'Something gigantic – powerful.'

'The Matron?'

Turnagin shook his head. 'No. From outside. Closing swiftly. Like an enormous summoning.'

Tayschrenn nodded at this. 'Yes, has the flavour of a summoning. But wide . . .' He cast his mind out to attempt to grasp some hint of the size of what approached. He could not believe what his senses told him. His gaze once more went to the mage of Meanas, whose astounded expression told that he too must have grasped what was facing them.

Turnagin sagged to a wall. 'By all the ancient gods . . .'

*

All four Crimson Guard stared at the sea. Blues crossed to Gwynn's side. 'There's magery there. I just can't place it.'

Gwynn nodded his distracted agreement. 'The aura is like Ruse, but different. Darker. Elder.'

'Gods it's huge,' Jacinth breathed. 'What is it?'

'I don't know,' Blues answered almost absent-mindedly, as he tried to grasp the scale of what he was witnessing.

418

'It's moving damned fast,' Black said.

'I've heard they do,' Gwynn murmured, squinting.

'What does?' Blues asked.

'These large waves. Some say they come from earthquakes – from Burn shuddering. Or Mael's wrath.'

'Looks like Mael's wrath,' Jacinth offered.

The great mass of foamed green-blue water continued to rise even as Blues stared, amazed and stunned. Its cresting top appeared to lean southwards, beginning to cave and curl, even as its base now engulfed the shore.

Gwynn had taken a step backwards. 'Blues . . .' he began, a warning note in his voice.

Blues nodded, unable to speak, for he now realized that he was no longer looking down at this titanic bulging mass of water, but level, straight outwards. And still it rose, swelling and burgeoning. The very colour of the sky now took on a green tinge.

'*By all the gods!*' Black breathed, awed.

Blues tugged on Jacinth's arm. 'Higher ground!' he shouted. 'Run!'

All four turned and ran up the slope, scrambling, panting. A chest-hammering bestial growl now reached Blues, as of all the avalanches and waterfalls he'd ever witnessed combined.

A glance backwards staggered him anew as he realized that all he had seen was as nothing compared to what was to come – for this titanic wave had hit the shore and it was doing what waves do when they come ashore.

It was about to break.

As he pulled himself ever upwards, scrambling, tugging at brush and rocks, his last glimpse over his shoulder showed the mountain-sized K'Chain Che'Malle artefact, a gargantuan moving construct as large as a city, now seeming like a toy at the foot of a towering wall of water half again as high.

*

Only Gianna's focused Ruse magics turned and maintained the *Glimmer* bow-first as it coursed, faster and faster, down a water chute that seemed to go on for ever. Brevin and Realt now grasped the tiller-arm more to stop themselves falling forward than to direct the vessel. The crew held lines, or lay flat upon the tilted deck. Torva had slithered down into the shallow hold amidships.

She glanced astern and felt a moment of intense vertigo: the towering wall of water behind them seemed the flat sea surface and she therefore somehow suspended sideways.

Torva dared raise his head from the cargo hatch. 'Travelling south,' he yelled, awed, eyeing the titanic mass of webbed and foam-laced water.

Brevin called from the tiller, exclaiming, 'It's cresting!'

Indeed, the very top was now curving forward, as any wave closing on any shallows.

'It's breaking on the shore!' Gianna breathed. 'That means . . .'

'It's getting even bigger,' Torva finished for her.

Gianna stared, mesmerized, somehow unable to look away from the cataclysm about to befall. 'What have I done?' she said aloud.

'Don't torture yourself,' Brevin answered. 'That shore's uninhabited. There's no one there.'

'And that thing has to be stopped,' Torva added.

'If it can be . . .' Gianna whispered to herself.

*

Cartheron climbed the mountainside, grunting his effort. He hadn't fully recovered from his long hike cross-country, and vowed now never to set foot on land again – just as old Admiral Nok seemed to have done.

Shouts of alarm pulled his head up and he stopped, peered north, and gaped.

For a confused instant it seemed that the entire northern sea was coming at him, as if tilted upwards; then the sight resolved into a titanic mass of water filling the entire mouth of the valley, from east to west.

The K'Chain Che'Malle artefact stood in dark silhouette before it, dwarfed.

He put his hands to his mouth and bellowed: '*Run!*'

Two troopers nearby heaved on a travois loaded with gear. Cartheron stormed over to them and yanked their hands from it, ordering, 'Run, by Beru! Just run!' He pushed them onwards.

Everyone he could see was now pelting uphill and he took a moment to look behind, searching for dawdlers. A few figures remained – but far too far behind for him to reach, or, probably, even to signal clearly. He cursed them, himself, everything: why was there always someone who wouldn't listen, or who had to find this or that? He put hands to mouth again, hollering, 'Run, dammit! *Run!*'

But thunder now drowned him out: a ground-shaking roaring as uncountable tons of water came churning southwards. He couldn't help but watch as the wave's towering crest now broke, falling. Atavistic panic drove him to run then himself, panting, scrambling up the rocky mountain slope.

The ground kicked him and he fell. Boulders came crashing down the valley side. The thunder of the end-of-the-world cataclysm erupting behind him struck like a blow to his head. He lay dazed for a moment, then self-preservation drove him up and he resumed clawing at the rocks, heaving himself onwards.

Troopers he met he pushed ahead, urged and pulled, cajoled to keep going. Some spoke, their mouths moving, but all he could make out was an avalanche roaring – that seemed to be getting nearer.

*

Tayschrenn rested a palm against the stone of the side-chamber and felt a strange new juddering in the artefact. He looked to Turnagin. 'You feel that?'

The mage tilted his head, listening and consulting his Warren at the same time. The fellow nodded. 'Something's coming.' He extended a hand out into the wide hall. 'Movement. Something's driving the air through here.'

'What could possibly—' Tayschrenn broke off as he sensed that *something*, enormous, Elder, descending upon him like a god's fist. He shared a glance with Turnagin who appeared as stunned as he imagined he must look: *Good, I'm not going insane . . .*

Both backed away from the entrance. Tayschrenn shouted to Dancer and the Sword, 'Back! Get back!'

'What?' Dancer asked as he warily backed up.

'Some—'

All three grunted, hammered backwards as the air itself punched them in the chest. Turnagin slammed into a wall, slumping; Dancer righted himself; Tayschrenn snapped up his Warren just as the stone floor fell out from under them as if the entire edifice had been kicked.

Tayschrenn reflexively used his Warren to protect them from the worst. Dancer collected a limp Turnagin while Dassem had somehow, amazingly, kept his feet under him the entire time.

The floor was now tilted, the air screaming about them, driving spikes of pressure into his ears. Then a roaring charged them like an avalanche and he threw up his Warren magics to bar the entrance – against *what*, he did not know.

It struck – a solid wall of water filled the hall beyond the portal. Monstrous pieces of equipment came crashing and tumbling past amid the flow, some striking his ward, and he grunted anew, sliding backwards until his back was pressed to a wall and he could yield no farther.

Dassem was with him, yelling something, but he barely noted any of his surroundings as he was entirely consumed in summoning and channelling the colossal forces needed to fend off the pressure of what seemed an unending ram of water. Around him he sensed the K'Chain Che'Malle energies that so frayed and scoured his mind shredding, fraction by fraction failing, diminishing: torn or smothered.

With each contraction of the Che'Malle energies he felt strengthened and he opened himself even more to his Warren without holding back, without fear of self-annihilation, for what choice did he have? None. It was all or nothing as an indifferent ocean of water sought to crush him like an insect.

He only became aware of his surroundings when he felt a gentle hand on his arm. He realized his eyes were squeezed tight shut. With an effort, he opened them, blinking, to see a wash of dirty water coursing through the hall opposite and Dancer at his side, sodden, studying him.

'High Mage?'

Tayschrenn nodded blankly, almost uncertain as to *where* he was.

Dancer gave him an answering nod. 'Well done, High Mage.'

He let his arms fall.

Dassem was crouched at Turnagin's side where he lay coughing and hacking.

Tayschrenn crossed to them. 'How are you?'

The scholar mage waved a hand to indicate his soundness.

The Sword straightened, eyed Tayschrenn up and down and crooked a half-smile. 'Indeed, well done, High Mage.'

He had no words; he just panted, weaving slightly.

Turnagin fought to rise; Dassem helped pull him upright.

Dancer waded out into the now ankle-deep stream in the hall, peered up and down, listening. 'No vibrations. All quiet.'

Tayschrenn nodded. 'The engines have ceased.'

'I thought you said they could burn underwater,' Dancer observed.

'They can,' Turnagin answered and pointed upwards to the floors above, 'but obviously the mechanisms that control them can't.'

Tayschrenn drew a wet sleeve across his brow. 'Or the Shi'gal may have shut everything down to protect all those mechanisms.'

Turnagin tilted his head in assent. 'True. Whichever. The artefact seems inert now.'

'What was it,' Dancer asked, 'all this water?'

They waded out into the hall. 'I do not know,' Tayschrenn mused, 'but I believe it may have been this Jhistal of which we have been hearing so much.'

Dassem grunted, 'Hunh. So, not some monster.'

'Which way then?' Dancer asked.

Turnagin peered at the rushing remnant stream of water pulling at their feet and gave a small half-amused laugh. 'Downstream.'

*

Blues stopped climbing and sat heavily, panting, his hands bloodied and aching, and surveyed the valley below. He called over his shoulder, 'Okay, everyone!'

A wide stream of murky water filled the valley from side to side, flowing south. Flotsam of logs and tussocks rolled and tumbled in the course.

The Che'Malle artefact rested at the mouth of the valley, canted, wreathed in plumes of steam that rose from its base and out of vents and cracks higher up. Waterfalls coursed down its sides and the flood washed about it.

Footfalls and Gwynn came to sit next to him. 'It appears to have been stopped.'

Blues nodded wearily. 'All it took was Mael's own wrath.'

'Someone in Falar possesses a formidable weapon.'

'Not something to casually throw around though.'

'No. Not casually.'

Blues looked to the man; his scavenged clothes were torn and dusty, his long hair unbound and wind-tossed. 'You will join Skinner, then?'

A sigh. 'Yes. If we can reach him. I won't pretend it will be easy.'

'Well . . . good luck.'

A curt nod. 'Yes. Thank you. And . . . you too.'

Gwynn waved to Jacinth in the distance, motioning west. The swordswoman eyed Blues for a time, then shook her head, and turned away.

Black came to thump down next to him. 'They're goin', hey?'

'Yes.'

'Too bad. What's our plan?'

Blues let out a breath, brushed the drying soil from his hands. 'Get a boat, I suppose. Head east.'

'Can't you walk us over there using your Warren?'

'Not *all* the way, no.'

'Got money to hire a boat?'

'No.'

'Gonna steal a boat?'

'Maybe, I suppose.'

'Know how to sail?'

'Not really. Just the basics.'

'Me neither.' Black scratched his thickening beard. 'Well, this is a bit of a pickle, isn't it.'

Both watched the coursing water for a time. It was shallowing, ever so slowly. Blues looked to the south. 'How'd the Malazans do?'

'Lotsa movement on the slopes. Maybe we should leg it too.'

Blues straightened, cuffed the dirt from his scavenged leathers. 'Yeah. I suppose so.'

The two headed north.

'Maybe we could sign on with a raider,' Black suggested.

'Maybe so.'

'Or maybe just take a raider.'

'Let's not get ahead of ourselves.'

*

Cartheron stood with Dujek while the Fist took stock of his command. They occupied a hillock that itself had been washed over, but which now stood out of the waters as an island amid a wide flood. Messengers came sloshing through the diminishing flow to report to Dujek who stood immobile, jaws tight, as flotsam of broken equipment and war materiel came floating past their position on its way downstream now, towards the sea.

'Could've been much worse,' Cartheron murmured in an attempt to soothe the commander's mood.

'Fucking disaster,' the man muttered, then waved to an approaching officer. Cartheron recognized the young captain, Ullen. 'You have the butcher's bill?' Dujek asked.

The captain saluted and offered Cartheron a nod. His black and grey surcoat hung soaked and torn and grey river-mud slathered him up to his thighs. 'Many are still missing and unaccounted for,' he began, but Dujek raised his hand, forestalling all such qualifications.

'Yes, yes. But . . .'

'Round numbers, the estimate is about a thousand all told.'

The Fist pressed his one hand to his brow to massage his temples.

'Could've been far worse,' Cartheron offered again.

'I want all you can salvaged, captain.' Ullen nodded, half-turning to go. 'Especially foodstuffs. And tents and such. We'll need shelter.'

The captain saluted and jogged off.

'I'll be lucky if I'm not tried and hanged for this,' Dujek muttered.

'There was nothing you could do – who could've expected this?'

The Fist just shook his head, looking desolate.

At this point Hairlock appeared, his robes sodden and muddied, tramping towards them from the east.

The Dal Hon captain Orosé came storming up on one of their few remaining horses. She threw herself from the mount, saluted. 'Scouts say the Che'Malle artefact appears dead.'

'I agree,' Hairlock put in. 'Wouldn't 'a thought it, but looks that way.'

Dujek grunted at the news. 'Any sign of our party?'

'None as yet. Should I send in a few scouts?' Orosé asked.

'No. No one enters – understood? That thing is under interdiction until I say otherwise. Now go keep an eye on it.'

The woman saluted, jumped back up onto her mount and urged it around.

Dujek looked to Cartheron. 'We'll give them a little time to get clear – if they can.'

Crust nodded his assent. 'We'll have to keep that thing under guard from now on.'

The Fist waved over a passing staff runner, called, 'What's that Thelomen doing?'

The young female lieutenant saluted. 'The giant?'

'Yes.'

'I believe he's helping in the search for the missing.'

Dujek nodded, impressed. 'Very good. And the Jhek Priestess? What news of her?'

'I believe the Jhek got clear, sir. Do you have a message?'

Dujek waved her off. 'No, not now.'

Cartheron watched the reborn river running northwards towards the sea. He shaded his gaze against the yellowing afternoon light glittering off the waters. 'Looks like you've made it – got to the coast.'

Dujek grunted again. 'Have to get some troops along there. If we can see the water then ships can see us. That's not good.'

'And then?'

'We have to make sure that thing's dead.'

Hairlock spat aside. 'I'll go take a closer look if you like.'

'Very well. Just don't enter.'

The mage grunted at the idiocy of that possibility and tramped off.

'And after this?' Cartheron prompted once more.

'Well, then we build boats, I suppose.'

Cartheron snorted a wry half-laugh. 'Yeah. I suppose so.'

'You?'

A shrug. 'Got to get back out to the *Twisted*. Don't know how I'm gonna do that.'

'Maybe you can oversee the boat-building, hey?'

Cartheron nodded. 'Suppose so.' He offered an informal salute. 'Guess I'll go round up the crew and we'll set to it.'

The Fist waved him off.

Chapter 28

THE *GLIMMER* SKIDDED DOWN THE NEVER-ENDING WAVE crest ever faster, its stern high and prow dangerously low. Gianna stared ahead, utterly fixed upon keeping them prow first down the steepening chute of water.

The ship struck minor wave after wave on its descent, slamming sickeningly, timbers bursting, equipment and even sailors dashed against railings and the fore-deck.

Thankfully, the chest was roped secure, else it would have been lost in the first smashing collision. Gianna had thrust her arms through these ropes, while Brevin and Realt had lashed themselves to the tiller-arm.

So long was their continued descent, so high must they have been, that it seemed to Gianna as if the entire Lure Sea had risen up to spit them out. And so certain was she of their impending destruction that she actually murmured prayers to Mael not to forget her and the crew.

One particularly brutal impact wrenched Gianna's arms sickeningly. The mainmast sheared, smashing to the fore-deck. Its shrouds and lines collapsed across the vessel.

Brevin bellowed commands, but her voice was lost in the tumult of wind and waves. The *Glimmer* rushed on, kept aligned only by Gianna's Ruse influence. The crew dared not release their grips and holds to deal with the wreckage.

Further impacts juddered the vessel and something flew into Gianna's vision for an instant, a cat-block or broken shard of spar swinging loose. She ducked but it slammed into her and she knew nothing more.

She awoke in the cool night, a reviving wind upon her upturned face. She blinked then winced, her hand going to grip her left shoulder – something was wrong there, the bones grinding with her slightest motion.

She realized she was still lying upright lashed to the chest. About her crewmen and women worked to clear the deck and assess the damage. She spotted Torva sprawling against the stern nearby, asleep, or worse.

Seeing her awake, Brevin came and crouched at her side. 'With us, I see.'

Gianna nodded weakly. 'What's the damage?'

'Plenty. Burst seams, busted planks. Got half the crew bailing. How are you?'

'Shoulder's hurt.'

'Yes, I can see. Looks like a broken collarbone at the least.'

Gianna gently laid a hand to the shoulder and summoned what small workings of Denul healing she could manage to mute the pain and encourage a knitting of the bones. Brevin watched, nodding to herself, then cleared her throat.

'Now that you're with us – I was hoping you could take a look at a few of the crew . . .'

'Of course.' She motioned to the ropes still taut about her.

Smiling, Brevin began unknotting the lines. Gianna looked to Torva. 'How is he?'

'Old. It was hard on him. Nothing broken, though, that I could see.'

Gianna struggled to rise but her vision darkened and she fell back. 'Can't stand.'

Brevin pressed a hand to her leg. 'Fine. You stay, I'll have them sent over.'

Gianna spent the next few hours dealing with multiple broken limbs and severe impacts to chests and bellies. Most looked to be recoverable, save for one savage blow to the head. Even with her limited knowledge and skills in Denul, it was obvious to her that with this woman shards of the skull had been driven far into the brain and that the internal bleeding was catastrophic. All she could do for her was dull the pain – she wouldn't survive the night.

While working on a sailor who'd suffered a blow to the side and broken ribs, Gianna realized she'd pushed herself far too hard in healing all she could and as her vision darkened she felt herself sliding down her own chute into unconsciousness and there was nothing she could do to stop herself.

She awoke to warm sunlight on her face and smiled at the pleasantness of it. As she lay, head back, the sunlight turned to cold shadow, then light again, and she blinked, frowning. She raised her head.

'Awake, hey?' Torva said from nearby.

She looked over; he was now sitting up next to her, yet he was peering up and away.

Shadow engulfed the *Glimmer*'s deck once more and she squinted up to see a tall black hull passing silently on calm seas; she blinked anew. 'What in the . . .'

'Black ships,' the old smuggler said. 'Black sails with a sceptre on 'em.'

'How many?'

'More than a hundred, I'd say. Malazan.'

'But the raiders didn't carry any such sigil.'

'They was just pirates. These must be their Imperial Navy. Impressive, but slow. Wide at the beam for man-o'-wars. Half troop carrier, half warship, looks like.'

'Our galleys could take these.'

'Aye, they coulda . . .' and he shook his head.

Gianna sighed as well. *Yes, they could've . . .*

Faces peered down at them from the passing vessels: wild-looking, foreign, in many shades of brown, deep mahogany tan, and even night-black. She noted not one red-haired head was among them and she snorted a humourless laugh.

'What is it, lass?' Torva asked.

'New invaders. Just not red-haired this time.'

Torva pursed his lips at that, saying nothing.

Brevin came to them, her eyes on the foreign vessels. She shook her head at the outrageousness of it. 'We're of no interest to them. Just floating jetsam and flotsam. And ain't that not far from the truth.' She crouched next to Gianna. 'Thank you for your healing. Was a true blessing.'

'Just did what I could – sorry I'm not more versed in it. We're in Old Guando Sea, aren't we.'

'Aye. Drifted for a time. But we're rigging up a fore-stay, and digging a few oars out.'

'They're headed west.'

'Aye. West. Cabil, maybe. Damned invaders.'

Gianna nodded to herself, thinking. 'Captain, I have a favour to ask. Could we head to Old Guando Isle?'

'The old abandoned capital, hey? That ruin?' She rubbed her wide jaws. 'Smarter to head to the nearest landfall. Back to Silver Caye maybe. But . . . we have the worst leaks recaulked, and the fore-stay's comin' along.' She gave a bobbed assent. 'Very well. Good a place as any to haul-up for a proper refit. And plenty out of the way, too. That's a plus.'

'Thank you.'

Brevin shook a negative. 'No, thank you, priestess. You saved a lot of lives last night, I'm thinking.'

And how many did I take? she wondered, but said nothing, lowering her head.

The captain squeezed her good shoulder. 'You rest up now. Be there in just over two days, I'm thinking – the way we'll be crawling along.'

Gianna couldn't help but stare after the passing foreign fleet.

Brevin followed her gaze and shook her head. 'Nothing we can do about that, priestess. Out of our hands. It's the cultists' worry now, hey? I wonder who'll end up being the worse of the two. Not like we've ever had any say all this time.'

Gianna nodded at the sentiment, but couldn't help but feel that there must be more she could do. She bit her lip then, thinking, *So this is how it begins: the best of intentions . . .*

* * *

Glinith was breaking her fast on a terrace of the Abbey when the priest Hedran came to her table and bowed. 'Yes?' she acknowledged, sipping her tea.

The fellow licked his lips, appearing nervous. 'Word from the mages of Ruse, Abbess. It seems the Jhistal has been summoned.'

She frowned. 'You are mistaken, surely.'

'No, Abbess. I fear not. The priests who have access to Ruse are certain.'

430

Glinith stared for a time, astounded. She almost dropped her glass. 'Well . . . where?'

'South of us. Lure Sea. Against this volcano – which the priests now insist was not a volcano.'

'It wasn't? Just what was it, then?'

'Two priests – adepts of Ruse – managed to get within sight of it as they withdrew from Pull four days ago. They claim it was moving. A moving mountain. And the only thing even vaguely like this in the records is a reference to ancient K'Chain Che'Malle artefacts. Their moving homes, or nests.'

'Preposterous. Wait – *four* days ago? Why have I not heard of this before?'

'Apparently they were researching it. Also, no one would give them a hearing.'

Glinith nodded sourly at that. Mallick had made it clear he wasn't interested in the damned volcano.

A priest attached to the council entered then, breathless. 'Abbess . . .'

'I am summoned to the council.'

'Indeed.'

She wiped her lips and rose, muttering, 'I should think so.'

The council chamber was an uproar of messengers coming and going and as Glinith entered she overheard mention of foreign ships, which startled her. She assumed all this had to do with the Jhistal.

She sat and Nuraj sent her a distracted nod; Mallick ignored her – which was usual for him. 'I have disturbing news of the Jhistal,' she began, but Mallick raised a pallid hand for silence.

'We have heard,' he said. 'However, a more immediate threat has appeared. It seems the *true* Malazan invasion has arrived.'

'Whatever do you mean?'

'I mean we have word from the priesthood in Belid, Fallen Towers, and Ictor of foreign – Malazan – vessels entering our waters and heading west – to us here in Cabil, presumably.' He turned to Nuraj. 'How many vessels can you muster?'

'I am sending word by way of the priesthood to all ports and isles that all war galleys be sent to counter this threat immediately.'

'I asked *how many*.'

Nuraj pressed a hand to his brow. 'If every one of the remaining vessels responds? Perhaps just barely enough.'

'If every one . . .' Mallick echoed, his voice hardening.

'Surely we are safe here in the capital?' Glinith put in. 'Our harbour is unassailable.'

Mallick eyed her strangely for a time then returned his attention to Nuraj. 'Make certain that *all* respond, Guardian of the Faith.'

Nuraj inclined his head. 'Yes, Proctor.'

'Then we are done. All we can do is monitor the gathering of the vessels. Have the harbour sealed, Nuraj. And muster all the Faith Militant to our defence.'

'Of course,' Nuraj answered. He stacked his papers and rose. 'If you do not mind, I have much work to do.'

Mallick waved him off. 'Of course. Thank you, good Nuraj. Good luck.'

The man bowed and exited.

Glinith now found herself alone with Mallick. The squat fellow eyed her across the table, his gaze half lidded. She rose as well, bowing. 'I, too, have duties to attend to.'

'Of course,' he murmured.

When she was at the door, he spoke again. 'Who,' he asked, 'do you imagine summoned the Jhistal when we could not?'

She paused, turning. 'I quite assure you I have no idea.'

'Really? No idea at all? I understand that no hint of a body has been seen among the rocks at the bottom of the Pool of Mael.'

Glinith's hand went to her throat and she shrugged. 'Not surprising that – as I understand it, the Pool opened onto the seas beyond.'

Mallick showed his greying teeth in a caricature of a smile. 'Of course. Understandable.' The smile disappeared. 'I want to know who was responsible for this and where he or she is – understood?'

She bowed her head. 'Of course, Proctor. I will bend every effort to it.'

'Do so. As *I* understand time is no longer on our side.'

She bowed again, more deeply. 'At once.' She exited then, with deliberate calm, trying desperately to disguise a gagging desire to be as far from the man as was physically possible.

* * *

It was a rag-tag, wet and weary mass of soldiers who encamped on the north shore of the mainland. Adding to their misery was the command from Fist Dujek that no fires be lit – as if any dry wood were to be found in any case.

Cartheron sat with the Fist on a desolate dune of clean-swept sand – a remnant of what may have lain on the spot a mere few days earlier – to watch the stars on a cold night. 'Why no fires for Fener's sake?' he asked of the man.

Dujek was staring at the dark waters north of them. 'Don't know if anyone knows we're here. Or our numbers. No need to go telling everyone ourselves.'

Cartheron raised a hand in understanding. 'Ah, I see. Hadn't thought of it that way. But the troops are hungry – as I'm sure you know.'

A gruff, 'Yes. Scavenged supplies are being handed out. It's all we have for now. Maybe tomorrow we'll get some fishing done. Or I'm sure there's drowned game about. We just have to find it.'

'And the next day,' Cartheron asked. 'What then?'

Dujek pulled his hand down his lined haggard face. 'We'll head west along the coast. Confiscate any boats as we go.'

Cartheron looked to the rearing dark silhouette of the artefact just to their south. 'Any word?'

'No. None yet. Got scouts watching on all sides. We'll maybe have a look tomorrow.'

Cartheron offered a half-salute. 'Very good, Fist. Try to get some sleep.'

Dujek guffawed and waved him off.

It was a quiet crew that Cartheron gathered together that night. All were muddy from walking through the churned-up sands and clay of the delta. Streams susurrated in the dark all about them – the waters still returning whence they came.

'No fires?' complained Creel, the first mate, his long legs stretched out before him. 'Not even a *little* one?'

'No. None,' answered Cartheron, tiredly.

'Wise not to disturb the dark,' murmured a familiar voice from the shadows.

Cartheron Crust pressed a hand to his chest in momentary panic. He sought out and spotted a diminutive dark figure, hands before him on a walking stick, and muttered, 'Gods! Don't do that!'

The figure emerged from the murk: a Dal Hon elder, grey-haired and wrinkled, in fine black silk trousers, shirt and vest. The crew scrambled to their feet. 'Emp—'

'Say not that word,' the elder warned. 'We know not if anyone is listening to the night.'

Cartheron nodded, 'Of course, Emp— ah, sor.'

Kellanved looked them all over. 'I have need of you now on the *Twisted*. The time has finally come. My much-delayed reinforcements have arrived.'

Cartheron nodded his agreement. 'Yes. Dujek made it.'

A negative wave of one limp hand. 'No, no. Not *them*. Others. Here now, finally.'

'Who?'

'You'll see. We go now.'

Cartheron opened his hands. 'But wait – Dujek needs to—' He cut himself off as the darkness swirled around them and the crew shouted their surprise. The ground moved beneath him and he stumbled, then found it was not the ground any more but wooden decking. The shifting murk diminished in waves until he saw that he and the crew were now on board the *Twisted* somewhere at sea.

Kellanved stood before them. He brandished his silver hound's-head walking stick to urge them into action. 'Do what you do to get us moving, please.'

Rather frustrated, Cartheron threw his hands wide. 'Just where are we?'

'What the Falarans name the Old Guando Sea, I believe.'

Cartheron was quite astonished. 'You've been here all this time?'

The Dal Hon elder got a sly look in his eyes. 'Well, not really *here* – to be precise. And not all the time.'

'And no Falaran vessel came for you?'

'Oh, yes. There've been three attacks upon the *Twisted*.'

Cartheron waited for further explanation. When none was forthcoming, he had to ask, 'And what happened?'

The walking stick waved in wide circles. 'They all . . . disappeared.' The Emperor made a little gesture with one hand as if brushing something aside. 'In any case – you have a heading.'

Cartheron squinted, not quite understanding, and asked, 'By all the gods, where?'

'West of course – the coast you were just on.'

'And why, in the name of Fener, may I ask?'

The walking stick pointed to the east. 'To guide our friends.'

Cartheron squinted and was quite astonished to see off in the distance multiple tall black hulls and black sails bearing the silver Imperial Sceptre sigil. Geddin, the steersman, short and bandy-legged, came to his side, announcing, awed, 'It's the southern fleet – under Nok. What's it doing up here?'

'I summoned him at the beginning of this little expedition,' Kellanved answered, sounding too smug for Cartheron's liking.

'And what about the southern forces in Fist?' he asked.

The Emperor shook his head. 'Nok evacuated most. Some are . . . held up. The south is lost to us. I've decided the north is our way forward.'

Cartheron couldn't help but mutter, 'Good men and women have given their all to the cause down there. You shouldn't just abandon their efforts.'

'One must remain flexible,' Kellanved pronounced, fluttering a hand. 'Now, I am rather busy. If you need me, I shall be in my cabin.' He turned on his heel and hurried away. The cabin door slammed behind him.

The Nose came to Cartheron. He was rubbing a finger along the considerable bridge of his namesake. In a lowered voice, he murmured, 'The ship's a wreck.'

'This ship's always been a wreck,' Cartheron answered tiredly.

'No. I mean now it's a *real* wreck.'

He waved him off. 'Put up what canvas you can.'

'Also,' The Nose continued, 'I wish to formally request transfer to another crew.'

'Duly noted.'

'But not your brother, that's for certain. And not one o' them new crop of captains, mind you. They only know how to polish their brass – not how to sneak along a coast so tight you lose a coat o' tar.'

'Guess that only leaves me,' Cartheron answered, keeping his voice straight.

The Nose rubbed his nose, his eyes narrowed in thought. '*Damn.*' He shambled off.

'Heading?' Geddin called from the stern tiller-arm.

'West,' Cartheron answered, and he pressed a hand to his brow; this was all becoming too commonplace. He'd probably have a heart-attack if Kellanved ever did something utterly predictable.

*　*　*

Dancer helped him navigate the broken rock and choked slanted passages of the lower levels of the now inert K'Chain Che'Malle artefact. He thanked the man many times, quite aware that he was now rather more of an impediment than an asset. For his part, leading him on through rough passages, taking his arm, or even taking his weight through narrow jumbled heaps of shattered stone, the wiry assassin merely inclined his head, murmuring, 'Not at all . . . High Mage.'

And Tayschrenn answered the acknowledgement with his own half-bow, somehow now at peace with his own self-doubts and constant second-questioning. For he had done it; he had held the breach. Somehow he had channelled the full potency of his Thyr Warren to hold up an entire ocean of water, and somehow, even at that moment, it had been strangely trivial, unexceptional.

In that extremity an entire wider universe of possibilities had suddenly revealed itself to him. Only in the extremity of such escalation, or testing, he now understood, could such a breakthrough be possible for any practitioner. He had been driven to the very edge again and again by his confrontations and he had risen to the occasion; that or he'd have been consumed by them.

Now, he no longer feared opening himself to the Warrens. Always before he'd been the mouse stealthily daring to steal just one bit of cheese. But no longer. He now saw things as quite the opposite. *He* was the master who would use these resources as he would – come what may.

He reflected, as he stumbled along, his head hammering, his vision still not quite recovered, that he had perhaps adopted something of the cavalier attitude of the blasted damned Emperor himself – and he shook his head at the utter outlandishness of it.

Was that the key? he wondered. In the end: not giving a damned fig?

He pressed a hand to his brow. *Ye gods, let us not get ahead of ourselves . . .*

His guide, Dancer, steadied him then, indicated the tunnel ahead. He blinked to focus his vision and saw golden daylight streaming in through piled wreckage of heaped shattered rock.

Dancer eased him down and he and the Sword waded onwards through pools of dirty water to begin heaving rocks aside. He sat with their guide, Turnagin, both still suffering the after-effects of exposure to the alien aura of the Che'Malle energies.

The scholar mage then raised his head, peering off into the distance, and half-snorted.

'What is it?' Tayschrenn asked.

'I can now sense it. *He* is close.'

'Who?'

Turnagin regarded him speculatively. 'The Master of Shadow. The Great Deceiver. The Usurper – his titles are many.'

'Your master,' Tayschrenn amended, pointedly.

A shake of the head. 'You have no understanding of Shadow if that is what you think. We are – how shall I put it – a herd of cats.'

Tayschrenn smiled appreciatively, and quite ruefully, at the image. 'Ah. I begin to see our mutual friend's difficulty.'

Turnagin grunted, rising. 'Quite so.' He motioned ahead. 'It looks like we may have a way out . . .'

Struggling down a descent of loose wet sands and mud, Tayschrenn blinked at the sunlight – rather startled, in some abstract way, to find himself alive and whole. Malazan scouts came climbing up the slope to take his arm and guide him down the long descent from the canted portal of the artefact. Past a swamp of pooled water, streams and churned sands, they came to the edge of the expeditionary force's encampment. Troops gathered to welcome them – though keeping a respectful distance – and to his surprise, Tayschrenn felt himself completely at home among them without making any effort, or conscious design, to do so.

'High Mage,' they greeted him, bowing.

Even Hairlock was there, eyeing him as if in disbelief. 'Made it out, hey?' he said, and shook his head at the unlikeliness of it all.

Ute and Missy, his attendants, appeared then, brushing others aside, to throw a blanket over his shoulders and steady him. 'This way, sor,' Ute murmured.

He leaned close then to whisper to the trooper: 'You have to tell me: just what happened?'

'Well, sor,' the fellow answered, guiding him onwards, a hand at his elbow, 'them Falarans dropped an entire ocean of water on the mountain. Filled the whole valley side to side. But here you are come through all that, hey? Took 'em both on, an' come through.'

Personally, he would've disputed that interpretation, but he kept quiet, beginning to intuit something of Kellanved's methods – that a little burnishing of one's reputation doesn't hurt.

*　*　*

The *Glimmer* made its way up the narrow channel that led to the old abandoned and ruined city and temple complex that had once been the capital of the region. Gianna knew the legends that an earthquake – Mael's displeasure – had destroyed it. After this, Cabil became the new centre of the Faith.

Brevin's steersman, Realt, expertly brought them up alongside the ancient stone jetty and Gianna came to Brevin. 'My thanks, captain. All I need is help unloading the chest and you can be on your way.'

The big woman just snorted and shook her head. 'Me 'n the crew had a talk and we've decided we're yours, Priestess.'

'Whatever do you mean?'

'I mean it's obvious you are the true High Priestess of Mael. And like any sailors, we're here to serve.'

Gianna had to smile at this rather tactful way of saying that like any *superstitious* and *cautious* sea-going sailors, they would give due obeisance to Mael.

'O' course,' Brevin continued, 'we'd like to take a run out to see my cousins in Gravid.'

Gianna smiled again, nodding, 'Of course, captain. And my thanks. Perhaps you could also look into what is going on in Cabil? Is there fighting? And also, the fate of any of those taken by the Faith?'

'I can have a poke around,' Torva put in. 'I still have a few old friends in the capital.'

Old smuggler and thief friends, Gianna silently clarified. But she gave her assent, 'My thanks, Torva.'

'First off, this here chest is a little too attention-grabbing, if you know what I mean,' Brevin offered. 'We'll just transfer the scrolls to a sturdy sea-duffel, maybe, yes?'

Gianna smiled again. 'Yes, Brevin. I quite agree.'

Other hands came out with bundles of odds and ends of gear and extra clothes and blankets. After transferring the scroll tubes into a duffel, they walked up the long, canted jetty to the shore of ruined stone walls and buckled stone-flagged streets, continuing uphill to the old fallen-in temple to Mael.

Round the curve of the inlet, away from the ruins, a collection of dories and wattle and daub huts denoted a small coastal village.

They came to a wide set of buckled foundation stones and top-pled columns of white marble. A hut of sticks leaned against one wall, a thin plume of white cook smoke rising from its roof of broken tiles. An old man, quite ancient, sat out front on a block of marble.

'Well, well,' he announced, eyeing them, 'I was told you'd come and now here you are. Let's have a look at you,' and he beckoned Gianna closer.

He peered up at her with red rheumy eyes, half-blind, then nod-ded to himself. 'Welcome, Priestess. Welcome.' He struggled to rise and gestured to the hut. 'You may sleep here.'

Gianna glanced back to Brevin and Torva; neither appeared impressed.

She crossed to them, let out a long breath. 'Well. Looks like I have quarters.'

'Not exactly palatial,' Brevin muttered.

'It is all I need.'

They set down the bundles and the duffel. Torva pressed her hand. 'Well, then. Good luck, lass. Take care. Be seein' you again, I'm sure.'

She hugged her old captain. '*You* take care, you old smuggler.'

Brevin cleared her throat. 'Yes, well. If you're sure of things here, then we will be going.'

'Thank you, captain. For all you've done.'

'We'll be back with news and supplies.'

'Mael willing,' Gianna added.

Brevin crooked a half-smile, bowing to her. 'Yes, Mael willing.'

* * *

Tayschrenn stood on the new sand shore of the delta together with the Fist, Dassem and Dancer. A chill wind buffeted him and he pulled tighter his cape, newly stitched and remade. It was late afternoon and the three stood watching a long line of black vessels coming along the coast, led by the unmistakable battered and derelict-looking *Twisted*.

'A welcome sight,' Dassem murmured.

'Very welcome,' agreed Dancer, sounding very relieved.

The Sword gestured as if to encompass all the vessels and turned to Dancer. 'How does he do it?'

Dancer gave a tired shrug. 'I don't know. Sometimes I think that while we're playing one hand, he's playing five or six. Other times I think he has no more idea than we.'

A small launch was lowered from the side of the *Twisted* and figures could just be made out clambering down. The launch headed for shore.

Fist Dujek evidently couldn't contain himself and walked out knee-deep in the surf to greet them. As the boat grated on the gravels and sand, Cartheron was first overboard, jumping into the surf. He and Dujek shook hands.

The diminutive figure of Kellanved appeared then, daintily stepping over the side and onto the beach. The Emperor walked straight up to Dancer and gave him a nod in greeting; then looked to the Sword and offered a sketched salute; he eyed Tayschrenn for some time, then inclined his head in greeting, murmuring, 'High Mage.'

Tayschrenn answered the half-bow.

Kellanved pointed his walking stick up the strand, announcing, 'A council of war is needed, my friends.'

'High time,' Dujek rasped in his gruff voice and waved everyone onwards.

A large tent had been set up close to the shore. Within, the mage Hairlock waited, his thick arms crossed at his chest. Otherwise, the tent was empty but for a few braziers glowing within for warmth. The Fist possessed no table nor chairs to offer, no maps to pore over; all had been lost in the flood. The off-shore winds whipped through, snapping the canvas.

'We should begin loading the troops immediately,' Kellanved ordered as he entered. 'Through the night.'

Dujek looked to his captains Ullen and Orosé, ordered, 'See to it.' The two bowed and jogged off.

'Will Admiral Nok be joining us?' Cartheron asked.

Kellanved shook his head. 'The Admiral has declined to attend. He prefers not to leave his flagship, the *Sapphire*.'

'Our target?' Dassem asked.

'Cabil, of course,' Kellanved answered.

The Fist pulled his hand down his face. 'Cabil? A tough nut from reports of that harbour.'

The Emperor fluttered a hand. 'That is why you, Fist, will land the majority of your forces on the south shore of the island and march overland to take the city from the landward side. Meanwhile, the majority of the fleet will besiege the harbour – making lots of noise and attracting a great deal of attention.'

Hairlock crooked a sideways knowing smile.

Cartheron shook his head. 'Just like old times.'

'May I accompany the Fist?' Dassem asked.

'Of course, of course. And,' Kellanved looked to Tayschrenn, 'I would like you on the *Twisted*. Will you attend?'

A touch startled, but also oddly pleased by the request, Tayschrenn bowed. 'Of course.'

'And will you accompany the Fist?' Kellanved asked of Hairlock, who gave a nod.

The Emperor peered about, rocking on his heels. 'Good, good. Then we are done.'

'No we aren't,' Cartheron growled. He jerked a thumb to the north. 'What about all these pirate and raider scum you unleashed throughout the isles? Some have declared themselves kings and queens.'

Kellanved tapped the silver hound's-head handle of his walking stick to his chin. 'Ah, yes. Served their purpose, didn't they? Sowed chaos and disorder throughout the region. Burned, looted, murdered. Seeded fear and uncertainty. Distracted and muddied the councils of our enemies.'

He planted the stick and laid his hands upon the hound's-head grip. 'But no more, Cartheron. We must demonstrate to these Falarans that the Empire does not tolerate piracy. Once we are finished with Cabil we will track down every one of these criminals and publicly hang them to prove our commitment to the defence of these isles.'

Cartheron felt his brows rising at the pure unadulterated devious ruthlessness of this and blew out a breath. *Poor bastards – never stood a chance against Kellanved.*

'And I would like you, Admiral Crust, to lead the punitive forces.'

He crooked a smile and inclined his head in assent. 'With pleasure.'

The Emperor peered about, a brow raised, then gave a curt nod. 'Very good. Then we are done. Except that, Fist, practise restraint in your actions. Bloodshed must be avoided if possible. Someone here possesses a powerful weapon – and I would not want them provoked. Understood?'

Dujek nodded, 'Understood.'

'Good. I shall be on board the *Twisted*.' He opened his hands. 'I leave you to it.'

Dancer followed Kellanved out and Tayschrenn watched while the two spoke for a time in the gathering dark on the way down to the shore. Cartheron and Dujek headed into camp, discussing logistics.

Dancer returned looking distracted. He eyed Tayschrenn and Hairlock, then asked, 'I have some last duties to discharge, High Mage. As imperial mage cadre, would you two accompany me?'

The two bowed.

Dancer headed south, towards the dark bulk of the artefact. Tayschrenn walked with him in silence, feeling oddly at ease with the long silence, and with himself. He knew the man would explain when he was ready. Hairlock thumped along with them, humming tunelessly to himself.

Near the cooling base of the artefact a large party awaited in the dusk. At its centre was the Bird Priestess in her litter, the sides pulled back to reveal her sitting cross-legged. Tayschrenn was a touch chagrined to see with her the renegade imperial cadre mage Sialle. Surrounding the litter was her usual grouping of bear-warrior guards. Also with the party was the Thelomen giant

Koroll – who greeted them with a broad smile on his jaggedly tattooed face.

Hairlock, Tayschrenn noted, was glaring at Sialle.

Dancer raised a hand. 'Bird Priestess,' he greeted her.

'Dancer,' she answered.

'I am here with a proposition before we take ship from these lands.'

'Oh?'

'Yes. I speak for the Emperor when I say that we will leave these lands in your hands – provided that you agree to undertake one duty.'

The Bird Priestess tilted her head as if intrigued. 'Oh? You will leave them in our hands, will you? And what is this duty?'

'To undertake to guard and watch over the K'Chain Che'Malle artefact. To keep any from meddling or interfering with it.'

Tayschrenn was surprised by the generosity of the offer, but knew it was not his place to speak.

The Priestess tilted her head to the night sky as if studying the stars, though Tayschrenn knew she was blind. 'I do not think these lands are yours to give or take,' she began, 'but that is beside the point right now. I should be angered, but I am not. In your coming you Malazans have disrupted everything. But you have also delivered something precious.' She held out a frail hand and Sialle took it. 'You have delivered a new Priestess to the people, and for that I am thankful. Therefore, I accept your offer. We Jhek will guard the artefact and prohibit all from entering – in a way, that has always been our task.'

'We Thelomen also pledge to ward the artefact,' Koroll rumbled, and the Priestess offered him a smile.

Dancer turned to Tayschrenn and Hairlock. 'It's decided, then. This bears Kellanved's authority. No reprisals. Is this clear?'

Hairlock's jaws worked, his lips tight. But then he shrugged, snorting his disdain. He muttered, 'Not important enough,' and walked away.

Dancer looked to Tayschrenn. 'Now, I'd like to speak privately.'

Tayschrenn half-bowed and followed Hairlock to where the squat mage now awaited him. He paused to glance back and saw the assassin next to the litter in some close conversation with the Bird Priestess. It appeared very private indeed – and so he turned away and motioned Hairlock off.

They walked together for a time in the night, splashing through shallow pools and streams, then Hairlock turned to him and grunted, 'Didn't think you'd make it out of the damned place. Surprised me, I tell you.'

Tayschrenn looked over to him, quite taken aback by the blunt admission. It was beginning to dawn upon him that this mage was a rather odious fellow.

But useful to the Empire.

Chapter 29

THE SECOND DAY OF THE HARBOUR SIEGE GLINITH WALKED down to the fortifications for a better view. She passed many servants, clerks, priests and priestesses standing at windows and open walkways; all eyeing the exchange of missile weapons. Glinith's stern clearing of throat sent all the gawkers scattering to return to their duties.

The first day of the besieging fleet's arrival, the most adept mages of Ruse had gathered together to perform a ritual to crush the vessels – as the Faith had done many times before. Once the ritual began, however, a stupendous lashing of power launched itself from the invaders' battered flagship to blast the circle apart. Few of the Ruse mages survived the assault. Since then the remaining adepts had been forced to keep their heads down, effecting minor pieces of magics only.

'A deterrent', Nuraj had called the demonstration.

Now the black-hulled Malazan man-o'-wars took turns in sweeping past to unleash shipboard scorpions, catapults and springalds that sent stones and bolts arcing up to strike the outer defences, doing – even to her untrained eye – little to no damage to the robust structure. Meanwhile, the permanent, wall-mounted counter-engines sent catapult stones, flaming pitch-coated incendiaries and long iron-tipped bolts raining down upon every vessel that dared such an approach.

Closer to the fortifications a flurry of messengers and officers of the Faith Militant led her to find Nuraj, Guardian of the Faith, at a command post on the innermost, and tallest, of the three harbour gates. The commander gave her a brief nod that she answered.

For a time she watched the siege in silence, then, when the man was not engaged in whispered intense conversation with some messenger or other, she ventured to ask, 'Why are they even trying, Nuraj? Can't they see it is hopeless? Our engines possess a far greater range than theirs.'

The Guardian of the Faith looked up, distracted and harried, to spare a glance to the waterfront. 'Hubris, I think,' he offered. 'This *Emperor* of theirs has obviously won many battles in the past down south – and now thinks he cannot fail. Foolish . . . but to our favour.'

Glinith nodded at this assessment, then ventured again, 'But surely those around him, the officers and such. Surely *they* must see the uselessness of this?'

Without raising his head, Nuraj answered, absently, 'No doubt he is a tyrant and all those around him are terrified of speaking the truth – and of then being punished for it.'

Glinith again nodded; *that* she understood all too well.

The morning wore towards noon without any appreciable progress in the siege. Glinith kept quiet so as not to distract the commander as he consulted with messengers and fired off orders.

An officer of the Faith Militant came rushing up and handed Nuraj a slip of paper that sent him surging to his feet. 'What?' he murmured. 'Soldiers on the island?' He looked to Glinith. 'I must see to this – pardon me, Abbess.' He gathered up his papers and hurried off with the officer.

Left alone, Glinith found the view had lost its interest, and so after a time she wandered back to the precincts of the Abbey. At her desk she spent the afternoon composing missives to be sent out to the various isles, all exhorting the faithful to lend support to the capital and to resist the invaders.

Towards evening, however, she began to be distracted by a growing distant murmur, a noise coming from inland, the city presumably. Annoyed, she rose and sought out a landward view of the city – which was difficult as few windows or openings offered such a less than desirable outlook.

Eventually, she found an open-roofed walkway that afforded such a vista and was surprised to see smoke rising from several quarters of the city, and townsfolk rushing about, crowding the streets far below.

446

A guard of the Faith Militant came running down the walkway and Glinith called to the woman, but she ignored her and ran past her as if she hadn't spoken. Glinith thought that astonishingly insulting and vowed to have a word with the proctors of the order regarding discipline.

She decided to send a messenger to Nuraj asking what the disturbance in town was about, and headed to her private quarters to draft the missive. Were the townsfolk that fearful? Didn't they know that there was no way the harbour could be breached?

She found the double doors to her private living quarters open and paused there, astonished. How could the servants be so forgetful? This was unforgivable – her personal rooms?

Within, she was further astonished to find the reception room a disordered mess. Several fine vases had fallen and lay shattered. A slim table knocked over. She noted that a number of rare pieces of artwork were missing from their spots in niches and on pedestals.

Mystified, she walked on and pushed open the door to her offices.

Here was not disorder, but mayhem: her papers cluttered the floor; side-tables lay overturned; every drawer had been pulled out and emptied onto the floor. She stood amid the wreckage, stunned. What in the name of Mael . . . ?

Noise from her bedroom drew her and she pushed open the door, which was hanging askew, to see a servant at her opened closet in the process of yanking clothes from hooks and hangers and draping the fine silks and brocades over her shoulder.

Glinith marched to her and spun her round. 'What in the name of Beru do you think you're doing?'

The servant-girl stared back, neither chastened nor fearful, but defiant, almost dismissive. She shook Glinith's hand from her shoulder and walked off without a word.

The Abbess stared after her, stunned beyond rage – beyond comprehension.

What is happening here? Has the world gone mad?

She walked out to the main hallway, peered up and down. Servants, clerks and priests were all rushing about. Some bore chests in their hands, others bundles of clothes, one or two carried absurdly large paintings.

A priestess hurried by, Tianta, and Glinith called after her, 'Stop! What is going on?' but the girl ran on, ignoring her.

A servant passed next, a young girl clutching a set of golden goblets to her chest, and she caught her arm. 'I demand that you tell me what is going on!'

The young servant-girl just calmly and deliberately slapped her across the face and ran on.

Glinith retreated to her quarters.

In the office she began clearing up all her scattered papers. Tomorrow, at the council meeting, she'd have harsh words regarding discipline for Mallick and Nuraj, that was certain!

As evening came, she noted a certain strange silence and she went to a window overlooking the harbour. It seemed the besieging Malazan ships had had enough, for they had withdrawn beyond range and rested now at anchor. Perhaps, she mused, they meant to begin a blockade of the capital.

Good. They had obviously seen the foolishness of any attack against their defences. She sat at her ransacked desk, searched amid the clutter for an ink pot, found it, and began composing a strongly worded complaint to the chamberlain of servants – had the man lost all authority? How could he be so negligent? This was all so utterly outrageous!

She was nearing completion of the letter when the tramp of measured marching footsteps approaching up the hall reached her. She stared, frozen, quill poised, eyes fixed on the doors to her offices until they were swept open and in came armed and armoured figures in blackened mail and half-plate, bearing the upright sigil of a sceptre upon their chests.

The leader of the contingent drew off his helmet, revealing a very dark face, scarred and sweaty. He glanced aside to an older, grey-haired woman with them, unarmed, in tattered servant's robes, who gave the man a nod.

The foreign officer announced, in strangely accented Falaran, 'Glinith of Tenak, Abbess of Cabil . . . you are under arrest.'

* * *

After Kellanved had called for a withdrawal from the active besiegement – or petty harassment, as Tayschrenn saw it, for all the damage it was doing – he stood on deck rocking back and forth on his heels, and humming to himself.

Tayschrenn remained watchful: three times he had had to raise his Warren to dissuade efforts by these Ruse mages to attack the fleet. And this was even after his first lashing out. After that they appeared to have learned not to congregate, but individual attackers persisted, and he had to continually demonstrate the foolishness of such acts.

Dancer, he noted, also remained on deck, his back to a mast, watchful as well. While they waited out of range of the capital's defensive engines, the Emperor turned to Tayschrenn.

He regarded him for some time, then said, 'That was quite the demonstration, High Mage. You appear to be coming into the potential I saw in you when we first met.'

Tayschrenn inclined his head. 'I received some unlooked-for advice from Nightchill – and even the mage Hairlock, come to think of it. That, and the unique challenges of this campaign.'

Kellanved nodded his agreement. 'Oh yes. Being challenged can do that. It seems that far more paths are open to you now, yes?'

Something in that phrasing almost startled Tayschrenn, but he had to agree with the sentiment. 'Yes. I suppose so.'

'Indeed, indeed. As I have found just recently as well. Recently I was forced to . . . extend myself. Now I can see further possibilities and potentialities – just like you.' He raised the walking stick to the city hidden beyond the sea-walls. 'Look. Smoke. Our troops must be inside. Excellent.' He nodded to himself as he watched, obviously quite pleased.

'Things do seem to be in hand,' he added, turning from the rail. He invited Dancer forward. 'The cabin, if you would, good friend. We have things to do.'

The two retreated to Kellanved's cabin. Tayschrenn remained on deck, continuing to watch for any massing of Ruse magics – or any hostile magery, for that matter – ready to swat it down.

The plumes of smoke thickened across the city. A dull, distant roaring reached him, as of thousands of voices raised in panic and general tumult.

Finally, as evening drew in, the deep blue flags of the Faith atop the tallest buildings – the famed Abbey of Cabil, Tayschrenn assumed – came down to be replaced by the black and sceptre of Malaz.

He nodded to himself and turned to congratulate the Emperor but found him still absent. Frowning, he went to the cabin door and knocked. He waited but no answer came. Finally, a touch unnerved, he pushed on the door; it was not locked. He swung it open to find the room empty.

Tayschrenn stood upon the threshold and shook his head. '*Dammit to all the Mysteries!*'

* * *

It was Gianna's habit each day to head down to the shore to dig for clams and hunt crabs amid the broken blocks of the ruin's old breakwater. It was here one day that she spotted a beaten-up old dory approach the shore, rowed by a familiar figure.

She looked to the sky in rueful amazement for it was the bald and pot-bellied ex-priest of Mael. She waved and the boat angled towards her. 'What in the name of all the gods are you doing here?' she called.

The fellow worked the oars to stay in place off shore as the waves rolled under him.

'Just come to say goodbye,' he shouted.

Gianna shook her head again. 'How did you know I was here?'

'Oh, let's just say the seas whispered it.'

She laughed, waved him in. 'Come ashore. Have dinner. Let's talk.'

'Oh, no. It's all right. I just wanted to thank you. That's all. Thank you.'

She had to frown. 'Well . . . I don't think I've done anything at all.'

'Exactly, exactly. That is as it should be. So, goodbye,' and he waved.

'Where are you going?' she shouted as he worked the oars.

He called back, 'To see the world!'

'But . . . what's your name, anyway!'

A shrug of his meaty shoulders. 'What's in a name? I have had many!' He raised a hand again in farewell, and she answered, waving as he drove the dory up the narrow inlet.

She watched for some time as the tiny boat diminished into the distance between the tall sheer cliffs. It seemed to her that the odd fellow somehow drove the craft with preternatural speed to disappear amid the waves.

Then she shrugged, pushed down the crabs that were determined to escape her wooden bucket, and headed up the shore.

* * *

Two figures, a man and a woman, emerged from a wooded slope and onto a field cleared for farming, to halt, looking bewildered. The youth tending the field approached. He could see the haggard lines of hunger on their pale dirt-smeared faces. And their clothes were equally haggard, torn and filthy. Oddly, though, each bore the heavy burden of a large leather backpack.

'What place is this?' the woman asked in a dry, croaking voice.

The boy pointed downslope, towards a distant coast. 'That's Old Ilk. You headed that way?'

'And the water beyond?' the man asked.

'That's a bay. Look Bay. Cragg Ocean's beyond.'

The two exchanged gleeful, almost fevered looks. 'We made it, Ayal,' the man said.

Closer now, the lad saw that the two were not so old after all, just obviously drained, and driven to the very edge of their endurance. They also bore a strange likeness to one another.

'Are there boats there in that little flea-bite of a town?' the woman asked.

The lad nodded. 'Oh, yes. Plenty of fishing out of Old Ilk.'

'Good. We'll need a boat.'

The lad laughed. 'Oh, none for sale. That's for sure. Every family needs their boat.'

The two exchanged glances once more. The man's hand went to the sack on his back as if to check for it.

The woman chuckled in a strange knowing sort of way. 'Don't you worry about that, laddie. Now, you wouldn't happen to have any water or food with you, would you? We'll pay.'

* * *

In the catacombs far beneath the Falaran capital of Cabil, Corporal Aragan sat at a small table, a tankard of watered Falaran wine at one elbow, and curling sheets of records at the other. He felt chilled in the musty and dark tunnels and, eyeing the mould

451

and dripping water on the chamber walls, he scowled his resentment. *Damned damp will be the death of me.*

Sighing, he raised his gaze to the trooper at the door and gave a curt nod. The guard opened the door and called up the hall, 'Next!'

A prisoner, a sack over his head, was frogmarched in and thumped down in the chair opposite.

Aragan noted from his blue robes that he was a priest – those robes now torn from a thorough search, and dirtied from his time in a holding cell.

Aragan pulled a hand down his face, sighed yet again, took a small sip of cold watered wine, and picked up a record sheet. He studied the list, cleared his throat of catarrh – *damned damp!* – and began: 'Brother Lethor, you are here because elements of the Malazan occupying force have spoken for you and you have provided intelligence of use to us. How we proceed from here depends upon how cooperative you continue to be. Do you understand?'

The pudgy fellow tilted his head within the sack. 'I do,' came a muffled answer. 'However, while I am Brother Lethor . . . at the same time I am not.'

Aragan let his head fall back to gaze at the leprous, mould-covered ceiling above. How he hated the ones who made everything more difficult than it had to be.

'You are jeopardizing your position here.'

'I understand. Please allow me to explain.'

Aragan waved a hand to invite him to continue, realized the man couldn't see it from within the hood, and through gritted teeth said, 'Do so . . .'

'In the sacking of the capital Brother Lethor suffered a mishap. He fell down a steep set of stairs, I believe. Therefore, I am here in his stead.'

Aragan set chin in hand and studied the man. Why was he talking himself into an early grave? 'And you are?'

'The one who provided all the intelligence he was good enough to pass along to you.'

Grimacing, Aragan nodded to the trooper, who yanked the hood from the man's head. The fellow blinked in the weak light of the single lamp.

'And you are?' Aragan demanded again.

The prisoner smiled then, revealing sickly grey-green teeth, saying, 'Someone who is here to cooperate fully with this new regime, I assure you.'

*　*　*

This new cell, Glinith noted, was no different from her earlier one. Some things, sadly, remained the same – despite the powers that be. She passed the time pacing its three-step length, as she had before as well. Three feedings came and went; three days, she assumed.

A number of times footsteps came and went up the hall, but never stopping at her cell. Always at others. And so, when another set of steps approached, she did not stir.

These, however, stopped at her door. She rose, adjusted her much-soiled clothes, crossed her arms and raised her chin – whoever this might be, they would not find her cowering.

A slot in the door opened and a voice spoke: 'Glinith of Tenak, Abbess of Cabil, the charges against you are many and severe.'

She arched a brow; how pathetically predictable. 'I demand to speak to—'

The clerk, or officer, spoke over her: 'You are charged with kidnapping, coercion, extortion, murder and blackmail. You are charged with imprisoning Rentil Orodrin, Celebrant of the Faith, to silence him. You are charged with coercing the Council of the Faith into threatening the island of Curaca with destruction, imperilling the lives of thousands. You are charged with putting your own overweening pursuit of power over the good of the Falaran people. These charges are serious indeed, and you will be held imprisoned until such time as the Provisional Council of the Isles decides your fate. What have you to say for yourself?'

Glinith could only gape. 'I'm sorry – did you say I imprisoned the Celebrant?'

'Yes. You conspired to do so. We have testimony to this effect from many sources. Some very high indeed.'

'These are all lies. Bald-faced, utter lies. I did no such thing. Utter trash.'

'We have numerous sworn affidavits from numerous sources.'

'Oh? And who do these individuals work for? Whose creatures are they? I will tell you who – Mallick Rel! That is who! He is the one you want. Those crimes are his! Not mine.'

She heard papers being rolled up. 'I did not come to argue. You have been informed of your charges. There will be a hearing, eventually. You may answer them then.'

The slot grated shut.

Glinith threw herself to the door, shouting, 'It was Mallick, I tell you! Mallick! He is the one! Him!' All she heard were footsteps receding.

She pressed her forehead to the chill and damp wood of the door. A laugh shook her then, rising in timbre until she cut it off, a touch alarmed. He needed someone, she now saw. Someone he could pin it all on. And not poor old doddering Orodrin. No, too sympathetic a figure by far. And obviously incapable! She chuckled anew – this time at herself. No, he needed someone who appeared scheming and ambitious. Someone who *was* scheming and ambitious; just not ruthless and ambitious enough!

She slumped into a straw-filled corner of her cell. That, she decided, had been her downfall. She hadn't been ruthless or treacherous enough. Unlike her friend Mallick. She had, she realized, actually, foolishly, assumed he'd keep to their agreement. How could she have been so naive?

She laughed then, anew. Laughing on and on. Until it became a sob, and she rocked herself, sobbing. Her face in her hands. Rocking and rocking. In the darkness, all alone.

Epilogue

IN THE DARKNESS OF THE ANTECHAMBER TO HIS LORD'S reception hall, Endest Silann waited. It had been some time since he and Feral had arrived at the Moon's Spawn; however, at Feral's request, he had put off his report to Anomander so that they could lay out their discoveries together.

This day word had come that Feral was ready. And so he waited, hands at his back, admiring the artwork adorning the halls – artwork he knew well, but which deserved admiration – until the clack of boots on stone announced Feral's approach.

He turned to see that she had had new clothes tailored, and had arranged for new accoutrements. Which was understandable, given that most had been scorched and crisped by her confrontation. She had gathered up a new weapon as well, now at her side. And her midnight black hair had been trimmed and skilfully arranged so as to minimize any hint of the lengths that had been burned away.

He inclined his head in greeting, murmuring, 'Feral . . . you look . . . resplendent.'

She passed without a word or glance to push open the heavy double doors.

He pursed his lips a touch at that, but shrugged inwardly; Feral would be what Feral was.

He followed, hands at his back, just behind.

They found their Lord in a side-chamber, at a table chiselled from the black rock of the Spawn, leaning over a scattering of parchment maps. He turned at their entrance and nodded a greeting.

'My Lord,' Endest murmured – and diverted his gaze from the deeper darkness at the man's side.

Feral simply returned the nod.

'My Lord, we are returned from investigating the K'Chain Che'Malle nest—'

'And the humans interfering with it,' Feral put in.

Anomander looked to her. 'Feral. It is good to see you returned. It has been . . . some time.'

She gave a small wave of a gloved hand, as if to brush aside such pleasantries.

'I took the liberty of asking her to join me in this errand,' Endest explained.

Anomander nodded. 'I hadn't anticipated such a thing, but you are most welcome, of course.'

'Lord Anomander,' Feral began, 'I understand Endest has already informed you that an upstart human mage has somehow gained access to Kurald Emurlahn and also somehow mastered the Hounds of Shadow.'

'I have sensed these things.'

'And that this selfsame mage has also somehow mastered the army of the T'lan Imass themselves?'

Anomander raised a hand for a pause. 'Firstly, thank you, Feral, for aiding Endest in his investigations. I must however take issue with your use of the word *mastered*. I wonder if anyone could possibly master such potent forces as the Hounds or the T'lan Imass.'

'They appear to serve his will – is that not enough?'

The Son of Darkness tilted his lean head as if granting the point, for now. 'Proceed.'

'I found these humans attempting to master the secrets of the Nest and the K'Chain Che'Malle themselves. When I intervened to stop them, they attacked me.'

'One of these humans is an unusually gifted mage,' Endest added. 'The purity and depth of his manipulation reminded me of an Adept. He faced Feral and survived.'

Anomander regarded her, clearly surprised. 'Indeed?'

Her mouth soured and she cast a sharp glance to Endest. 'I was taken by surprise. I did not anticipate such strength. However, we are at least now forewarned of such capability.'

The Son of Darkness simply looked away for a time, thoughtful. 'And the Hive, or Nest?'

Endest answered: 'I sense it has since returned to quiescence.'

'So perhaps they over-reached,' Anomander mused.

'Or failing to master them, destroyed them instead,' Feral ground out.

The Son of Darkness clasped his hands before himself and leaned back against the table. 'You appear to be working towards a point, Feral.'

She gave a curt nod. 'Indeed. The intelligence we have gathered regarding this upstart, this self-styled *Emperor of the Malazans*,' which she spat with scorn. 'Manipulation of Kurald Emurlahn, mastery of the Hounds, mastery of the T'lan Imass, and now meddling with the K'Chain Che'Malle – the pattern is clear.'

'And that is?'

Feral lifted her chin, announcing, 'War and pogrom against all Elders – including us.'

'Now, Feral—' Endest began, but she snapped up a hand to silence him.

Anomander pursed his lips. His gaze was directed downwards. After a time, he said, 'A serious accusation, Feral.'

'The pattern is clear.'

'Cloth can be cut to fit any shape,' he murmured.

'It is your duty to protect your people against any threat. You must act.'

The Son of Darkness seemed to wince. '*War* . . .' he whispered, and shook his head.

Feral watched him narrowly, poised, ready to speak again, but waiting, judging.

Endest glanced between the two, feeling oddly alarmed.

'Very well, Feral,' Anomander said at last. 'You make a strong case. And you are correct – it is my duty to act to protect my people. I will keep an eye on these Malazans.'

Feral's high tensed shoulders eased, and she inclined her head in assent. 'Very good . . . m'lord.'

Anomander then looked to Endest. 'Thank you for your service in this. I know such errands are not to your taste.'

He bowed. 'Honoured, m'lord.'

Feral bowed as well. 'M'lord,' and turned to go.

'You will not be leaving us so soon?' Anomander called after her.

She turned. 'I fear I must. I have . . . other business to attend to.'

'Well, do return if you can. You are always welcome.'

She offered a shallow bow. 'My thanks . . . m'lord.' And she marched off, pushing open the heavy door.

Walking away, her newly made and fitted boots striking the polished stone of the floor, a tight, satisfied – almost savage – smile grew on Feral's lips.

Endest remained behind. His Lord stood in silent thought, eyes downcast once more. A slight frown creased his forehead.

Eventually, after a long silence during which Endest suspected that his Lord had perhaps forgotten he was even still present, he dared murmur, 'But . . . war . . . m'lord?'

Anomandaris blinked as if brushing away other visions, other thoughts, and he returned to studying the maps cluttering the wide table. 'We shall see, Endest,' he answered. 'We shall see . . .'

* * *

The fishing boat was intercepted long before reaching the harbour of Aren. Seven Cities sailors jumped aboard, knives bared, and they kicked the crew of six Falarans together at the stern.

'Falaran dogs!' one growled. 'Why are you here? What do you want? Fish?'

'Treat our guests with respect,' spoke up one of the crew sitting hidden at the very bow.

A sailor turned on him, knife readied. 'Get over here, damn you! This boat is now property of the Holy city of Aren.'

This last one stood, revealing leathers of Seven Cities cut, horn-gripped knives at his hips in similar fashion.

The Aren sailor advanced upon him, readied for attack. 'What is this? A renegade? Fool to have come! You know the price of exile! The chains of servitude.'

This one extended his wrists. 'By all means – dare to place a hand upon me.'

The Aren sailor advanced, warily, knife extended. 'It's for the fishes with you. I will—' He paused, frowning, the curved blade

458

lowering slightly. 'That is . . .' He fell to his knees then, the blade clattering to the timbers of the hull. 'By all the Seven! It is *you*!'

'Hakal!' shouted another Aren sailor, 'are you gone mad?'

The one named Hakal turned upon them, snarling, 'To your knees, idiots! It is Imanaj D'Shren! Our Holy Champion is returned to us!'

'Is it . . . true?' one sailor asked of this newcomer.

'I am Imanaj,' this one answered.

All the Aren sailors fell to their knees.

Hakal himself wept, kissing his blade and sheathing it. 'Praise to the Seven!' he called to the sky.

Their entrance past the breakwater into the harbour proper of Aren was announced by great horns blowing from the walls above. Thousands lined the battlements, waving and cheering, and instead of stones and crossbow bolts falling from above, flower petals and silk scarves floated down upon their boat.

The Falaran fishermen and women of War Isle blinked at one another in astounded wonder. Then they gaped at the rising curtain walls before them of the Seawall of Aren, proper. Curving barrier after curving barrier rose higher and higher – far taller than those of Cabil, or Strike. And the Falarans stared in disbelief.

Imanaj came to them then, smiling. 'Welcome, guests. Thank you for bringing me home. Behold, the Seawall of Aren. A wonder of the world. For over a thousand years it has stood against attack.'

Brother Rendren, who had accompanied Imanaj, blew out a breath. 'Are we to be your prisoners then?'

'No. As I said. Guests. You will be rewarded for your time and trouble. I will see to it.'

The fishing boat docked at a wharf. An honour guard of forty Aren soldiers met them there, and in their midst, an elderly woman draped in robes of shimmering cloth of gold, a slim crown of gold upon her grey hair.

Imanaj climbed up onto the wharf then knelt before her. He murmured in obeisance, 'Ismara. Queen of Aren . . . High Priestess . . . Mother.'

The woman raised her hands high and announced, her voice strong and carrying, 'Praise the Seven!'

An answering roar sounded from the walls. Standing, Imanaj

raised a hand to the battlements, acknowledging the crowd – and their cheering was redoubled.

The woman wrapped her arm through his and guided him back up the wharf. The honour guard fell in about them. 'You are returned to us, son. For this I have prayed. For this I give all thanks to the Seven. But I cannot say I understand why you left us at all. Is it so unpleasant here?'

An indulgent smile. 'No, Mother. I just needed time. Time to think.'

She tightened her arm round his. 'And you returned! I am so thankful. I shall sacrifice twenty oxen on the city altar come the morrow.'

'One should suffice, please. And these Falarans who brought me – they must be rewarded and sent on their way.'

'Of course! I shall drape them in gold!'

Imanaj gave a small laugh. 'They would look rather foolish fishing while draped in gold. No . . . we have many captured Falaran vessels in our docks, do we not?'

'Of course.'

'Give them our finest and send them home.'

The queen nodded to a priest shadowing her. 'It shall be done.' He bowed and ducked away.

She guided him onwards towards the formal waterfront doors – twin iron leaves three man-heights tall – opened only for ceremonial occasions. 'You are just come from Falaran waters, son. Tell me – what of these rumours we are hearing of invasion? Invasion from the south?'

He nodded. 'I have seen them. These Malazans.' He gave a dismissive wave. 'They are no threat to us.'

ADDENDUM

Note *upon the Addendum*
from a sub-sub-sub-librarian:

*Your humble servant offers an overlooked manuscript
discovered some time ago in the basement annex of the
extension of the Imperial Archive. Its provenance appears
authentic. However, after due diligence, this servant's
efforts to uncover any administrative records of an
Imperial Historian Feroot, have, so far, to this date,
met with a peculiar lack of success.*

OCEAN

WOAD

Coast

Woad

WHT Strait

Dhab

DHAB STRAIT

Trapp

Heft

Torvo

Bada

Chenang

Jick

Tenak

RUBBLE ISLE

Lurk

Clump

Ship Graveyard

WALK SEA

SPARROW PASS CUT

Walk

Shoals

SPARROW PASS ISLAND

Strike

SLEEP ISLE

WAR ISLE

OLD GUANDO SEA

OLD GUANDO ISLE

Flood

STROM SEA

Belid

Fallen Towers

Belikân

Victor

Iguan

Delanss

Wett

(LAND'S END SEA)

STRETCH OCEAN

STRIKE OCEAN

ICE SEA

As compiled from diverse sources
by Imperial Historian Feroot

ABOUT THE AUTHOR

Born in Winnipeg, Ian C. Esslemont has studied and worked as an archaeologist, traveled extensively in Southeast Asia, and lived in Thailand and Japan for several years. He now lives in Fairbanks, Alaska, with his wife and children. His novels—beginning with *Night of Knives*—are all set in the world of Malaz that he cocreated with Steven Erikson. *Dancer's Lament* was the first book in the Path to Ascendancy sequence (which continues the story of the turbulent early history of this epic imagined world), while *Forge of the High Mage* is the fourth.

To find out more, visit ian-esslemont.com and malazanempire.com.